AGAINST THE SHOALS

AGAINST

THE

SHOALS

T.K. SZEPESI

Print ISBN: 978-1-54399-223-6

eBook ISBN: 978-1-54399-224-3

This book is dedicated to my daughter, Sarah,
without whose love, support, and faith, this book
would never have been written.

PART ONE

THE WATERSHED

CHAPTER 1

The days aren't discarded or collected, they are bees
That burned with sweetness or maddened
The sting: the struggle continues,
The journeys to and come between honey and pain.

—Pablo Neruda, *Still Another Day*

New York City. March 12th, 2012

I ducked under the tape, walking towards the only house lit up like a klieg-blitzed movie set. Senator Monnehan's townhouse. On any other day, with its limestone façade and three sets of tall, narrow windows, it was probably a warm and inviting home. Tonight, however, it telegraphed "stay away." A uniformed cop lingered in the oversized entrance, the door slightly ajar.

Fishing out my business card, I said, "Nicholas Conor. I'm here at the request of Mrs. Monnehan."

The cop squinted at the small print, identifying me as a lawyer. "Please wait here, sir."

He disappeared inside. Leo O'Shaunessy had called me thirty minutes earlier on behalf of Mrs. Monnehan. He was a senior partner at the law offices of O'Shaunessy, Warren, and Rosen, one of the largest firms in the city. It commanded small fortunes from the privileged few – the Monnehans among them.

"Who's in charge?" I asked

The uniform returned, motioned me to follow.

I stepped onto an ocean of gleaming white marble and looked up at the most imposing staircase I'd ever seen: double curved stairs joined at the landing in a graceful arc. The hall had a cool arrogance about it, a haughty display of glitz.

Linda Lippi of the New York coroner's office was standing beside a massive table showcasing a riotous flower arrangement. The petite woman had a stellar reputation as the Chief Medical Examiner. Right now, she was talking to a tall man in a dark suit. I noticed the discreet bulge of his holstered gun. Security? Another detective? The man in charge? Linda spotted me and touched his arm. The man turned and gave me the once-over. He looked to be in his early fifties, robust and obviously in shape, his face either tanned or naturally dark. Altogether an impressive figure.

The man strode towards me, his right hand extended. "Detective Tom Lachey," he said. His large hand clamped around mine. "That was fast. I heard you were coming from Brooklyn."

"No traffic. I was lucky."

"We're ready to bring Monnehan down. I'll give you five minutes."

"Thanks. Appreciate the time."

"Just make it quick. All hell's breaking loose."

I studied his face. Couldn't read much.

Moses Stringer, the forensic genius of the NYPD, was descending the stairs, followed by uniforms and white coats steering a gurney with what I assumed was the body of the now-deceased Senator Andrew Monnehan.

I turned to Detective Lachey. "Could you point me to Mrs. Monnehan?"

He gestured toward an enormous archway to his left. "In there."

I entered the library, the vaulted space soaring two stories. I felt the softness of the Oriental rug under my feet. The room and its contents screamed money.

There were at least six people in the room. A gaggle of plainclothesmen and two more uniforms stood in front of the fireplace, but it was O'Shaunessy in the far corner of the room that caught my eye. Even at this hour, the short trim man was perfectly turned out in a three-piece charcoal suit and a pristine white shirt, with a jaunty red bow tie at his neck.

The woman who must be the new widow had her back turned towards me. O'Shaunessy, a head shorter than the woman, tilted his bespectacled face as his head tilted up as he spoke, and seemed to be endeavoring to make a point. I could tell from his perturbed expression that he was coming up short. O'Shaunessy noticed me, and looked relieved. "My dear, here is Mr. Conor. I'm sure he will agree with me on this."

The woman pivoted gracefully to face me, shoulders drawn firmly back, hands taut at her sides, her chin raised. She was the picture of self-control, but it was a vibrating, tense restraint. Then without understanding how or why, I felt something flash from within, a sliver of an image, a memory. I stopped short; deep inside my spine something hummed. Suddenly the room drew dark and I was tumbling.

I was wet and cold. I couldn't breathe. I had been running toward the docks, toward the boathouse at the end of the pier, the rain bitter and the merciless wind whipping against my bloody cheek. And then I saw Padrick, his black hair plastered to his head, the overhead streetlight carving shadows into the white of his face, his eyes blazing blue and fierce.

I felt the rush of blood as I refocused on the woman. She stood still. Except for a fading bruise on her left cheek, which no amount of make-up could hide, she was perfect. The long white line of her neck, the elegant curve of her cheeks, the slant of her stunning green eyes, all made her seem unreal. Her eyes widened for the briefest of moments.

Then her right hand rose to finger the brooch pinned at her throat. Her gaze never left mine. I let out a quick expulsion of air, a sudden jolt of energy and then, very carefully, I walked over to extend my hand. She was still staring at me as our palms touched.

"Nicholas Conor, Ma'am." My voice sounded raw.

"Madeline Monnehan. Thank you for coming so swiftly, Mr. Conor. I'm sorry for the ungodly hour."

"It's alright." My heart was trying to resume its normal pace. *What the hell was going on?*

O'Shaunessy piped up. "Thanks for being here, Nick. It seems I got here a little late myself. Maddie's already made a statement. I've asked her not to say anything further, but she doesn't—"

"I've already confessed to killing my husband." Madeline Monnehan's eyes never left mine. "I don't know how much more damage I can do."

"Well, what's done is done, but the less you say from here on, the better," I said.

She nodded gravely. The bruise on the left side of her face grew more discernible against the growing pallor of her face.

"We don't have much time. I'd like to tell you what's going to happen next," I said.

"All right." Her face remained impassive, her voice like soft, black velvet.

"In a few minutes, you'll be taken to the precinct where you'll be processed. You don't need to bring anything except your ID. They'll take your prints and photograph you when you arrive, and I'll meet you there shortly after. Then we'll talk."

She was following my recitation carefully, watching me with inscrutable eyes. I continued, "We'll get you out of there as soon as possible. In the meantime, Mr. O'Shaunessy is right: I strongly advise you to say nothing until we get a chance to talk tomorrow..." I smiled wryly. "I mean, later today."

"Excuse me, Mrs. Monnehan," Detective Lachey's harsh baritone interrupted. "It's time." He was holding a pair of handcuffs.

"Is that really necessary?" My voice regained its tenor.

"It's all right, Mr. Conor," Mrs. Monnehan murmured, extending her wrists. I heard the slight catch in her voice, but her face remained expressionless as the cuffs locked into place. The detective and my client retreated.

I started to follow, but O'Shaunessy caught my arm and held onto it. I was taken aback by the anxiety I saw in his eyes.

"Nick, if you can minimize the damage, I…we would really appreciate it. It's…a tragedy. If anyone can fix it, you can, right?" He spoke with urgency, like an anxious relative pleading with an attending surgeon for assurances or comfort.

"We'll do our best. We've got a pretty solid batting average," I added.

"Yes, yes," he muttered, his tone distracted. "I'll leave you now. I know she's in good hands. You don't know her, but she's…" O'Shaunessy fumbled for a moment. I thought I heard him say "extraordinary," but his voice was lost as he turned away and left.

CHAPTER 2

Black beneath the eye can see
Yet no further than the circle.

—Maddie Walker, *Against the Shoals,*

As I sped back down the dark, empty West Side Highway, I thought about that night. *I haven't thought of that night for years. What the fuck was that?* I felt the old familiar dread stirring within me, my body vibrating like a tuning fork. It had been ages since I'd had an episode of what I called "the hundred feet"—an unstoppable freefall through a hundred feet of hell—furious rushes of pain and despair. Something about Madeline Monnehan had taken a hammer to my carefully constructed world. I forced myself to take long, deep pulls of air.

Making partner at the thriving firm of Stetson, Stetson, and Conor had its high points, one of which was my penthouse. The apartment consumed half the top floor of my building, and overlooked the Hudson River. I've always loved the feeling of openness, the sense of drama of this space. Surrounded by breathtaking vistas of city and the river, I felt suspended between earth and sky. I stepped inside and tried to breathe in the quiet. *Inhale–exhale, inhale–exhale.* I couldn't still the pounding in my chest.

Padrick… What was it about Madeline Monnehan that had thrust Padrick back into the light of day? I walked over to the bathroom, opened the medicine cabinet and gulped down four ibuprofen tablets. I stared into the mirror, my stark, jaw-clenched reflection glaring back at me. I wouldn't let myself plunge into that dark again. *Breathe, just breathe.*

The grief surged like a wave. I forced my hands to let go of the sink. Seven years of therapy and decades of discipline had taught me quick coping mechanisms—controlled breathing, a six-mile run at dawn every morning, Sal's Gym three times a week, and a shitload of work. Lord knows I had plenty of practice.

I showered and changed. In less than twenty minutes I was behind the steering wheel of my car, and my head was clear by the time I walked into the Nineteenth Precinct. It was just after 2:30 a.m. If I hadn't known better, I would have thought it was the middle of the day. The bullpen seemed to be more feverish than usual: lots of men, lots of guns, lots of empty coffee cups. The room was buzzing with the shrill, incessant ringing of telephones, the din of cross voices, and the thumping of the Talking Heads. It seemed as if the entire squad had been called in.

Bloodshot eyes turned towards the entrance and followed my progress with unconcealed interest. The night desk operator glanced up as I approached the counter. He sighed, a long, pained sound. "Yeah, yeah, you're here for Monnehan. Detective Lachey is waiting for you."

"News travels fast," I answered.

"It'll be a miracle if we don't get a dozen shithouse reporters in the next ten minutes. This kind of headline is bigger than Musk's high-speed Hyperloop," he growled.

He pushed the buzzer. "Up the stairs, second door to your right." He went back to shuffling papers on his desk. I felt a momentary kinship: a long night for both of us.

I walked into Detective Lachey's cubicle. It was empty. The miniscule space held two chairs opposite a cluttered desk, which, I was sure, had not revealed its surface for quite some time. On top a lone filing cabinet were two framed photographs, one featuring Lachey shaking the former Mayor's hand, the other, a Citation for Bravery.

I was just about to turn away when Detective Lachey entered. "You're early," he said, his voice as weary as his eyes. "The photo equipment was on the fritz, so I just finished the preliminary paperwork a few minutes ago." He pinched the bridge of his nose with his thumb and index finger, sat down, and opened a thick manila folder. "Paperwork will be the death of me."

"Do you mind if I ask you a few questions?"

Detective Lachey continued leafing through the pages in front of him. "I can tell you the bare facts, which I'm sure you'll find out in no time."

"How and when was the body found?"

"The night operator received a 911 from Madeline Monnehan at exactly 24:08. She claimed to have shot and killed her husband. An ambulance was dispatched immediately."

"And when did the police arrive on the scene?"

"About fifteen minutes after that."

"Mrs. Monnehan called from home?"

"That's right. Anything else?"

"That's all for the moment."

"Levinson!" Lachey barked. A uniformed cop, who looked all of sixteen, appeared at the door. He cast an eager glance in my direction. "Escort Mr. Conor down to Interview Room B."

Detective Lachey stood and shook my hand. A man of few words.

"Thanks. See you in a few, Detective."

Madeline Monnehan was seated at a wide stainless steel table; an oversized, prison-issue jumpsuit hanging off her slight frame. The unforgiving overhead light made the purplish bruise on her cheek stand out. She looked exhausted and a little shell-shocked, but she managed to offer me a tight smile.

"Hello, again, Mrs. Monnehan."

"Mr. Conor." She lifted her gaze to my wet hair. I could sense the weary undertones she was trying to disguise as she spoke.

I crossed over to the bare table and laid my briefcase on the scratched surface. I took out a legal pad and sat down across from my client.

"Mrs. Monnehan, before we start, I need you to know that what we say here is confidential. By law, this room is bug-free and absolutely private. Anything discussed stays between us and doesn't leave the room unless you want it to. There's a rule of evidence that forbids me from disclosing anything you tell me, regardless of whether or not you decide to engage my services. It's called attorney-client privilege, so you can talk to me about what happened last night freely and without worry. I'm never going to use whatever you tell me to your disadvantage. Do you understand?"

Madeline Monnehan absorbed my words quietly, then nodded.

"I'm going to help you navigate through the next few hours and make sure your rights are protected. Is it okay with you if I record our session together? No one will have access to the recording except me and my team."

"All right."

I continued slowly and deliberately. "In the event that you do hire us to represent you, I may need to discuss your case with other lawyers, witnesses, experts, and private investigators. If there's any particular information that you do not want me to reveal, you would need to let me know and I'd certainly respect your wishes in the matter. Is that clear?"

She nodded.

"The way I like to do this is simply to let you tell me what happened. I'll take a few notes. Then I'll ask you some questions. Will that work for you?"

"Yes."

I scrawled the date and time on my pad: Wednesday, March 12th, 2012. 2:49 a.m. "Mrs. Monnehan, why don't you talk me through the events of last evening?" I softened my voice. "I know it's difficult, but it's very important that we establish the facts surrounding your husband's death."

Madeline Monnehan spoke slowly, choosing her words carefully. "I suppose I should go back to a bit earlier in the day. Yesterday morning, Andrew called me from his office here, in New York, and told me he was leaving for D.C. The new tax bill had taken a great toll on every member of the committee and they'd been holding countless meetings. Andrew had been going back and forth for the past two months. He said to expect him home by late Friday night. I told him I would go to our cottage on Long Island for the next few days to do some writing. So I packed a couple of things and went out to Sag Harbor later in the day."

The account was clear and concise. For a moment I almost forgot that we were discussing the events leading up to the fatal shooting of her husband.

"You drove?"

"No, I took a train and had someone pick me up from the station."

"Who was that?"

"Anthony, the groundskeeper out there. Our driver had left earlier due to a family emergency, so Anthony picked me up and drove me to the cottage."

"Around what time did you get there?"

"Maybe 5:30 in the afternoon" I felt her eyes on me as I jotted down the salient facts.

"Okay, go on."

"Almost immediately after we arrived at the cottage, I realized I'd forgotten my insulin in the city. I'm a diabetic. In addition, I discovered I'd left my writing at home. I decided to take the next train back to New York. I thought I would spend the night at home and head out again in the morning. A few hours from now, actually."

"Did you call or text anyone to let them know your change of plans?"

"I called Andrew's office in DC to let him know I'd be heading back to the city. As far as the staff knew, there was no need to. The house was empty. I had given our New York staff Wednesday off, since I didn't expect either myself or Andrew to be back before Thursday."

"When you say New York staff, who do you mean?"

"Helen Morley, our housekeeper, and Mrs. Piacelli, our cook."

"Okay, so you took a train back to New York?"

"Yes. I missed the 6:02 train. I caught the 7:25, arriving in the city around 10 p.m." She drew in a long, even breath and continued, "I took a cab from Penn Station."

"Did anyone see you come home?"

"No, I don't think so. Well, actually, I stopped at a coffee shop before heading home. It's at the corner of my block and they know me there. I don't know if they saw me go home, but I was there."

"And then?"

"I bought a sugar-free muffin—the last one—went home, and took a long bath. I was exhausted."

"No one was at home at the time?"

"That's correct. I was just leaving the bathroom when I heard a crash downstairs. I realized I had forgotten to set the security alarm. I waited for a few minutes and didn't hear anything. I thought maybe I had imagined it. Then I heard footsteps and I knew someone was in the house. I was petrified. I made myself reach into the nightstand by the bed and pull out Andrew's handgun." She took a shuddering breath and grew quiet.

"Take your time."

"I stood in the doorway, frozen. I don't know how long I stayed there; my heart was beating so fast I thought it would burst." She laid a hand on the table and contemplated it for a moment. "I realized I couldn't just stand there, waiting in the dark with a gun in my hand. I needed to do something. I turned on the hallway lights and called out a few times. No answer. I went downstairs and checked every room in the house: the kitchen, the library, Andrew's study, the living room. I even went into the laundry and the housekeeper's rooms. I thought perhaps Helen had returned for some reason. But there was no one. Everything was quiet and in order. I assumed maybe I had just imagined it, so I switched on the alarm and went upstairs.

"When I turned out the lights in the hall and stepped into the bedroom there was a large, hulking form near the foot of the bed. It was dark… I froze. I couldn't move or yell or speak." I watched as her eyes widened with horror. "I was terrified. The shape turned and started to come toward me. I didn't have time to think. The man kept moving towards me. My hand tightened on the gun and I fired…," Her voice trailed off.

She leaned forward, laid both her hands on the table, palms up. It looked like a silent cry for help.

I surprised myself by reaching over to touch her hand. "Would you like to take a break?"

Madeline Monnehan released her breath and suddenly the stiff lines of her shoulders softened. For one single moment she seemed fragile.

"No, I'm fine."

Her voice grew tighter. "The man was crumpled at my feet. I turned on the lights. He was face down in a pool of blood. There was so much blood. It was awful. Then I saw…" Her eyes appeared to fixate on a scene replaying in her mind. Her voice broke with the first hint of helplessness. "…Andrew's pinstriped shirt and shiny Gucci loafers and my knees buckled. I was shaking… He was so still. I knew he was dead, but I checked his pulse anyway. It was no use. I killed Andrew. I killed my own husband." Her breath caught and she closed her eyes. Her face was as white as paper.

"I'm very sorry, Mrs. Monnehan."

She took a long shuddering breath. "Thank you."

"Whenever you're ready."

She seemed lost in thought; she looked up at me, unseeing. "Yes?"

"We can continue whenever you're ready."

She took in a long breath. "I don't know how long I stayed with Andrew. It was a while. I was shaking. I couldn't make my legs move. Then I went into the bathroom. My hands were covered in blood. I cleaned up and I must have returned to the bedroom, because the next thing I knew, I was sitting at the edge of my bed staring down at my dead husband. Then I called 9-1-1."

"This was at 12:08 a.m.?"

Her tone sounded flat. "If you say so."

"I'm assuming the gun was registered." I asked.

"Yes, Andrew received some threatening calls and decided we needed a firearm for additional protection."

I turned off the tape recorder.

"I can't help but notice the bruise on your cheek." I stared hard into her eyes. "Is there something you'd like to tell me about it?"

Instinctively her fingers touched the ugly bruise and she shook her head. "It's an old contusion; I was careless opening an overhead cabinet. As you can see, it's almost gone."

I studied Madeline's face. It was true, the tell-tale mark was in its last stages, but its image struck a chord and I made a mental note to have Madeline Monnehan's health record checked out. I was sure Detective Lachey was already on it. Spousal abuse accounted for many homicides.

She tucked her hands back in her lap and sat still. I waited for her to ask the usual questions about what to expect, what the next step was, when she would see me again. But she remained silent.

When I spoke, my voice was even. "As you know, Mr. O'Shaunessy contacted our firm on your behalf and asked us to represent you. Is that what you'd like?" I paused, waiting for a response. When none was forthcoming, I continued, "As I said earlier, I'll be here for the next few hours, regardless of the decision you make."

A flicker of hesitation crossed her features.

I smiled wryly. "I haven't had to pitch myself for quite some time. What's important for you to know is that I'm good at representing my clients once they retain me."

"Leo says you're a star."

"Twenty-four cases in five years and just one single loss, in an extremely complex multiple homicide case. If you follow that kind of news, the Lloyd Pritchet case garnered a few headlines."

She gave me a searching look.

Against my better judgment, I felt compelled to state, "I, myself, served as a deputy district attorney in Brooklyn for four years, prosecuting hundreds of hard-core cases involving homicides, sex crimes, assault, and narcotics. In the past seven years, since I joined the firm, I've been utilizing that experience in a number of high-profile cases. I'm very selective about my cases and I only work with clients I believe in."

She gave me a quick smile, brittle as glass. "So, would you like to represent me?" The words were uttered in a smooth and easy cadence. They seemed to imply that any response I cared to offer would be acceptable. She leaned forward and I caught a whiff of her scent, a subtle whisper of spicy orange blossoms. Her eyes were level and direct, but I noticed her right-hand curl and press against her middle.

I was finding it hard to separate my thoughts from my initial gut reaction. I had felt drawn to Madeline Monnehan from the first moment I laid eyes on her, but I sensed trouble. I tend to put great stock in my inner voice: it's usually right. And in this room, at this moment, that voice was screaming: Madeline Monnehan was bad news.

Then she shifted slightly in her seat and a quick graceful shudder traveled down the length of her body in one fluid ripple. I became conscious of the slender curves of the figure hidden under the cloth, naked and defenseless. Suddenly I felt the need to reach into that will of steel, to find out what lay beneath all that self-control. I felt my senses vibrate, I could almost hear the buzz.

Madeline's question lingered in the air. Almost against my will, I heard myself respond warily. "Yes, I would."

When she finally spoke, her voice was smooth, betraying nothing. "All right then, do I have to sign any papers, an agreement for retaining you?'

"It's not necessary for now, Mrs. Monnehan. We'll be representing you at the bail hearing and when you're released, we'll meet in my office. We'll go over the issue of my fee and what I will do to earn it." My voice sounded clipped and cool.

In a soft voice, she breathed, "It's Maddie."

I let a moment pass. "All right, Maddie, we're going to be led soon to a room where Detective Lachey and his partner will interview you in my presence."

"I understand."

"Are you familiar with the Fifth Amendment?"

"Yes, I know what it means."

"I want you to exercise your right to silence."

Maddie answered calmly enough. "All right, if that's your advice."

"It is."

It took less than ten minutes for us to enter the interview room, for Maddie to assert her Fifth Amendment right, and for Lachey and his partner to exit the room.

I watched Maddie carefully. "I'm going to call the District Attorney's office as soon as it opens. I'll get you the earliest bail hearing. We'll proceed from there. In the meantime, don't talk to anyone and don't worry; you're in good hands."

She said, "Leo O'Shaunessy has my Power of Attorney; he can sign anything you need. He'll be able to assist you with any inquiries."

I stood up, gathered my belongings, and opened the door. My smile suggested we should ignore the fact that the air between us was charged with an inexplicable tension. We were locked in a course neither one of us had anticipated, or desired. I let her walk out in front of me. I felt the stir in the air as she passed by, our bodies almost touching.

I was thinking about those long slender fingers with their tapered nails; the hands matched the woman, long and lovely, and yet strong and capable. *Capable of what?* Whatever thoughts or emotions coursed through the head and heart of this woman, she kept them well in check. And I knew, somehow, that what she had chosen to tell me was not the entire truth.

CHAPTER 3

In a night, or in day,
In a vision, or in none,
Is it therefore the less gone?
All that we see or seem
Is but a dream within a dream.

—Edgar Allan Poe, *A Dream Within a Dream*

My sneakers are silent on the pavement. I love running, especially track at school—the one sport I excel at. I hear a car's engine behind me, slowing down. I don't care. I keep running. I turn my head to look. My reflection flickers across the black-tinted windows, but I know who's sitting behind them. Crawley the Asshole has been reminding me he's got me in his sights. I have no idea why, but I'm sure he'll let me know in his sweet old time. In the meantime, I know I shouldn't stop. Keep on moving! Keep on running! I feel the sweat gather between my shoulder blades, and I'm starting to feel my lungs constrict, but I'm not slowing down. And then I zip around the corner, sprint through an alley and through the gate, and I'm at The Commons. The car stops. It can't follow, vehicles are forbidden. I'm still running. My lungs are about to explode.

"Hey, slow down, O'Rourke. Where's the fire?" A strong hand grabs my shoulder. Mr. Cuccinelli from the third floor. His wiry eyebrows are

creased with concern, but he has a warm, toothy smile, and I stop, catching my breath.

It's hard to talk. "My brother…Padrick…he hit a home run. NYPD's Finest won!" I gush. I don't mention the black Caddy following me, or who's inside.

"Ah," Mr. Cuccinelli grins and lets go of my shoulder. "Si, si, that brother of yours, he iss a good athlete, no?" Mr. Cuccinelli speaks with a halting accent. Ma says he's from the old country, not Ireland, not our old country, but still from over there, from another foreign place.

I smile at his bright eyes. The car is forgotten. The bully gone. The dark windows, the danger behind them. "Oh, yeah!" I answer. "But I run faster!"

I woke up flailing for air, every muscle in my body aching with fatigue, but as usual, sleepless nights only stoked the need to run. I put on my running shorts, a long sleeve t-shirt that had seen better days, and my new Nikes. I crossed the street and headed toward the Hudson.

I started slow, but then my strides accelerated and I was off. My legs pumping their furious, familiar rhythm. Following the runner's path, I let the punishing pace take over, a combat zone where the body takes charge and muscles and blood and lungs are the sole means for mastery of self. This uncompromising prescription never failed.

By the time I returned to my building, the dream was forgotten and I was ready to dive in.

Andrew Clive Monnehan, born in 1955 to Mildred and Brandon Monnehan of Greenwich, Connecticut, was the youngest of four children. After three pregnancies, which produced three petite, freckled daughters, Mildred finally presented her husband with his heir apparent. When Andrew Monnehan was born, his father's wealth was immense and his holdings diverse. The fifteen-thousand-square-foot mansion in the gated Greenwich Connecticut community of Conyers Farm was a veritable showcase for his wealth. The shrewd Monnehan Sr. had also invested in a French seaside villa in Sag Harbor and a townhouse on East 75th Street for when business called him to New York. If

Monnehan Sr. lacked pedigree and appropriate lineage, he made up for it by chairing well-publicized and popular charities. He capitalized on his business acumen to gather an impressive coterie of well-connected politicians and government officials.

The numerous photographs chronicling Andrew's childhood and youth showed a fawning mother, an interchangeable series of nannies and tutors, and an astounding array of leisure activities. He graduated from Choate, was accepted at Yale, where he majored in political science, then went on to graduate from Harvard Law School. After seventeen years of specializing in corporate law at Murphy, Cranston and Shaw, Monnehan, at forty-two, turned his eyes towards politics.

He ran almost uncontested for a chair on the New York City Council, becoming the most outspoken proponent of women's rights and a pro-choice advocate. It was only in his race for the U.S. Senate, in 2006, that Andrew Monnehan encountered his first real political difficulty. But here, Monnehan Sr. stepped in with his limitless funds to drive a campaign unparalleled in resources and political pull to secure the seat for his son.

Compared with the flood of information about Andrew Monnehan's charitable, political, and professional activities, there was little about his private life. His picture did appear in some newspapers and magazines escorting beautiful women from the Washington scene. In fact, there was one major article in *Esquire* that pronounced the Senator one of the ten most eligible bachelors in America.

It was, therefore, a social upset of tidal proportions when, out of nowhere at the age of fifty-five, Senator Monnehan announced his engagement to Madeline Walker. The collective shock in the Washington circles was due largely to the belief that Madeline Walker, twenty years his junior, was an inappropriate consort to the popular and handsome Senator. Her sole distinction was her newly published collection of poetry titled *Against the Shoals*.

As it turned out, the small volume won the Pulitzer Prize the week following the engagement notices, and Madeline, or Maddie, as she was known to her colleagues, catapulted to fame. The whirlwind courtship and subsequent nuptials of the new couple culminated in their move to the Senator's home on East 75th Street, and what followed was a union much discussed and photographed by a frenzied media.

My phone rang as I was looking at a photo of the grinning Senator embracing his beautiful wife. Shit, the woman had a face born to steal a man's breath.

"Conor here."

My assistant, Annika, was at the other end of the wire. "Nick, I just got your message. I was in the shower. You said urgent, what's up?"

Annika Ormond had been my associate for the past six years; her brusque manner and her brook-no-nonsense style disguised a brilliant legal mind and organizational genius which made her indispensable.

"We have a new case and I need you to get in touch with your contact at the D. A.'s office. We need to be discreet, but fast."

"Who's the client?"

"Madeline Monnehan. Arrested last night after confessing to the shooting of her husband, the Honorable Senator from New York, Andrew Monnehan. I met with Mrs. Monnehan and she claims she shot him out of fear for her life. Mistook him for an intruder. She's being held for bail. We'll push for released on recognizance. But in the meantime, find out who the prosecutor is going to be, wake that sleeping dog of ours ASAP. He should start working the case."

"Got it. So, we need to call Paul Ribisi's office," Annika said, "You think he'll be heading the hearing? I need to call the morgue and find out when we'll have the autopsy results. I'll call Oscar to meet us at the office. I'll have to file a request to visit the scene of the crime, which incidentally was where?"

It was always a guess which Annika would come up for air; she could run on, ticking off all executive matters in mere seconds.

"The couple's residence on East 75th Street. I'm assuming Ribisi will prosecute. He's itching for headlines. I don't think we'll go to trial but if we do, this case is his ticket to the elections. We also need to get into the residence. Also, can you get me info on the presiding judge at the arraignment? I'm pushing for today sometime."

"No problem. Are we still meeting at the office at the same time?"

"Yes, see you soon."

I hung up and called Paul Ribisi's cell phone, which I'd had on speed dial for the past year. Usually, the New York Assistant D.A. would not be available before nine, but with such a high visibility case, I thought Ribisi would already be stoked.

He answered on the first ring. "I know, Nick, as early as possible. Let me get to the office first. I spoke with Detective Lachey, but still need to make some calls. Give me an hour." He cleared his voice. "Trust me; I have as little interest in keeping her with the general population as you have."

"Thanks, I'll wait for your call." I hung up and the phone on the desk rang. I barked into the receiver, "Conor."

It was Annika. "Arraignment is set for 2:45 pm in front of Judge Ramsey. I talked to Oscar. He'll be in the office as soon as he 'showers, shaves, and consumes his morning nourishment,' and I'm quoting him verbatim…what do you suppose he considers a nourishing breakfast?"

Before I could answer, the other line started ringing.

"Hold on, Annika."

I picked up the second line. It was Ribisi. "2:45 in front of Judge Ramsey." No hello, no greeting, the life of a very busy man.

"See you then."

I snapped back to Annika, "How do you always beat Ribisi to the punch?"

"Connections are my middle name, Boss. That's why you pay me the big bucks. Anything else?"

"Try to work out a reasonable timeframe for all our pending cases. I have to advise the General I've taken on the Monnehan case."

I heard Annika's quiet chuckle. The reference to Stetson Senior as the General was a private joke between the two of us, but when the shoe fits… "In the meantime, find out anything you can about Andrew and Madeline Monnehan and I mean anything. I also need the Long Island Railroad schedule from yesterday."

"I called Lippi's office, nothing yet. Anything else?" She paused for a moment and then continued, "I'm assuming you need all of the above for this afternoon?" There was a slight hint of sarcasm in Annika's voice, but the tone was good-natured, and I knew she would come through. She was pure gold.

"Yes."

"You know I only do this because of your baby blues."

Annika was happily married to a successful corporate accountant with whom she had adorable twin girls, so all her perky remarks about my eyes, my abs, or my status as a "player" were merely fruits of her subversive sense of humor.

I let the silence roll and then said, "See you at the office, then."

"Okay, Boss, see you later." I could almost feel the smile at the other end.

CHAPTER 4

Power and redemption carved into my skin.
No looking back, just holding fast.

—Maddie Walker, *Against the Shoals.*

James Stetson Jr. 'Jim' (he hated to be called James) was standing by the window of his office, staring out into the city as it came to life. He turned around and his heavy gaze searched my face. Jim was only a year older than me, but looked weighed down by the shackles of age. His receding hairline and his slight paunch contributed to the overall image of a man past his prime. I knew that lately he was flailing, both in his professional and personal life.

I also knew that Jim's hunger for acknowledgment was unfortunately spurred by my success. There was no doubt that his skill and determination matched mine, but his father's approval seemed beyond Jim's reach. I wondered, not for the first time, whether my partnership in the firm was detrimental to their relationship. Yet whenever I brought up the subject of leaving, Jim balked. Whether I stayed or left, Jim said, his father's opinion of him would remain unchanged. All he could do was white-knuckle it.

Jim and I had been roommates while studying law at Emory in Atlanta. Transplants from New York City, we had forged a close friendship, somehow recognizing that we had both been indelibly shaped by our troubled pasts. I was juggling the ferocious load of coursework, research, and exams, but was slowly losing ground to my demons. Jim found me one night standing on top of our roof, dispassionately contemplating the drop. Out of his depth, Jim called one of his father's old friends, Dr. Alan Michelson, Director of Psychiatry and Behavioral Sciences, at the university. The doctor showed up within the hour, talked me off the roof, and sedated me for the next eight hours.

The next Sunday morning, I found myself sitting across from the Doc on a two-sail sloop, swaying gently on the Chattahoochee River. Usually curt, bad-tempered and obdurately unresponsive, I suddenly found myself talking. It was like listening to the slow, halting words of a total stranger. We must have sat there for hours. Perhaps it was the familiar lapping of the water, the sights and the smells so entrenched in my memories, or maybe it was an unacknowledged need to finally open up to someone. Whatever it was—the dam was breached. I remember fixing my stare on his benign eyes and spewing out the sludge of toxins in my gut. The Doc barely moved, and never once interrupting the flow of anguish and rage. When I finally stopped talking, the sun was already low on the horizon. I felt stunned, exhausted, and mortified. The Doc steered the boat back to the dock and ever so casually informed me that he expected me the next day in his office.

The Doc taught me how to use my body as a weapon against the inner turmoil. Even as a child, I knew that there was something deep and unyielding inside me that would emerge in moments of fear or anger. The Doc showed me how to marshal that flinty coldness. He taught me that I could channel my energies against, what I called, "the hundred feet." That I could literally remove myself from crippling emotions. When memories of Da and Ma, my sister Moira and Padrick clung like algae around my ankles, I learned to will myself back to what was real. I was healed inasmuch as I maintained my rational modus operandi. But there was a price: I was loath to, and in truth, quite incapable of forming deeply felt attachments.

The Doc not only helped save my sanity but gave me back my life. And I never forgot that it was due to Jim that I had become, if not a full-fledged card-carrying member of the Kumbaya Society, then at least a productive son of a bitch who never threw in the towel. It was a fair trade.

Jim's rumpled suit looked slept-in. I raised my brows. "You're in early."

He ignored the implied question. "How did it go with Monnehan?"

"She's hired us."

He nodded. We looked at each other; the unsaid hanging between us. We were in for a media blizzard, and we knew it.

"She claims self-defense." I paused for a heartbeat. "Mistook him for an intruder." Without omitting a single detail, I gave him a full report of my interview with Maddie.

Jim went to his desk and sat down. The worry lines on his forehead disappeared as he watched me. We've always had this, the steady under-standing, the to and fro of colleagues who bounced ideas off of each other and knew they had each other's back. Jim had an analytical mind. Reductive reasoning was his forte, and he could excise superfluous facts with the ease of a surgeon.

"What do you think?" I asked Jim.

"I suppose you'll be pursuing her timeline," he said. "Also, the Senator's movements. Why did he return so suddenly, so late? Why return at all?" We both knew that we had to tread carefully. Pleas of self-defense were almost always smokescreens, and it was better to base a defense on a damning truth rather than on a half-cocked elaborate lie.

I turned to leave when he muttered, "By the way, did I mention you look like shit?"

"Back at you, Jimbo."

We smiled wearily at each other. "I'll be in my office for the next hour if you have any thoughts," I said as I made to the door. I damn well had to make Maddie Monnehan's story stick, and if there were any inconsistencies, I needed to find them early in the game.

As I passed Kim's desk, she called my name. "Call for you on line one. A Mr. Carlisle regarding Senator Monnehan?"

"Police?"

"No, the Senator's personal assistant."

"Take a message."

Back in my office, I jotted the name Carlisle on a new legal pad, writing the number '1' on its front page. It would be the first of many in the Maddie Monnehan file. I wondered if Mr. Carlisle knew to what extent his personal and professional life was going to be scrutinized. There was little we would not find out, as soon as our in-house detective Oscar dug his long bony fingers into the late Senator's affairs. I realized that I felt little compassion towards the deceased. But surely no one deserves to die for being a political blip.

Annika's bright face popped through the doorway to my office. "Busy? I'm early."

"Come on in. I was just thinking."

"Not a bad idea with a three-ringer like this one."

"Have you ever met the Monnehans?"

"You must be confusing me with your latest arm candy. I don't cavort with 'they and them'."

She smiled. A pair of wide, intelligent brown eyes dominated Annika's lean features. Although she came to the firm in her thirties, already married with two small children, her competence and commitment were never in question, and her endless energy, which I exploited mercilessly, was a tremendous asset. It helped that we liked each other and were comfortable with one another's foibles.

"Well, I hope Oscar is in form today," I grunted.

"Did I hear my name?" Oscar's lined face peeked in the open door.

Oscar Flamoix had been the in-house private investigator before Jim and I even joined the firm. He was a hound dog. Not only did he resemble one, with his long face and droopy eyes, but he had the canniest skills in subterfuge and unearthing clues. As rumor had it, he had quit the police force in the middle of a flourishing career and had, to my knowledge, never explained why. I felt a kinship with Oscar, perhaps because Padrick had been an officer of the law, and I always suspected that Oscar remained one at heart.

I motioned him in. "Oscar, good of you to join us."

He stepped in, but remained silent.

"Senator Monnehan was shot at his home last night. We're representing his wife. She's confessed to the shooting and claims self-defense. Says she mistook him for an intruder. We're going to have to hustle to the site immediately. The media's all over this. Her block is probably surrounded by ABC, NBC, CNN, and every other damn initial by now."

"All right. Let me get the camera."

"The bail hearing's later today."

"She was with her husband?"

"No, he came home in the middle of the night. I'd love a witness."

"You got it. I'll get the details from Annie O." In Annika's second week at the firm, Oscar complained of whiplash trying to catch up with her relentless lists of requirements. He nicknamed her after Annie Oakley, the quick-draw sharpshooter, but the moniker was more a nod of respect than of irritation, and much to Annika's chagrin, stuck.

After a quick pause Oscar added, "You know, I met Maddie Monnehan before she got engaged, back then she was Maddie Walker."

Both Annika and I stared at him with astonishment. It was hard to imagine Oscar and Maddie Walker in the same context.

"Seriously?" asked Annika.

"Yeah, on her book tour. I stood on line for an hour at Barnes and Noble just to get her autograph." He turned to me and asked, "Have you read her book?"

"No, but I plan to." It would be interesting to get into the head of Maddie Walker Monnehan.

"I'll bring in my copy, just don't lose it. I treasure the inscription on the first page."

"Never would have pegged you for a poetry sap," I said.

CHAPTER 5

You cast my heart as sharp as razors
I walked in your shadow- fire and ice.

—Maddie Walker, *Against the Shoals.*

Assistant D.A. Paul Ribisi was seated at the prosecutor's table, flanked by two men. His smile was friendly and generous, but it never reached his eyes. When I first met Ribisi, I recognized the cold-blooded tenacity and passion that seemed to be the hallmarks of most outsiders. Neither one of us even entertained the notion of failure.

Ribisi was a head shorter than me, a few years my senior, and had mastered the art of radiating power and authority: he dominated any room he entered. His slicked-back hair, custom-tailored suits, and condescending grin had become a familiar sight in the social tableau of the city. His meteoric rise within the ranks of the Prosecutor's Office was a case study in ambition backed by talent and political acumen. Habitually hobnobbing with the powers that be, he was going places and he knew it.

We acknowledged each other with curt nods.

Ribisi's second was the bright Harvard graduate George Bennett. He was young and gangly, his unprepossessing manner mitigated by sharp blue eyes and a high wide brow. The third person at the prosecution table was an earnest man in his forties, whose name was either

Smith or Smyth and who was making some notations in the binder in front of him.

The courtroom was filled with a mix of press, lawyers, and law officers. My eyes caught Oscar's; he was sitting in the cheap seats and gave me a short nod. Annika and I sat at counsel's table. There was a single legal pad in front of us. I felt a slight buzz in my head—the low hum of nerves—and then the familiar, cool wash of adrenaline.

Homicide cases could incur a No Bail policy, if intent was established. The rule, of course, was flexible, and bail amounts were determined by the presiding judge. Because Maddie herself had called the police and had voluntarily submitted to arrest, I was hoping that might be sufficient grounds for Ramsey to release her on her own recognizance.

"All rise!" cried the bailiff. "The court is in session. The Honorable Judge Ramsey is presiding."

The Honorable Judge Seymour T. Ramsey cut a distinguished figure with his wavy silver hair, tall stature, and austere features, but his appearance was his only claim to distinction. His career had stalled in his mid-fifties, planting him on the backburners of the Supreme Court system. His timid decisions marked him as a lightweight. However, I was not entirely certain that his shortcomings were going to work to our benefit.

The judge sat down and we all followed suit.

"Docket 9742, the People versus Madeline Monnehan," stated the court officer.

I became aware of the unnatural silence that had settled over the court. There seemed to be a small collective hush as all eyes turned towards the far corner of the hall. Maddie Monnehan was led up from the holding room into the chamber. She was wearing something blue, the simple lines of the dress accentuating the long, lean body underneath. Her face was composed, her expression impassive. She stood motionless as she was uncuffed. The packed courtroom seemed spellbound; all eyes were riveted on the defendant.

Maddie looked at me unflinchingly, acknowledged Annika with a brief nod, and then turned slowly to look at Ribisi. It was a direct gaze, assessing him impartially but with a hint of speculation. There was something cold beneath Ribisi's scowl as he met her eyes. Something disturbingly personal and antagonistic flared up in that glance, and I felt the figurative squaring of my shoulders. Ribisi was itching for a fight, and not necessarily for professional reasons. Then I sensed, rather than saw, the stillness that came over him, the quick recovery of deliberate detachment. The practiced prosecutor quashing the visceral reaction. It was but a mere moment, even shorter. Maddie, impassive and indifferent, kept staring into his silence.

Ribisi was the first to slide his eyes to the floor, and his discomfiture sent a small wave of pleasure through me. Welcome to the club, chum.

Maddie Monnehan and I stood side by side.

"Mr. Ribisi?" the judge's voice was clipped as he motioned toward the prosecution's table.

Paul Ribisi cleared his throat as he stood up. "Your Honor, we hereby charge Madeline Monnehan with murder in the first degree. Due to the severity of the crime, we request a 'No Bail' ruling." Somber and resolute, Ribisi took his seat, never once looking in my direction.

I looked at the charging document in my hand. Christ. First-degree murder! Where did that come from?

I raised my eyes to level them on the judge. "Your Honor, these are the first criminal charges ever brought against my client. Furthermore, Mrs. Monnehan voluntarily surrendered to the detectives in charge. She is of stellar character, is a world-renowned Pulitzer Prize-winning author, and has strong community ties. She is by no means a flight risk. We request the court's indulgence in releasing her on her own recognizance."

Ramsey's eyes lingered on Maddie's face with undisguised interest; he started slowly. "The court is well aware of Mrs. Monnehan's accomplishments and standing in the community. However, we cannot ignore the severity of the charges against her. Bail is set at three million dollars."

I felt a quick stab of anger; the high bail was more than I deemed appropriate. Was the Honorable Judge a little swayed by the amount of publicity the case was about to generate?

"Your Honor," I said quickly, "We urge a reconsideration of the bail order. Mrs. Monnehan had surrendered voluntarily to the detectives in charge. She has cooperated fully with the law and will continue to do so. We will arrange for appropriate friends and associates to provide testimonies supporting Mrs. Monnehan."

"You may appeal the court's bail order," offered Ramsey tersely and then consulted his calendar. "Grand jury date will be determined as soon as possible. The D.A.'s office will be duly notified, and so will Counsel for the Defense."

I touched Maddie's elbow. I knew she did not expect the prohibitive bail, yet there was not a trace of emotion in her face.

"Don't worry. I'm sure O'Shaunessy will come up with the funds," I offered. "When bail is posted and you're released, call my office. I'd like you to come in as soon as possible."

"Okay." Her voice was as flat as mine. She turned abruptly as the guard reached her side. I turned and I looked at Annika, "I guess Ramsey is going to play hardball for a change,"

"He knows which side his bread is buttered on. If Ribisi wins the coming election, which is probably odds on, Ramsey is assured another term on the bench." Annika stuffed the pad into her briefcase.

Her wry voice echoed my thoughts. As the prosecutor, Ribisi had a lot riding on this case. He was in possession of some god-damn information and it was going to be lethal. This could well become a juggernaut of a media blitz: a murdered Senator, a beautiful Pulitzer Prize winner of a wife… As "hot stories" went this could take the cake. If the indictment went on to trial, Ribisi would become a household name.

I pronounced evenly, "If there's a good time to be indicted for murder, this isn't it."

We pushed through the throng of journalists gathered on the front steps, mumbling a continuous litany of "No comments" until we reached Oscar's car. National and local stations were extensively represented. The death of a Senator by the hand of his famous and beautiful wife charged with his murder—the case promised prolonged and salacious coverage.

"How did it go, Boss?" asked Oscar, glancing at me in his rearview mirror as I heaved myself onto the back seat.

"Find out what is the connection between the Monnehans and Ribisi." I said and closed my eyes.

* * *

Oscar closed the door behind him. The telephone rang, I recognized my sister Moira's soft voice, "Hey, Nick."

"Hey." I felt the quick twinge of remorse. "I didn't call this morning. I'm sorry, I know I promised."

"It's okay. I know how busy you are…." Her voice trailed off.

"I'm never too busy for you, *a ghrá,* you should know that. I just got waylaid by this case and completely forgot to return your call. Are we on for lunch on Monday?"

Moira and I met every two to three weeks. Eaten by my overwhelming guilt, I often dreaded these get-togethers. Moira, on the other hand, looked forward to them. Yet my sister had never once initiated a single meeting. In fact, Moira had asked so very little of me over the years that I sometimes felt not only all-consuming guilt, but also utter shame.

Tending to Da was a duty she had taken on willingly, stoically, and against my express wishes. If it were up to me, I would have long ago left the miserable son of a bitch to his own devices, dropped him off somewhere, and let loneliness and oblivion take care of what remained of his wretched life.

When my father was diagnosed with severe chronic rheumatoid arthritis, Moira opted to move back from Manhattan to Brooklyn to be near him. She divided her time between work as a counselor at the Brooklyn Academy of Music and Da's needs, and no amount of persuasion or displeasure on my part had convinced her to quit taking care of the bastard.

My only contribution to this dreary state of affairs was financial, which I willingly would have quadrupled if I could excise Da away from Moira. But she was adamant about keeping him at home.

Moira choose her words carefully. "It's Da. We need to talk."

"All right."

"I need you to come and see him."

I let out a short laugh.

Moira repeated patiently, "I need you to come home and see him."

Twenty-four fucking years I hadn't laid eyes on the bastard. Now, my sister's voice, soft with a hint of steel, a jolt of unexpected punch.

"Home?" I couldn't help the acerbic tone.

"He's sick."

"I know. The asshole's been sick for sixty-seven years."

"It's his liver, advanced cirrhosis," she went on quietly. "I guess we all knew this was coming, he never stopped drinking. I finally got him to the doctor this week. He looks terrible. He's not a candidate for a transplant."

Yeah, not even a fucking heart transplant would fix the bastard. "I gather the prognosis is bad," I stated dryly.

"He's going to be totally bedridden soon and they say he'll need round-the-clock care."

"Do you need more money?"

"No, I need you to come see him. It's important."

Da's image flashed against my eyes. The square jawline, the cold black stare. The hard and brutal strength of a well-aimed fist. I swallowed against the foul taste. "Sorry. Can't."

"All right, Nick. We both stopped feeling sorry for ourselves a long time ago," she snapped.

"Sweetheart," I said, "sooner or later the man will have to be carted off. Things will get increasingly difficult for both you and him. Professionals need to take over. Why don't you look into institutions that might take him? Cost is no object. I'll take care of it."

"But to move him from the only place he knows and feels secure…?"

I wanted to laugh. Wasn't this the man who had single-handedly inflicted a reign of terror on us? The man under whose shadow none of us had ever felt secure? What Socratic irony that we now had to make him feel safe and sound.

"Just come and see him, Nick. It's time. I'm not asking; I am telling you. You need to come see him before it's too late." There was a definite stubborn edge in that calm voice. "It'll be okay, you'll see. I'll talk to him. Come Saturday night. I'll make your favorite stew and a grand shepherd's pie."

It was clear that Moira wasn't going to let it go. I thought for the hundredth time that I could never make amends for Moira's lost life. If this was some little measure of atonement, I would tolerate Da for a measly two hours.

"All right, Moira. What time?"

She let out a sigh of relief. "Thank you. Seven o'clock?"

"I'll be there." I paused, then added, "The fucker will probably out-live us both."

"Watch your language! He's still your father," she said in that soft voice.

"Yeah, which is why I took Ma's name."

"In any case," she said, "he is our father."

"I wonder if Satan's spawns honor their sire."

"I don't think Satan was permitted to beget any children," she said lightly.

"If only that were the case with Francis Angus O'Rourke."

"Then I wouldn't have you for my big, brilliant brother, would I?" Moira's warmth sluiced over me.

I knew I had to work just a little harder at deserving it.

"All right, sis. See you tomorrow."

I set the telephone gently back on its cradle and opened my hand to find deep scarlet grooves imprinted on my palm. My sweet sister, Moira. How could one love another so deeply, yet dread that person as if one's immortal soul were in jeopardy? There were days that were easier to handle, but there was never a day without the guilt.

I was about to face the son of a bitch for the first time in over two decades.

CHAPTER 6

As flies to wanton boys, are we to the gods.
They kill us for their sport.

—William Shakespeare, *King Lear, Act I, Scene I*

My friend, Greg, picked up after one ring.

"After exhausting all manner of modern communication, I decided to drop by personally, but you were still out," Greg said without a greeting.

"My doorman told me."

"Twenty-four-hour babysitter, eh?"

"Yeah, something like that." I smiled into the phone.

I heard no responding levity in Greg's voice as he cleared his throat and said slowly, "We just got the new release sheets from upstate. I wanted to tell you that your good-old-friend Crawley's been released. Yesterday afternoon. He's since disappeared into the belly of the beast, somewhere in Brooklyn, I hear." Another long pause. "You know you're number one on the Crow's list."

"Yeah, sounds like my life just got a shade more interesting. Guess I've got to start setting my alarm." I realized too late that my last remark was a mistake.

"It's two goddamn buttons! You can't push two buttons?" Greg sounded pissed and worried at the same time. "Why do I bother to hook up your place if you're not using the freakin' system?"

"I am, I am. Just…twenty-four-hour doorman, remember?"

"Screw the rent-a-cop. Push the two buttons!"

"Okay, man. No worries, I will."

"Watch your back, Nick. He's a mean piece of shit."

"I don't think he'll come looking for me here."

"I was thinking more like you looking for him."

I knew he called it right. I hated Crawley. I could not and would not let it go.

"I have a full plate without looking for outside distractions." I wondered whether my voice was convincingly even.

Greg sounded skeptical. "Be careful, that's all I'm saying."

Hugh Crawley aka The Crow, was my personal nemesis. From the moment he lasered his nasty slits of eyes at Padrick and me more than thirty years ago, the Crow and I were set to circle each other with deadly purpose. Ten years ago, while serving at the D.A.'s office in Brooklyn, I participated in a sting operation in which Crawley was finally apprehended and indicted. I succeeded in having him charged with assault with a deadly weapon, found guilty, and sent to Attica Correctional Facility. The twin engines that had driven me to become a lawyer—the pursuit of justice and trust in the spirit of the law—had finally paid off. After years of skating around the law and eluding indictments in at least two murder investigations, Crawley was finally behind bars. Karma was a bitch.

I threw together a sandwich, pulled a cold Amstel off the refrigerator shelf, and went out on my terrace. The air was brisk, but unusually mild for March. I gulped down my meal and rested my head against the chair back. I was done in, more mentally than physically. I could go for days with little sleep, but the past twenty-four hours had exhausted me. Nothing was as it had been; nothing was as it should be. First,

Maddie Monnehan. Then, Moira's adamant demand to come and see my bastard father, and now—Hugh Crawley.

I pulled out my cell and called Oscar.

"Took you long enough," he answered gruffly. Like Greg, he dispensed with polite greetings.

"Just got in, what's up?" The matter of Crawley could wait till Oscar returned.

"I had some luck with the super of the Senator's apartment building. A friendly little chap who liked to talk. The short and short of it is that the Senator had a coterie of friends who were frequent visitors at his place. His chief aide, Aubrey Carlisle, seems to have been a regular. The super says he might have stayed overnight on more than one occasion."

"And the apartment?"

Legally I could not be privy to how he accessed Monnehan's apartment. Oscar was prudent enough not to share any details. But I also knew that the picking of locks was one of his innumerable talents.

"No problem there. Fancy place. From what I could tell, totally furnished with choice antiques and completely stocked with the finest wines and liquors. The man was a total sybarite. And he certainly was into fashion. He had more silk ties than I have jelly beans in my jar."

I smiled. Oscar was a devout Jelly Belly gourmet. There were never enough of those colorful suckers to satisfy his craving.

"I think the Missus spent very little time in that place. One or two blouses in the closet, a few toiletries in the corner of the medicine cabinet, also a robe and a pair of women's running sneakers. But that's all."

I started to form a mental picture of Senator Monnehan. "Anything else?"

"I need to stay for two more nights at least. Carlisle is out of the office tomorrow, and I want to speak directly to Monnehan's office staff."

"How about a laptop?"

"Nada" was the short reply.

"Okay, call me when you have something." Then I remembered. "Did you find any records in the apartment?"

"No, nothing there, no letters or papers. Looks like his study was cleaned out. I couldn't even find the utility bills. Either he kept his paperwork at the office, or someone beat me to the punch." Oscar sounded miffed.

I sighed. I would have loved to see the Senator's telephone and credit card statements. I knew I'd have to delve into his personal affairs if I was going to plot out a sound defense strategy for his wife.

"I'll endeavor to follow Euripides's words," Oscar muttered slyly.

I grinned. "What is: Omnem movere lapidem for 100? 'Leave no stone unturned.'"

"I was saving that one."

I chuckled. "Freshman year, Classics 100. You'll have to do better than that."

"Where there's life there's hope," Oscar retorted gruffly.

"You're reading Cicero now?"

"Just revisiting, no need to get excited."

I had yet to find a gap in Oscar's mastery of Greco-Roman literature. I found his reservoir of knowledge astounding. He loved to ferret out information and hoarded data. Oscar was Basque by birth, as he never failed to point out. Not French, not Spanish, but a full-fledged Basque on both his maternal and paternal sides. He spoke English, Italian, Spanish, Basque, and French, had a quick mathematical mind and a sharp eye that missed very little. His one fatal flaw was his love for what he called the "nectar of the gods," the sweet gold liquid of an aged cognac. Once in a while, Oscar would drop off the face of the earth, only to reappear freshly shaved and primly dressed and as communicative as a turtle. In any event, Oscar Flamoix was a man to be reckoned with, and I was happy to consider him an ally.

* * *

I woke up at the crack of dawn and for a few moments lay still, waiting for my newly recurring dream of Padrick and the old heartache to give way. I looked at the empty space next to me. Often, it seemed, I woke up surprised to find the blanket and sheets mussed strictly on my side, half-expecting to hear my brother's deep breathing next to me. It was always at moments like these, when my half-awakened mind— that traitorous keeper of memories—would thrust me back down the rabbit hole.

I put on my running gear, took the elevator down, and lunged into my morning routine.

The river on my right smelled of seaweed and fish as I inhaled the familiar stench. It was an odor I grew up with and knew inside out. It was the smell of my childhood and had become the smell of my worst nightmares. The steady pounding of my running shoes and the lapping sounds of the river washed over me. I felt the welcome whoosh of my mind as it slowly sank into blankness. I was halfway through my route when the thought of Crawley intruded.

It's the first day of summer vacation! Ma, Moira and I are going to take the train to Coney Island. It's only two stops, but it might as well be a world away. I love the ocean and the sand and the sun, but we rarely get to go to the beach. Most days I have to go with Da on his fishing trawl. But today is different! Da is away for three whole days and we are free! Ma is already busy in the cramped kitchen. Her cheeks are flushed and her eyes shine bright. She looks young. In my head I take a snapshot of this moment.

Jones Beach is half-full when we arrive. It's still early. We lay out the wool blanket on the sand near the water. I strip to my trunks, throwing my t-shirt and shorts on the ground, barely hearing Ma's warning to be careful. I race into the water and dive head-first into the frothing surf. I swim further and further out until I leave everything behind. I flip over onto my back and stare at the astonishing blue expanse above. Makes me forget any other color exists in the world, makes me forget everything else.

When I finally come back to Ma and Moira, Ma's darning what looks like a small blouse. Her fingers are never idle. She smiles quietly when she looks up. My sister, Moira, is completely rapt in a new book. Moira and I are barely a year apart, but it's like we're from different planets. Moira has an open and warm smile for everyone. I, on the other hand, never give anything away. And I'd walk on rusty nails before I'd admit it, but I'm jealous of her.

Then I think of my big brother Padrick, who is going with his class-mates today to the New Jersey shore. Padrick will be starting his senior year at Lincoln High School in the fall. Robbie says he's practically out the door already. I grin when I think of Padrick. This time next year, he'll probably be as far away from Brooklyn as I am from the moon.

As I shake the water out of my hair, I spot Crawley at the far end of the pier. He scares the shit out of me—makes me feel small and weak and out of control. I hate the feeling. But I'm drawn to him like those bluefin tuna suckers Da hooks by dangling herrings.

I start walking toward the pier. I can make out the creepos I secretly named Mutt and Jeff. There are six boys in the group surrounding Crawley, and they're all staring down at the rocks at the end of the pier. Crawley is just a year younger than Padrick, but he's vicious and strong like a pit bull. He's taller than me by more than a foot. Freaky "Creature from the Black Lagoon."

On the days that Crawley, the bully, does attend school, most everyone avoids him. I try to keep away, but he and his flunkies are always after me. When Crawley and the dickheads find me, I never run. I stay and fight them; any blow that catches Crawley is like getting a small gold star. Crawley loves that I fight because he can prolong his pleasure and when I return home, I stay clear of Da's path. Da wouldn't appreciate me being thrashed. It's not the brawling that he would object to. Christ, Da could give lessons in ass-whipping. He would beat me up just for losing.

Crawley doesn't know it, but I once witnessed Padrick give him an awe-some wipe-the-floor-with-his-face trashing after he caught Crawley ganging up on Charlie Beecham, the smallest kid in my class. I know Crawley hates Padrick, not only because Crawley was forced to eat crow, but also because Padrick is his absolute opposite. Padrick is my Rock Star! Crawley hates everyone, but he hates Padrick the most. Every time I catch Crawley looking at my brother, I can feel my skin crawl.

Without turning around, Crawley drawls, "Nicholas Nickleby, come join us." The sixth sense of the predator. "And where's your knight in shining armor?" Crawley sneers.

I give Crawley a blank look. I've had excellent practice. I smile with my lips closed. My hammering heart is wedged in my throat.

"So, Nickleby, what do you think?"

Shit. I'll die before I show him how scared I am.

"Think?"

"The jump. You stupid, or what?"

Last year, on one of the few days I spent at the beach, I saw the lifeguard pull out some dumb swimmer from beneath the pier. The body of the boy was twisted at the waist and there was a lot of blood. He looked like one of Moira's rag dolls as he was laid out on a stretcher. Somebody told me that he took a dare and dove into the water, trying to clear the jutting boulders. Since that incident, the lifeguard posted a sign forbidding swimmer from jumping off the pier. But, like all forbidden fruit, every other numbnut keeps trying to sink his teeth into it.

Crawley's pig face is gloating. He knows I won't be able to resist.

I shrug, "Says here it's forbidden." I point to the large, yellow sign attached to the pole.

"So?" he scoffs. "You always follow the rules, or are you just chicken-shit?"

I walk over to the rail and look down. The eddying waters churn like a whirlpool. The boulders' jagged edges look like the teeth of a Great White.

I sling my legs over the rail. My heart slams into my throat. "I will if you will," I say.

"After you, Nickleby." His laugh sounds like a snort.

I'm thinking of Padrick. He'd never let me jump. I say a silent prayer as I raise my arms above my head, bend my knees and push off the edge, head first. I clear the furthest boulder! My left ankle grazes the sharp tip of the tallest rock, but I don't feel any pain. I'm floating on a bubble of mad, mad, mad glee. I'm okay! I feel like pumping my fist in the air. As I surface, I see the figures of two lifeguards sprinting towards the end of the pier. Crawley and his boot-lickers scatter like rats. I am in deep shit. I see the taller lifeguard gesturing at me furiously. I swim to shore, leaving a thin pink trail on the water's surface.

When I let myself collapse on the sand, I see the nasty cut curving from my ankle to my shin. There's a lot of blood, but I'm more scared of what's to come. Jesus! Will they call Da? He's away, but he'll find out somehow. He always finds out. Always.

I had absently passed the halfway point of my morning route. I'd have to speed up if I was going to make it back in time for my meeting. I turned around and quickened my pace. I was tense before the day had even begun.

I arrived in the office at 8:30, late for me. The effects of two previous sleepless nights clung to me, thoughts of my sister, my brother, the flash of dreaded memories, all congealed to generate the dull insistence of a throbbing headache, a stinging dryness in the eyes.

Annika knocked on the door and walked in, leafed through her notebook, and started in: "Except for the fact that we know that Madeline Monnehan was born in 1975, she seems to have sprung out of a seashell like Botticelli's Venus." She paused for effect, but sensing I was not going to play, continued, "Her registration forms at Yale are the first paper trail of any official records. She graduated in '94, got her Master's Degree from Princeton in '97, and a Ph.D. in literature from Berkeley in 2001. Since then, she's taught comparative literature at a number of leading academic institutions, starting with a seven-year stint at Berkeley. In 2008, she moved to the University of Chicago for two years and then to Washington, where she lectured at Georgetown

University. Her book of poems *Against the Shoals* was published in 2009 and catapulted her to instant literary stardom. Colleagues, and academia in general, talked about her work as haunting, angst-ridden poetry, using such adjectives as "dark" "subversive" and "volatile". Shortly after meeting Andrew Monnehan, she moved to New York where she was offered tenure at NYU. Apparently, she and the Senator kept seeing each other and in April of 2010, when she was awarded the Pulitzer Prize in Poetry, she exploded into the public eye, an instant celebrity combining brains with beauty. They married in June, 2010, after six short months of dating. First marriages for both. Twenty-year age difference, thirty-five and fifty-five." Annika stopped reading and glanced at me again. "Both waited long enough to get hitched. I've been looking at pictures of the couple. Maybe it's me, but neither one strikes me as passionately in love. Theirs was a strange union, don't you think?"

I returned her stare impassively. I was not going to speculate.

She continued, "In the past nineteen years, she changed her address seven times."

"What about family and friends?" I asked.

"Zilch. As I said, the lady appeared from nowhere. The trail is dead or buried." Annika closed her notebook, leaned forward, and looked at me intently. "I've been at it for more than seven hours. I even called in some favors at the DMV in California, thinking a license there would give us another route. Would you believe, she didn't even apply for one until she moved to New York?"

"What did she put down as place of birth?"

Annika opened her pad and after leafing through, raised an eyebrow. "Budapest, Hungary."

"What about the Senator?"

"He's an open book. A product of the silk-stocking set, he led a well-documented life of privilege. We have hours of taped appearances, both professional and social. The man loved the limelight."

"Any red flags on his finances?"

"The man was flush," answered Annika. "He was the only son of the late Brandon Monnehan and had not only inherited a sizable bequest upon his father's death six years ago, but managed to invest prudently over the years. He spent lavishly, especially on his new, beautiful wife. He was known to have hosted some of the most sumptuous parties in the Capital, except she was rarely in D.C."

"Oscar's back. Let's see what he's got," I said.

"Can't wait to hear all the unsavory details of the Senator's arrest for possession before he met Maddie."

"There's been more than enough written about it."

"Yes, but glossed over quickly, wouldn't you agree?"

Before I could answer, Oscar came in with his usual loping gait and took a seat. A wide grin was plastered over his normally hard-edged features. "I have some dirt on the late, rest his soul, Senator."

I studied him curiously. "Try to contain yourself, Oscar; what have you found?"

"First of all, the Senator was maintaining a swinging bachelor pad sans the missus. His 'get-togethers,' as one acquaintance called them, were extremely sought after. Best food, best alcohol, some lightweight recreational drugs. An absolute free-for-all."

I nodded slowly, noncommittally. I knew Oscar was not done.

"These 'get-togethers,'" he continued with one eyebrow raised, "anything but clothes parties,' were by invitation only to a select few."

"Sex parties?" Annika asked.

"Oh yeah. The guests were for the most part older and pretty diverse—bi, gay, hetero-flexible trans, you name it. According to some accounts, the place was hopping with beautiful half-naked women and men, and although cell phones were banned, there was no limit to available amenities."

It was my turn to ask. "Amenities?"

Oscar waved a hand dismissively, as if he'd been attending such parties for years. "You know – toys, body paints, costumes, lubricants, booze, drugs, and anything that could improve one's erotic experiences." Oscar was finally winding down. "What set his parties apart was his penchant for men. Lately, however, he appears to have been more into domination with women."

"I find it hard to understand how this type of hedonistic lifestyle could be kept under wraps."

"Apparently, it was an open secret within the circles he moved in, but since his coterie included some prominent personalities, he had enough clout to keep the lid on. The guest list was extremely selective. Senator Savich, Senator Gomez, Governor Linus, even a Supreme Court Justice. One of Monnehan's closest friends and his most frequent guest was Berrigan, the World News Editor of the *Washington News.* The man had friends in high places."

"Anybody who might testify?" I needed a live body to come forth, not just hearsays or second-hand accounts.

"Nary a soul," said Oscar, unable to disguise his displeasure.

"Was Monnehan linked to anyone in particular?" I asked.

"Publically, he's been a good boy since he got married."

"How about that DUI and possession of coke incident in October 2007? That was a major shitstorm, if I recall."

"Being a first-time offender, jail time was suspended, and upon paying $1,100 in fines and court fees, he was released on one-year probation. The Senator successfully completed his probationary period and the court dismissed the case. He then had the arrest completely expunged from his record. But someone in the precinct had the foresight to make a copy, which is what you're looking at." He tapped his fingers against the report.

I had long ago stopped marveling at Oscar's extraordinary access to all sorts of confidential information.

"D.C. has a custom-made drug court designed to funnel low-level addicts into rehab rather than long-term jail time," I said. "The power of politics—the hubris, and vanity of the politicians who wield it. Had Monnehan been arrested here, in his home state, he would have faced far more serious consequences."

"Well," said Oscar, "he might have eluded the justice system, but the public outcry was extreme. He had to quell a torrent of ridicule, not to mention scathing news articles from both critics and supporters. He left the capital with his tail between his legs and remained invisible for a year."

Oscar, deadpan and cool, concluded, "The Senator was back in Washington in January 2008, fully rehabbed."

"And married Madeline Walker two years later," I added contemplatively.

"Makes sense, don't you think? The man had set his sights on being re-elected. He must have been under pressure to establish a quick, wholesome 'family man' image."

A long silence.

"Anything on Aubrey Carlisle?"

Oscar stretched his long legs and said, "He was the Senator's right-hand man. My guy in the D.C. Metropolitan Police Department referred to him as 'Monnehan's houseboy.' He was at the Senator's beck and call, seems to have actually kept the place running while Monnehan was away."

Oscar held up a manila envelope and put it on my desk—his usual report, including interview transcripts, relevant documents, and a timeline with dates and locations precisely laid out. He said, "I also included the photos you and I took of the residence on 75th Street. It's lucky we got there before items were packed off as evidence. Let me know if we're going to pursue any of the leads in D.C. For now, I'll start digging up what I can here. Annie O is on me like white on rice."

Annika and I studied the photos in silence. I looked at the 8x10s that Oscar dropped off. Some of the pictures featured Oscar in the frame, others included me, both of us holding a ruler or a tape measure, a practice employed by all experienced defense lawyers visiting crime scenes. The Monnehans' bedroom was spacious and elegant, reflecting balance, symmetry and restraint. The king-size bed was covered with a silky white duvet, but the pleated bed-skirt was splattered with reddish-brown stains. The plush, white carpet was saturated with the same dried-out muddy color.

Unlike the serenity of the bedroom, the study was cluttered with every expensive piece of furniture and bric-a-brac. The kitchen was a sleek chrome-and-black affair as welcoming as a steel vault. Oscar even captured the view from the large French doors leading to the backyard. The stamp-sized yard featured a Japanese garden complete with a diminutive Koi pool, equally neat and tidy.

What kind of marriage did the Monnehans have? Two professionals at the prime of their careers, living in that god-awful showcase of a house. The place was devoid of heart and warmth.

I attached Oscar's materials to the first three-ring binder of the Monnehan case and turned to Annika. "The General requested to be present for Maddie's interview and I've asked Jim to join us as well."

"Any ideas about the sudden interest on Stetson Sr.'s part?"

"Might relate to O'Shaunessy. They've been buddies for a long time. Or, perhaps he's just interested in seeing what all the fuss is about."

"You are certainly interested," Annika added acerbically.

"She's a client."

CHAPTER 7

Any fool can know. The point is to understand.

—Albert Einstein

The office was served with the One-Ninety-Fifty notice, which was simply an announcement that Maddie's case was scheduled to be presented to a Grand Jury. I served my own CROSS-One-Ninety-Fifty which reserved Maddie's right to testify before the Grand Jury. Whether I did or did not want Maddie to do so, the option had to remain open. We had five days.

I tried to figure out what Ribisi was willing to part with. In this case, it was entirely the prosecution's show. The preponderance of the evidence did not support the felony charges – self-defense could have been clearly posited on both sides. However, here we were, and I had no clue what had induced Ribisi to go with Murder in the First. I recalled New York Judge Wachtler's famous pronouncement that a Grand Jury would "Indict a ham sandwich."

Unlike trial juries, which decide whether a suspect is guilty, a Grand Jury panel consisting of at least 16 out of 23 jurors, merely needed to determine that the evidence was legally sufficient and that it provided probable cause to prosecute a suspect on felony charges. Ribisi opted to present his case to a Grand Jury in lieu of a preliminary hearing. It was a smart move: he had little time to solidify his evidence and provide our office with all the prerequisite discovery mandatory for a full hearing.

Since the function of the Grand Jury was deemed to be an investigative tool of the government rather than an adversarial institution, secrecy in the Grand Jury has legitimately become indispensable. Its proceedings needed to be conducted behind closed doors, without the presence of a judge and attended by select government representatives, eliminating any possible leaks. Unlike a preliminary hearing open to the public, Grand Jury proceedings barred me from appearing with my client, cross examining the prosecution's witnesses, or questioning witnesses favorable to Maddie's defense. Besides submitting a written presentation with Maddie's sworn deposition and our motion for dismissal, I had little recourse but to wait for the court's decision. If I were to advise Maddie to testify, I would be forced to stand outside the room for the duration of the proceedings.

While I was aware that most defense lawyers would not put their clients on the witness stand, my own unshakeable reasoning argued that Maddie would make a formidable witness and I wanted the jury to weigh her testimony against Ribisi's presentation of DNA data, ballistics information and the testimonies of the police investigators and forensic experts. On the other hand, the notion that Maddie would be alone in the room, testifying and laying herself bare without legal protection, was troublesome. The need to tread cautiously was intense. I could hardly ignore the fact that I was plagued with unsettling feelings. If I let Maddie bear testimony in front of the Grand Jury was I potentially putting her in harm's way? I was wrestling with unwanted and unfamiliar misgivings, running on resolve, doubt and an unfathomable need to protect.

My team was assembled and waiting for me in the conference room. Stetson Sr. and Jim followed me in, and we all took our seats. I looked at the faces of Annika, Dennis Morton, a thin-lipped Washington import with a keen grasp of key issues in any legal conundrum, Trevor Sicario, an unflappable logician certain to poke holes in any legal argument, and Matthew. Before I laid out my game plan for the New York City Grand Jury hearing, I gave everyone a rundown of my interview with Maddie. By now, everyone in the room was apprised of O'Shaunessy's quick posting of the exorbitant bail, and of Maddie's subsequent release. I proceeded to fill them in on Oscar's findings on Senator Monnehan's extracurricular activities in his Washington pad.

Six pairs of eyes were riveted on me. When I was done, only Oscar and Annika remained unshocked. The others were still digesting the startling news about the late Senator when Annika asked, "Do you think Maddie was aware of her husband's activities?"

The sixty-four-million-dollar question.

I felt my chest tighten. "Ummm…I don't know. We will delve deeper into the particulars of the marriage, at a later time. For now, Ribisi's office shows no interest in the Senator's activities in D.C. The prosecution has been strictly focused on the crime and Maddie Monnehan." I paused for a moment then continued, "Oscar has just informed me that Andrew Monnehan and Paul Ribisi had a past association from the time they practiced law together at the firm of Murphy, Cranston and Shaw."

"It was a strong professional relationship," Oscar interrupted. "Ribisi was mentored by Monnehan when the former joined the firm as a young attorney, and according to records, the two spent quality time before Monnehan left the office." Oscar drew a thumb over his left brow, the only sign of uneasiness I had ever witnessed in him. "The fact that the people are ready to assert that Maddie had killed in cold blood is proof that Ribisi is privy to more than any of us is aware of. I venture to say that Monnehan and Ribisi had an ongoing relationship but kept it under wraps for either personal or political reasons."

"Can we have him recused on grounds of personal bias?" asked Annika.

I shook my head. "Our motion to disqualify Ribisi would be predicated on an old business connection, fifteen-years old, to be precise. We can't claim more than that, and that previous link does not constitute sufficient grounds."

Breaking the heavy silence that settled in the room I said, "We're going to submit a written presentation to the Grand Jury for the dismissal of the charges. We're going to poke holes in Ribisi's discovery and provide written testimonials that would have a favorable impact on the Grand Jury's decision."

"Ribisi is required to present enough evidence to establish a 'probable cause' for Maddie's indictment of 'murder in the first'. We need to collect and process all the evidentiary documents for the case." I turned to Matthew, Trevor, and Dennis. "That is your primary job. You'll need to decipher the key documents and the prosecution's discovery. As you all know, sometimes it's all about the pre-trial motions. Let's have no surprises. I know that the prosecution will likely not present all its evidence against Maddie, but since the rules are more relaxed than at a trial, Detective Lachey will probably be allowed to testify. His testimony will establish what Maddie had told him during his interview with her prior to her arrest. Ribisi will likely call witnesses to present the state's physical evidence to show that there was 'probable cause,' so I'm certain he will call Lippi and Stringer."

"Our Grand Jury Packet will center on Castle Doctrine, which was incorporated in some form into the law of most states, New York being one of them. It establishes Maddie's legal rights to act in self-defense in her own home. Maddie is entitled to establish an affirmative defense; a solid case of self-defense is the very definition of affirmative defense to murder charges. By invoking the Castle Doctrine, we will present an iron-clad rationale for Maddie's actions. As we all know, New York State law designates a person's abode as a place in which that person has certain protections and immunities. In Maddie's case, deadly force would be considered justifiable homicide if she acted out of fear of death or serious bodily harm."

I tamped down the urge to shove my hand through my hair and scanned everyone's faces. It was time to quit stalling. "I've decided to call Maddie to the witness box. I will work with her, so she'll know what to expect, but I have no doubt she will be a much more credible witness than any legal argument we will present to the Grand Jury."

Before I could continue, Annika added wryly. "At the end of the day, however, the jury will hear the state's evidence and probably decide there is sufficient evidence to require Maddie to stand trial."

I agreed. "Hoping the jury will be convinced that a murder indictment was hastily founded and has no merit is something we will leave to fools, dreamers and first -year rookies." I looked at my watch. "I've asked Maddie to come in, she should be here in a moment."

As if on cue, Maddie showed up promptly at 9:00 as requested. She wore a simple gray pantsuit and a tailored white shirt that did wonders for her skin. She wore no jewelry except for an unusually large man's watch on her left wrist. She seemed calm. It occurred to me that I had yet to see her ruffled or off-balance.

I rose to my feet. "Hello Maddie, please have a seat."

Her movements were easy as she took an empty seat across from mine.

"Thank you for coming in so promptly," I said.

The beautiful eyes were direct and disturbing. "Of course. After all, we're dealing with my defense."

"You seem unperturbed."

She smiled graciously. "I prefer to grieve privately. I've never equated a blatant display of tears with genuine sorrow."

I made the necessary introductions when Maddie said, "I see I've succeeded in mustering the top talent of Stetson, Stetson and Conor." There was a faint sardonic undertone in Maddie's voice. The room had fallen silent. It was Jim who answered with his innate grace. "Nothing but the best for you, Maddie. It's Nick's show, Dad and I are here only to offer assistance if need be. I hope it's all right with you."

"Perfectly." She nodded courteously and added, "Leo is unable to attend, so we can get started, but before we commence, could I ask everyone to please call me Maddie?" Gone were the dark circles around her eyes, as well as the last of the bruise visible the night of the shooting. Reed slim, perfectly turned out in that simple gray suit, she seemed rested and composed, and utterly beautiful. And although she was smiling, there was a sense of aloneness around her. She seemed to be in a room all by herself.

I said levelly, "Maddie, in our initial interview you recounted the events leading to your husband's death. I'd like to go over that account one more time. This time there'll be additional questions, at the end of which I'll outline our plan for your defense. Afterwards, you and I will discuss the Grand Jury."

"I understand." Her level gaze wandered slowly from face to face, as she spoke.

It was hard not to stare. Her allure was palpable, and I thought wryly that if we ever did go to trial, selecting as many male jurors as possible would be a boon. Of the six of us, only Annika seemed impervious to Maddie's charms.

I studied her as she recounted the events of the night of March 11th, repeating her previous account about going to Sag Harbor, deciding to return for her meds, missing the 6:02 p.m. train, arriving in the city around 10:00 p.m., buying the muffin at the diner on the corner, all the way up to calling the police.

The words rolled unhurried, the statement precise, thorough and exact. Too exact. My sense of unease grew, it grew at odds with Maddie's cool and collected voice. In my experience, almost all witnesses varied their accounts over time, adding flourishes or confusing the order of events. Maddie's account was almost verbatim the one she had given me. Of the ones present in the room, I was the only one who heard the meticulousness of the echo, the repeated phrasing, the seemingly unrehearsed pauses. I felt it in my bones – she was too polished.

When she was done, she looked around the room and then stared directly into my eyes. I wished I could ignore the warp and woof of that insidious attraction. I had long ago come to realize that physical allure was a short-lived fuse. As much as I was tempted to succumb to that velvety spell, there was something prickling at my neck.

"Maddie," Harold Stetson's gravelly voice cut through the silence, "is there anything that the prosecutor could have to contradict the accuracy of your statement, witnesses, train tickets, anything?"

She eyed him cooly and answered with a simple, "No."

"I'm asking only to make sure that you're certain. Nick here is going to base his case on the information you've just provided."

She leveled her gaze at the camera recording our session, her voice even and unperturbed. "As far as I remember," she said, "everything I told Nick and repeated here is the truth."

I turned off the camera and looked at her. "Maddie, let me lay out what we have so far. The prosecution's case consists of a very clear admission on your part." I paused. "But it doesn't matter what the prosecution's case is, it doesn't matter what the physical evidence shows, I'm going to present the jury with an alternate narrative that will use the evidence to tell a different story and reveal you to be an exculpable victim yourself. We're going to build a strong defense around the premise that you acted out of fear for your life."

I looked around the room and saw Jim's eyes locked on his father's face. I was gratified to see Matthew taking notes and totally focused on my every word. "Besides our own investigation into the hard evidence, we'll be interviewing your friends, colleagues, and anyone associated with you and your late husband. We will demonstrate that there was no intent to kill, no criminal intention."

Maddie said quietly, "What the court refers to as *mens rea*."

"That's right" I responded. "'A guilty act does not convey a guilty mind.' That is an ironclad legal premise and we will build our case around it."

"Self-defense?"

I nodded. After a long silence, I continued, "There are some anomalies in the fingerprint analysis."

"Anomalies?"

It seemed to me that Maddie's open look clouded for a fraction of a second. "According to forensics, there's evidence of some partials. Some smudged and unidentifiable prints found on the gun."

"Wouldn't they be mine?" Maddie asked slowly.

"Apparently they have determined that some of them aren't."

"Do they know how the prints got there? I mean…I'm not the only person who handled the gun."

"Fingerprints evidence sometimes is inconclusive. Lab technicians cannot always determine irrefutably when or how fingerprints got on a gun. The prosecution will definitely be looking into when and how the gun was handled prior to the shooting."

I looked hard into her eyes. "We'll have our own forensic expert who'll shed light on these irregularities. Can you get us a list of everyone who might have handled the gun?"

She nodded absently, then asked, "Would these partials…Do they confuse the issue of the rest of the prints?"

"No. Your fingerprints, plus the GSR—the gunshot residue—lifted off your sleeve and hand clearly establish you pulled the trigger."

I watched as Maddie tilted her head. She appeared to be deep in thought.

Harold Stetson suddenly spoke up. "I've looked through the data on file, there's also the issue of the ballistics report. The bullet itself was recovered from your husband's chest, there were some irregularities concerning the point of impact."

Deliberately, without haste, I said. "We're still waiting for full discovery."

Maddie raised her gaze to meet mine. I continued, "I'm wondering if your husband called you that day to let you know of his change of plans."

"No. My cell was off. A dead battery" she answered. "But as soon as I arrived at the cottage, I used the landline to call and let him know I was heading to New York for the night. He never picked up, so I left a message at the office."

"Any ideas, Maddie?" Annika stepped in smoothly. "Any ideas why your husband returned home that night? Why he was lurking in the dark in his own house?"

"No. No idea." She remained perfectly still. Then she asked evenly, "The timing of his return is important, isn't it?"

"Yes, very." I answered. "We need to corroborate his movements."

"You need a witness who could come forth and place Andrew at a certain time at the house that night?" Maddie offered.

We all stared at Maddie, willing her to add something. Anything. Matthew raised his face from his papers to study Maddie with interest.

"Yes." I said. As I gazed into those mesmerizing eyes, I knew she would add nothing more. I accepted the realization that I was matched in wits and will power. The thought was unsettling. I definitely did not want to stumble upon new discoveries during trial.

Harold Stetson rose and walked over to Maddie to say his good-byes. Jim rubbed his bald pate thoughtfully, then rose as well. The room cleared except for Maddie and me. I looked up to find her staring at me.

"Well, that leaves you and me." I said.

She watched me silently, her face showing nothing but faint courtesy.

I was aware of the quality of aloofness which surrounded her, the sense of resolve underneath those lovely features. I locked my eyes on her face and that tingle of attraction shot through me, a sudden coiling in my gut. Maddie seemed to stiffen and I wondered if she too felt the spike – the quick pull. I willed my eyes to look away and picked up my notebook. "My people have been lining up more than a few ducks. I wanted to cover other information face-to-face."

"I'd like to talk specifically about you today. The prosecution might question you about your past history." There was a quick glimmer of something in her eyes—not a reaction, but the willful refraining from revealing one. "Facts might come up that we need to be aware of and be prepared for." I watched her watching me. "We need to know if you've ever been at odds with the law."

Maddie smiled easily and without rancor. "I've never had any run-ins with the law. I never even got a parking ticket."

"You were never married before, according to our records."

"No."

"Never even came close?"

"No."

"Yet after barely six months of dating, Andrew Monnehan proposed and you accepted."

"Yes."

"You know, you're not on the witness stand yet. It's okay to elaborate a little."

"What would you like to know?" she asked calmly.

"It seems as if he swept you off your feet."

"Perhaps it was I who swept him off his feet." The voice was deceptively soft.

I could well believe it, but knowing what I knew about Monnehan's proclivities, the union between these two didn't line up.

"How did you two meet?"

"Through a mutual friend." She noticed my interest and added, "The friend's name is Christopher Logan."

"Presently the New York State Attorney?"

"Yes."

"Anything I should know about the relationship between the two of you?"

"He's a good friend," said Maddie dryly.

I flashed her a friendly grin. "Would you describe your marriage as happy?"

"Happiness is for children, Nick. We had something that many couples don't have but would like to have."

"And that is?"

"Willingness to venture into new territories, to be equally engaged in our interests, and to never become complacent with each other."

"And love?"

"There are all kinds of love," Maddie said softly. "Our marriage was based on mutual respect and trust. We were never bored, nor did we ever take for granted any of the pleasures we were able to share with each other. Striving to please one another is also a kind of love."

I wondered where the bodies were buried, for I was certain the relationship had more holes than Swiss cheese. I wondered whether Maddie truly believed what she was so pragmatically professing.

"You had no misgivings about signing a pre-nup?"

"No."

"It was then that you met your husband's lawyer, Leo O'Shaunessy?"

"Yes."

"The night your husband died, you called O'Shaunessy."

"Yes."

"Doesn't strike me as a first choice." I ventured levelly. "Why Leo O'Shaunessy, why not your friend, Mr. Logan?"

She looked directly into my eyes. "I didn't want to get Chris involved. Anyway, Leo is extremely capable." Her mouth curved into a wry smile. "Look where I've wound up following Leo's recommendation."

I closed the open folder and said, "The hearing is in five days, in the meantime try not to overthink your testimony. If you have any questions, or feel unsure about anything, don't hesitate to call." I thought

I saw a flash of something in her eyes, uncertainty, wariness, defiance? Then it was gone.

All grace and reticence, Maddie rose to her feet. "Thank you, Nick."

"You're welcome."

"I'll be at the cottage, you can always reach me there."

Maddie extended her hand. Fingers touching, our eyes locked for the briefest moment. Every synapse in my brain started firing. I gathered my papers. When I looked up, Maddie was gone.

CHAPTER 8

In my mother's house the light was lost and
gone forever
Buried in mirrors which looked and wept.

—Maddie Walker, *Against the Shoals.*

I approached The Commons, as they were colloquially known, the original plaque proclaiming The Great Communal Village of Sheepshead Bay having long ago been ripped off the entrance gate. Our apartment complex was built in the late 1950s—another failed exercise in the social experiment of offering attractive and affordable living for low-income families. There were nine ungainly brick buildings, uniform in their ugliness, consisting of six floors each, ten apartments to a floor. The long, barracks-like structures were configured as spokes of a wheel shooting off a small central hub. This blighted place was home to the first sixteen years of my life. I grew up here, the middle child of Francis Angus O'Rourke and Molly Fiona Conor. My brother Padrick was my senior by seven years and my sister Moira was born barely eleven months after me: Irish twins.

The passage of time was obvious. The place had fallen into disrepair. It had never been a happy place, but now the dilapidated buildings wore a mantle of sadness and despair. This was the landscape of my childhood, home to a few sweet memories, but for the most part, the birthplace of nightmares and abuse. I hated the place. But sometimes at night, when Padrick would turn in our shared bed and I could see the comforting rise and fall of his chest, hear his breathing—deep and peaceful—I would feel safe. Then, I could float away into my dreamland. Padrick was always telling me that dreaming was the heart of achievement, and that achievement was within reach of each and every one of us. Shutting my eyes and drifting away, I would feel cocooned in the promise of tomorrow. In the mornings, I held onto that sweet kernel of hope as long as I could, fighting against the sound of Da's voice and the brutal vise of fear.

The evening air smelled the way I remembered. A pungent mix of beer, burnt oils, cigarettes, and beans wafted through open windows. As I approached the center of the housing project, my steps grew shorter and my pace slower. I walked towards Building C, rounded the corner, and reached the last door on the ground level. Our tiny apartment consisted of two narrow bedrooms, a sitting room, and a windowless kitchen. Ma and Da occupied the rear bedroom and the three of us children shared the other. When Da's brother Rob arrived in America, he took over the sitting room. Thus, the six of us were crammed into a space barely fit for four. Yet, it would not have been half bad if Da was not such a miserable son of a bitch.

I stood at the door, willing myself to knock, when my uncle Rob swung it open, his face instantly plastered with a broad, happy grin. "Nick, my boy!" He dropped the black garbage bag at his side and embraced me in a crushing bear hug. "You're a wee bit early, but that's grand!" He moved back to look me over. "Not the worse for wear, Boyo!"

"Hi, Robbie," I said quietly. "You're looking good, yourself." He was dressed in a pair of neatly pressed jeans, a green U2 t-shirt with the legend "Wide Awake in Glastonbury," and a pair of ratty black sneakers. He looked old and worn-out.

"Flattery gets you everywhere, but not straight-out lies." He let out a cackle and touched his brow. "I know how I look, my boy. The sea air, sun, and water will do it to you every time." He grinned. His ruddy, weather-beaten features showed the merciless lashing of years at sea, the wrinkles nearly swallowing his bright eyes. But his laughter and endearing Irish brogue remained intact even after twenty-eight years in the United States.

"I was just about to drop off the trash. Why don't you go right in?" He lowered his voice. "You better be hungry; she's cooked up a storm." Rob picked up the plastic bag at his feet and passed by me.

I entered the dim hallway and saw Moira in the kitchen doorway, wiping her hands on a dishtowel. She lifted her hand in a gesture of apology, as if to say, "I know it's tough, but you need to be here." I opened my arms and she came rushing in.

"Nicki, I'm so happy you're here!" she said as she disengaged herself. Two things struck me at the same time: her use of the nickname I haven't heard in ages, and the fact that she had cut her hair short. For years, Moira's hair hung like a blond shroud shielding the left side of her face from the pitying eyes of strangers. Her cropped bob did nothing to conceal her scarred features—sickly, pallid patches of skin furrowed at the edges of her jaw line, the mottled skin stretched unnaturally across the left cheek and down to her neck. Like rubbery pancake batter, it was lumpy and uneven. Her left eye, a milk-colored orb, stared into mine, the left edge of her mouth drooped slightly in a frozen grimace. No number of surgeries could reconstruct her features to their original beauty. This was the face of my sister Moira, the face that would have remained whole and beautiful had it not been for me. Each and every time I saw my sister's face, I was totally undone. I saw her lips moving, but heard nothing except the same, silently frothing mantra: "I'm sorry…I'm sorry…I'm sorry…."

The first lifeguard to reach me grabs me by my upper arm. He looks at his companion. "We should call the police. They'll handle him."

The only thought going through my head is perhaps we can keep it away from Da. He'll beat me senseless for messing with the authorities. He has a thing about uniforms. We finally reach the lower level of the lifeguard stand.

It's dark and cool inside and I start shivering, either from cold or from fear. Neither man seems concerned. I'm dripping and bleeding, but I remain silent.

"Sit!" commands the tall one. I sit on a stool and now tremors take over. I can't control the shaking. His eyes scan my face. "Carl, go get him a blanket before he passes out," he says.

Carl leaves and the other looks down at my ankle. "Let me look at your foot."

I don't move. Let him bend down, if he's interested.

Carl returns with a thin blanket and some bandages. He's agitated. "There's some trouble at the end of the cove, Jim. I think we gotta leave the boy here."

Jim throws the blanket over my shaking shoulders, hands me the gauze and says, "Stay here if you know what's good for you! We'll be right back." He gives me a look, which he probably thinks of as ominous, and leaves with Carl.

Da did not raise stupid children. I wait till they disappear and sprint like a good little rabbit, running as fast as my legs will carry me. I'm running to Ma and Moira. When I reach our spot, I'm shaking again; they aren't where they're supposed to be! I look around frantically. How long has it been? I start running to one end of the sandy stretch, then to the other. I weave between blankets, chairs, and well-oiled bodies, but can't find either of them. Finally, I take a few calming breaths and start walking towards the road. I'll wait till nighttime and then head back home. Then, unbelievably, I spot Moira sitting on a low stone wall by the roadside.

"Where've you been, Nicki?" Moira cries, her eyes swollen and red. "Ma's so worried. We were looking for you everywhere. For hours!" She notices the trail of blood as I hobble towards her and her small face screws up. "Oh, Nicki! What happened to you?"

"It's no big deal, I got cut on some rocks. Where's Ma?" I ask.

"She's still out there looking for you. She told me to wait here in case you showed up and tell you to stay put 'til she returns."

I sit down next to Moira and she takes my hand in hers, clasping it tightly. "I was so scared, Nicki. I thought something really bad had happened to you."

I look at her delicate eyebrows as she frowns into my face. "I'm sorry. I'm sorry I scared you and Ma." I tug her hand closer and squeeze her fingers. Moira's smile is something else; it could melt ice in the frozen tundra. I can never get over how beautiful she is. When she grows up, I'll probably have to beat off more boys than I can handle.

We sit quietly. Moira hands me my t-shirt and I pull it over my head. I take the blanket from her bag and wrap it around our shoulders. I wrap the gauze bandage around my ankle, and we sit hunched together waiting for Ma. When I look up, I see a different sky from the one that greeted us this morning. The sun is low, emitting little warmth. The beautiful blue has been gobbled up by muted shades of orange and purple. And beyond, the dark is waiting. Ma must be frantic by now! After what seems like hours, I see her figure clambering towards the road. She looks dejected and worn out. When she lifts her head and sees me, a look of love washes over her face. She runs toward me and grabs me so tightly it hurts.

Then she cuffs my neck and stares intently into my eyes. "Don't you ever! Ever! Do that again! I don't care why or how!" Her voice is high and shaking. "Don't you disappear on me like that ever again!" Then she hugs me again and kisses the top of my head. I nod, pushing my face against her bosom, and feel tears of relief. After a full minute, Ma says "All right, then. Let's go home." Her eyes widen as she sees my foot. "Arun, let me look at that. What happened?"

I pull away. "Not now, Ma, I'm okay. Let's go home. We can't do much out here."

It's almost night-time, my least favorite time of day. We walk slowly through the Commons' gate. When we reach our building, the light in our apartment is on. All three of us stop as if we've slammed into a giant brick wall. Da is home! Ma raises her hand and clutches her chest. I don't see her face, but I know mine is wearing the same look, the wild look of an animal ready for flight. I hear Ma inhale softly, then she squares her shoulders and without a glance or a word, walks forward. The front door is unlocked. We enter the small, airless hall. Three little mice with nowhere to run.

"Shut the door," Da says in that deadly voice that heralds all of my night terrors. He's sitting at the kitchen table, an almost-empty whiskey bottle next to his glass. His eyes are glazed with that mad look, and I know it's going to be bad. Real bad.

"Frank," Ma raises both her hands imploringly. "Frank, the children! Not in front of the children…."

"Shut the fuck up," he answers without raising his voice.

His eyes never leave her face. "Pretty Molly Conor, what good are ye?" His breath hisses between his teeth. "A man comes home after two days of hard work. Call him dumb or crazy, but he's entitled to some respect! You dried up piece of shite. Some nice warm dinner to start with." His voice is rising like the growl of a feral dog. "But instead, what is waiting for this dumb fuck?" I see the thick veins in his neck bulge.

Da is beyond reason. I seriously think of grabbing Ma's hand and dragging her and Moira outside to run for our lives. But before I can move, Da jumps out of his chair. For a big guy, Da can move pretty fast. He flings his right arm and his palm makes a terrible cracking noise as it connects with Ma's right cheek. Ma lets out a sharp scream from shock and pain. The impact snaps her head backwards and she falls to the floor with a low grunt.

I feel Moira's thin shoulders bunch up as she starts to sob. I lift my hand off her back and step forward and cry, "Please Da, it's my fault. It's all my fault! We wouldn't have come home so late…" Those slits of eyes turn in my direction. I hear the quaver in my voice, but it doesn't matter. All that matters is that I reach Da through his red-hot haze of rage and violence.

"Don't you give me any lip, you good-for-nothing little weasel!" Da's voice is now a roar. His blow knocks my head sideways into the wall. The room around me splinters into a thousand jagged edges and for a moment, I can't see. My neck and right temple vibrate with heat and sound. When my eyes clear up, I see Ma trying to scramble off the ground.

"Frank!" she screams, with tears running down her cheek. "Stop it! Stop it!" She rises with painful effort; her upper lip is cut, her cheek is red and already swollen, and one of her eyelids is bleeding. "Your dinner is ready. We didn't know you were coming home today. But your dinner is ready." She smiles tremulously at his furious face.

"Here." She moves away from him towards the icebox, never taking her eyes off of his face. "It'll take just a minute to heat up the stew, and the potatoes are almost ready, I just have to boil the water." Her hands are trembling violently as she scurries around. She puts two heavy pots on the stove and turns on the gas.

Da hasn't moved. I think he finds it hard to focus now. Perhaps if we keep very still, we'll be spared. Moira and I inch our way towards Ma, who is busy stirring the stew. She doesn't turn to acknowledge us; she knows that the slightest move can unleash a tsunami of terror. We huddle together in frozen silence as the minutes tick by.

"You dried-up bitch," Da is swaying forward. "Pretty, pretty bitch." His voice is low again. "My wife…honey won't melt in her mouth."

It's Moira who makes an ill-fated sound, a cross between a sob and a hiccup. Da's eyes sharpen with malice. "Where've you three leeches been today?" Da is not only a drunk, but a miserable mean drunk. He hates it when people around him are happy. Moira tries to speak but her mouth opens without a sound. My heart jumps into my throat. I don't know if I should answer or risk Da's wrath by keeping quiet. Da is still looming over

Moira, so I rush in—my voice small, barely above a whisper. "We went to the…"

Moira clutches my arm and whispers frantically. "No, Nicki…" The fury in Da's face transforms it into an unrecognizable, scary mask. He's back in that free-fall, stomach-dropping roller-coaster ride.

He hollers at Moira's tiny, petrified face. "Why you little Miss Perfect! Little Miss Muffet! When I ask a question, you better come up with an answer."

"Frank," Ma turns to him, shielding both of us with her small body. "Frank, please, sit down."

"Don't you tell me what to do in me own bleedin' house."

He steps forward. His hand is raised. "No!" screams Moira and she flings herself between Ma and Da. His fist punches her squarely between the eyes and before any one of us can grab it, her small body careens backwards and hits the large pot on the stove. I would gladly cut off my arm if I could stop hearing the hissing sound of boiling water as it gushes and flows all over Moira's face. Her howling ricochets around us as she crumples to the floor with her arms slung over her face. I hear Ma shriek, a high-pitched wail that comes from deep inside her belly. It seems to go on forever.

Ma drops to Moira's side, shushing and cooing, while she gently lifts Moira's arm off her face. I think Ma's going to faint at that moment, but she hangs on. She meets my terrified eyes and commands me very calmly, "Nicholas, go to Mrs. Bialystok next door. Tell her it's an emergency and to call an ambulance. Tell her there has been an accident involving serious burns to the face. Tell her to ask them to hurry."

Moira stops screaming as she loses consciousness and I run for help. I'm running and I'm sobbing now, crying like a baby. I can barely see through my tears. I feel like I'm going to throw up, I don't stop, I bang on Mrs. Bialystok's door.

When I return, Ma's still sitting on the floor, cradling Moira's head and looking at nothing. Da's sprawled on his chair; he's staring blankly at the opposite wall. His face is ashen, his cheeks gray and sunken, and his eyes *lifeless like those of a small dead rat. His body seems to have lost its substance. My cheeks are wet, but I no longer make any sound. It's as if all the air has been sucked out of the kitchen. I sink to the floor next to Moira and try to ignore the screeching in my head. We sit silent and numb, waiting for the ambulance.*

"I'm sorry," I whisper. "It's all my fault. I'm so sorry, I'm so sorry," I whisper over and over, but no one answers. I know it's my fault. If it weren't for me, we wouldn't have come home late. We'd have made it home before Da, and dinner would have been ready. Please God, please God! Please God, make it go away.

CHAPTER 9

Out of suffering have emerged the strongest souls;
the most massive characters are seared with scars.

—Khalil Gibran, *The Prophet*

Moira was holding both my wrists, pulling me towards the sitting room. I heard Da's voice. The sound of it still, after all these years, made my jaw clench. He was propped up against some pillows, watching television. I picked my way around him. Da didn't glance my way at first, but emitted a hard snort at the back of his throat. He then lifted his mean eyes and gave me a belligerent stare.

"Well," his voice rasped, "Look who's here, the prodigal son."

Moira stepped in front of me. She placed her palm gently on Da's hand resting limply on the arm of the chair. "Da, we talked about this. You promised."

"I promised not to make a scene. I can still have me say!" came the biting response. The voice hadn't changed, but the wasted man in front of me seemed like a ghost of himself. The great hulking body disappeared into the supporting pillows around him. His once- robust arms hung useless, capped by a pair of gnarled hands, the right one, deformed. I regarded him carefully. Drink and age, sickness and malevolence, his body reeked of decay.

"Da, this is a special evening, Nick hasn't seen you in a very long time," said Moira softly.

Da's sharp laughter sounded like a bark. "Well, he can see me now." He raised his bad hand, fingers trembling with impotence. "Proud! Are ye? You righteous bastard. It's a good thing ye stayed away all these years, ye ungrateful shite. Don't think I couldn't have taken ye down, even with one hand." He was running out of breath. His face darkened, suffused with blood, his mouth sucking on his own spittle.

I glanced at him coldly, then saw Moira's anguished look and touched her shoulder. "Why don't you give him a minute to deflate? A glass of water might help."

Moira left for the kitchen, and I took a long look around.

Save for the 40-inch flat screen and a new maroon sofa, not much had changed. Same afflicted site where the four of us tiptoed on eggshells like prisoners of war, careful not to set off the monster, I felt the slow bleeding of memories, I sensed them all around me.

I joined Moira in the familiarly crammed kitchen. "He's barely able to sit up," I said.

Moira whispered, "We'll talk after dinner, okay?"

I willed myself to walk over to our old bedroom. I felt the erratic beating of my heart. The room was Moira's now – walls painted yellow, and covered with riotously bright water-colors – but the past lay in wait. For a second, yesterday and today coexisted, the space clamped around a palimpsest of bittersweet memories. I didn't hear Rob's footsteps approach.

"She's done marvels with the room." His lips twitched sheepishly. "She has her own apartment now, not too far away, but still, she wanted to make this room cheerful for when she visits."

"Da's still in the back room?"

"No, it's mine now. He sleeps out in the sitting room so he can have his TV. Can't move much."

"How long has he been like this?"

"A few years now, maybe five or six." Rob slung an arm around my stiff shoulders and continued softly, "He practically never moves."

I remained silent. I could feel no pity for Da. Not now, not ever. For years, all my waking moments had been spent trying to decipher his unpredictable scowls, monitoring the nuances in his voice, trying to detect the slightest signal of an impending detonation. Living in constant fear does something to you. You can surrender and break, as Ma had done, or become immutable and hard, like Padrick and I.

Moira came to fetch us. We moved the kitchen table and set it in front of Da, who sank into a morose silence. Moira and Rob started to lay the table with all that Moira had prepared, and we sat down. The first course was a leek and potato soup. After a few spoonfuls, I felt my throat tighten against my will. It's uncanny, the power of food to transport you to another place and another time. One minute I was sitting in this sham of a family reunion, the next I was standing behind Ma who was quietly stirring a pot of potato soup. I pushed the bowl away.

"It's wonderful, the soup, Moira, but I can't eat it right now."

"Ye sit there, fuckhead! And eat what Moira has been slaving on all day," snapped Da.

"Look, old man," I felt the slow icy rage, "keep a civil tongue in your mouth, or I'm up and going."

Moira shot me a pleading glance, but I was staring at Da. I was waiting for him to blast me to hell and I was more than ready to leave. Hell! I was itching to leave.

He grimaced spitefully, his voice guttural and low. He spat at me. "Ye think yer a better man?" He kept on slurping the hot soup. He lifted his gaze, and I stared into those malicious eyes.

"I always thought so, you miserable excuse for a man. I never once hit a defenseless creature. I never once hit a woman." I felt the crackling freeze as it oozed around me. There was so much ice, I thought the air would shatter like glass.

He narrowed his eyes. "Ye never hit a woman, because ye never loved one! Ye never loved a woman with all yer heart till ye thought ye would die if she was not yers." His voice broke and his gaze slithered away. "Ye know shite about this kind of love, what it does to yer insides. It burns ye and twists ye day by day."

My eyes remained unflinchingly on his face. No amount of words could express my contempt for this man. "Your great big love killed her." I spat, "I stopped calling you 'Da' after that night…" A quick glance of support at Moira, "At eleven years of age, I decided you could not be a father. You could not be *my* father. You were only a brute force we had to hide from till we could get out."

Moira said, "Please…"

"No," I said coldly, "I'm done. This time for good. I'm here to give him my parting shot. I hope he rots in hell for what he did to Ma and Padrick and you."

In the light, Moira's good eye reflected a pool of pain. "And you…" she whispered.

Da's face turned to granite but he did not utter another word. The hard chomping of his jaws as he continued chewing was the only sound in the room. After I had managed to choke down the rest of the meal with as much appreciation as I could muster, I helped Moira clean up. Rob left for his favorite pub, and we left Da to his favorite TV show: *Off the Hook: Extreme Catches*.

I noticed how tired Moira seemed. "Why don't I walk you back to your place?" I asked.

She swiped at an unruly strand of hair. "No, I'll stay here tonight, I'm too tired." Then she added, "It was good that you came." She did not add "for the last time" but she didn't have to. The bastard's days were numbered.

"I don't know what good it did, *a ghrá*," I said tiredly. "Except that we do need to discuss what to do with him."

Moira laid her hands on my shoulders and kissed me softly on the cheek. "I think maybe we should talk somewhere else. Why don't you come to Brooklyn, meet me at the Academy on Monday night? I'll be done teaching by 6:30."

I hugged her, breathing in the clean smell of soap. "Okay, I'll meet you there."

CHAPTER 10

Hundreds of fins swoosh cutting to the bone
Wires in their gills slice red and blue.

—Maddie Walker, *Against the Shoals.*

True to form, within days of his release, Crawley gave me the finger by sending his goons to break into my apartment. Since they trashed the place, I regarded it as a good excuse to redecorate—and to heed Greg's advice to upgrade the security. I chose to stay away from the apartment while it was being dolled up and rewired. The suite at The Essex House was better than I had anticipated. It had all the amenities of a luxurious apartment with the added advantage of in-house service.

I walked over to the tall window. The day looked much too enticing to order room service and stay indoors. It was another Saturday evening and the human traffic milling on East 59th Street was a sight to behold—a colorful panorama of energy and zest, men and women jostling elbows on their way to Central Park or to the designer boutiques on Fifth Avenue.

I grabbed my jacket and headed down to the Grand Army Plaza. The Pulitzer Fountain in front of the Plaza Hotel was resplendent with color and sound. It was on days like this that the city's unequaled glamour and vibrancy shone the brightest. No place in the world could rival New York. I often thought that the experience of visiting the city fell short of actually living in it. One missed the chance to unravel the infinite possibilities of a metropolis that thumbed its nose at any single classification.

I remembered that Maddie had mentioned going out to Long Island that weekend. On impulse, I pulled out my cell and dialed her number to let her know that I'd be in South Hampton the next day, just a stone's throw away from her cottage. I tried to sound professional as I scheduled time to interview her and her staff. There was no earthly reason for me to drive out to Long Island. No reason at all. Except…I wanted to see her. When I hung up, I felt foolish, edgy and strangely animated. I headed back to my suite.

Grabbing a soda from the minibar, I scrolled through the music on my phone, landing on Roberto Alagna and Bryn Terfyl's duet from the *Pearl Fishers* by Bizet. I loved the melancholy beauty of the music— it never failed to evoke memories of my brother. But now, like the seductive heroine of the opera, Maddie lodged herself like a splinter in my mind.

I walked over to the desk, turned off the music and unwrapped the book left by Oscar earlier. On the front page of the slim volume was a hand-written inscription to:

> To: Oscar Flamoix
> —an ardent and erudite reader –
> Thank you for likening me to what Robert Browning called a poet.
> But consider this—the poet's words need the lightness and the winged imagination of the reader to complete the story.
> —Maddie

I studied the slant of the forceful letters, the bold scroll. No feminine touches or soft curlicues here.

The first poem was simple, short. Its title "The Shoals" tapped into some familiar, oblique unease.

> When the sand reaches the knee the little minnows
> swim faster
> Whirling loops they swoop and cluster.
> Hundreds of fins swooshing cutting bone
> Wires in their gills slice red and stone
> Weave in the melee to never rise.
> Against the shoals you must pay the price.

I rebooted my laptop and when the monitor came alive, I trawled through the various definitions of the word "shoal":

A **shoal, sandbar** (or just **bar** in context), **sandbank,** or **gravel bar** is a somewhat linear landform within or extending into a body of water, typically composed of sand, silt, or small pebbles

1. A large number of fish swimming together. "A shoal of bream."
2. (Informal) A large number of people. "A rock star's entrance, first proceeding with his shoal of attendants."
3. A hidden danger or difficulty. "He alone could safely guide them through Hollywood's treacherous shoals."
4. *Verb* – become shallower

I knew all about the shoals. They might have held a different meaning for Madeline Walker Monnehan, but it seemed to me we were both standing fast against them. Her words spoke of elusive and disturbing dangers from without and despair from within. Something dense hung in the air around me, as I reconciled myself to the realization that Maddie and I had somehow traveled the same inroads; two solitary souls pressing on against the pain. The thought that I would be seeing her the next day welled inside. The uncertainty of a moment ago faded away and I was filled with an unfathomable sense of anticipation. Later that night, four hours into tossing and turning, I was fully engaged in second-guessing my plans and cursing my inexplicably idiotic compulsion. I made up my mind to call first thing in the morning and politely extricate myself from driving out.

The next morning, while reading the newspaper over coffee and toast I realized that despite my midnight resolve to cancel my meeting with Maddie, nothing would prevent me from driving out to see her. The urgency I felt had nothing to do with her case and everything to do with a need to just be with her. I was lying to myself if I thought that I was pulled into her defense strictly on a professional level. This was that familiar yet unpredictable law of attraction which kept nudging at my insides. Here I was, like an over-eager, love-struck teenager contriving reasons to bike past the house of his first crush. It occurred to me that I was setting things in motion, but I didn't know or care what those things might be.

I reached the town of Sag Harbor fairly quickly. It seemed only a few travelers chose Sunday mornings to commute from the city. After a few wrong turns my beast of a car, that beautifully powerful prowling Jaguar, found Maddie's cottage. Hidden from view, the place was ensconced at the end of a winding lane. It was charming—a cross between a country home and an elegant French chateau. The square, symmetrical shape of the country house was capped by a series of hipped roofs of varying heights. The tall bay windows were highlighted by red bricks set into the stucco. The villa, or cottage, as Maddie referred to it, had a romantic aura, straight out of *Beauty and the Beast*. Splashes of color danced around me, heralding early spring. I would never have imagined Maddie in this setting, but strangely, nothing seemed more fitting for this woman.

The front door opened and Maddie stood at the entrance. I couldn't see her expression, but my smile never wavered, and when I reached her, I saw it mirrored in her face. For a single minute I felt young—not as I had been in my youth, but as I had always imagined one would feel when facing one's future with the enthusiasm of a child.

"Hi," I said simply.

"Hi," she answered, with the same lightness. Her grin now said that it was all right, whatever tension we had felt in each other's presence, it was all right to enjoy the moment. For an instant I was startled, for I knew we were both glad to see each other.

"Would you like to come in?" she said. She had lost the smile but the tightness she had always exhibited with me was gone.

"Sorry, I'm a little late. I got lost," I said as I followed Maddie through an elegant entry foyer which led into a large, open space flooded with sunlight. Indoor and outdoor seemed to flow together. No matter how often one entered this place, I thought, one could never grow immune to its sense of serenity and warmth.

Maddie walked ahead and perched on the arm of a large amber-colored sofa. "Can I offer you something to drink?" she asked.

"Thanks, I'm all right for now. Perhaps later."

"How would you like to proceed?"

"I'd like to talk to Agi first, then Anthony and Lou. You and I can talk at the end."

Maddie straightened with quick grace. "I'll get Agi for you."

I watched the long, straight back as she disappeared towards what I assumed was the kitchen. Maddie returned with Agi, holding a silver tray.

"This is Agi," Maddie said.

Agi set a tray down on a side table and smiled at me. I smiled back and said reassuringly, "This won't take long. I just need to ask you a few questions."

Maddie said something in a language I didn't recognize and left us. I heard her climbing the stairs towards the second floor as I studied Agi, a short, compact woman of indiscernible age with large blue eyes and curly, reddish hair. She eyed me with the same intent curiosity. We smiled at each other. Reserved friendliness.

"Why don't we sit?" I said. "I'm going to tape this interview to ensure the accuracy of our conversation, but nothing we discuss will leave my office."

"That's fine," Agi said and waited patiently while I switched on the mini digital recorder and confirmed Agi Spolen's name, address, and occupation and the date and time of the interview.

I was curious. "Before, when Maddie spoke to you, what language was that?"

Agi grinned. "I'm Hungarian, and Maddie still remembers her native tongue, so she likes to practice it with me."

"How long have you lived in the United States?"

"Eighteen years, this coming April."

"And you've been working for Maddie for how long?"

"Eighteen years, this coming April."

"You were fortunate to have found Maddie so soon after your arrival."

Agi waved her hand expressively. "I did not find Maddie by accident. I came specifically to be with her." She looked at me, her face open and guileless. "I knew Maddie's mother. We were childhood friends. We never lost touch, even after Maddie's mom went to America. So when Maddie reached out to me, I came as soon as I could. There was nothing for me back home, and I wanted to be with Maddie."

"Is Walker a common Hungarian name?" I asked.

Agi's lips curved. "Mr. Conor, you must know that it's a pure Anglo name."

"What was Maddie's mother name?"

"Ilonka Erdos."

The corners of my mouth lifted in response. "I guess I'll have to ask Maddie how she came by the name 'Walker' then."

"I guess you would have to ask her," agreed Agi with a twinkle in her eye.

"Do you mind if I also take a few notes?" I pulled my pad from my briefcase. While all her answers would be recorded and filed in my memory, I appreciated the pauses in conversation that scribing afforded me. I often used the time to better observe reactions.

"Were you here on the afternoon of March 11th when Maddie arrived from the city?"

"Yes."

"Were you expecting her?"

"She called earlier to let me know she was coming."

"What time did she call?"

"Around twelve or so."

"It was a surprise visit?"

"Yes."

Agi would make a great witness. I usually coached my witnesses to never offer more than the requisite answer and never embellish their responses.

I went through Agi's statement fairly quickly. She confirmed Maddie's time of arrival and subsequent departure, the fact that Lou was gone and that it was Anthony the groundskeeper who took Maddie back to the station.

"Maddie told us she forgot her insulin in the city." I levelled my eyes on Agi's face. "Why didn't she ask Anthony to take her back to Manhattan if it was that urgent to retrieve her meds?"

"Anthony usually leaves by 4:00 or 4:30 in the afternoon. His chores as a gardener and caretaker are over by that time. Anthony is never here that late, he's needed back home. Maddie would never ask him."

"Yet he was here that day, later than usual?" I asked evenly.

"Yes. Lou asked Anthony to stay. As it turned out, as soon as Anthony and Maddie walked in, Anthony had to drive her back to the station."

A full and detailed answer, this time. Agi was making sure, I thought, that I had a precise and accurate picture of the day.

"You don't drive?" I asked.

"No," said Agi. "Believe me, if I could, I would have driven her back to the city myself. Maddie is diabetic; it's important for her to never miss her regular medication. I once witnessed Maddie in insulin shock and it was terrifying—for both Lou and me. I'd rather see her turn back and get her medicine than witness her having a similar episode."

This was the most emotional response elicited from Agi. I could see that she was genuinely upset.

"Are there no local pharmacies where Maddie could get her prescription filled?"

A small furrow appeared between Agi's brows. "That's what I've always disliked about living in the boondocks. Everything closes at 5 p.m."

"There's always the emergency room," I proposed gently.

"Yes." Agi said impassively. "But Maddie also mentioned that she needed to pick up some of the work she left behind."

"Work?"

"Maddie prefers editing on paper, rather than on the computer."

I wondered if Maddie had left New York in haste. It seemed out of character for someone as composed and in control as Maddie to have forgotten two such essential things. "I see," I said. "Must have been frustrating for Maddie to turn around as soon as she'd arrived."

I moved on. "When was the next time you spoke to Maddie?"

"I did not speak with Maddie until after her release on bail."

"You were at the cottage all that time?"

"Yes."

"What about Lou? I understand he was away when Maddie arrived."

"Yes."

"He took the Monnehans' car. Is that usual?"

"I'm sure Lou cleared it with Maddie before he left."

"Which was around what time?"

Agi's forehead wrinkled in concentration. "I think it was between three and four o'clock."

I was interested in the different comings and goings of the household members. I saw a fleeting expression of concern on Agi's face and added a big question mark in my notes.

Agi remained silent. You can tell a lot about someone when that someone chooses silence over words. Agi's affable demeanor remained the same, but I sensed a growing wariness.

"How about Senator Monnehan? How often did he stay at the cottage?"

"He rarely came out."

"Why's that, do you think?"

A discreet shrug. "I don't think he cared much for the beach or the town." There was no disapproval in her tone; it was a mere statement.

I studied her for a moment, wondering if she'd elaborate, but Agi remained quiet.

"Yes, I gather he preferred the city," I offered.

"I think so."

"He seemed to be very active socially. Loved the bustling city life," I added helpfully.

Agi's expression did not change.

"You were with Maddie when she met the Senator?"

"Yes."

"A whirlwind romance?"

I could tell that she wanted to remain silent, but was aware of the need to respond. "I guess the Senator fell in love and saw no reason to wait."

"And Maddie?"

Agi's eyes were unguarded as she studied me. "I think Maddie was ready to settle down."

"You came with her to New York after the wedding?"

"Yes."

"To the townhouse in the city?"

"For one night only. The next day, the Senator and Maddie brought me to Sag Harbor."

"I think we have covered the questions I had. If anything else comes to mind, please don't hesitate to call. Thank you for your time." I handed her my card.

Agi rose swiftly to her feet. "You know, Mr. Conor, I understand that you are confirming Maddie's and our movements that day, and you will find out that we are all eager to answer your questions. We were all shocked and saddened by events that followed. What happened was a tragic accident." She turned on her heels and left before I could compose a suitable response. Underneath her courteous and genial manner, I knew that Agi viewed me as an interloper, and her loyalty to Maddie was clear.

Agi returned with a tall young man with a full head of black hair, a strong hooked nose, and the whitest teeth I'd ever seen. He shook my hand with a strong, callused grip. "Anthony Martinez," he pronounced, all the while looking me over.

Agi left without a word and I said, "Thanks for coming to see me on your day off, Mr. Martinez."

He nodded. "Anthony, please. No problem, Miss Maddie explained to me that it's important for you to speak with me." He flashed those pearly whites again. "So, here I am."

I smiled disarmingly, trying to meet charm head on. It was easy to get Anthony to talk. He had an open, unaffected manner and was voluble by nature. His father used to work the Monnehans' property and when his health deteriorated, Anthony took over. He was friendly and willing to answer all questions pertaining to his job, his family, and the Monnehans. He confirmed Agi's statement: Yes, Lou asked him to pick Maddie up, and yes, it was around 5:30 when he did. He thought that Lou had to leave for a family emergency and no, he didn't ask why. He tried to get Maddie to the station in time for the 6:02, but wasn't sure she had made it. Anthony liked to talk, but besides the bare facts, there was not much I could glean from him, so I thanked him and asked him to send Lou in.

I thought I was ready for anything, but when the slight, frail-looking old man walked in, I was taken aback. He appraised me calmly as he thrust a sturdy hand into mine and said, "Louis Kertés." Even his voice sounded old and used up, but the accent was unmistakable. Agi and Lou hailed from the same proud Magyar background.

"Please have a seat, Mr. Kertés. I understand that you can offer little information about the afternoon of March 11th, since you were not here." I smiled. He didn't return my smile and waited silently for me to proceed.

"On the afternoon of the 11th, you had to leave. What time was that?"

"Three-thirty."

"And Mrs. Monnehan was okay with your leaving?"

He stared at me quietly and for a moment, I thought he wasn't going to answer. But then he said, his voice tight, "I could not reach Maddie, but I asked Anthony to pick her up."

The impassive eyes stared at me unblinking. Agi and Lou had perfected the art of silence. I wondered if it was a Hungarian thing.

"I'm sorry to hear that you were having family problems," I offered sympathetically.

A quick blink of an eye was all I succeeded in provoking. "A storm in a teacup," he answered in a voice that sounded like sandpaper.

"How long have been working for the Monnehans?"

"Twelve years."

"You are an American citizen, I assume?"

"Yes."

"You have family here?"

I saw the quick flash of something close to anger in his face, but he answered civilly enough. "Yes, I have a sister in Connecticut."

"Is that where you were going that afternoon?"

He paused and then asked tersely, "Mr. Conor, what has my family got to do with Mr. Monnehan's death?"

I smiled coolly. "Nothing at all, Mr. Kertés. I'm just curious by nature." I let my smile grow wider. "The hazards of my profession, I'm afraid."

He looked at me and said very slowly, "I have no more information about that afternoon, Mr. Conor. Is there anything else?"

I sensed my own growing irritation. "Yes, one more question, Mr. Kertés. Did you like Mr. Monnehan?" I was as surprised as he was, and the question hung in the air between us.

He said slowly but very clearly, making sure I understood him, "I did not know Mr. Monnehan well, but the little I knew of him, I did not like very much."

"Why is that?"

"He looked to me all made-up."

For a minute I was startled. The old man had locked in on something I had sensed. "Made-up?"

Lou Kertés stared at me with unflinching eyes, then rose to his feet and shrugged. "I don't know, maybe it's an American thing, or politics, what I saw was just veneer." He pressed his lips into a thin line and muttered, "I like real."

I extended my hand. I looked down at the tough and heavily scarred hand that lay in mine. This man, as small and as old as he looked, was a formidable friend in Maddie's corner.

"Thank you, Mr. Kertés."

Lou left the room, his narrow shoulders stiff and unyielding. Maddie appeared a minute later.

"You have good people on your side," I said.

She answered simply, fully acknowledging what I had implied, "Yes, I'd trust them with my life."

"Well, that leaves you and me," I said. "Would you like to sit down?"

"It's such a beautiful day. It feels like summer," said Maddie. "I was thinking that perhaps we could sit on the veranda. The ocean is quite spectacular today." She added almost hesitantly, "We can have a quick lunch while we talk. Agi is preparing something light."

I walked over to the large windows that enclosed the room. The cottage stood on a bluff overlooking the Atlantic, an expanse of cerulean blue so overwhelming it seemed surreal.

"Sure. That sounds like a great idea. I didn't realize I was hungry till you mentioned food."

We walked onto a wrap-around porch, partly tucked under overhanging timbers. But Maddie chose a table set in the sun. The clean smell of the ocean permeated the air, so different from any I had known, perhaps because of Maddie's scent in the air. All of a sudden I realized there was no place on earth I would have rather been at that moment than here, in the sun with this woman.

Agi showed up with a tray holding a large salad bowl, some herb-crusted salmon, and a freshly baked baguette. Maddie helped set the table and we sat down to eat.

Breaking off a piece of bread and dipping it into a small dish of olive oil, Maddie turned to me and said, "If you have any questions, Nick, go ahead. I can eat and talk at the same time."

"You forgot your meds and your work." I willed my voice to sound detached.

"Yes."

"You don't strike me as absent-minded." I dipped my bread into the olive oil.

I felt her eyes linger on my bent head. Her tone was calm, her voice unhurried as she answered, "No, I'm generally pretty focused."

"But on March 11th you walked out of your house forgetting two essential items."

Maddie looked me in the eye. "Mrs. Morley and I had a miscommunication. I thought she packed the meds, she thought I packed them. As for my papers, I simply grabbed the wrong folder. I prefer writing in long-hand."

I let it drop. The sun touched the curve of her cheek. I fought the roiling need to touch that warmed skin. I looked away and took a bracing breath. "You missed the 6:02 train bound for Manhattan."

"Is there a question somewhere?"

I speared an asparagus and continued. "What did you do while waiting for over an hour for the next train?"

"I read and jotted down some ideas for some new poems. Sometimes the best ideas come unexpectedly in incongruous places. Even in waiting rooms of train stations."

"Did you see anyone you know?"

"I don't know many people in this area."

"How is it that you don't know people in your town? I understand that your husband was pretty social?"

She stopped eating and looked thoughtful as she responded. "Yes, Andrew liked to socialize. But most of the people I met through him were from the city or from D.C. He very rarely came out to the cottage. It was too remote and isolated for him. I, on the other hand, relish the quiet… I'm hard at work on a new book."

"What about your teaching at the university?"

"I have an abbreviated curriculum this semester." She smiled tightly. "Helps with the requisite introspection all us writers thrive on."

"OK, coming back to your return to the train station, did you talk to anyone while you were waiting?"

"No." Maddie put her fork down. "What is this all about, Nick?"

"I want to verify the timeline of your movements that evening. It would be helpful if we found some corroborating witnesses to testify to your taking the 7:25 train." I pierced her with a cool level look. "Perhaps the conductor?"

She stared at me for some time. "What possible reason would I have to lie about the time I boarded the train? I bought the ticket at the ticket machine and had I known I would need the stub, I would have held on to it." Her voice turned edgier. "Unfortunately, I don't own a crystal ball, so it's gone."

We were no longer light and easy. "Juries are funny sometimes. Chances are they wouldn't even think twice about your comings and goings. But if the prosecutor finds a discrepancy in your alibi, your entire narrative will be suspect." I heard the hardness creep into my voice.

"I see." She studied me silently for a moment. "Is there something that's bothering you about my account of that night?"

Nothing I can put my finger on. "No. I just like to try to tie up all loose ends."

"I believe I was the only person waiting. I took that train just as I told you and arrived in the city at 10:05. I reached home about thirty minutes later, having stopped on my way to buy a sugar-free muffin, and walked into an empty house."

I gave her a quick, questioning look. The feeling that Maddie was being only partially truthful lodged in my mind. I wanted to grab her by the shoulders and shake her; it was an alarming urge. A sick realization had dawned on me: I was as tangibly inveigled as if I had been skewered to a stake. I felt the immediate staggering desire to have her.

It took only a minute for cold discipline to jerk me back. I lowered my gaze and took another bite of salmon. It pleased me that my voice was calm. "This is really delicious. My compliments to the chef."

We continued to eat silently. Trying a new tack, I went for a non sequitur. "I read somewhere that you have quite a nice collection of artwork?"

Maddie seemed startled for an instant. "Yes, I've tried to buy some interesting pieces over the years. Interesting to me, that is."

"It seems to me that some of them must have required a pretty penny," I ventured.

"Some were real steals at the time, believe it or not. Only a few involved a heftier investment. My mother left me a small trust fund when she died. I had access to the monies when I turned eighteen."

She stood up abruptly, her face turned away. "Would you like some more water?"

"Thanks. I'm okay," I said softly. Maddie was already pivoting away and into the house. When she returned, she carried a basketful of strawberries and a tall pitcher of iced water. Her expression was calm as she sat down, but soon she was absently pushing at the food on her plate.

Barely thirty minutes later, I left Maddie standing in the doorway, the sunlight streaming at her back. Something unknown stirred at the corners of my mind. I strode away, unsure of what had actually transpired. For the first time in a long time, I felt raw and vulnerable. Doors were slowly opening, locked chambers suddenly flooding with light. There was silence everywhere, as if all living things were holding their breaths. Only the even crunch of my footsteps cut through the stillness.

CHAPTER 11

The dead were and are not. Their place knows them
no more and is ours today…but now all gone…gone
as utterly as we ourselves shall shortly be gone, like
ghosts at cockcrow.

—*G.M.* Trevelyan, *An Autobiography and Other Essays*

It was Monday afternoon and Annika, Trevor, and I had just
returned from the downtown court. This is how one should live one's
life, I thought, as I looked out the window of my office. After two years
of mind-numbing legal convolutions, battling Stuben and Dewey's
shameless practices of relentless obstruction, delaying motions and
continuances, we had finally won the case. This last case, the latest test
in resolve, stamina and perseverance had finally paid off. Justice and
redemption. This was what I had longed for, that exhilarating comple-
tion of a task well done, a sense of moral vindication. This moment, as
rare as it was, sustained me. Like prick points of light against black, its
touch was as warm as a handshake.

The General walked in and sat stiff-backed in the seat facing me.
His thin-lipped smile creased his hollow cheeks. "I congratulate you
and your team on winning the Dewey case. This victory will certainly
bestow upon you a prestigious mantle. I think, Nick, every sad sor-
ry-eyed bastard with a sob-story of malpractice is going to bang on

your door. Ha! You've become, what my assistant, Greta, calls a 'poster boy' for the abused, used and the down-trodden."

I couldn't tell whether it was a compliment or an insult so I opted for a "Thank you, sir."

He rose laboriously to his feet. Before he turned to leave, he started to say, "If only James—" but then stopped and walked out without another word.

I kept still. There was nothing I could have said, and Stetson Sr. left without another word. I had a fleeting flash of Jim's harried expression, his constant restraint against pressure from within and without, and I sighed. I, too, had to face my demons. I was scheduled to meet with Moira on Tuesday evening to resolve what to do with Da. God knows I had wasted no thoughts on my father, but it had become clear to me that he was deteriorating fast and that Moira needed my help. I would do anything for Moira, even if I wished the son of a bitch dead.

Hemingway wrote that "The world breaks all of us. But some are stronger at the broken places." Ma was broken irrevocably, long before I or Moira had arrived. Padrick, on the other hand, had grown strong. Like those legendary *Gulag* survivors, who withstood inhuman conditions to emerge immutable and victorious, my brother had become granite and steel. With the passage of time, however, I had come to realize that Padrick's greatest achievement was his capacity for love—the love he shared with Ma, Moira, and me. His body might have been beaten, his psyche scarred, but his heart remained intact. He was beautiful, my brother. While he was alive, he knew how to bolster my resilience and nurture my dreams. At the time when I needed it most, he gave me the greatest gift of all: hope.

Late that night when I entered my suite at the Essex, I knew that I was heading towards another sleepless night. I pulled out a pair of sweats and a Pink Floyd t-shirt still folded in one of the shopping bags and put them on. I uncorked a bottle of Pinot Noir and sipped the blood-red liquid as I gazed out into the shadowy expanse of Central

Park. I watched the lucky pedestrians having somewhere to go, or someone to go to, and felt as remote and lifeless as the most far-flung star above.

I settled comfortably under the strong light of the floor lamp and picked up the small volume of Maddie's poems. It was this iconoclastic collection, this unforeseen shocker that turned the high-powered klieg lights on an anonymous writer and made her a household name. Hours, or what seemed like light-years later, I was done scouring the pages. I drank the last of the wine and turned off the light. Maddie's verses were intimate reflections on suffering. "Shame and fury bled the lilies on the wall" or "In my mother's house the light was gone and lost forever" echoed in my head, strangely and frightfully familiar. With every phrase, I felt the knife twist harder into my chest. It was as if she, conjuring her words, had reached a hand into my heart and pulled it out for all to see. Like Maddie, I was "stripped of faith and bare of hope."

Maddie's poetry and its disturbing images of rearing wild beasts, monsters grinning behind weeping mirrors, "Black beneath the eye can see," pulsed in the air around me as I sat listening to the beat of my own memories. Oscillating between the fury of Nyx, mother of doom and destruction, and the despair of a child, Maddie painted images of agony as brutal as my own. This Madeline Monnehan was a woman who had waded through the fires of hell and survived to tell about it. Not just tell, but hurl it in the reader's face, unleashing images as ugly as Cronos, the cannibal god, eating his son. More than once, I, too, had sat "On Death's lap." Reading Maddie's poetry, I felt as if I had dipped into what seemed like her mantra of pain, only to discover that it mirrored my own.

I was sixteen when I first stared into the darkness within. "What water is there to cleanse ourselves?" Nietzsche asked. I knew nothing would wash me clean, nothing would ever be the same for me. I learned to shut down and deflect – control had become paramount. I now knew that Maddie was as skillful at "hiding in plain sight." There was little one could divine of the real woman beneath the self-possessed demeanor she presented to the world.

Sitting in the dark, I tried to fight the sick sensation of falling in space.

I booted up the computer and trawled the various websites following and discussing Madeline Walker Monnehan. Annika was right: Maddie seemed to have moved around quite a bit. I wondered what prompted the frequent moves, whether it was personal choice or a compulsion to never be still. What one colleague had referred to as Maddie's "audacious peregrination, surreal and bizarre," was, I sensed, more than a poet's conceit. A journey that I suspected both Maddie and I had experienced.

Head and heart warred relentlessly. Like a cruel, heedless child, this treacherous hunger to yield to desire kept on defying logic and mocking reason. I was punchy with fatigue, irritable and raw as I finally let go and slipped into shallow sleep. I dreamed of Padrick dying, and I woke up, the pain of the dream slicing through me. A feeling of utter wretchedness washed over me as I lay between sweat-drenched sheets, The goddamned nightmares were back with increased ferocity. "The past is never dead. It is not even past," Faulkner wrote. I realized how weary I had become of reliving my past, of shadowboxing with my memories. I desperately wanted to bury my dead.

I forced myself to lie in the dark, to feel the stillness haul me under. It seemed barely an hour later when I heard the annoyingly shrill sound of the telephone.

"What?" I growled with all the hostility I could muster.

"Hi, it's me." Moira said softly. "Da suffered a seizure and was rushed to Maimonides Medical Center in Borough Park."

It was fewer than thirty minutes later that Moira, Rob and I crowded against a narrow hospital bed framed by raised handrails. Da's ghostly white face was almost unrecognizable. His features were grotesquely concave. He was hooked up to several monitors, and an IV was attached to his misshapen right arm. It was the odd stillness of his body that was most startling. If not for the steady beeping of the heartbeat blips, one would easily have thought him dead. I jammed my fisted hands into my pockets. The quick flash of an image, of another body stretched lifeless at my feet, sliced straight into my guts.

All I feel is pain. It's a furious night – the rain, a relentless roaring curtain. I'm sixteen, I'm scared and I'm running to Padrick. His back is toward me. He's staring into the dark waters of the bay. Behind him the hulking shadows of fishing boats and their precariously listing masts are lurching against their moorings. I hear the shrill echoes of my voice as it swirls frantically around me. I'm shouting into the wind. Padrick turns and at the sight of my bloody face and dangling wrist, his jaw tightens and his eyes freeze. I'm gasping for air, trying to speak, when a hand from behind shoves me forward and I fall at my brother's feet. The Crow and his homies have reached my brother faster than I'd anticipated. Crawley's pathological hatred of my brother, his obsessive pursuit of Padrick is almost as tangible as the stinging wind against my bloody cheek. It dawns on me that this must be what hell is like.

Padrick stands still, watching the tight group around Crawley. I can see every rivulet of water as it streams down Padrick's face. He turns his head as if to look at the pier, but I know what that gaze means. I've seen it often. It's a sweeping glance, taking in the scene around him, a practice born of street smarts.

I struggle to get up, but at that instant two lightning blows rip into my side, and I double over, falling to my knees. Again, I try to breathe against the searing stab of pain. Padrick's face blazes with anxiety and rage, and he charges towards me. I realize through the haze that he should stay with his back to the rails but it's too late! He's suddenly surrounded on all sides. Bill Mahoney and the short, dark-skinned thug grab Padrick from behind, before he has a chance to twist away.

"Long time no see," Crawley drawls.

Padrick strains against Bill's elbow, which is wedged against Padrick's windpipe. He cannot speak, but I see the fingers of his left hand push the silent emergency button on his radio.

"Help me out here, Officer," the Crow continues. "You're here, after all, to protect and to serve." I can hardly see through the blood and tears and rain. Crawley looks as if he's undulating behind a wavy glass wall, his face lit eerily by the yellowed street light.

Through clenched teeth, Padrick's voice is barely audible. "I wouldn't hand you a dime to call an ambulance if you were about to croak in front of me."

"That's too bad. I've come to make a citizen's arrest." He points his finger in my direction. His face is a mask of malice and smugness.

Bill Mahoney grips Padrick in a chokehold, while two others pin his arms back. The little Italian is hopping from foot to foot, a quick, dizzying tap dance.

"Antonioni, why don't you relieve this 'officer of the peace' of his weapon, so there'll be no accidents, "says Crawley.

The frenzied dance halts as Antonioni unholsters Padrick's service revolver.

"And the stick, too." Crawley's voice turns colder.

Anthony removes the night stick and stares at the Crow. The moments tick by.

Padrick's legs are braced to push back, but the one behind him kicks his knee from behind. Struggling for air against Bill's beefy arm, Padrick tries to twist away, but it's no use, he's practically immobilized. Antonioni pulls at Padrick's right arm, stretching it as if to shake it.

"Rusty?" The name barely escapes Crawley's lips before the man next to Crawley grabs the stick, comes around, and swings it in the air. He brings it down on Padrick's arm. I hear the crunch of Padrick's bones and see him slump in pain.

Crawley's fist catches Padrick with a stunning blow. His broken arm hangs useless at his side. I can't move my head and the throbbing in my side burns like a bitch. I'm savagely ill, then I heave my shaking body to its knees as I try to stop the panic. I'm wiping away the bile. Blood is still pouring down over my half-shut eye. I look helplessly as my brother stumbles backwards and I see the crowbar in Crawley's left hand. I think my lungs will burst as the scream rips me apart. The crowbar swings with brutal force and crashes into Padrick's neck. Padrick's head snaps back and he crumples to the floor without a sound.

I watch Crawley throw Padrick's unconscious body into the water. Sinking, legs first, Padrick vanishes under the dark water and I hear this animal howl pierce the night air. I realize I'm hollering as I wrench free of someone's restraining arms. I try to plunge in after my brother, but I'm dazed; all I can do is crawl on all fours towards the water's edge. I feel Crawley's hands grab me from behind, but instead of pinning me down, he picks me up like a rag doll and throws me in after my brother. I feel the water's icy shock and then I sink into the blackness.

Padrick's body glides down silently, as graceful as a diver. Disoriented, I reach my brother. He's as still as death. I can see the brutal open gash in his neck. Red blood clouds swirl and billow around us. Padrick's right foot had gotten wedged between two boulders, trapping him like a swaying blown-up dummy. I swim next to him and open my lips against his, desperately blowing the last of my breath into his mouth. I push upward to the surface and gulp in as much air as I can. Diving back in, I can see Padrick's eyes open but he's barely conscious. I fill his lungs with air again and try to pull his trapped foot out.

Padrick's eyes open wide. He's staring at me, fully aware of where we are and what is happening. I look hard into his eyes, greedy for any morsel of consciousness. I see the feeble jerk of his leg as he tries to free his foot. I know he's holding on through sheer willpower. We're running out of time. My good hand shakes uncontrollably. It's useless; I'm not strong enough to dislodge Padrick. I feel the skin of my fingers tear as I pull against the rocks. My lungs are burning and I know I need to surface once more.

When I dive back down, I see Padrick shaking his head lightly: it's no use. The dark is all around us, I can barely make out the expression on his face. I hold my brother tight and he tries to smile. His eyes stare calmly into mine. Then the glow in them dims. His eyes lose the last of their light and he's gone. Something alien rattles in my throat as I cling to Padrick's torso. I slip Padrick's watch off his wrist, slide it onto my own, and swim back up. Once I break water, I hear a disembodied roar. I'm howling into the night. The pier is empty as I clamber to the top, body convulsing with rage and shock. I'm frozen. I think I will never get warm again. This is what death feels like.

When Jerry arrives with the rest of the squad, he finds me curled up like a child at the edge of the pier.

"It took too goddamn long to get here." Jerry curses. "We got the 'officer in distress' alarm when O'Rourke pressed the button, but fuck, fucking hell! It took too goddamn long!"

I'm shivering so violently I think my jaw might break. I can barely hear Jerry's words, I don't see a thing. I'm staring at the spot where I met Padrick's eyes for the last time. I push Padrick's water-logged watch, into Jerry's startled eyes. "It took six minutes, only six." I croak hoarsely.

Jerry's eyes swing to the watch, its face shattered by a policeman baton at precisely 9:54 p.m.

I point to the swirling water beneath "He's in there." Gasping against a pain so vicious I can barely breathe. "I couldn't...I couldn't pull him...I left him there." I'm sobbing now, my body wracked with so much pain, it is inconceivable that I could survive it.

The night that Padrick died blasted a hole in me whose true depth I understood only years later. Like the aftershocks following an earthquake, the ripples never subsided. Watching Padrick die, I had witnessed not only the end of a life unfulfilled, but also the death of all those bright futures we'd woven together. I brought death to Padrick's doorstep, and I lost the most important person in my life. Like Cain, I became a marked man, my guilt tattooed into my heart.

All at once, I thought of Maddie at the office going through her Q and A's, of Maddie taking on the Grand Jury in the morning, and I was filled with a renewed sense of purpose. These feelings for Maddie, new and terrifying, were filled with promise—a promise I needed to believe could be had. I thought of the cottage, of Maddie's face as she waited and watched me stride towards her. The moment when we smiled at each other: the sound of keys unlocking the prison door.

* * *

In the morning, on another sun-kissed day, Maddie and I showed up at court. We made our way to the entrance, surrounded by reporters jostling to get a better shot, shouting out inflammatory questions. I never understood the compulsion to yell out questions and shove microphones in defendants' faces when everyone knew no answers would be forthcoming.

Maddie seemed unruffled and inscrutable. She wore a black suit, severe and beautifully tailored like a bespoke man's suit. The white tailored collar of her shirt stood stiffly against her cheeks and was pinned together by a beautiful old cameo brooch—the one I had first seen the night we met. Her face remained carefully blank; there wasn't the slightest indication of anxiety or apprehension. It was I who felt tense and edgy.

When Maddie finally emerged from the courtroom I couldn't tell if my gambit had been a smart move. She was as composed as when she had entered the courtroom, and on exiting could offer no way of predicting whether the jury would issue a True Bill vote—an indictment—or a No Bill, a motion to dismiss.

Ribisi came out soon after, looking relaxed and pleased with himself. He extended his hand to shake mine and seemed clearly confident of an indictment. I knew him well enough to know that it was not an act, and swallowed hard against the sinking feeling in my gut. I waited for him to leave and then turned to Maddie. "The grand jury's decision will be reviewed by a superior court judge. We've submitted a motion to 'inspect and dismiss' if the jurors vote for an indictment. So although these proceedings were secret during Ribisi's presentation, they will be reviewed by a judge and ultimately turned over to my office for discovery purposes."

"How long before we hear anything?" she asked.

"It can take a few days, sometimes a few weeks, before we have a decision. In the meantime, we'll be preparing your defense. You should return home and leave things in my hands. I'll be in touch as soon as I know."

We walked out of the courthouse into the sun, past the scrum of hopeful journalists pressing for sound bites. I spotted Oscar's car waiting for us. My hand resting lightly on Maddie's elbow, I steered her towards the car. We settled against the car's padded seats, and I saw Maddie close her eyes for a moment. Her scent seemed to swim around me, as light as air.

"You're going back to the cottage?" I asked softly.

"Yes." Maddie glanced at me. "You believe the jury will indict, don't you?"

Keeping my tone as even as possible, I responded with a simple, "Yes."

I watched her eyes register the implications of my answer. When she spoke, I could detect the weary tones of bewilderment. "Ribisi read the counts out loud: murder in the first degree, manslaughter in the first degree, murder in the second degree, criminally negligent homicide, reckless endangerment with intent to cause harm, aggravated assault. He listed the entire alphabet soup—from Class A felony down the line."

"It's common practice," I said calmly. "Don't worry about it, it's insurance in case Ribisi or I decide to negotiate a plea agreement and reduce the charge of murder in the first to a lesser offense. It's a well-known fact that the vast majority of people charged with felonies never end up in trial. Ribisi is just covering his ass."

"Plea bargaining often takes place while a case is pending in the calendar, isn't that so?" asked Maddie coolly.

"Yes."

"I don't want to change my plea of 'Not Guilty'."

"All right. So far I don't know whether Ribisi is even contemplating the option."

"Regardless, if he approaches you, I'm directing you not to enter into any deal."

I looked into her eyes and said, "Even if I advise you to the contrary?"

An unequivocal "Yes."

It was a minute, at least, before I spoke, but my voice was rock-steady when I said, "Okay. I'd better win, then."

Maddie said nothing. She looked at Oscar's back. His eyes intent on the road, he was deliberately trying to distance himself from our conversation, although I knew he was picking up the slightest nuances. Maddie leaned forward and asked him, "Can you please drop me off at the house on 75th Street? I need to pick up a few things."

She turned to me with a courteous smile, as cruel as a slap. "I'll stay at the cottage until you need me." I alighted with Maddie, my hand firm on her elbow as I ushered her up the steps through the tight group of paparazzi, who seemed to be camped there at all hours of the day. I stood silent as I watched her unlock her door. She didn't glance in my direction, but I heard the subdued "Thank you" as she disappeared inside.

I settled into the passenger seat next to Oscar. We remained silent for the rest of the ride, but just as we arrived at the office, Oscar turned to me. "Got a minute?"

I nodded. "Sure."

"I wasn't present when Maddie came into the office." He was watching me carefully, but I could tell nothing from his tone or expression.

"Yeah," I concurred. "We'll have to make sure you're here the next time she comes in. Actually, I'd like you to attend all future meetings with her. If nothing else, I could use your magneto-sensory divining rod."

"Well, my magneto-sensory thing, as you call it, is detecting something off."

"We just started working on the case, Oscar. Let's get our bearings first."

Oscar responded gruffly, "It's your bearings I'm talking about, Nick."

First Annika and now Oscar.

I met his eyes. "What do you mean?"

"If I had a tuning fork, it would start humming the moment her name touches your lips."

I smiled broadly. "A bit fanciful for an old dog like you."

Oscar's gaze was steady and kind. "You're right, Nick, I'm an old dog; so respect my experience, if nothing else."

"What is it that we're talking about?" I asked.

"It's none of my business, but a blind man could see that you're going to get hurt."

"You're talking about something you've inferred about Maddie Monnehan and me?" I asked.

"Yes."

"And you've inferred it how?" I asked coldly.

"From your reaction, every time her name is mentioned. Like just now, Nick. Relax your jaw muscles."

My nod acknowledged his point. "All right, Oscar, I'll try to remember that I've lost my poker face."

He asked gently, "Is there something you'd like to talk to me about?"

My voice sounded reassuringly cool. "If there is, Doctor Flamoix, I'll let you know. In the meantime, let's get to what I do need from you."

Oscar suddenly said, "Do you know what true love is, Nick?"

I said nothing. It was hard enough to navigate the undercurrents between Maddie and me.

Oscar gave me a penetrating look and said, "If you believe Aristophanes, it's the unique experience of finding your other half. He believed that we were created as four-legged creatures sundered in the middle by Zeus because he feared our power." Oscar laughed softly. "Can you believe that a god like Zeus was fearful of being overpowered by humans? Anyway, we poor mortals basically embark on an eternal quest to find our other half. It's an exercise in futility for most of us. But most of us do." He gave me a shrewd squint. "It must be excruciating to battle the gods…"

I had to laugh. "Is that what you think I'm doing?"

Oscar shrugged; he scratched his chin and gave a heavy sigh. "I've never known anyone as bottled up as you, Nick." A pause and then in a voice as warm as a hug, he said, "You know I'm like a sponge, whatever I soak up stays between us." He waited.

I was saved from answering by my cell phone vibrating. I smiled tightly at Oscar as I slid out of the car.

CHAPTER 12

Shame and anger bled the lilies on the walls.

—Maddie Walker, *Against the Shoals.*

We decided to have Da's body cremated on Saturday. I refused to participate in any pretense of praying for his soul or for absolution for a man who deserved none. I had long ceased believing in God. God would not have permitted the unchecked violence within the four walls of our home. But if He did exist, I would have asked for a divine decree that Da spend eternity in purgatory, doing penance for the rottenness of his soul. On Sunday, Moira, Rob, and I drove to Sheepshead Bay where Da had spent most of his adult life. We were silent on the way. Da's dry bone fragments, pulverized into ashes, sat in the front seat between Moira and me.

At seventeen, I had vowed to leave this place and never return again. But now, twenty-four years later, browbeaten by Moira, I had ventured into the past. I had discovered that one could indeed go home again, literally and figuratively, and that I could face down a memory I had buried more than two decades.

The chair was splayed sideways on the floor, its seat splintered and its back legs split like broken twigs. Ma was hobbling on one foot, dragging the other, grotesquely twisted at a sickening angle. She was trying to sweep the food and shattered fragments of plates off the floor. Her hands were shaking so badly that the dust-pan was weaving and pitching as if carried on the wind. Incoherent words tumbled through Da's slack lips. The smell of cheap whiskey burned my nostrils.

They both froze when I entered the narrow hall. Ma limped towards me with slow mincing steps. Her face was misshapen and already starting to turn blue. One of her eyes was completely shut; a thin trickle of blood was streaking from her left ear down her neck. The broom clattered to the floor as she held her palm against my chest, looking desperately into my face. "It's all over, a mhuirnin. It's all over. Nicholas! It's all right!"

I looked past her at the wretched face of Da, his mouth sucking in air, his chest heaving in loud drowning gasps. He was staring at me balefully. I pulled Ma aside, but she clung to my shirt. "Nicholas, he didn't mean it. Nicholas!" she wailed as I rushed towards my father, balled my left fist and hit his jaw as hard as I could. Ordinarily, I would never have had a chance against Da's great bulk and strength. I was still a scrawny kid, all thin arms and legs, too short for my age and no match for him. But Da was so drunk that he was barely standing, and surprisingly, my blow hit him hard and square. His body crashed down like a giant oak. He made a sickening noise as his back hit the floor.

I curled my arm around Ma's waist and half-dragged her to the sofa, where I laid her down, scarcely conscious. I called the ambulance on our new shiny black telephone, the sense of déjà vu misting over my eyes. Then I returned to Da's prone figure. He came to and tried to stagger to his feet. I watched his efforts as one watches a slimy bug crawl towards its dark hole. Most people associate rage with heat, they talk about blood-curdling fury. But at that moment I was as cold as a funeral slab. I went into the kitchen and opened the small drawer.

When I came back into the hall, Da was still on all fours, shaking his head in a futile effort to regain his senses. I knelt down next to him, my face inches away from his.

"You will never raise your hand against my mother again." In one fell swoop, I brought the hammer crashing down on his right hand, which was *splayed on the floor. There are twenty-seven bones in a human hand and I heard the shattering of every one of them. He let out a crazed howl. I said nothing when Moira walked in and saw us. Very calmly I returned the blood-stained hammer to its drawer, and sat on the sofa near Ma while we all waited for the ambulance.*

We took Rob's boat out into the bay, and I watched as Moira and Rob scattered the ashes. When Moira finally cast the urn overboard, there was nothing left of Da. I watched the small pot float and bob on the water until it was finally swallowed up, the last pathetic scrap of a vile life. My insides twisted with bottomless hatred toward a man the world called my father. I thought back to my childhood days spent on these waters. Scurrying and hauling, wet and cold, my fingers swollen and bleeding. Working on Da's boat every weekend from the age of five, huddling under Padrick's protective eye, and trying to stay clear of Da's wrath. There was never a moment of respite or relief. If a man's home was his castle, Da's boat was his kingdom.

I looked out at the water and remembered how insidiously the smell of sweat and fish—and fear—would lodge in my nostrils. On the way home, my eyes would burn with salt and tears, but my hand was always nestled in my brother's large, callused palm.

I glanced quickly to my left, my eyes drawn to Pier No.8 where Padrick spent the last moments of his life. We had not had a happy family, but we had each other. As the memories bubbled up, I saw myself, a child of six or seven, the house temporarily cleansed of Da's stench and me freshly scrubbed and shooed to bed. I remembered waiting for a flash of white teeth and a quick, affectionate poke and the books Padrick read aloud while lying next to me.

A hard, physical longing to hear Padrick's deep voice swept through me now with a searing pain. When I lost Padrick, I lost the one beacon that could have pointed me towards a happier life. I became a success, for sure, but I had lost what he had tried to gift me with: a sense of hope and love. I wondered if Maddie held the key to recovering what I had lost.

* * *

It did not take weeks; it took only five days for Maddie to be indicted for murder in the first. Trial date was set for August 12th in front of the Honorable Seymour Ramsey.

I called Maddie. "We knew it was coming. Not to worry. Our office is on top of things, we've been following leads and going through lab reports and forensics." I paused to wait for a reply. When none came, I continued, "Ribisi has been open and accessible with discovery, but we'll be doing our own investigation." I was picking my words carefully. "We're going to investigate everything up to the hour, up to the minute of the shooting. Whatever is necessary to win our case." I added softly, "We'll be investigating you as well."

"I told you what happened that night. What else do you think you'll find?"

"Whatever we don't know can hurt us."

"There's nothing to find out."

"Whatever we don't know can hurt us," I repeated patiently. "The prosecution will go to great lengths to substantiate your indictment. Make no mistake about it. They'll pursue the same avenues that we will. The only difference is that they have at their disposal resources that far outweigh our own." I could almost feel the waves of Maddie's resistance racing along the wires.

I felt this sick feeling spreading through my body. "You need to tell me what the prosecution will find."

"There's nothing to find."

I tried to hide the weary undertone. "Why don't you come into the office tomorrow morning and we'll talk?"

"All right, Nick. See you at your office at 9:00."

We had a full staff meeting that evening. Oscar, Annika, Dennis, Matthew, Trevor, and my two interns, Josh and Gladys, who brought in their laptops. I could never understand the new crop of attorneys who preferred to take notes on laptops rather than paper.

I examined each face and nodded. This was a good team. I pulled out the three-ring binder of scene and autopsy reports. "This is what the prosecutor provided the grand jury," I began. "These are the documents required by law, which, at best, offer us a glimpse into the prosecution's theory of the case. Now we must gather all available evidence and evaluate it in Maddie's best interest. We lost at the hearing, but we're not going to lose at the trial."

Annika picked up smoothly, "The prosecution's burden is to present an airtight case of first-degree murder, which means proving motive and premeditation. They might have stumbled on a motive." She cast a quick glance in my direction, "I'm referring to the pre-nup agreement that Maddie signed that accorded her a mere $100,000 a year as her divorce settlement. The Senator's estate, which she would otherwise have received as his widow, is worth in excess of one hundred million dollars." She paused briefly and then added, "But they sure came up short trying to establish pre-meditation."

I nodded in agreement. "Annika is right. We have nineteen weeks, till August, to rebut their conclusions and shake loose both their motive and premeditation arguments. This is a fact-finding undertaking." I turned to look at Oscar. "You're now the man of the hour, Oscar. You need to concentrate on what Ribisi can or cannot prove. Collect every bit of data on the Monnehans. I need telephone records, both landline and mobile, financial statements, and any evidentiary confirmations of Monnehan's movements on the day and night of March 11. Check Maddie's timeline as well.

"It would be helpful to find a witness to confirm Maddie's arrival at the house around 10:30 or so; same goes for anyone spotting Monnehan." I stopped, dragged my hand through my hair, and smiled briefly at Annika. "Annika, let's have the Senator's staff from the New York office deposed. We'll eventually obtain all the statements from the D.C. office as well. You'll be responsible for collating the material. Also run the reports from the domestic staff at both the Manhattan residence and the cottage in Sag Harbor."

I looked at Matthew. "Matthew, you and Trevor, together with Josh and Gladys, will review the crime scene and lab reports. I'd like you to follow up with Lippi and Stringer. I want you to study every single piece of evidence, listing all the problem areas that we'll need to tackle. I've already examined the scene of the shooting with Oscar. You should also acquaint yourselves with the place. Make arrangements with O'Shaunessy to let you in to the premises. I'd like diagrams and measurements, especially of the master bedroom." Matthew and Trevor nodded in unison while the two interns instantly reached for the binder on the table.

I asked Annika, "Would you find out if Dr. Morgan is available to conduct independent forensics next week?"

Annika nodded, then added, "I've been interviewing friends and family. Monnehan had a large group of friends; Maddie, not so much. They did share a few friends in common: the McGuires and the Watkinses, who incidentally were the last four people to see the Senator the night before he died. So far they've contributed very little. Let's see if Maddie's indictment will loosen their tongues." Annika met and held my eyes. "We don't want to be blind-sided when the time comes."

Her voice had a hard, emphatic tone. I knew that Annika's initial distrust of Maddie had only intensified.

"We'll have our own experts refute the state's theories. We need to remember that this case is about burden of proof."

When everyone but Oscar had filed out, I took a deep breath before asking ungraciously, "What?"

Oscar let the silence linger and then said, "That was some rah-rah speech. Ever thought of motivational speaking before you became a lawyer?"

"What is it, Oscar?" I asked testily. "I'm too tired for clever banter."

"I meant it as a compliment." He sighed. "You must be beat. You've lost your sense of humor."

"Is there a point you're trying to make?"

"Actually, I'd like to make sure you know that Dennis will be useless in pumping his friends for information. The guy is too uptight."

Oscar let the remark hang. His basset-hound instincts never failed to amaze me. I heaved a sigh. "I promised Dennis we wouldn't involve his friends at the Capitol, if we can help it. He's pretty loyal to them. He'll be okay interviewing the Senator's staff. They'll trust him, after all, he's one of them."

Oscar shrugged and stood up. "Okay boss, I guess you know what you're doing."

I hoped that as long as I knew what I was doing in my professional life, I could also police the chaos that raged in my personal life. Professionally, I would have to eliminate every seed of doubt in the hearts of the prospective jurors. But misgivings had taken root in my own mind. I had to admit that it wasn't hard to imagine Maddie's slender fingers curled around the butt of a .45 Beretta. I was powerless to rein in my own fears about Maddie's version of the events. And yet, she filled my heart with such a fierce need to protect her that nothing else mattered.

CHAPTER 13

Not all those who wander are lost.

—J.R.R. Tolkien, *The Fellowship of the Ring.*

It was late. I relished the quiet that settled in the office and started making my own list of priorities. I was less concerned with the scientific findings; the science in this case was not infallible, and both the prosecution and I knew it. I was more concerned with what Ribisi's investigation could turn up, and how these discoveries could impact Maddie's account. I knew that the criminal justice system was not especially good at finding the truth. But I believed in jurisprudence.

I needed to talk to O'Shaunessy; his submitted affidavit was clear enough, but the inclusion of his associate, a Mr. Marvin Mollis, was confusing. As a rule, surprises in any case were anathema, and I, however, was overly sensitive to any perceived or unforeseen unknowns. We had three months of unearthing evidence, but from very early on, I learned to brace myself against any unprompted glancing blow that would set my ears ringing for days. Being vigilant was by now imprinted in my DNA. I picked up the phone and dialed O'Shaunessy's number.

I had the handset propped against my shoulder when Maddie walked in. The room was instantly filled with a brief, stunned silence. I slowly replaced the phone in its cradle. The air pulsated around me as if tiny particles were suddenly energized. Maddie's initial expression of determination and willfulness was replaced by a look of a sudden uncertainty.

My voice sounded too loud. "We were scheduled for tomorrow, I thought."

"It occurred to me that I did not want to wait till tomorrow. Do you have time to talk now?"

"Sure. What's on your mind?"

Maddie laid her handbag on the desk, shrugged off her raincoat, and dropped it on the chair next to her. Her movements were measured and unhurried. There was just a faint hint of tension, now that she seemed to have decided to stay.

I smiled gently. "Why don't you sit down, Maddie?"

She sat down as straight as the chair she was sitting on. She said quietly, "When you called me earlier, you mentioned investigating me and my past."

A long silence stretched between us, neither of us willing to break it. She was watching me and behind that fierce green gaze I saw the glimmer of something. Calculation or dread or the resolve to ignore both. Then something shuttered over her eyes and she turned her head and looked around. She took in the wide windows, the muted colors, the plush soft-cushioned sofa with a pair of armchairs flanking it, the black and white photographs on the wall.

"This is a nice office." She finally said. "Sleek clean lines, still," she turned to smile at me. "Looks lived-in."

I relaxed into my seat, waiting.

"I dislike talking about myself." She began, "I thought maybe you and I can cover that part of the process." She did not add "without the others" but I understood what she meant.

"Just a few basics, Maddie."

"All right." Her face was unreadable and smooth as glass.

"You were born in Hungary?"

"Yes, in Budapest."

"When did you leave Hungary?"

"In 1983. I was eight years old."

"You came with your family?"

"It was only my mother and me." She grew quiet and then added softly, "She died six years later. Leukemia."

"I'm sorry. It must have been devastating. You were what? Fourteen at the time?" I tried to quiet the quickening of my heart; here was the first crimson thread that bound the two of us together.

I spoke slowly. The words did not come easily. "I know what it's like to lose someone you love." I stopped but then added almost in spite of myself, "You're left with a black hole, sucking all matter and energy."

For a second the world went still. *What the hell was I doing? Where did that come from?*

Maddie searched my face. "From the moment I saw you, I knew that there was something in you I needed to watch out for. You're far too astute." Her quick smile was intended to lighten the mood, but it couldn't erase the import of her words, nor mine.

She turned her head towards the window, fixing her gaze on something only she could see, something more within than without. "My mother was everything to me. When I lost her, I lost myself and my entire world."

"I lost my brother when I was sixteen." I heard my voice, quiet and careful, continue and complete what Maddie had left unsaid. "In the end, in order to survive, you had to forget who you were. You had to reinvent yourself."

I saw the brief, stunned look in Maddie's eyes before she lowered her head. It was so quick that I might have missed it, had I not been so intently scrutinizing her face. When she looked up, her expression was schooled once more. The innocuous, brittle laugh she emitted gave me pause. I had hit a raw nerve.

"I never thought we had anything in common," she said.

I smiled gently. "No one has a monopoly on pain, Maddie."

"The past for me, Nick, is never dead. It's the bedrock of everything I feel, think, and write about." She took a breath and added, "I am who I am today because of the things that happened to me and the things I did. I can't get rid of any of that."

Fucking hell. To hear my own thoughts thrown back at me was the height of sophist irony. Someone up there had a twisted sense of humor.

"Maddie, believe me, I understand." I laughed, a short bitter sound. "Of all the gin joints, in all the towns, in all the world, she walks into mine."

She smiled at me tentatively. "*Casablanca?*"

"Maddie, what you just said describes me too. I've been hobbling along with the baggage of my past for more than two decades? I ruined my sister for life, I maimed my dad, and I killed my brother. *I've been holding on, traipsing through my life, knowing full well that I was crippled myself."* I leaned back, away from the desk light.

"I hated my father," I added in a flat and dead voice.

"I had a stepfather," she said. "I, too, hated him."

"I would venture to say that hating a step-parent is more understandable than hating the man responsible for giving you life." I focused my eyes on hers, forcing hers to meet mine.

"It depends on who the step-parent is, who the birth father is, and on the intensity of the hatred, wouldn't you say?" she said coolly.

"When I was sixteen I attacked my father, I wanted to kill him…"

There was still no expression on Maddie's face. She didn't seem shocked or repelled. She sat silent, absorbing my confession. I wondered if she was trying to find the right words of commiseration, but all she said was, "Sometimes the pain is too much. One can be pushed hard beyond one's limit."

"I learned long ago that my childhood had nothing in common with the canonical American Norman Rockwell family. It's tough but you learn to survive."

I wondered what surviving meant for Maddie. I knew what complex constructs of survival I had erected. All of a sudden, I felt the crazy desire to stop talking and just sit across from this woman in silence and longing. But inside me there was this sudden need to open up, to touch and be touched.

I continued deliberately. "My father was a violent man who made our lives hell. I failed to protect my mother from a lifetime of horrendous abuse. The only way I thought I could stop the beast was to hurt him so badly that he could never harm her again."

"And your brother?"

I felt my throat constrict; it was hard to form the words. "I was young and stupid and being bullied by a psychotic schoolmate. I thought my brother would make things right." I stopped. The onslaught of memories barreled through me. "I realized later I was the bait, my brother was always the target. I led that monster to his doorstep and got him killed. And that monster was never brought to justice for his murder."

I saw a faint softening of Maddie's mouth, and I continued tightly, "I know you're going to tell me that I wasn't responsible for his death. You're going to point out that I was a child, that I didn't slash his neck myself and throw him in the bay to drown."

"But you didn't, did you?" said Maddie. The gentleness of her voice was a shock.

I waved my hand angrily. "I know all the answers, Maddie. I was in therapy for more years than I can count, learned all the catch phrases. It was that psycho, Crawley, who killed him; it was the thugs, Bill Mahoney and Ed Tutts and Jaime Luis and Rusty Luria and Anthony Pasquale, the thugs who enabled the Crow and carried out my brother's execution." I touched my brow tiredly. "But then, answer me one question, a question I ask myself over and over: If I hadn't run to my brother for protection, would he still be alive today?"

Maddie lowered her head; she seemed lost in thought. When she finally spoke, it was the question I knew she would ask: "If you felt that way, how could you…what did you do so you could go on?"

I shook my head in wonder. "I guess I was lucky in a way. I witnessed acts of such senseless cruelty and evil that they changed me. I longed to make things right. I knew that as long as I had breath in my body, I would fight the corrupt, the wrong, the bad." I paused, trying to articulate an idea that I had always felt but had never given voice to. "I wanted to spend my life pursuing those who caused suffering in others." I took a deep breath; it was becoming easier to speak. "I knew then that I wanted to study law. I guess you can say that the law gave me an out to save myself."

I paused and gave her a hard look. "But you know, Maddie, my life was a ruined life. I survived, but I was never the same. Since my boyhood, I see everything from the outside, never the inside. I am separate and apart."

There was such an intense silence between us it was almost tangible.

"How old were you when you left home?" Maddie finally asked.

"Sixteen."

I reached over and touched her hand. I felt the tension and the quiver of the long fingers. I watched her eyes widen as she studied my face, and I knew she felt the pull. It seemed to me as if we were live-wired to one another, but in the next moment she withdrew her hand without a word.

"I left home when I was sixteen," I said quietly. "After my brother's funeral, I packed my few belongings and went over to my friend Greg's place. My mother was already dead. I couldn't stay. I couldn't catch my breath inside the four walls of our wretched home. I couldn't abide my father for one more miserable day. Each day I was dying a little. I lived with Greg's family until I graduated, then left for college and never looked back."

I saw Maddie's throat work as she swallowed hard. But she was brave; I'd touched that steely courage in our first handshake. I knew she was afraid but that she would give us this moment, because it was the right moment and the right thing to do.

"I was almost fourteen when I left," she began. "I watched my mother die. It took her a long time. Two long, miserable years." Maddie's voice lowered to a whisper. "At the end, she didn't look much like my mother, just a shell, as dried out as my paper dolls." I heard the heaviness in Maddie's voice, the suffering and her inability to get past it.

Maddie's features seemed to tighten. She continued flatly, "We had been living with my stepfather, a doctor, for four years."

It occurred to me that I didn't want to hear the rest.

"When he first raped me, I lost consciousness. I was twelve at the time."

I felt the sudden drop in my stomach.

"When I came to, he raped me over and over until I blacked out again. He derived great pleasure not only from my subjugation, but from the physical pain he inflicted. I was a thin, undeveloped kid and he was a genius at devising new ways of causing pain." Her voice was tight. "Sometimes the pain was so great that I thought I would not survive it…They say that what does not kill you makes you stronger. Well, I guess I'd have to thank the "good doctor" for making me as strong as I am today."

She fell silent, her shoulders held by what seemed like sheer will.

"Maddie—" I choked on her name.

"And I had no voice…I had to endure it all in silence, lest my mother find out and scream bloody murder. He would have thrown us out in a minute."

Maddie grew quiet, and I thought thankfully that her recital of pain was over. But she went on. "You see, my mother had just returned from the hospital, diagnosed with leukemia. A life-sentence. She was facing a torturous regimen of radiation and chemotherapy and blood trans-fusions, and maybe a bone marrow transplant. The treatments were to be on-going." She tried to stifle the break in her voice. "I knew that as long as he had access to my body, he would be willing to pay for my mother's treatment."

I didn't know what she could read in my face, but I didn't try to hide my compassion or my anger.

"Do you know what agonies a child can suffer at the brutal hand of a sadist?" she asked, her voice curiously indifferent, as if she were talking to herself.

I felt my jaw clenching. "Yes."

"His smell used to set my blood boiling." She stared sightless into the air, as if she had forgotten I was there. Then she raised her head and looked directly into my eyes. "You spoke of evil, Nick." She smiled and said, "I could draw you a picture of evil. Whenever I saw his face, I saw the shape of evil."

She continued with a clear and cool tone. "I had no-one. It's a terrible thing to be so utterly helpless, so alone…There was no one I could talk to, no-one who would believe me, no-one who could help. You have to remember that at the time child abuse was terra incognita. There were no reported cases of incest or sexual abuse. Pedophiles were invisible, living among men but as unknowable and alien as werewolves or vampires." Her eyes went flat, but her voice grew softer "But then my mother died, and I was free." She took in a long breath and exhaled.

"Eventually I wound up in Washington where I struggled over my poetry – words providing catharsis. I had finally found my voice – I was no longer helpless… I discovered an intoxicating power, one that allowed me to set free all that rage and hate."

Those clear cold eyes were trained on my face. "As much as I need the past to disappear, it had simply metastasized within me. I am who I am because of it."

Maddie finally grew quiet.

There was a yawning ache in the middle of my chest. I wanted to take away Maddie's pain and her memories of it, but I knew there were no words for what I wanted to say. I walked over to her, leaned over her right shoulder, and lay my lips against the hollow of her neck. I felt her pulse quicken. My heart pounded furiously as I pulled her out of the seat and turned her around.

I saw the moment of uncertainty, the instinct to resist as she took a stumbling step back. I pulled her hard, then kissed her, pressing her body against mine. She was mine, and the instinct to love and protect roared in my head. I felt her moment of hesitation and then the give as her arms rose to pull us even closer. I let my fingers slide down her neck to her collarbone, to her breast, to her hip, and she softened into my arms. A little choking sound, muffled against my neck, sounded like a sob.

There were so many reasons that this was a disastrous idea. It was not so much the considerable ethical dilemma that stared me in the face: the prevalence of sexual relations between lawyers and their clients, it was, after all, the legal profession's "Dirty Little Secret," as one Law Review article had declared. No, it was the threat to, and the undermining of, my own personal principles. I knew myself to be safe as long as I stayed within the parameters my mind had long ago set. Yet she had been drawing me in. My fascination and attraction to Maddie were both incomprehensible, yet utterly irresistible.

She tore her mouth away and pushed her palms against my chest, her face pale and frightened. "No," she whispered. "No. This is not going to happen."

I tightened my arms around her and looked into the green of her eyes as it blurred and hazed over. *I want you*! I wanted to cry out. *I've wanted you from the first moment I laid eyes on you. I want you, whether you want me or not. For the first time I know what it is to feel a hunger with no name. I want to feel your naked body against mine. That is what*

I want. But what I said was, "Don't be a coward, Maddie. I know you. I see you and you know me and see me."

Maddie's face grew wary, then she turned to gaze blindly away. Against the backdrop of the night, her features gleamed like alabaster. The glow of the desk lamp cast shadows on the planes of her face. I found it impossible to look away.

"Night light suits you," I said softly.

Her eyes darkened. "Don't let my looks fool you. I'm not as fragile as I look."

"Don't worry, Maddie," I said quietly. "I'm not as soft as I sound." I let my arms relax and smiled gently. "This thing between us has been brewing for a while. I just didn't expect it to be this strong."

I took two steadying breaths and pulled her towards the sitting area of the office. Her hand was ice as it nestled in mine. She was watching me intently. Whatever she saw in my face made her stiffen. She stood in front of me, defiant and proud, both fragile and strong. Her eyes hard, her voice naked of emotion, she said slowly, "I don't know what you see when you look at me, but I don't want it. Just because I'm attracted to you physically doesn't mean I'm going to do something about it. Sex is not a priority for me."

I sensed the slow build-up, my frustration turning into anger. I stepped closer, and pulled her toward me, the length of her body stretched against mine. I felt the crackling of electricity as it coursed down my body and up through hers. The air blasted out of the room as I kissed her. She went rigid, then a sound like a moan escaped Maddie's lips as the stiffening of her spine gave way to a fierce hunger equal to my own. She leaned into me, her arms grasping my shoulders in violent response.

If I could or wanted to resist, it was at that moment that I stopped fighting the fall. I heard the rugged flutters of Maddie's breath as she struggled for air; her lips, helpless and open. The hiss of my breath sounded like drops of water hitting a hot grate. Maddie pulled my head down to meet her mouth again. The feel of Maddie's skin, the deep rich scent of spice and orange blossoms. I pulled back for an instant. I wanted her eyes on me. I wanted her fully aware; we were past doubts or denials. I kissed her again, gently this time, and we moved towards the sofa, never breaking our lips apart.

When we fell onto its soft cushions, I felt Maddie tremble. We lay stretched out as I twisted my hands in her hair. For one brief moment we were still, holding each other's eyes. I was braced over Maddie's slender body as it quivered and arched like a plucked bow. Then, tearing at her clothes, I pressed her against the soft cushions, all the while filling my hands with everything I could reach and touch. I yanked her head back to look at that white slender throat, at her breasts exposed to my lips. It seemed more than I could bear. And then I sank into her body, falling helplessly into a pleasure as acute as pain. Her long, slim body began to vibrate as her hands began to move against my shoulders, fingers clawing into my back, her lips swollen and desperate, teeth scraping along my throat. Maddie's passionate abandon, matching my own, sent me reeling. The air around us sizzled and roared. I ran my hand over her breast, down to her hip as she strained against me, her body shivering like a pulsing wire and then I pressed my palm against the damp heat between her thighs. She screamed my name as I shuddered with release.

Afterwards, out of breath, the blood pounding in my ears, I buried my face in Maddie's neck, at peace for the first time in days. I rolled off her body, long-limbed and perfectly relaxed. I thought I heard a sound between a moan and a sigh. Incredulous and light-headed, I laughed softly. I felt as if I had just ingested some miraculous elixir: a pitcher of the coolest, purest spring water after an endless trek in the desert. I turned and looked down at Maddie, her eyes were watching me, direct and alert. She lay naked, one long arm stretched out at an awkward angle, the palm open and upturned. A gesture of supplication.

I said lightly, "I've been loving you a little more every time I saw you, but it's only now that I can say what I didn't admit even to myself." I kissed her temple softly and whispered, "I once was lost but now I'm found."

I saw a look of bewilderment cross Maddie's face as she tried to stiffen against my embrace, but I held on firmly and kissed the corner of her mouth. She became very still, then exhaled softly. "Nick, we have to talk."

I felt the struggle in her body. The planes in her face seemed to tighten. "I did not want this," she said tonelessly.

"I did."

She closed her eyes. "Men are so predictable."

I raised myself on one elbow and touched her breast with my palm, my thumb on her nipple. I felt the beginning of a shudder. "Was this… predictable?" I asked.

Maddie's eyes flew open. "No," her voice barely above a whisper.

I bent down to her lips, our breaths mingled. "Let's agree, Maddie, never to lie to each other."

Maddie moved away and sat up, the remnants of her blouse held tightly to her breasts. It was a gesture of self-defense. She said in a low and steady voice, "I knew when I met you that we would wind up here."

"I didn't." I smiled ruefully.

Maddie's naked shoulders were turned from me, and I reached out and forced her backwards. She lay against my arms, her body twisted as I bent over her. I felt a brief stab of shock. What I saw in her face was a drained passivity—her eyes as hard as jade. Maddie returned my gaze, fully aware of what I was seeing in her face. She bowed her head in a strange gesture of resignation.

"What is it, Maddie?" My voice was barely above a whisper.

She stared straight at me, letting me see the hardness and the anger. After a moment, she whispered, "I cannot. I will not."

I asked again, trying to stay calm, "What is it, Maddie?"

She emitted another spiky little laugh. There was a note of sadness in it, but she didn't answer. I knew that a door had been shut against a space I couldn't enter. There were words I thought I would never allow myself to think or to feel, let alone express. Now in the dark, next to this tense body of a woman on the verge of flight, I was thinking that I wanted her, I needed her, that I wanted to take her with me, away from whatever it was that we were both carrying as chainmail around our hearts. And that I would love this woman for the rest of my life, no matter what happened next.

I raised my hand and traced the graceful line of Maddie's neck, sliding it slowly down the curve of her bare shoulder, down to her breast. I held her glance. "I want to see you," I said quietly. "I want to see you tomorrow, and the day after, and every day and every night. I want to see you like this, naked in my arms." I continued, "I didn't think I could feel this way, ever."

I felt my lips twist into a little smile. "I didn't think I could ever be free…" I let the word roll off my tongue, savoring it. "You see, Maddie, you have to be free in order to need; you have to be free in order to desire, you have to be free in order to lo–"

Maddie raised her hand, a small jerk of the wrist stopping my words. Suddenly there were lines of bitterness in her face. Her mouth closed in a thin grimace. She didn't look like a woman who had just made passionate love.

I knew I shouldn't move. "Maddie?"

An expression like a smile of pain crossed her face but then disappeared. "I'm sorry, Nick. I never anticipated someone like you." She spoke dispassionately. "I've always known that there was something missing in me, a capacity that most people possess with no effort, as if by birth. I knew I was missing it…and it was all right." I heard the quiet plea in Maddie's voice. "I can't do this! I don't know how!"

I knew that I, I who had nurtured this cynical heart, now needed to make Maddie see and feel the rightness of what we had between us. I said tenderly, "It's all right, Maddie. I didn't anticipate what is happening between us, either. But it feels so right." I watched her close her eyes. Leaning over her I whispered softly, "We'll take it slowly, my dear. It'll come to us."

I watched Maddie's eyes lose that feral look and heard the small sigh as it left her lips.

Touching my lips to the slow-beating pulse in her throat, I inhaled her scent and murmured, "Close your eyes." The words fluttered strangely against my chest. "Stay, dearest. I'll drive you back later."

I took her in my arms and kissed her lips. I held her for a long time, giving her time to recover. We did not speak on the way to her hotel, we were both deep in thought. But before she turned to slide out of the car, I caught her hand and raised it to my lips. The gesture took me by as much surprise as it did her. I watched her glide out and walk straight-backed to the entrance. I had spent the evening falling in love with a woman of dangerous power, utterly irresistible, and maybe more broken than me.

In the morning, shaved, showered and caffeinated, I found myself humming softly along with the jingle on the television screen. I had but three hours of sleep, yet I felt light and vigorously alert. The image of Maddie floated into my head. I thought that if I had somehow earned redemption, the feelings I felt for Maddie were going to be my salvation. I felt my heart skip; it was as if it was coming alive for the first time since Padrick died. As unbelievable as the odds were, I had found in Maddie a rare reflection of myself. The thought that I would be seeing her tonight welled into my bones.

As soon as I sat behind my desk, I called Maddie. The telephone rang for a long time and just when I was about to hang up, she answered. Forget the face that could launch a thousand ships, I thought: it was this voice. A siren's call that could lure an entire armada to self-destruct.

"Hi," I said lightly. "I was thinking of you all morning. This is the first moment I've had to myself."

There was silence on the other end. I continued against the slight constriction in my chest. "I have appointments till late in the evening, but I'd like to come and see you afterwards."

"I'm about to check out," she said. There was no greeting, warmth, or acknowledgment of what had transpired between us the night before. Her tone was polite—addressing a total stranger.

"You're returning to Long Island?"

"Yes."

"I'd like to come out tomorrow, then."

The silence took on a life of its own. She finally said, "No. I don't think it's a good idea."

"I thought we agreed to be honest with each other."

"That's exactly what I'm doing, Nick," she said with the first note of anger I'd ever heard in her voice. "Can you at least grant me that?'

I remained silent, trying to reconcile this icy aloofness with the fierce abandon of last night. I knew it was this contradiction that made her irresistible to me.

"All right, Maddie," I said, my tone easy and calm. "We'll play by your rules."

"It's not a game, Nick."

"I know," I answered. *Do you?*

The isolation, the vacuum, the barrenness were gone. The world seemed to have tilted on its axis, and I was now racked with confounding sensations of love and hope. I was in over my head, my heart, my soul.

I met a woman and nothing has been quite the same ever since.

CHAPTER 14

A paper face Madonna holds fast to the coral in
her hand
Reaching for the dream so long held dear.

—Maddie Walker, *Against the Shoals*

It's been three weeks since I had seen or spoken with Maddie.
Since that telephone conversation in which she and I had maneuvered
through minefields of words left unsaid. I spent all day Sunday talking
to Oscar and Greg and Moira. Time well spent, yet at the end of day,
I had to face up to the truth: images of Maddie kept intruding into
my every thought. The eyes, impossibly green and unfathomable, the
soft cream of skin flushing pink in arousal, the shape of her mouth.
Something caged solid within me had suddenly been released. This
startling ache was a small price to pay for a savage new freedom to feel.

What was it that Maddie was hiding? Beneath Maddie's seemingly
factual account, I recognized the tell-tale signs of a talented confabula-
tor. And perhaps it was not the sin of lying so much as the sin of omis-
sion that Maddie was guilty of. What was it about her and Monnehan
that she was so fiercely covering up? I needed to know it all in order to
do away with the fear, the pain and the past. I was going to mount an
unbreachable defense. It was finally this and nothing else. Everything
hinged on proving Maddie's innocence;

It was this feeling that underlay my thoughts as I entered the Four Seasons Restaurant. Chris Logan, New York State Attorney General and Maddie's good friend, was already at the table chatting comfortably with a tall, distinguished-looking gentleman. When I had called him to set up a meeting, I had suggested lunch, as I wanted to see him in an informal setting. It was always helpful to observe a witness in surroundings that lulled him into a false sense of security.

Chris noticed me and motioned me to his table adjacent to the pool—well known as the prime location. Nothing less would do for the illustrious and influential Attorney General of the State of New York. The two of us were about to enjoy a "power lunch," a phrase coined in 1979 by the then-venerable *Esquire*. Chris Logan flashed me a thousand-watt smile, rose elegantly to his feet, and stuck out his hand. At least six feet two, with broad shoulders and a full head of black hair, Logan looked like an ex-athlete who still worked out daily. His attractive features were dominated by steel gray eyes, which took me in with unusual focus and intensity. An impressive guy, radiating authority and power. With his breeding, intellect, and charm, one could well understand how he had become a formidable force in city politics. I was certain the golden boy of New York City was already laying the foundation for a grander and more ambitious undertaking.

I smiled back. "Thank you for meeting with me, Mr. Logan. I know how busy you must be."

"Chris, please." He smiled disarmingly. "Would you like something to drink?"

"Just a Perrier, thanks." As if by magic, two waiters materialized by our side.

I sipped my water and enjoyed the remarkable hush of the room. The large high- ceilinged space had a timeless elegance, which thankfully had not been tampered with for over fifty years. I had always appreciated its minimalist design, Mies van der Rohe's ode to the concept of "less is more."

We engaged in the requisite small talk while eating our salads, trading stories about prosecutors, lawyers, and judges who had crossed our paths. I discovered that I liked Chris Logan and hoped that I wouldn't have to destroy the nascent, amiable connection we found ourselves cultivating.

It was only when our coffee was served that Logan finally addressed the ghost at the table.

"So, you're handling Maddie's defense," Logan began easily. "I don't know if I can help you in any way. I wasn't even in New York when it happened."

This was one charismatic man—with a touch of steel underneath. I kept my tone easy, "As I mentioned on the phone, this is just an informal inquiry about your relationship with the Monnehans, nothing to do with the shooting. I try to cover my bases and your name came up as a close friend."

"And as I told you, Nick," another deprecating smile, "I'm a good friend of Maddie's, but I didn't know Andrew Monnehan that well. Strictly a professional relationship."

"So what did you think of Maddie's marriage to Monnehan?"

"I was a little surprised, to tell you the truth," he said with equanimity.

"Surprised?"

A quick shake of his head. "It all happened pretty fast."

I tried to read Logan's face. "I understand that it was you who introduced them in the first place."

"I introduce lots of people." A brief pause. "They don't always end up married."

"A whirlwind romance?" I said.

"You could say that."

"No harbored misgivings or regrets on your part?"

I could see the involuntary tightening of his jaw and the slight twitch he could not control. I was dangerously close to alienating him. Whatever Logan was trying to hide, I needed to unveil it.

"What is it that you are implying, Nick?"

"Nothing at all," I answered quickly. "It's just that Mrs. Monnehan is a beautiful woman; it would be hard for any man not to be captivated by her." I smiled abashedly. "Even I am not immune to her charms." I took a long breath. "Look, all I'm trying to do is to establish the best legal defense I can, and that entails, among many other things, delving into private and personal matters. If my motion to dismiss fails, we'll be heading for a trial and all kinds of personal baggage will crop up. It would be better if my office found out early anything that could do harm to her case."

Chris Logan laughed with ease. "Maddie *is* a beautiful woman." He paused and gave me a serious look. "It's not what you think, Nick. Maddie is just a good friend."

But there was something there. Nothing in Logan's convivial manner hinted at a hidden agenda; still, I had the sense of an incredibly fine-tuned performance. I wondered if the upcoming elections had anything to do with his caginess. I had little interest in his political aspirations, but I had to find out the nature of his relationship with Maddie to determine if Logan was a ticking time bomb ready to explode in our faces.

"Well then," I smiled. "I'm glad that we've had this conversation. I hope you don't mind if I contact you in the future?"

Logan rose unhurriedly to his feet, all boyish charm and courtliness as he shook my hand. "By all means. Call me if Maddie needs anything." He pointed to our table. "My office took care of the lunch. It was a pleasure."

I returned his smile. "For me as well."

When I returned to the office, I called Oscar on his cell and gave him Logan's name to add to his list. Then I summarized my own perceptions and feelings about him and wondered again what it was that made me uneasy.

It was nearly midnight when I finally returned to my apartment with its newly installed, state-of-the-art surveillance system. I tossed back two fingers of malt whiskey and four ibuprofens and collapsed onto the unmade bed. My last thought was of Maddie and that stubborn tilt of her chin, the proud set of her shoulders as she turned to leave, but it was Padrick who again rose from the dead. Once more, I was leaning against the shed, drenched, face wet with sweat and tears and blood. Once more I was watching the rain slick down a young girl's golden hair. When I bolted awake into the predawn gloom, fully clothed, I tried to understand the recurrence of that dredged-up image of a girl – a memory that would not let go. Maddie and Padrick seemed to intertwine themselves within the swirls of my mind.

I showered, shaved, dressed, and was in the office before seven o'clock. By the time Kim walked in, I had downed my second cup of coffee. I retired to the conference room, where my task force was slowly assembling. Oscar was the first in with his large leather-bound writing pad; Dennis followed with a DVD player and two discs in hand, Annika in tow. Matthew and Trevor and the two interns entered, each with an armful of documents. We all waited for the defendant.

When she walked in, it was as if the room, previously shrouded in shadow, had been blasted with an overdose of light. I wondered if Maddie knew the effect she had on people and figured that she was not only aware of it but had learned to use it. Looking fresh and well-rested, Maddie greeted everyone by name. She sat down and leveled her gaze at me expectantly. For a moment, I felt as if we were alone. I let go of the wariness in my gut and smiled. This was, after all, my home turf.

"There's a big gap between 'probable cause' and 'reasonable doubt,'" I began. "The burden of proof is on the prosecution. Ribisi has opened a Pandora's Box with the charge of first degree murder, but he is far from being a fool, which raises the question, 'What does he know or think he can prove, that we don't?' Ribisi is a damn good prosecutor, and this case affords him a great vehicle to shine. He's smarter and better prepared than any District Attorney I know. Obviously, he knows much more than he's letting on, and his people are looking for every corroborating piece of evidence to guarantee him a win. Our scrutiny of the case is still scant, to say the least."

"Maddie, every one of us in this room is dedicated to your defense and is bound by attorney-client privilege." This time I made sure Maddie felt the underpinning of warmth in my voice as I continued, "Nothing you choose to say here will ever leave my office, and will be used only to further your case and ensure a quick and full acquittal." I broke off and looked directly into her eyes. Then I said, "Maddie, we need to have a clear picture of your relationship with your husband. Did you know he was filing for divorce?"

Chin held high, Maddie met my eyes. "How did you come by this information?"

How come you never answer my questions directly? And how come you never told us about it?

"O'Shaunessy's office was apparently approached by your late husband to start divorce proceedings. Were you aware of it?"

"No."

The room stilled.

"Were there issues we haven't touched upon that might paint your marriage in a different light?"

Maddie's face revealed little as she replied, "I told Andrew that I was going to leave him. I guess he did not take it well. Apparently, he was the only one allowed to do the leaving. If he spoke to O'Shaunessy about a divorce, it must have been in response to this conversation."

I heard the syllables fall like precisely measured drops of blood. I said nothing for a moment, then asked, "When did you tell him this?"

"About a month before he died."

I met Annika's narrowed eyes and noticed Oscar making a note in his book. "Why didn't you tell us about it till now?"

I saw that Maddie was considering her response carefully. "Because it had nothing to do with the night of the shooting and because I agreed to grant Andrew's request to wait until November, after the elections."

Silence hung heavily across the table.

"Why?" asked Annika.

Maddie gave her a long, deliberate look. "Why what?"

"Why did you decide to leave him?" It seemed Annika's irritation trumped even her most ingrained manners as she pushed on. "Why did you marry him in the first place?"

Everyone heard the pugnacious undertone in Annika's voice.

"I married him for reasons of my own, reasons that would probably not meet with your approval."

"Money and status," Annika offered almost amicably.

Maddie's eyebrows arched slightly and a broad, beautiful smile crossed her face. She waved an elegant hand. "No, Annika, money never interested me that much. Don't misunderstand me. I appreciate wealth, but it was never crucial to my well-being. While I don't like being poor—I know what that's like—I'm self-sufficient and can provide for myself quite adequately.

"As for status, I never rely on others for my sense of self-worth. I could never understand people whose self-esteem depended on whom they associate with, or their position in the social hierarchy." Maddie's gaze met mine. "It might be considered egotistical, but I value others only in so far as they appreciate me for who I am."

The large room was humming with intensity as all eyes were riveted on Maddie with a mixture of fascination and curiosity. Perhaps because of the simplicity and straight-forwardness of Maddie's response, I found myself believing her.

"All right, then, why did you decide to end the relationship?" I asked.

"Because I realized I had made a mistake. Not an irrevocable one, but one I needed to fix."

Annika heaved a sigh, and Maddie looked at her curiously. "You're unhappy with my answer."

Annika said in a crisp voice, "Yes, I am. The prosecution will find out all the dirty laundry hidden by either you or your husband. Ribisi will definitely pursue the Senator's initiating divorce proceedings and unearth all the unpleasant tidbits. So, Mrs. Monnehan, why don't you help us help you and tell us what we need to know?"

Maddie's clear and genuine laughter pealed across the room. Leaning back against her chair, her face held a look of pure amusement. "Annika, first I'd like you to call me Maddie. Second, I applaud your candor. I never thought lawyers were capable of being so blunt, especially when dealing with their own clients."

Oscar, who had been as still as a totem pole until now, said in an even voice, "Maddie, I don't think you realize that we can, and will, find out anything and everything that might support or contradict your affidavit. I'm the investigator in this case, and let me assure you that I'm very good." Oscar locked his eyes on Maddie, who was studying him with interest. "Once Nick lets me loose, I'm bound to find and tell all."

The silence that followed was fraught. I let it hang. I needed Maddie to understand that we were embarking on a different journey now, and that if she wanted us to represent her, she needed not only to cooperate, but be fully proactive.

Maddie nodded. "I married Andrew because he offered me what not many could or would have." Her voice was as sharp as a gutting knife. "He offered me sa…"" Her voice broke; it was her first moment of weakness. She recovered immediately. "He offered me a home and security."

Sanctuary? Was that the key? Sanctuary from what? Why?

"My life until I met Andrew was quite different from what most would consider 'settled.' I moved a lot. I had no roots and no attachments. When I met Andrew, I realized that I had lived a solitary life, perhaps even a barren one."

Maddie's voice was cool, steely; I could see nothing in her face except the intense expression of a scientist explaining a pure, uncontrived problem. "He let me peek into a different kind of universe. I found him charming and witty. Like me, he was self-sufficient, but unlike me, he was social, well-liked, and led an engaged life. I found him quite appealing. He pursued me, and I decided to accept."

"You were introduced to Andrew by Christopher Logan."

"Yes," she said coolly. She was already anticipating my line of questioning. She looked at me for a moment, then added, "Chris is an old friend."

"You met Mr. Logan in San Francisco?" I asked, knowing full well that she had.

"Yes."

"You continued your relationship even after your marriage?" I persisted.

"Yes."

"How did your husband feel about that?"

"About my friendship with Chris?" Her eyes met mine with a spark of mockery, which I knew was observed only by Oscar.

"Yes," I continued. My voice was as pleasant and unthreatening as I could make it. "After all, Mr. Logan is single and attractive. It wouldn't have been unusual for a spouse to feel threatened by this man's attentions to his wife."

"Chris and I have been friends for quite a long time and probably will remain so in the future. If Andrew was anxious or unhappy about my friendship with Chris, he never mentioned it."

I smiled offhandedly. We had plenty of time to excavate the nature of Maddie and Logan's connection. I continued smoothly, "Were you aware of your husband's intentions to have a prenuptial agreement before you agreed to marry him?"

"Yes."

"Did you mention it to anyone?"

The derisive smile was in full bloom now. "Are you asking me if I discussed it with anyone in general, or with Chris in particular?"

I returned her smile, nice and easy. "Did you solicit anyone's legal opinion or consult with a lawyer about it?"

"No."

"No family member or a friend?"

"I have no family and any friend's opinion wouldn't have been pertinent."

"No family at all?"

"My mother had a distant cousin on her mother's side living in New Jersey, but we've not kept in touch."

Oscar lifted his eyes from his pad. "Do you recall the cousin's name?"

Maddie's eyes flared for the briefest instant before she answered calmly, "I was eight when my mother and I arrived in the United States. I'm not at all sure I knew their surname at the time. We stayed with my mother's relatives for only ten days. All I remember from those days is that Sandor and Marta were less than welcoming and were desperate to rid themselves of two more mouths to feed. She was in the late stages of pregnancy and there were three young kids running around. They couldn't wait to see us leave."

Oscar shuffled through some papers. "Your maiden name is Erdos, I understand."

"Yes."

"But you go by the name of 'Walker'?"

"Yes. It's my name. I've been Madeline Walker for some time now."

Oscar continued in an unhurried, even tone, "Nick has filled me in about your mom's and your itinerant life; it must have been hard to keep moving around."

Fully alert now, Maddie was taking her time answering. "It was all right."

"But you must have settled someplace, eventually?" Oscar said.

"Not really."

"But you must have," I interjected with a hard edge. "At least for the last two years of your mother's illness?"

I felt six pairs of eyes turn towards me. Annika's glance was the only one filled with anxiety.

Maddie stared at me coldly, her high cheek bones tinged with a touch of color. "Yes. We were settled for a while." Her voice could have chipped ice.

"You left San Francisco for Chicago, then Washington, D.C. Anything we should know about that?"

Maddie shrugged. "Georgetown offered me better terms and a chance for tenure."

"But you actually left for NYU after barely three years?" It was Annika again, as unruffled as Maddie.

"They made me an offer I couldn't refuse." Maddie smiled. "I still commuted to Georgetown twice a week, honoring my agreement with the school."

Oscar looked at me for a moment. "I'm wondering, Nick, if I could ask Maddie to recount the events of the night of the 11th of March. I'm aware that she already gave you a full statement, but I wasn't here at the time, and I missed it. It would be most helpful if I could follow her account, rather than read the transcript."

It was clear to me that Oscar needed more than Maddie's words. His interest lay more in the pacing of the words, the nuances and cadences of the phrases, the shades of feelings that Maddie's verbal account would provide.

I nodded and turned to Maddie. "Would you mind, Maddie? It could also be useful for Dennis to hear your story."

"All right," she said indifferently, and without the slightest bit of hesitation began outlining the events of the day and night of March 11th. When her account drew to a close, it was past two in the afternoon. I decided we needed a break, along with some sustenance and fresh air. I adjourned the meeting and suggested reconvening in an hour. When the room emptied out, I looked at Maddie and said, "Except for your testimony at the trial, this will probably be the last time you'll need to recount the events of that night."

"It's all right," Maddie said quietly, "I understood what Oscar was after. It's his job."

"I want to protect you, Maddie, not only because I'm a damn good lawyer, but for my own personal stake in this," I said as I watched for any reaction on that hard, heart-stopping face.

"I know," she said simply, her exquisite eyes lucent and bottomless.

"I need you to be honest with me."

"All right."

"Why do I feel you're not telling me everything?" There was an edge in my tone I could not suppress.

"Everything? What is everything, Nick? Can anybody know everything about someone other than themselves?"

"Don't be coy, Maddie, it doesn't suit you," I said impatiently.

She lashed out. "You're my defense attorney; you know everything you need to know in order to defend me. Do so!" The unrestrained and harsh tone revealed how controlled Maddie had been until that moment.

Somehow, we had wound up on opposite sides of the net, and I was at a loss. For a fleeting moment I wanted to grab Maddie and shout that I'd be damned if I'd let anyone hurt her again, but then I stepped back from this mad compulsion. I rose to my feet and gathered my notes. I said softly, "I will, Maddie, I will."

It was well past the lunch-hour when Maddie and I took a table at the front of the low-key Olympia. The Greek restaurant was a stone's throw away from the office, and although its décor could have used some updating, the food was generally good and the service quick. Oscar, Matthew, and Annika were already seated in the back of the restaurant, engaged in a heated argument that I knew had nothing to do with the menu. We ordered two Greek salads and just then Maddie's phone started to chirp. She looked at the displayed number and stood up. "I need to take this," she said.

I nodded and stared at her back as she stood by the front door holding the phone to her ear. There was something in her perfect stillness that unsettled me. I saw Annika glance back and forth between Maddie and me. By the time Maddie came back, our salads were on the table. She seemed slightly off-balance as she took her seat.

"Everything all right?" I asked.

Deliberately keeping her eyes lowered, she picked up her fork and started to eat. She seemed to be processing some piece of upsetting information. She looked at me slightly bewildered, as if she needed to register my question and my presence.

"Nick," she said, and for a heartbeat, her eyes met mine with something that resembled helplessness.

I held out my palm, fingers outstretched to touch her hand. "What is it, Maddie?" I asked cautiously.

"Would you mind if I don't continue this afternoon? Can I cut today's session short?" She pulled her hand away and smiled. "I need to take care of something." Her smile never reached her eyes.

"Sure, we have tons of work to do. You can come in tomorrow."

Maddie rose. "Do you mind taking care of the check?" she asked, and without waiting for an answer, gathered her handbag and said, "I'm sorry, but I really have to go."

As I left the restaurant, Annika appeared at my side, quick as a defensive linebacker, and we walked to the office, neither of us saying a word. Oscar caught up with his long, loping strides and stopped me before entering the lobby. "I saw Maddie leave," he said. "I'm guessing the interview session is over." Oscar looked at me, waiting.

"We're left to our own devices for now. We'll continue with Maddie tomorrow morning."

"See you tomorrow then." And Oscar was gone. Annika examined me with mild curiosity. "Is there something going on between you and Oscar?" she asked, glancing over her shoulder at Oscar's retreating back.

"Nothing a day of sleuthing won't take care of," I answered smoothly. I sensed Oscar's unease. Both Annika and Oscar were hovering around me like oracles of doom and gloom, and although some part of me appreciated their concern, I, for the most part, wanted them to leave me to my own affairs.

CHAPTER 15

Beloved, we are always in the wrong,
Handling so clumsily our stupid lives,
Suffering too little or too long.

—W. H. Auden, *In Sickness and in Health*

It was past two in the morning when I heard the doorbell of my apartment ring. Half awake, unable to shrug off the clinging comfort of sleep, I groped my way in the dark and peeked through the hole over the door chain. Maddie's face appeared through the glass.

"I convinced the doorman to let me in. He was certain you'd be delighted with the surprise," she said. "I need to talk to you, Nick."

I grabbed her wrists and pulled her in. I felt my pulse beating like a drum, a quick fierce stirring in my groin. I was charged, all at once, with a violent flow, a sheer hunger to feel her. Maddie breathed out my name. Whether this was a dream or a nightmare, I was past caring. I wanted to forget everything. At this moment, in the dark, we would become Aristophanes's four-legged beasts. *Beware ye Gods!*

And then I was kissing Maddie, taking and claiming. Her gasps for air were the only sounds in the room. I pressed her against the door, her rain-soaked clothes cold against my bare chest. I moved into her with the length of my body. She arched against me with the same desperate greed. My hands were quick and impatient—almost rough—as I tore at the buttons of her jacket, then her blouse, then her bra. I plunged my fingers into the heat and wet of her as she opened her legs for me. I lowered my lips to her throat and felt the vibrations snaking along the slim lines of her body. I heard the exhale of her breath, and felt her fingers fisting in my hair. We were never going to make it to the bed, I knew. Stripped naked, Maddie clung to me and then I lifted her hips around my waist. In an instant I plunged into her, thrusting with such savage need, I thought she could not bear it. But then Maddie sank her teeth into my shoulder, and I felt her shaking as pleasure sliced through our bodies.

Then I carried Maddie, strangely compliant, to my bed. Nothing mattered at that moment but the feel of her warm skin against mine. Whatever had driven her to me in the middle of the night, whatever she needed to tell me, could wait. I wanted her warm and safe in my arms. I threw the soft comforter over her still body, and closed my eyes, waiting for the tremors to subside.

The shrill sound of the telephone tore at the air, tinny and insistent. I shrugged out of a dreamless sleep. The room shimmered with bright sunlight, and the space next to me was empty. Maddie was gone. Except for a small indent on the pillow, there were no signs of her ever having been there.

I recognized Oscar's gravelly voice as he said, "Good morning, sleepy-head. Thought I might catch you early in the office, but I guess you needed your beauty rest."

"What time is it?"

"Almost quarter to nine, late by your standards and mine."

"I'll be there in thirty minutes."

"I'm not waiting," Oscar countered. "Dennis and I are about to take the 9:50 to Washington. I wanted to ask you something before I'm off. Did you know that O'Shaunessy has a son?

"A son?" I repeated. I wasn't fully awake.

"Yeah, the boy is tucked away someplace exclusive and secure."

"What do you mean?"

"I just found out that that's where the old man was for the past two weeks. The boy apparently has been boarding at *Twin Oaks*, a Minneapolis behavioral health facility."

I sat up, fully alert now. "What kind of a behavioral health facility? Drugs?"

"I don't know. I didn't look into it too thoroughly. I was just pissed that no one would tell me where O'Shaunessy was, so I followed it up. Made some inquiries. But from what I could dig up, the place offers long-term care for a host of psychiatric and behavioral problems."

I couldn't begin to fathom how Oscar came by this bit of information, but I felt a pang of compassion for the old fox with his jaunty bowties and sprightly walk.

"Anyway," Oscar muttered, "just wanted to let you know why the poor bastard was MIA for the past two weeks. I'm off now."

"Okay." I threw back the covers, wincing at the sharp stab of pain in my shoulder. "Call me when you have something."

"Will do."

I let my thoughts wander from O'Shaunessy's personal troubles to mine and Maddie's. We were on the brink of a precipice—neither one of us ready to relinquish control, nor strong enough to withstand the gravitational pull. I wondered what had made Maddie leave with such urgency yesterday, and what had brought her to my doorstep last night. Then I smiled with a mixture of pleasure and pain as I saw on my shoulder the bite-mark she'd left behind. I hoped the blossoming bruise remained there for a long time.

CHAPTER 16

There is nothing alive more agonized than man
of all that breathe and crawl across the earth.

—Homer, *The Iliad*

The office nestled between two imposing luxury buildings on Park Avenue, and its modest entrance was tucked away, hardly noticeable from the street. The doctor's name was emblazoned on a discrete gold plate, burnished on a solid oak door. The door opened easily, and I walked into the small waiting room. It was furnished with a russet-colored sofa, which had the look of an oft-used and much-loved piece of furniture, and two black sling-back chairs set around a small coffee table. The place looked comfortable without any concession to trendy or even expensive décor. It was so nondescript as to make you settle in with ease and without wariness. I waited for no more than five minutes when Dr. Melanie Desoto opened the door to the inner sanctum and extended her hand.

"Mr. Conor, won't you come in?" The doctor's voice, soft-spoken with a slight musical lilt, was friendly; her expression courteous and professional. She was a tiny woman, barely reaching my shoulders, with soft brown hair curling carelessly around a delicate, oval face. Her eyes, the color of rich dark chocolate, were alert and intelligent; their gaze frankly appraising without the slightest hint of coyness. She shook my hand, her grip surprisingly strong and motioned for me to take the chair next to hers

Dr. Desoto didn't waste much time. "You made it sound important, Mr. Conor." Her dark eyes probed mine, skimmed over to my briefcase and moved back to my face. Her manner, as cordial and open as it was, suggested little tolerance for bullshit. "What exactly is the nature of this meeting, Mr. Conor?"

"I understand that your specialty is treating victims of abuse. I neglected to mention earlier that I needed to ask you specifically about sexual abuse."

"Ah…" The doctor leaned back. "I see." She looked at me again, her eyes clear and watchful.

"I wanted to ask you a few questions if I may," I repeated.

"I'm not usually solicited as a professional witness. I'm assuming it's about a case?" The lilt was a little more pronounced. Dr. Desoto leaned back against her chair. She looked trim and professional as her eyes totally focused on my face.

Compared to the musicality of Dr. Desoto's voice, mine sounded flat and stark. My face must have registered some kind of emotion, because when I spoke, I was noticing an expression of heightened attentiveness on the doctor's face. "I find myself needing to under-stand the pattern of behavior in an adult who suffered sexual abuse as a child," I added carefully. "This is more personal than professional."

"I see."

We stared at each other. I felt the tight coiling inside, the tense muscles, I thought that the emptiness of sound probably resembled that of the silence of deep space.

The lilt and the gentleness cut through the quiet. "It will be very difficult to make observations without the benefit of a client, you understand?" Desoto said without a flicker of contention. Just stating the obvious.

"Yes."

"I'll be able to talk about it only in the broadest sense and basically discuss concepts as mere theoretical theses."

"I understand."

"Can you tell me, is it a man or a woman we're discussing?"

I breathed through the ache. "A woman, Doctor."

"Why don't you tell me what concerns brought you here?"

My voice sounded hoarse as I acknowledged out loud what had been wordlessly swimming in my head for weeks. "I'm in love with a woman who experienced abuse as a child."

Dr. Desoto nodded calmly. There was a look of infinite sadness behind those eyes, a tapestry of countless heartbreaking confessions. I wondered what it took to listen to, and absorb, day in and day out, the stories of victims as they shared their personal tales of horror. Unimaginable cruelties and suffering laid wide open and bare. This office, a black box, echoed with the pings of hundreds of cries, yet the psychiatrist exhibited neither callousness nor inured professionalism. Desoto's keen eyes were kind and thoughtful, and she exuded an air of warmth and courage. Her manner suggested that there was nothing she could not listen to or accept. If the room was a black box, Dr. Desoto was the black cube in its center: able and willing to acknowledge and absorb the anguish and affliction of others without emitting a single negative spark. Remarkable, I thought as I eyed her admiringly.

The doctor waited for me to elaborate, but I thought my statement had fangs all by itself.

Dr. Desoto nodded and asked, "Do you know if it was both sexual and physical abuse? Sometimes it has strictly to do with sexual gratification, however warped."

I heard the edge in my voice as it came out, brittle and hard. "Both."

The thin smile lines bracketing the doctor's mouth tightened slightly, but her gaze never wavered from mine. Dr. Desoto started speaking in a detached manner, an academic extrapolating on an issue. "Frequently, "she said "I have found that adults who survived child abuse manifest a variety of sexual and emotional psychoses. Like in Post-Traumatic Stress Disorder, the scars run deep, and if not treated can fester and mutate within the mature personality, giving rise to complex phobias and obsessions." Desoto's face looked tired as she added, "What you can often find among these survivors are the manifestations of corroded psyches, of emotional barricades, sometimes deformities of spirit and morality. If you're familiar with the sad case of The Elephant Man, then these invisible aberrations of the psyche would be like the pitiful physical malformations of David Merrick: warped and agonized. Unfortunately, we often witness the perpetuation of this type of violence on the children of abuse victims. The abused become abusers themselves, continuing a vicious cycle, often inflicting the same kind of pain on their own children."

I thought of Maddie and Moira and myself: all our soft potential — like molded clay — had twisted and deformed like the burnt stumps of tree trunks.

The doctor continued in the gentlest tone, "Emotional and physical trauma applied on the fragile psyche of a child results very often in artificially constructed coping mechanisms. Once the child reaches adulthood, these mechanisms and any manifestations of stress-related disorders can become subtler as he or she learns to cope in day-to-day life. Symptoms of PTSD are prevalent among these adults, and become part of the fiber of their personalities. They can also mimic other disorders such as depression, anxiety, alcohol and drug abuse, to name a few."

Dr. Desoto studied me, unblinking. "You carry and handle yourself very well, Mr. Conor."

I smiled in acknowledgment. "Years of therapy, Doctor."

"But you are here about sexual abuse, which, I think, is not in your history," she prompted kindly.

"No. Not in my case," I answered tiredly, "but I would like to know if the prospect of a relationship with a sexually abused person is within the realm of the possible. And what one could do to alleviate the stress and the fears of someone associated with such experiences."

Dr. Desoto's features retained their grave and composed expression as she contemplated my question. "You obviously know that survivors of abuse face a myriad of problems in relationships and experience great difficulties in trusting other persons again. Sexual abuse is the worst kind of trauma. The rape of a child is about control, power and humiliation. It would take an inordinate amount of discipline to regain control over the shattered psyche, and a terrible sacrifice to relinquish that control voluntarily to another person. It's basically asking the victim to lay down his or her life-critical defenses and surrender."

"I love her, Doctor." I swallowed hard.

"Yes, I can see that," she replied. Dr. Desoto rose to her feet and glanced towards a large lithograph hanging on the opposite wall. "We are all swimmers in the murky waters of the mind, Mr. Conor. We study, examine, analyze, and explore mental illnesses – their roots and causes and effects, in the hope of finding viable treatments and potent remedies. But we are still far from able to unlock the mysteries of mental pain with simple remedies and without contradictory theories which are being supplanted every few years."

I turned to look at the picture the doctor was staring at. It was a large print of a simple drawing, almost child-like, and quite disturbing. An image of a pair of blood-shot, unblinking eyes, sketched against a blank sand-colored field. Devoid of any contextual reference to the human face, without a mouth, nose, eyebrows and eyelashes, the wide eyes seemed surreal, frozen in a trance. Whether from shock or hypnotized by some unseen horror, the image evoked feelings of anxiety and disquiet.

Dr. Desoto turned to look at me; her voice was thoughtful. "I keep this print on the wall facing me so that it reminds me of all the mute voices that are never heard. All the cries that remain silent."

I nodded. Maddie's voice echoed in my head as I heard the savagery of her words: "I had to endure all of that in silence. I had no voice." I sank into the picture, the transfixed stare drawing me in with its eerie silence. The strangely dissimilar blue irises, punctured by black holes - cut into me with their expression of an unknowable, deep sorrow.

The doctor asked, "Did you ever hear of the artist August Natterer?"

When I shook my head, she explained, "This is one of his works, done around 1911 or so. Records were pretty hazy then, and since his own doctor collected most of his works, we only have his records to go by. All we know is that he was a German engineer who succumbed to an onslaught of mental illnesses and remained hospitalized in a mental asylum for the rest of his life. He left behind an extraordinary and rich array of drawings and paintings in which he captured his delusions, hallucinations, and visions."

"What is it called?" I asked, fascinated.

"My Eyes at the Time of the Apparition," Dr. Desoto answered with a trace of sadness. She took her seat again and glanced at me. "There's something unreal and frightening about it. I think of it as an image of a child, ghost-eyed and trapped in pain; someone bound by a mental straitjacket."

The second uncomfortable silence settled in the room; we were each engaged in morbid and painful reflections.

Dr. Desoto let out a small sigh. "I would like to meet her," she said.

"I don't know if she'll agree." I paused to gather my thoughts, groping for the right words. "She's very strong, Doctor. Composed and extremely clever. She has superb powers of deflection and is in control of herself most of the time."

The doctor was eyeing me patiently. I felt as if she was carefully raking my words together, sifting through them and culling an image. I continued with a firmer voice, "I spent most of my life experiencing pain, shame, and guilt. I learned to practice the art of self- detachment, thinking I could never connect truly to another human being." I raised an unsteady hand over my brow. "I met a woman, and nothing has been quite the same ever since. She clings to something which renders her unknowable and unreachable even to herself. Whether she knows it or not, she is a walking powder keg of pain and rage." I smiled ruefully as my voice gentled. "She's trapped herself in a self-imposed prison. The need for self- preservation trumps everything and everyone."

The doctor contemplated my words with the same innate compassion and intelligence she exhibited while talking about her patients. She said kindly, "For some people, isolation and self-preservation go hand in hand. They become the only tools for survival."

"Life sentence without parole." I forced a brittle smile.

Dr. Desoto nodded solemnly. "Yes, for some."

"I'll be damned if I'll let it stay this way!" The edge of vehemence bled into my voice.

For the first time since we'd met, a slow smile bloomed in Dr. Desoto's eyes, easy and understanding. It felt like the handshake of a brother-in-arms, a comrade standing shoulder-to-shoulder fighting a common enemy "You now know and understand what makes me come to the office, day in and day out." Dr. Desoto said. "I have not laid down my arms yet, and neither, I see, have you."

"I don't know how to lose," I said dismally.

The calm eyes locked into mine. "You said 'most of the time.'" The doctor raised an eyebrow.

"What?"

"You said she's in control most of the time. When does she relinquish it?"

I exhaled harshly. "The wanting between us is huge." It was liberating to admit to another human being the sheer depth of this insatiable hunger. "But it's always a struggle. Even her surrender to pleasure is wrought with pain. The release of control is transient, brief, and she fights harder the next time." The doctor closed her eyes for a moment, as if listening to some distant melody. When she opened them, there was a singular expression in her eyes, a gathering light. Her voice was steady, almost amiably conspiratorial. "You'll do fine. Stubbornness and patience, and love…These are great weapons against any malady."

I felt the tiny teeth of fear snag my insides. "I need to win this… I don't know if my stubbornness and my feelings are enough. I don't know how to use them. I don't know how…" I let out an uneven breath.

Dr. Desoto stood up and walked around the desk. She laid a small hand on my shoulder, barely a touch. "Just love her" she said softly.

CHAPTER 17

From a certain point onward there is no longer any turning back. That is the point that must be reached.

—Franz Kafka. *The Trial*

The month of May had rushed by with the intensity of a wildfire—nothing left in its wake but determination and fierceness of purpose. My mind clear, I worked steadily through each hour of each day as I put my team through its paces. Maddie and I were poised precariously across a silent chasm. The yearning was relentless, the need inside grindingly ferocious, but I was busy, and I knew we had to stay away from each other. At this point, a week had not passed by without photos of the Monnehans blasted over the cover of some magazine. I certainly did not want to turn my relationship with Maddie into a new paradigm for celebrity coverage. Discretion was a must; besides, I was orchestrating organized chaos, and I needed to be patient. We needed to endure these waiting months; we had to survive and outlast the trial. Pushing my papers aside, I took out my cell and called Oscar. I wanted to walk him through my plans for the next day. When it went to voice mail, I hung up.

It was close to ten at night when I rounded the corner outside my office building. I was more than pleased to take in the comforting normalcy of the street after another exhausting day. As I stepped off the curb, my cell phone rang and I reached into my pocket to answer it.

"Don't move, Asshole, if you know what's good for you!" growled a gravelly voice next to my ear. I tried to throw off the arm pressing against my back. I couldn't move; it was like shoving at a brick wall.

Someone behind me drew close and whispered, "Long time no see, Nicholas Nickleby."

The sound of Bill Mahoney's voice set off alarm bells in my head. Providence, with its quirky sense of humor, had upstaged my plans. According to my intel, the Crow was still engaged in a turf war against the rivaling Russian-led Cribs. I had not expected him to take his eyes off the target and venture into the risky business of a personal vendetta. For the second time in my life the Crow had preempted me.

Before I could respond, Mahoney grabbed a fistful of my hair and rammed my face into the unyielding roof of the car. I felt something warm and wet run down the side of my face.

"Get in the car," Mahoney ordered without raising his voice. The ringing in my ear was morphing into a loud clanging, as tinny and shrill as the sound of an oncoming siren. I could barely hear Mahoney's words. He yanked my arms backward, any additional tug, I thought, would dislocate my shoulders. I slid helplessly inside the dark interior with Mahoney following suit.

"Don't try nothin' stupid," he ordered in that flat, dead tone. "I'd love to tell Crawley that you were dumb enough to resist. Nothin' would beat the pleasure to lay a few on you, you piece of shit."

I tried to breathe through the pain. There was a peculiar absence of sound—a white noise—everything around me disintegrated into a bouncing hiss of wire brushes as they scraped a pair of enormous cymbals. The swarthy guy sitting shotgun was grinning at me wildly with a mouthful of gold braces. The driver, older and heavier, dark bushy eyebrows framing a pair of deep-set eyes, gave me a once-over and turned his attention back to the road. Mahoney and I took up the back seat and the car slid noiselessly into the moving traffic. My brief-case was tossed to the front seat, but my cell was in the left pocket of my jacket. I knew I needed to distract Mahoney long enough to make good use of it.

The right side of my head was throbbing like the taut skin of a ket-tle-drum, but the ringing in my right ear was slowly subsiding. I won-dered dispassionately whether my eardrum was ruptured. My cheek started to swell, and I knew I was bleeding hard. I tried to draw in long, careful breaths, waiting for my head to clear up. I felt the deliberate slowing of my heart as I let the cold inside me take hold. The pain and the icy rage welled up like glacial water widening the cracks. If I had to die this night, I thought, I'd be damned if I wasn't going to take the Crow with me. I was finally going to have my *High Noon* moment.

I hoped we were heading for Brooklyn. I needed time. Time to dis-tract Mahoney and try to set things in motion. I tried to remember all I'd learned of Bill Mahoney. I knew he had avoided charges of dealing, but had served two and a half years for possession. I knew Mahoney had a younger brother who was currently in jail for the same crime. I knew his mother had left his father when Bill was only six. I decided to tackle Mahoney's relationship with Crawley.

"You still Crawley's houseboy?" I quipped.

"Shut your fucking mouth!"

"I guess nothing makes the heart grow fonder than absence," I con-tinued calmly.

This time Bill turned to face me. "I told you to fucking shut up!"

"I mean you were parted for six long years, must have been brutal," I said and winced as Mahoney's hand snaked around my neck and grabbed hold of my larynx. "If you don't shut up, I'm going to cut out your tongue," he snarled.

Gold-capped teeth swiveled around and a nasal voice whined at Mahoney, "Hey, the boss said to leave him untouched."

"Mind your own business."

During this interchange, I snaked my hand into my pocket. My fingers touched the phone, gripped it and held on. Barely breathing, I was clutching the small life line against my thigh and kept my eyes glued to the road ahead. I felt Mahoney's gaze turn and study me in the dark. His eyes glinted with satisfaction as he relaxed his angry hold and leaned back into his seat.

It was only when we reached Surf Avenue, a block from Nathan's Famous, that opportunity smiled. Two cars sat in the middle of the street, blocking the road. Standing in the middle of the road, pugnaciously close to one other, two wild-eyed drivers were screaming verbal abuse, which seemed to escalate by the moment. The cops were going to be called—definitely not the best-case scenario for Mahoney. Our car was now blocked in by the stalled traffic behind.

"Watch him!" Mahoney growled as he pointed towards me. He lit out of the car and stepped threateningly between the two testosterone-fueled men. While the driver and Jaws were busy watching the scene, I carefully snaked my fingers around the screen of my iPhone. I let my fingers inch their way around the familiar buttons and muted the sound and dimmed the glare. I visualized the screen and tapped the CALL button twice, hoping desperately that Oscar's tip had worked. I waited for the phone to redial my last call. I coughed loudly just as Oscar's voice came on the line. I leaned quickly forward to call out as loudly as I could, "So fellas, you guys are new with the Crow."

Jaw's squeaky voice floated from the front. "You heard what Mahoney said, shut the fuck up!"

I was thankful for the silence on Oscar's end, but to further clarify matters, I persisted: "I know this area, you're not going to get away with it. This is Coney Island. The place is crawling with cops."

Jaws reached around and slapped me hard in the face. The blow echoed within the silent confines of the car. "Listen you dumb fuck, don't say another fucking word or I'll sic Mahoney on you."

I felt the ringing in my ear grow perilously loud. I finally managed to hiss between my lips, "I thought you said the Crow wanted me to himself."

"A little slap here or there just tenderizes the meat, nothing the shoemaker would object to," he sneered. I hoped the conversation was loud enough for Oscar, whose nimble ears matched his nimble brain and who, I knew, was listening quietly. Mahoney slid back into the car. Out in the street, the two drivers slunk sullenly back into their cars. Mahoney must have used the magic words.

The car lunged forward and we drove on. I had done what I could. I hoped it was enough.

We finally stopped and Mahoney grabbed my arm and pulled me out of the car. I was dragged up the rickety steps and onto the pier.

"It's so like Crawley to hang out at an amusement park," I shouted, raising my voice against the ceaseless roar of the waves.

Crawley, the newly minted kingpin, stepped out of the shadows, a hoodlum in full bloom. He was built like a cement truck. At least six and a half feet of muscle and brute strength. His square head literally rested on top his massive shoulders—the neck was gone. He shot me a blank stare, a little manic gleam in his eyes. The hands, the size of overstuffed boxing gloves, were clenching and unclenching. Muscles corded and bulged like ham sausages straining against their outer casings. The open collar of his shirt revealed a large tattoo of a dragon's gaping jaw. The enormous arms were entirely etched with snakes, bats, spiders, and black swastikas. They were literally blue and green; no skin was visible under the intricate and gruesome artwork. Apparently, prison life afforded Crawley the opportunity to hone his bulk into formidable strength. He looked like he could bench press a car.

I looked at the Crow's face, as malleable and empty as a Halloween mask. He looked whacked out on crack or meth. He folded his arms across his body, steroid induced biceps and a barrel-like chest.

A snarl. "Nicholas Nickleby… Welcome."

I felt his words sink into the pit of my stomach. Everything came rushing back. Every cell in my body was vibrating with a cold mist of rage. It spread inside me like Methane Hydrate, that icy, cage-like structure surrounded by molecules of water. No wonder that explosive gas was called "Flammable Ice." I wanted the Crow dead, pulverized, obliterated. I felt the blinding electric shock course through my body, the small shockwaves as every nerve ending surged with frenzy. I took two bracing breaths and willed my mind to regain clarity.

"I'm not alone, Crawley," I said, trying to keep my voice even and calm. "You remember Greg, my friend, don't you? He's a cop now. He'll be coming along soon. This time you won't get away with murder."

I felt my own hand flexing in my pocket. I tried to relax my stance and force my brain to focus. Padrick had always cautioned me to fight smart. In this case, the odds that brains could triumph over brawn seemed laughable, but I was playing for time. I hoped Oscar, wily and smart as ever, had set things in motion.

I saw Mahoney's worried look. "That's right." I turned to him. "Aiding and abetting is fifteen to twenty."

"Shut the fuck up. No one is coming," uttered Crawley in a dead voice.

I looked at him with as much contempt as I could muster. "How does it feel, Crawley, to have your men do your dirty work? You don't ever get your hands unsanitary until the last minute, do you? Makes you feel like a man, does it?"

Crawley glared at me. "Keep on talking, you glorified suit. I don't need any of my men to take you." He snickered. "I can take you with one hand tied behind my back."

"Like you did with Padrick?" The pain of the name caught my breath.

Crawley smiled a big, malicious, tooth-bearing grin. "Your brother, he was different. He knew how to fight. Besides, he was carrying. I had to take him down before he stepped up."

I forced my voice to level out but it was still hoarse. "Is that why you had three guys hold him down while you beat him to death?"

"I had to do what I had to do," he observed indifferently.

I was hoping that my words would keep him off balance; I was familiar with his mind-numbing predictability. Goading him was my only chance.

"That's not how I see it." My voice was just above a whisper. "You're all show. Underneath you're just a little boy crying for your mama." There it was, that uncontrollable fury, the scowl transforming Crawley's ugly face into something feral. I went on, my voice full of derision. "You were what, Crawley, eight, when she left?"

He stepped forward, his weight shifting to his left foot, and he shot his right arm right at my face. I was ready. I dodged the full impact of the fist, but the sheer force of something like a rushing tide hit my body. I was flung backwards. I smelled the metallic scent of blood and tasted its salty tang on my tongue. I kicked Crawley in the crotch, but he only stumbled for an instant, and then he came at me again. My right hand snaked into my pocket and grabbed the twenty-five quarters wrapped in a coin tube, my trusty, ever-present defensive weapon, and I aimed it deep into Crawley's belly. I felt the nasty punch of metal meeting his left kidney all the way up into my shoulder blade, and I heard Crawley's soft hiss of pain as he doubled over. I followed my right with a clean left undercut to Crawley's chin, but his momentary floundering was short-lived, and the narrowed slits of his eyes locked into mine as a vicious elbow hook sank like a battering ram into the soft tissue of my neck.

I doubled over with the blow, yet stayed mercifully on my feet. I kept my head low, waiting for Crawley to close in. My body coiled upwards as I swung my fist in a solid arc connecting with his nose in a mind-numbing crunch. Anyone else would have gone down, but Crawley staggered a little, head snapped back, and held his ground. His dead eyes had a startled look, and his hand went to his bleeding nostrils. His recovery time was surprising, as he came back at me, his right elbow jamming into my ribs and his left hook aimed at my face. I dropped like a felled tree, my back against the rough planks, a morbid *déjà vu*.

I watched Crawley's large feet from the corner of my eye; he was holding a huge crowbar. His calling card. He was swinging it rhythmically in his right hand as he lumbered to stand over me. I tried to raise my head, gasping for air; there was a roaring in my ears. I was beyond pain, beyond fear, beyond exhaustion; I knew I was about to die. Crawley was taking his own sweet time. His smile grew wider as he watched my efforts to hoist my body. He was a model of pure psychopathology. I felt every muscle strain as I stumbled blindly to my feet. Crawley caught me with a stunning blow and then coldly, almost indifferently he swung the crowbar. I turned sideways, awkward and helpless, raising my left arm to ward off the deadly blow, and I heard a crunch. I saw the white streaks of bone and tissue poke through flesh and skin, my arm splitting in half like a ripe melon. The ground was rushing hard to meet my body.

I held on to consciousness, my clenched teeth fighting the blackness. I knew I was staring into death's face. I thought dimly of the article I had read that morning, about the wonder of existence, and the fact that the universe was about 14 billion years old. I was forty-one years old and this was not how I wanted to end my life. I thought of Padrick, who was only twenty-three when he died, and I thought of Maddie. Then I thought of nothing as Crawley's distorted features were inches away from mine, his lips curling in a small, savage smile. His preternaturally huge fist was poised to deliver the death blow. My hearing started to fade. I closed my eyes and let the darkness win. I thought I heard the sound of a pop as I passed out.

It was a shock to feel my eyes flutter open. I was alive. My body was wracked with pain; it spread like waves of fire. I waited for my vision to clear. I was staring with glazed eyes into Greg's face leaning low over mine, the blurred edges of the streetlight casting a golden halo around his head. An incessant noise kept drumming in my skull. My head was pounding so severely that I could not keep my eyes open. I tried to push myself up, but waves of vertigo threatened to spin me back into darkness.

"Where are you hurt?' Greg's voice sounded faraway and frantic. "Nick, where are you hurt? I can't see through the bloody mess. Damn it!!" Greg clutched the collar of my shirt and drew closer.

My swollen lips could barely move. I listened to my wheezing voice as if it belonged to someone else. "I think I have some broken ribs, and my left arm is broken. My head feels funny. I don't know about the rest." My speech was slurring and then my voice died.

"Don't you go to sleep, Nick! Do you hear me? The ambulance is on its way. You stay awake and look at me! I'm going to stay right here." I felt the deck's rough wood-plank against my cheek; I was fighting to keep my eyes open. My foggy brain lurched, trying to process what I was looking at: it seemed like a solid tree trunk was lying next to me. Greg's voice cut in. "Nick. Do you hear me? Look at me, damn you!'

I moved my head carefully. The pain was unbearable, any minute now I was going to let go.

"Don't move your head!"

"What happened?" I whispered.

"We got here in the nick of time." Greg's voice sounded funny. "You arrogant bastard! I told you he was going to come after you! But no—no protection for you! You had to do a Dirty Harry!"

I heard him draw in a long breath. "As soon as Oscar called, I got my squad to follow your GPS. I was praying your battery wouldn't die out and that we'd get here in time." Greg raised his hand to rake his hair. "Fool's luck! If it weren't for Oscar, you'd be dead right now."

I closed my eyes and groaned. "Where's Crawley?"

"Right next to you. Shot once through the head."

I smiled weakly. "All those hours spent on the shooting range paid off."

I never heard Greg's answer. I swam gratefully into the black.

CHAPTER 18

Every why has a wherefore.

—William Shakespeare, *Comedy of Errors*

I heard the muted sound of the rhythmic blips, a long way off. Trying to open my eyes, I thought for a moment I was dead at last, but then my ears tuned in to the all-too-real uniform, beeps. With hearing restored, I realized I was in too much pain to have died. I cracked my eyes open and gazed at the wavering, eerie strobes of light flickering over me, the room a ghostly green. I tried to turn my head and was instantly beset by a wave of nausea. A short stocky woman wearing bright blue nursing scrubs approached my bed.

"You're awake!" she said, flashing a warm smile. "Welcome to the land of the living, Mr. Conor. I'm Candice. I'm on the graveyard shift and have been taking care of you for the past two nights." Nurse Candice had a wide forehead and pale blue eyes that looked weary and strained, but beamed kindly.

"You're in New York-Presbyterian Weill Cornell Hospital. Try not to move."

I smiled weakly. I couldn't move if my life depended on it. I felt the tube being removed from my throat, and the loud hissing noise stopped. I was breathing on my own – short little breaths, stiff wire bristles swiping metal.

She lifted my hand to check my pulse and grinned as she spoke, "You've been out of it for the better part of two days."

It hurt like hell to breathe. I looked at Nurse Candice mutely, my chest heaving as I tried to push away an immense ball pressing against it. My throat was on fire: tiny sharp blades were ripping my windpipe apart. I wondered whether my vocal chords would cooperate if I tried to speak. I opened my parched lips tentatively, but she laid a quick finger against my mouth. "You have a pretty bad concussion and a hairline fracture at the base of your skull. We've used some restraints to limit any sudden movements while you were unconscious."

I closed my eyes and waited for the onslaught of pain to subside. All at once, memories of the fight slammed into me. The sudden impact of something like a 400-horsepower beast of machinery, the final seconds of consciousness as I waited to die. The incomprehensible sounds of a medic as he leaned over me, screaming into my face.

"I'm going to unhook the restraints," she said, "but you must remember to lie very still."

I felt the welcomed release of my wrists and legs but my head, like a lead-filled appendage, refused to move. Nurse Candice lowered her face towards mine and said gently, "You can move your legs. Your left arm is in a cast. Both the ulna and radius were broken. You were lucky that our Dr. Somner, head of the Department of Orthopedic Surgery, was on hand to operate on you."

I managed a whisper, more like a scratchy croak, "My sister?" My throat throbbed.

The nurse laid a comforting hand on my shoulder. "Try not to speak. From the bruises on your neck, we thought your larynx was damaged. You need to refrain from using your voice."

I touched the heavy, swaddling bandages around my head. The nurse drew my hand away gently. "You had a nasty gash on the side of your head. You have more than a few sutures, and we're still unsure about the inner ear. She smiled as she noticed my frown. "You have a ruptured spleen, a collapsed lung, and three of your ribs were fractured and are tightly bound. They'll probably cause you a lot of pain. There's the IV on your right to provide pain relief. You're lucky to be alive, Mr. Conor. Try to get some sleep. That's the best therapy for now."

I woke into blazing daylight looking into Moira's robin's egg blue eyes. She smiled a sweet, tremulous smile.

"Oh, God, Nicki," she half-choked, as she swiped at her quiet tears.

I smiled weakly and lifted my hand towards my throat.

Moira nodded. "Yes, I know, you're not supposed to speak. Just blink once for 'Yes' and twice for 'No.'"

A scarily guttural sound escaped my lips as I tried to utter a simple "Hey."

"No," Moira said as if addressing a recalcitrant student. "I told you, no talking! Use your eyes." She placed her hand over mine and brought it to her unmarred cheek. "I was so scared, Nicki. You almost died. I thought I'd lost you! Thank God for Greg. He's been here every night." Moira's teary eyes roamed my face anxiously, reassuring herself that I was there with her, alive and breathing. "Are you in a lot of pain?" she asked.

I blinked twice. This tugging need to protect Moira, which I never did, which I never could, was like a dead weight on my heart. Trying to smile, I thought of the wreckage of our lives. We were like the last survivors of a catastrophe that had decimated our family and left us crippled. But then a thought fluttered in my mind: *we were alive.*

"We made it, *mhuirnin,*" I whispered and held her as best I could. Lying there, under the stark, harsh hospital lights, body racked with pain, I felt the happy lightness of being alive. Yes, I thought: we could make a go of it, Moira and I.

Then I closed my eyes and drifted off.

The next time I opened my eyes, I was staring into the luminescent green of Maddie's eyes filled with concern and relief. Complete affirmation. First, the wild flash of realizing I was alive, then gratitude for the gift of life, and now this.

When she said "Hello," the sound of her voice was like the gentle swell of a distant sea. A wave of infinite longing rolled over me. I was suddenly aware of what this life of mine could be – a life outside that dark tunnel, a life in the sunlight. Not since childhood, and maybe not even then, did I feel so intensely the joy of being alive. I smiled, reached for Maddie's hand, lifted it to my face and kissed it.

"I met your sister, Moira." Maddie broke the silence.

My eyes flew open, and I watched Maddie's face settle into an expression I hadn't seen before. She spoke in a musing tone, her eyes straying from mine to stare down some distant thought. "I knew someone, a long time ago, someone who told me about his sister, whose face was burned…" A pause, as Maddie sifted through the memory. "I don't think he ever mentioned her name, but she would have been around my age. Your brother, the one who died, what was his name?"

A memory, a face, a laugh, but now just that: only a memory, not a searing knife lodged in my chest. "Padrick," I whispered and smiled.

There was such a long silence that I thought Maddie hadn't heard me, but then she withdrew her hand and looked at me with a baffled expression. "Your brother…I met him…I knew him." Her voice lost its evenness, and the husky undertone, which I loved, grew patchy. "I met your brother a long time ago. I was fourteen at the time…"

I was watching the film unspool, frame by frame: the image of a girl; the long, wet, golden hair; the proud, taut shoulders. The dark rain sluicing down over a pier, blacker than the blackest night.

I nodded, ignoring the pain thumping against my skull, my voice gravelly and halting. "I saw you once," I whispered. "I saw you one night on the pier, in the rain as you walked away. I never saw your face, but when you and I met for the first time, when you turned to meet me, that flicker of an image floated towards me." I took a long breath. "Every time I saw you, memories of that night rushed back…I didn't understand why…You see, my brother… The night I saw you… Padrick was killed that night…" My voice died. There was a roar in my head.

We stared at each other, stunned by the vagaries of fate which had thrown us together against all odds.

Maddie saw the unasked question in my eyes, and a ghost of a smile touched her lips. "I met your brother, or more accurately, he found me, huddled around a burning barrel. Four homeless derelicts of undetermined ages and dubious characters, and a fourteen-year-old girl. We must have been a pretty sight, dregs of humanity that we were. It was the dead of winter, and I had just arrived in New York maybe two or three days earlier." Maddie's smile had a tinge of bitter sadness as she continued, "The men were as indifferent to my presence as to everything else around them."

She lifted her eyes and stared at the memory. "Your brother… Padrick…" The sound of his name on her lips resonated like a gong hit with a mallet. "He was a policeman. He had come down to check on the men. I saw the dark shape of his uniform stride towards us, and I started to walk away. The men were all adults; they could handle themselves with the law. I was a girl, a child, really, and I got scared."

I lay transfixed, listening, as I tried to wrap my head around the fact that Padrick and Maddie had known each other. She continued, "I wasn't quick enough, or perhaps he was faster than I had anticipated, but he caught up with me." Maddie grew silent. I kept my eyes closed.

She continued, "He took me to a shelter, a type of home for itinerant youths, runaways, and juvenile delinquents. He promised to relocate me as soon as he found a suitable place." She gazed down at me. "He was extremely kind but very determined…very persuasive." She added a little uncertainly, "I don't know if that's the right word, but he made me listen and I almost believed I could trust him."

"Almost?" My heart hammered against my bruised ribs.

Maddie averted her face. "I wasn't in the trusting business then," she said tonelessly.

Not then, not now.

"That night on the pier?" I asked in a half-whisper.

"It was a few days later; I came back to tell him I was leaving the city." Another inward glance. "He told me, in no uncertain terms, that it was a bad idea. He was angry. He told me he was on track with some people who could foster me. I walked away, sure he would follow me. When he didn't, I sighed with relief. I never saw him again."

Against my closed eyes, I replayed that horrific night, the painful chain of events that cut down my brother's life. Had I not shown up at that moment, had I come but a few minutes later, Padrick, as strong-willed and determined as he was, would have followed Maddie and would have cheated the Crow and fate. I would have missed him and he would have been alive today.

"He died within an hour," I forced out.

"I'm sorry," Maddie whispered.

I felt the hardness of my stare, almost as hard as plutonium or stron-tium or "kryptonite." Something unyielding and primordial. *Sorry... Sorry...Sorry...*I felt my chest compress under the familiar mass of guilt and remorse. Neither of us said another word. And I floated away.

When I awakened, it was dark. I was in another ward, and Maddie was gone.

PART TWO

THE TRIAL

CHAPTER 19

Today is only one day in all the days that will
ever be.
But what will happen in all the other days that ever
come can depend on what you do today.

—Ernest Hemingway, *For Whom the Bell Tolls*

September 15th, 2012. New York City

Oscar let us off at the corner, but as we approached the New York Supreme Court building, we were blitzed by a mass of TV and newspaper reporters, all jostling for a look, a photo, a sound bite. I pushed through, against the current, all the while holding onto Maddie's arm, shielding her as best as I could. It was a relief to enter the dimly lit, cool hallway.

Anticipating the interest in the case, Judge Ramsey had requested the large ceremonial courtroom, which nonetheless was crammed with standing-room-only spectators. The maple furnishings looked tired, the walnut planks of the well-trodden floor and matching benches were slicked by the passage of time. Two flags flanked Judge Ramsey's bench, and the large inscription "In God We Trust" was centered behind the judge's chair.

The room was cloyingly hot. I looked back to see the row of gawkers—permanent fixtures in any celebrity trial; the ranks of enterprising reporters who had managed to commandeer seats; the perennial sketch artists. Directly behind Ribisi sat the Monnehan contingency: Mildred Monnehan, mother of the victim, primly coiffed and dry-eyed, and her three daughters, sitting with men I assumed were their spouses. I made out some of my colleagues—those with whom I had negotiated plea bargains and those against whom I had litigated tenaciously and, more often than not, successfully. As I swung my gaze around, my eyes met the stolid, blank stare of Ribisi's investigator, Alfie Braddock. I nodded coolly and smiled, a quick and easy smile, and he turned briskly away. Oscar was watching the exchange with his usual alertness. *Our hounddog versus their hyena.* Directly behind us, I noticed Maddie's publisher, Bobby Hershing, one of our character witnesses, and Leo O'Shaunessy, whose spine was so rigid his back barely touched the bench.

"All rise, the Honorable Judge Seymour Ramsey is presiding," boomed the bailiff's voice, and Judge Ramsey stepped out onto the dais. The room fell silent as the judge took his seat.

"Be seated," Ramsey said, as he shuffled through a pile of papers on his desk. "Bailiff, please call the case."

"Docket 9942, the people versus Madeline Monnehan," stated the court officer. The judge peered over his reading glasses. "I see that the prosecution and defense attorneys have opted for a balance of power." He nodded towards the three at the prosecution table—Paul Ribisi, George Bennett, and his stalwart clerk, then looked at Annika, Matthew, and me.

Maddie and I stood still. She was facing the judge on charges of first-degree murder and looked incredibly calm. She was wearing a dark gray suit and a white blouse beautifully tailored, suggesting an air of festive formality. The familiar cameo brooch sat distinctively on the right lapel. It was clear to me that Maddie regarded the pin as a kind of badge. Not for the first time, I wondered if by understanding its significance, I could solve the mystery of the woman wearing it.

Ramsey addressed Maddie, "Mrs. Monnehan, you are hereby charged with Murder in the First Degree, how do you plead?"

"Not guilty, Your Honor."

Ramsey narrowed his eyes at me. "Mr. Conor, any other preliminary motions, before we begin the *voir dire*?"

"No, Your Honor."

"Then let us proceed. Bailiff, call in the first panel."

We began the process of selecting jurors, asking a series of basic questions. I'd opted to have no jury expert, no focus groups, no background checks, and no expert psychiatrist to consult with in jury selection. From experience, I considered them overrated and over-compensated.

Since I didn't rely on experts, I approached jury selection with uncommon intensity and focus, relying on my own perceptions, my serviceable memory, and the perceptiveness of my associates. Once in a while, Annika, her eyes glued on a prospective juror, would slide over a sheet of paper with shorthand notations, comments that revealed her invaluable skill at assessing the pros and cons of each answer. We had learned to perfect this non-verbal dialogue over time. It was a thing to behold, this laser-sharp teamwork–more art than science.

Ribisi took a long time to ferret out the people he wanted on the panel, and I weighed in with my own preferences. It was a delicate *pas de deux,* in which neither one conceded nor revealed his hand—a battle conducted with finesse, white gloves, and impeccable manners. By the end of the third day, we had our twelve jurors. Seven women, five men, and four alternates. Eight Caucasians, four African Americans, two Asian Americans, and two Hispanics.

The following morning, we made our appearance in front of the Supreme Court.

Judge Ramsey looked somber as he regarded the jurors and said, "Ladies and gentlemen of the jury, I would like to remind you that the following statements from both Mr. Ribisi and Mr. Conor, the prosecutor and defense counselor in the case against Madeline Monnehan, will not constitute evidence. They will each simply proffer statements, which they will then endeavor to prove. I believe that you understand the gravity of this case and will adhere to the stringent rules that prevail. You are not to talk about the case to anyone outside the jury room; you are not to engage in discussions until all the evidence has been presented. Most of all, you are not to read, listen to, or watch anything related to the trial. You have a pivotal role in these proceedings, so treat your duties with the respect they deserve."

Ribisi rose elegantly to his feet, blue suit impeccably tailored, lavender striped tie winking with panache, and a high voltage smile bestowed on each juror as he approached the jury box. He started in a firm, confident tone. "This is a case of murder masquerading as self-defense," he said. A good opening—strong and catchy. I could envision tomorrow's headlines emblazoned with the phrase. I wondered if George Bennett, who was known for turning a pretty phrase, was responsible for it.

"On the night of March 11th of this year, Mrs. Monnehan shot her husband to death. This she admitted freely and clearly to the detectives on the scene. She later amended her statement to include a claim of self-defense—which her lawyer," he turned to look at me, making certain all eyes followed his, "might, or might not, have advised her to do. We will also submit the transcript of the defendant's telephone call in which she confessed to shooting her husband." Ribisi walked back to the prosecution table, making a show of looking at his notes. I was too familiar with Ribisi's courtroom tactics to be fooled by the studied pause. I knew he not only committed to memory the words of his opening statement, but also choreographed the pauses. They were Ribisi's way of giving the jurors time to mull over the transcript of Maddie's taped call, time to digest its import.

Glancing up from his notes, Ribisi scrutinized the jurors. "We intend to show that Madeline Monnehan not only killed her husband, but did so with intent and malice. We will show that Mr. and Mrs. Monnehan were experiencing matrimonial difficulties prior to the shooting. We will produce witnesses to attest to the fact that Senator Monnehan was in the process of severing the ties between himself and his wife, a fact that the defendant failed to disclose to either her own lawyer or to the state's attorney. We intend to prove that Mrs. Monnehan was aware of the impending divorce initiated by her husband. We will show that the public affront of her husband's disenchantment with their marriage, the blow to her prestige and newfound standing in society, in addition to the impending loss of the life of luxury she had become accustomed to, had driven the defendant to the edge. Mrs. Monnehan decided to eliminate her husband from her life. We will show that despite the defendant's claim that she strongly abhorred handguns, Mrs. Monnehan had spent time at a shooting range, acquiring enough proficiency to handle the gun in her possession."

Ribisi paused as he looked at the jury and then at the judge, aware of the total silence greeting his words. He was wielding the baton and save for a single, strangled cough in the back, the hall had an air of riveted anticipation.

"Ladies and gentlemen, we will show that Madeline Monnehan planned and executed an elaborate scheme, including asking this court to believe that her husband's death was a tragic accident. We will prove that the one clean shot to the Senator's heart was a cold, premeditated act intended to put an end to his life."

I watched Ribisi, my features schooled in an expression of disinterested attention. I knew he was about to wind down and waited for his well-known penchant for finishing with a flourish. As expected, Ribisi cleared his throat, furrowed his brow, and casting a grave, disparaging look at Maddie, said: "Madeline Monnehan used what she is known for: her intelligence, a steely composure under pressure, and above all, her writer's imagination, as she wove and spun a plausible story of self-defense to cover up a pre-meditated homicide. Ladies and gentlemen, after you hear all the evidence, you will have no choice but to reach the conclusion that the defendant killed her husband knowingly and deliberately. There will be no doubt in your minds that this heinous act was premeditated, and that Madeline Monnehan is guilty of first-degree murder."

I had to concede that Ribisi's opening statement was eloquent and powerful. He sat down and Bennett leaned over to whisper in his ear. There was a satisfied gleam in Ribisi's eyes when he glanced in my direction.

Judge Ramsey looked at me. "Mr. Conor," he prompted.

Like a heavy-weight coming out of his corner, I felt a rush of adrenaline. I disregarded the tightening bands across my chest, the ever-present insidious pain I had grown accustomed to; I was tired of shadowboxing. This was the last leg of the journey I had embarked on when a slender woman turned to me with equal measures of defiance and need. As I rose to my feet, I locked eyes with Maddie. The promise of all that I could have took my breath away.

Then Ribisi and I exchanged sharp glances. Purportedly, we faced each other on equal footing, but the match was definitely rigged in the prosecution's favor. The preponderance of evidence weighed heavily on the State's side. Yet Ribisi was unaware of one crucial fact: against my heart lay the whisper of a talisman. I was poised to lay claim to something more than a verdict of innocence. I was going to win this case because there was never any other alternative.

Like many defense lawyers, my opening statements were customarily short and concise. But this time I needed more than a terse opening, I needed to not only present the jury with an overview of the case, but to engage them in a persuasive story which I hoped would smooth my road to the verdict of "Innocent." I had spent the better half of the previous week constructing my presentation to the jury. As I spoke, I kept my voice deliberately low. I wanted every juror to focus his or her undivided attention on my face and hang on my every word. "Ladies and gentlemen of the jury, the prosecutor has the burden of proving, beyond a shadow of a doubt, that the shooting of Senator Monnehan was not accidental. The State must establish the fact that a self-defense argument is without grounds. If, by the end of the trial, the prosecution fails to do so, it is your duty to return a verdict of 'Not Guilty.'" I walked over to the jurors, my expression earnest and deliberate. "Ladies and gentlemen of the jury, the human response, when threatened with a looming danger, is to react instantly. Maddie Monnehan acted in self-defense. Thinking that she was about to be attacked by an intruder in her home, she used the surest means at her disposal and shot the unknown assailant. In Maddie Monnehan's mind there were but a few seconds between mortal danger and survival. Thus, we must consider the state of mind of Mrs. Monnehan, the speed of the event, and the time frame of my client's reaction."

I paused briefly and injected a conversational tone into my voice. "Imagine that you have entered your home and found an intruder lurking, threatening your safety and the safety of your family. Ask yourself what you would do if, in your mind, you had only a few desperate seconds to decide. Who among us would not fight back in order to survive?" I saw the involuntary wince on the face of Mrs. Wilkinson, the housewife from Queens. Her family, consisting of three daughters, aged ten to fifteen, resided in a less-than-safe neighborhood. Miss Thackeray, the accountant, was pursing her lips in reflection as her dark eyes scrutinized Maddie. Emily Long, the youngest person in the box, lowered her eyes in uneasiness. I was gratified by the initial reactions on the faces of the men, who were all eyeing Maddie with a mixture of fascination and speculation.

I continued in a sharper and more authoritative voice. "Furthermore, Maddie Monnehan was legally entitled to defend herself. The Penal Law clearly allows the use of deadly force to repel an imminent attack such as robbery, kidnapping, or rape. The threat, as Mrs. Monnehan perceived it, was imminent and deadly. The New York State legislature recognizes what is known as a castle doctrine, also known as a castle law, or a defense of habitation law. This is a legal doctrine that designates a person's abode or, in some states, any legally occupied place, like a vehicle or workplace, as a place in which that person has certain protections and immunities. In certain circumstances, the person is entitled to use force, including deadly force, to defend himself or herself against an intruder, free from legal responsibility and prosecution for the consequences of the force used.

"Maddie Monnehan was at home when she confronted an intruder and was within her rights to use force to defend herself. Unfortunately, the intruder turned out to be Senator Monnehan, whose death was a truly tragic accident." A pause, and then I added in the softest tone, "A tragedy whose devastating impact, I can assure you, is felt by no-one more desperately than by Mrs. Monnehan herself." I took a long breath and leveled a frank stare at the jury box. "Ladies and gentlemen, I hope that you will bear in mind these salient facts. I trust that after reviewing the evidence, you will find Madeline Monnehan innocent of the charges. Thank you."

Court was adjourned.

* * *

Detective Tom Lachey, clean-shaven and alert, appeared in court on the fifth day of the trial. He was dressed in a dark suit that fit his tall body well. Looking competent and confident, Lachey took his seat on the stand and faced Ribisi, who verified the detective's credentials. Lachey was an experienced witness who had testified in more homicide prosecutions than any other officer in his squad. Most jury panels found for the prosecution and culminated in convictions. Ribisi's expression was earnest and respectful as he drew near the witness.

"You are the detective in charge of the investigation, are you not, Detective?"

"Yes." The intelligent, broad face remained impassive.

"Can you please describe for the court the events of March 12th of this year?"

"I entered the residence of Senator and Mrs. Monnehan at 12 East 75th Street at…" he looked down at his notes, "twelve-thirty-one a.m. on March 12th. Officer Markham, the first man on the scene, was waiting for me. I walked up to the master bedroom on the second floor, where the response team was already hard at work. The paramedics dispatched to the scene had spent some time with the victim. Once Senator Monnehan was declared dead, the medical examiner was requested. Dr. Lippi, the coroner, and Moses Stringer, the police forensic expert, and I arrived at practically the same time to find Senator Monnehan lying face down on the floor of the master bedroom. After conferring with Dr. Lippi, we waited for the photographer and the forensics team to start collecting evidence."

I could tell how lethal Lachey's calm manner was. So far it was quietly instilling confidence in the listeners and winning points with the judge.

Ribisi walked over to my desk and handed me five photos, then handed copies to Grimaldi, the foreman of the jury, who dutifully passed them along. Ribisi then projected the photo of Monnehan's prostrate body on the large television facing the jurors and the judge. "Is that how you found Senator Monnehan?"

"Yes."

"What did you do then?"

"I put my task force through their paces. I needed them to process the crime scene as quickly and efficiently as possible. My team collected the evidence: we cut out the rug under the victim's body for blood analysis. The forensic technicians collected hair, dusted for fingerprints. They bagged the pistol and sent the evidence to the police lab for analysis."

Ribisi walked to his desk, picked up a gun sheathed in a clear plastic evidence bag, walked back to Lachey and asked, "Is this the gun you found?"

Lachey inspected the gun through the plastic, turned it over once, and nodded. "Yes."

"And where was it found?"

"It lay right next to Senator Monnehan's body."

Ribisi picked up the plastic-enclosed firearm and returned it to the prosecution's desk. "Your Honor, we would to like submit the gun as exhibit B."

He took a quick look at his notes and turned back to Lachey. "Did your people conduct a luminol test?"

"Yes."

"And what did you find?"

"There was no blood anywhere else except for the area where the victim was lying. And some splashes against the foot of the bed covering."

"What did you do then?"

"I went down to speak with the victim's wife."

"Mrs. Monnehan was downstairs?"

"Yes. She was sitting in the kitchen."

"What happened then?"

"I informed her that her husband was dead."

"What did she say?"

"She said she already knew that, she checked his pulse after she shot him."

"Did she say anything else?"

"No." Detective Lachey cast a quick glance in my direction.

"Was Mrs. Monnehan's lawyer present at the time?"

"No." There was a weary note in Lachey's voice.

"So, Mrs. Monnehan was alone when she told you she killed her husband?" Ribisi asked with the same grave and respectful tone.

"Well, there was a woman officer in the kitchen preparing some tea. Mrs. Monnehan's lawyer joined us almost immediately."

Ribisi shot me a glance and asked pointedly, "Mr. Conor joined you before Mrs. Monnehan was done talking with you?"

"It wasn't Mr. Conor who walked in, but Leo O'Shaunessy, the family's counsel," said Lachey tonelessly.

Mr. Angus Mork, the second juror from the left, squinted slightly as he viewed Ribisi with a sudden, alert wariness.

"Did the defendant add anything more?"

"No."

"So, basically, without prompting or questioning, Mrs. Monnehan had openly confessed to the killing of her husband?"

"Yes." His dark eyes remained implacably fixed on Ribisi's face. There was not a hint of concern or nervousness in Lachey's relaxed jaw or brow.

"All she said was that she had shot her husband?"

"Yes."

"Did you ask her what happened?"

He looked at Ribisi, then me. "No."

"Why not?"

"I hadn't Mirandized her yet, and I didn't want to compromise my investigation."

"What happened next?"

"I read Mrs. Monnehan her rights and asked her if she understood them."

"And did she?"

He glanced at Maddie. "Yes."

"Mrs. Monnehan was shortly taken to the station?"

"Yes."

"So, as far as you know, everything the police did was beyond reproach?"

Lachey replied with a resounding, "Yes."

Ribisi, energized and quick of step, approached the detective. "Detective, in your investigation, did you pursue the issue of the gun and the Monnehans' familiarity with it?"

"Yes. Both Senator Monnehan and Mrs. Monnehan were members of the Shore Shot Pistol Range in Lakewood, New Jersey. We checked the club's attendance records and their names showed up on twelve different occasions."

"Twelve?" exclaimed Ribisi. "That seems to be a true commitment to target shooting, wouldn't you say?"

"Objection, Your Honor. Beyond the scope," I said dryly.

Ramsey impaled me with his light eyes. "I will allow."

Ribisi repeated his question.

Detective Lachey thought for a full minute and then answered, "I guess it shows that they wanted to get proficient in handling a gun."

"Objection," I called out.

"Overruled."

"Would you say that twelve practice sessions at a shooting range would allow Mrs. Monnehan to be comfortable handling a gun?"

"Yes."

Ribisi smiled at his witness, nodding his thanks. "That is all for now, thank you, Detective." He directed his gaze at Ramsey. "We reserve the right, Your Honor, to redirect at a later time."

"Very well, Mr. Ribisi." The judge glanced in my direction. "Mr. Conor?"

I smiled at Lachey as I approached the witness box. He didn't return my smile.

"Detective, you and I have previously gone over the events of the night of March 12th, isn't that so?" I asked companionably.

"Yes."

"I did not ask you before, but I'm assuming that Mrs. Monnehan was alone in the house when you arrived on the premises?"

Lachey narrowed his eyes a fraction but answered coolly. "Yes. Except for the EMTs and my men, there was no one else. We checked the entire house."

"So, Mrs. Monnehan was alone when she told you that she shot her husband?"

I saw Lachey's guarded glance. "Yes."

"She told you she had shot her husband?"

"Yes."

I gave him a long, deliberate stare. "Did Mrs. Monnehan say anything else?"

"She said, 'I called 9-1-1; I told them what happened.'"

"Anything else?"

"No." There was a note of caution in his voice. Lachey knew where we were heading.

Instead, I changed direction. "How did Maddie Monnehan seem to you?"

Lachey turned to meet my eyes. If he was startled, he hid it well, taking several seconds to think about it. "She seemed calm. Cold."

"You mean emotionally detached or physically cold?"

"I don't know. It could have been both."

"So, when you say that Mrs. Monnehan seemed to be cold, how did you come by that conclusion?"

When there was a long pause, I decided to help him dig the hole a little deeper. "Was it cold in the kitchen, Detective, as far as you can remember?"

"Maybe."

My voice grew a shade softer. "She was shivering. Do you suppose Mrs. Monnehan was exhibiting signs of shock?"

Lachey sighed. "She seemed calm."

"You mean, she was not sobbing hysterically or wringing her hands?" I asked politely.

He stared at me coldly. "Yes."

"Hugging oneself and shivering, these are some of the signs of shock, isn't that so, Detective?"

He let the question hang in the air a bit too long, but was staunchly honest when he answered. "You could say that there were signs of her being under some kind of stress."

I changed tack. "Mrs. Monnehan responded to you as soon as you informed her of her husband's death?"

"Yes."

"When she spoke to you, she was not Mirandized?"

A baleful stare as Detective Lachey seemed to summon his patience. I gave him a thin smile. I would bring up the issue of the Miranda warning as many times as I was allowed. Repetition, a useful Chinese torture method of drip, drip, drip, ensured the jury's full attention to crucial points.

Before Lachey could respond, Ribisi rose hastily to his feet and yelled, "Objection, Your Honor. The witness has already testified thoroughly to the chronology of the events. That particular question has been asked and answered. I request the court's immediate ruling on undue repetition of testimony."

I looked at Ramsey. "Your Honor, the purpose of my bringing up the Miranda Rights is to lay the foundation for further questioning."

Ribisi countered, "We have a taped transcript of Mrs. Monnehan fully admitting to the shooting; whatever she told Detective Lachey has been corroborated by the defendant's own words to the sergeant on duty."

"We have submitted motions to dismiss Mrs. Monnehan's call to the station, Your Honor." My voice was patient and cool.

Ramsey narrowed his eyes. "Your motion was denied, Counselor."

"I'm aware of that, Your Honor, but again, it goes to the issue of my client's state of mind, and I will be reminding the jury that Mrs. Monnehan was not Mirandized when she first spoke to Detective Lachey."

"This is a waste of the court's time," retorted Ribisi.

I sighed audibly. "We are not contesting Mrs. Monnehan's telephone call. On the contrary, we will eventually submit it as Exhibit A for the defense, but for now we would simply like to ensure the jury's understanding that when Mrs. Monnehan first spoke to the detective, she was unaware of her rights." Whether Ramsey sustained the prosecution's objection didn't matter. As the old adage goes, it's impossible to unring a bell.

"Overruled, Mr. Ribisi," said the judge. "The court has a definite interest in the order of events."

"Thank you, Your Honor." I smiled into Ramsey's severe features. "So, Detective, when did you advise my client of her rights?"

I saw a wince cross Lachey's face, but I thought it was more unhappiness with himself than with me. "Had I known that Mrs. Monnehan was going to come out and admit to the shooting the first instant I saw her, I would have Mirandized her immediately." He cleared his throat. "I knew about the phone call she made to the station, of course, but I felt that my first duty was to advise her of her husband's condition."

"You Mirandized Mrs. Monnehan only after she told you that she had killed her husband?" I asked smoothly.

Aggrieved, but in control, Lachey said. "Yes."

"Which means, as we all know," I turned to face the jurors, pointing my open palms towards their box, "that whatever Mrs. Monnehan had said before that point is null and void."

"Is there a question somewhere?" Ribisi retorted.

I grinned, but didn't look at Ribisi when I said, "I'll rephrase. Isn't it true that not only was my client in shock and not in a condition to make statements of any kind, but that whatever she said to you before your Miranda Warning cannot be construed as a true and valid confession?"

Judge Ramsey interrupted before Lachey could answer. "The jury will disregard Detective Lachey's testimony regarding his dialogue with the defendant before he advised her of her rights."

I nodded. "Thank you, Your Honor."

I drew nearer to the witness box, not to intimidate the witness, but to focus the jury's attention on Lachey rather than on me. "Tell me, Detective, did you call a physician to see to the defendant?"

"No." Lachey frowned. "Except for a small bruise on her left cheek, she wasn't hurt, and she didn't seem to need medical attention."

"You determined that how?"

"Look," Lachey's voice grew louder, "she was sitting in the kitchen waiting for me. She looked as if she was ready for an interview."

"You mean she was all made up and dressed to go out?"

For the first time, he hesitated. "No. She was unhurt, and as I said already, she seemed self-possessed and calm."

"Can we agree that we can substitute 'calm' with 'quiet and unresponsive'?"

"All right." Back to terse and familiar ground.

"Wouldn't it be possible that the same manner you call calm was actually an outward manifestation of disorientation? After all, she had just witnessed the tragic death of her husband."

"Maybe." Lachey shrugged.

"A lethargic manner combined with uncontrollable shivering… Hmmm…Couldn't these point to the possibility that Mrs. Monnehan was in shock?" I asked contemplatively.

Lachey stared at me. "Her manner was calm when she told me she had shot her husband."

"Could Mrs. Monnehan have been, in effect, shut down as she sat there, traumatized by what had just transpired?"

"Objection." Ribisi's voice dripped with sarcasm. "Beyond the scope. The witness would have to have a medical degree to answer the question."

"Sustained."

There is more than one way to skin a catfish. "But you did ask Dr. Lippi to have a look at Mrs. Monnehan before my arrival?"

"Yes."

"For what purpose?"

"Just to make sure that Mrs. Monnehan was all right."

"You were making sure that besides the bruise you mentioned, there were no defensive marks on my client?"

Lachey eyed me carefully and his tone was deliberate. "At that point I had no idea what had happened, I wasn't thinking self-defense or accidental discharge or homicide. I just wanted to cover all the bases and make sure Mrs. Monnehan herself was uninjured. I had yet to interview her and find out the details."

"I see. According to Dr. Lippi, was Mrs. Monnehan injured in any way?"

"Just the bruise, which Mrs. Monnehan said she got when she hit her head against a cabinet."

"Detective," I asked again, "would you agree that Mrs. Monnehan was at that point experiencing some sort of emotional or mental breakdown?"

"She seemed unresponsive, as I said. I cannot testify as to her state of mind," Lachey replied tersely.

"Have you ever witnessed trauma survivors, Detective?"

"Yes."

"Would you concede that you may have misinterpreted Mrs. Monnehan's quiet manner, and instead of a display of composure, it was a trauma-induced response?"

Lachey returned my stare. "Yes, it's possible," he concurred in a low voice.

I turned away from the box, then pivoted to face Lachey again and asked, as if an afterthought, "Tell me, Detective, at that point, did you know why Mrs. Monnehan shot her husband?"

"No."

"Isn't it true that you were made aware of the fact that Mrs. Monnehan was charged with first-degree murder only after you had met with the prosecutor?"

"Yes."

"As lead investigator, did you conduct your investigation to support Mr. Ribisi's case?"

Before Lachey could answer, I saw Ribisi lunge to his feet, and I waved my hand in surrender. "I withdraw the question."

Ramsey shot me a displeased look. "Mr. Conor, I warned you at the beginning of these proceedings that I will not allow any slurs to be cast by either side."

"Sorry, Your Honor." I met the darkening scowl on his face with a thin smile. "I did not mean to malign the prosecutor's office."

Across the space between us, I saw Annika's lips twitch in approval.

I walked over to our table and asked Lachey as casually as I could manage, "Did you discover Mrs. Monnehan's proficiency level when you checked out the attendance dates at the gun range?"

"No."

"So the number of target-shooting sessions wouldn't necessarily indicate a person's competence as a marksman?"

"No. But after twelve visits, she could definitely shoot someone if she wanted to," retorted the detective. I heard the muffled sounds of laughter in the back. Served me right for asking an open-ended question.

"Thank you, Detective." I nodded, unconcerned. "Nothing further," I said as I turned around.

"Redirect?' asked the judge.

"Thank you, Your Honor." Ribisi rose unhurriedly to his feet. He looked intently at Lachey. "After you read Mrs. Monnehan her rights, did you try to question her as to what had happened?"

"Yes."

"And?"

"She remained silent."

"You mean she refused to answer?"

"Objection," I interjected coolly.

"Sustained." Judge Ramsey looked at Ribisi. "Counselor, please refrain from leading the witness."

"Thank you, Your Honor," Ribisi said. "Still, Mrs. Monnehan did not answer your questions?"

"She did not."

"She did not answer any of your questions at the station either."

"No."

"Detective Lachey, in your investigation, did your finding at any time verify Mrs. Monnehan's claim of self-defense?"

"No."

"Isn't it a fact that during your investigation, the case against Mrs. Monnehan became much more evident of murder?"

"Yes."

"As a veteran police investigator, is there any doubt in your mind that the department followed procedures properly and appropriately?"

"No. No doubt."

"Thank you, Detective, that is all."

"The witness is excused," said the judge.

Court was adjourned.

CHAPTER 20

Your battles inspire me—not the obvious material
battles but those that were fought and won behind
your forehead.

—James Joyce, Letter to Henrik Ibsen, *Selected Letters*

"At this time, Your Honor, we would like to call Dr. Linda Lippi to
the stand."

Linda Lippi walked quickly to the box and took her seat. She was
relaxed, and her intelligent hazel eyes were steady as she regarded Ribisi.
I heard the rustling in the room; Lippi's presence in any court elicited
respect among her colleagues and awe among the non-initiates.

Ribisi went through Dr. Lippi's credentials with methodical care.
She was indeed formidable, both in experience and qualifications. Her
voice was clear as she recited her *curriculum vitae,* her expression pleasant and professional.

I knew that the medical examiner would testify that Monnehan had
been dead for more than an hour before Maddie placed the emergency
call. I was aware that, based on her testimony, Dr. Lippi was about to
debunk Maddie's version of how the shooting went down. Lippi was a
straight shooter, extremely competent and honest. This was a woman
I respected and knew to be reliable in her findings. There was nothing

to be gained by going at Linda Lippi, but I had to try to poke holes in her testimony to lessen the damage.

Ribisi began by asking Lippi to report on her findings.

"The deceased was a male of fifty-eight years." Lippi's tone was dry and self-assured. "He was shot once in the chest. The single bullet was fired at close range. The cause of death was hypoxia caused by pneumo-thorax, set off by a single bullet that penetrated the aortic arch of the heart, most likely causing instant death. In layman's terms, the lungs collapsed and the body was deprived of oxygen. Time of death was between nine p.m. and eleven p.m., give or take half an hour. There were no defensive wounds, and I found no skin particles under the clipped fingernails, indicating no resistance." Lippi did not add that in all likelihood, this scenario indicated that Monnehan was either taken by complete surprise or knew his assailant well enough not to resist.

The doctor's report covered the cause of death, the victim's injuries, and the time of death all in less than a minute. She continued, "The gastrointestinal contents indicated that the Senator's last full meal took place about two to three hours prior to his death. The toxicology test showed a positive 0.6, consistent with two glasses of wine. There were also traces of sildenafil citrate."

"Sildenafil?" asked Ribisi.

"Better known as Viagra. The victim's blood showed traces of the drug."

Dr. Lippi grew silent and looked expectantly at Ribisi.

I sensed Maddie's sudden, icy stillness. I knew that somehow the last piece of information was important. I was careful to keep my eyes fixed on Dr. Lippi and was thankful when Ribisi asked, "Can you tell us, Dr. Lippi, how you determined the probable time of death?"

"Time of death is determined by the stiffening of the musculature of the corpse due to chemical changes in the body, what we call rigor mortis. It begins three hours after death and can last up to twelve, until it starts to dissipate. In Senator Monnehan's case, the body was just starting to exhibit early stages of rigor mortis."

"So he'd been dead two to three hours by the time you examined him?"

"Approximately."

Ribisi closed in for the *Pièce de Résistance* "Doctor, can you please elaborate on the entry of the bullet and your conclusions?"

"The entry wound was rimmed with gray powder burns," answered Lippi unequivocally.

Ribisi's eyebrows shot up suggestively. "Meaning what, exactly?"

"It indicates a gun fired at close range."

"At close range…" repeated Ribisi soberly, as if marveling at this unexpected bit of information. "How close would a shooter have to stand for these burn marks to be evident?"

"It would require a distance of two to three feet, perhaps less, to deposit burn marks on a victim's skin."

"Maddie Monnehan had to have been extremely close to her husband when she shot him?"

"Close enough to distinguish and recognize the face of the victim."

"Objection, calls for speculation."

"Sustained," Ramsey assented without raising his eyes from his notes.

"But he was shot at point-blank range?"

"Yes." Terse and absolute.

"Can we go back to the Senator's other injuries?"

"All right."

"Can you elaborate on the broken nose and the bruise on the forehead indicated in your report?"

"As I have already suggested in my conclusions, both occurred posthumously. There was no evidence of bleeding. Once the heart stops beating, blood is no longer pumped through the body."

"How do you suppose the deceased incurred these injuries?"

Dr. Lippi turned her thoughtful gaze in my direction as she answered, "The force of the bullet's impact knocked the victim's body to the floor, causing both injuries."

"I see. Was there anything else unusual about the markings of the chest wound?"

"Yes," answered Lippi, so matter-of-factly that it almost obliterated the significance of what followed. "In my examination, I found two pieces of evidence that show there was a downward angle to the trajectory of the bullet as it entered the body."

Ribisi nodded with patent deference to his witness's expertise. "Can you please tell the court how you came to this conclusion?"

"The shape of the bullet's entry was irregular. We call this phenomenon a *stippling*. The stippling of the wound led us to believe that the bullet entered the chest cavity at a downward angle. The lack of symmetry of the entry wound is indicative of a disparity between the height of the shooter and the deceased."

"What you are saying is that the entry wound was not round, and that this 'stippling' indicates a diagonal trajectory of the bullet's path?"

"Yes. The angle of the bullet's path will determine the point of origin. In this case, the deceased was either shorter than the shooter, or not fully upright when he was shot."

"You mentioned that there were two pieces of evidence to support your theory," prompted Ribisi.

"Yes. The second is the fact that the bullet entered the victim's body, but never exited it. That is usually the case with a downward impact such as this one." Lippi glanced at me, her eyes unreadable. "The fact that there was no exit wound further supports the theory that the bullet penetrated at a downward angle."

There was a long, pregnant pause while Ribisi turned to look at the jurors, who were transfixed. They seemed to follow him completely. As competent and self-assured as his witness, he knew not to smile. Nonetheless, he could not hide the satisfied glint in his eye as he turned to look at Maddie. As testimonies go, this one was patently damaging. "Thank you, Doctor; you have been more than thorough," he said.

I rose slowly to my feet. "Dr. Lippi, it is your testimony that the existence of the powder on the deceased's chest indicates that he was shot at close range?" I asked with a polite and easy tone. I had to walk a thin line between deferring to Lippi's expertise and undermining some of the pivotal points of her testimony.

"Yes," came the unequivocal answer.

Lippi gave me a considering look. "Like I told Mr. Ribisi, generally speaking, the evidence of a charcoal-gray circle of powder around the bullet's entry wound means the shooter would have to be no further than two to three feet away."

I drew nearer to the witness box, standing in the middle of the "well"—the space between the defendant's table and the judge's dais.

"A distance like this?" I pointed my finger at the space between Dr. Lippi and myself. I noticed the look of curiosity on the judge's face.

Dr. Lippi looked down and agreed, "Yes, but no further than that."

"Could the defendant have advanced at the same time that the intruder lurched, or to use your own words, pitched forward towards her?"

"Perhaps."

Lippi sounded pensive and I forged on, slightly encouraged. "Is it possible that in the dark and in a panic, Mrs. Monnehan fired reflexively, unable to determine the distance or the identity of the intruder?"

"Objection, Your Honor, calls for speculation," Ribisi called out.

I turned to the judge. "I'm merely asking this witness if, in her professional opinion and according to her own testimony, such a scenario is scientifically possible, Your Honor."

Ramsey looked at me with interest. "I'll allow the question."

I looked at Lippi. "Would you like me to repeat the question?"

There was a slight smile behind Lippi's alert eyes. "Thank you, no need. The answer is that various scenarios are possible. Only the defendant and the victim could tell us what really happened."

"But would such a scenario explain the bullet's mark on Senator Monnehan's chest?" I persisted.

"Yes," said Lippi

"Is it conceivable, Doctor, that were we standing in pitch black darkness, you would find it hard to recognize me at this distance?"

Lippi took some time before she finally said, "I don't know. I can't answer that satisfactorily. It depends on the circumstances." She eyed me with amusement as she added, "I think, though, that I would recognize you anywhere, Mr. Conor."

There was a low rustle of laughter in the courtroom, and Lippi smiled at me pleasantly.

I returned her smile, stepped back, and picked up my notes off the table.

"Doctor, I would like to ask you about the findings of GSR on the defendant's hands. Can you explain to the court what it means and its impact on any crime investigation?"

Lippi eyed me speculatively, but answered without hesitation, "Gunshot residue, also known as cartridge discharge residue—CDR— is residue deposited on the hands and clothes of someone who discharges a firearm. It is principally composed of burnt and unburnt particles from the explosive primer, the propellant, and possibly fragments of the bullet itself. I collected samples from the skin on Mrs. Monnehan's hands and from her blouse, and they showed positive." For the first time Dr. Lippi turned towards the jury, her tone conveying that this conclusion was not to be questioned.

My voice and expression betrayed nothing as I inquired amiably, "Isn't it true, though, Doctor, that there can be false positives in determining gunshot residue?"

"It can happen, but very rarely."

"Isn't it so that such residue can be transferred from the clothes of a gunshot victim or by being in proximity to someone who has fired a gun?"

"Yes, false positives can be caused by transfer of GSR from the body by mishandling, or when the body is heavily contaminated. But neither condition was true in this case," replied Lippi, just as agreeably as if we were sipping Oolong tea, expounding on its superiority over Earl Grey. "The number of particles from secondary environmental contamination is usually extremely low, and was not the case here."

"How about if the person had washed his or her hands prior to the swab collection?"

"That can result in a false negative."

"Are you aware that Mrs. Monnehan washed her hands after checking her husband's pulse?"

"Yes. But there was still a sufficient quantity of lead antimony and barium present to conclude that the particles found on Mrs. Monnehan's hand were consistent with gunshot residue."

"How about Mrs. Monnehan's clothes?"

"She was wearing a shirt tucked into slacks at the time."

"Any gunpowder marks on the sleeves?"

"Some."

"More than on Mrs. Monnehan's hand?"

"Yes."

"So when the defendant knelt down to check the body of her husband, there could have been a transfer of the particles onto the sleeve of her blouse and onto her hands?" I persisted with the same courteous tone.

"There was still enough physical evidence on the skin itself," replied Dr. Lippi.

"What if the person was simply in the vicinity of a gun going off?"

"Yes, that could account for a false positive," conceded Dr. Lippi, "but since Mrs. Monnehan was acting alone, I fail to see how that is relevant in this case."

I smiled; I'd finally wedged my foot in the door. "I simply wanted to make sure that the jurors understand that the GSR test is not infallible. When the time comes, we will address this issue again."

I went back to my notes lying open on the table. It was a good cross-examination, and like Ribisi, I needed to take full advantage of it. I wanted to establish a nice and easy rhythm. I turned back to Lippi, hoping she saw the respect in my smile. "Doctor, let us examine your time-of-death report. Time of death is determined by livor mortis and rigor mortis in addition to the gastrointestinal contents of the victim's body. Isn't that so?"

"Yes."

"Could you explain to the court in layman's terms what livor mortis means and what it indicates?"

"What is known as livor mortis starts twenty minutes to three hours after death," said Lippi in a dry professorial tone. "When the heart stops beating, the blood pools in the lower parts of the body and is expressed by purplish-red staining. The intensity of the color depends upon the level of the hemoglobin in the blood."

"Isn't it a fact that both livor mortis and rigor mortis can be altered by manipulation of body location and temperature?" I asked courteously. "Extreme cold can set both processes back and affect the estimate of the time of death, isn't that correct?"

"Yes. It's not an exact science, but given the pallor, rigidity, and discoloration of the lower extremities, I believe that the heart stopped pumping at least two hours before we arrived at the scene."

"Let me put out a hypothesis." I paused for a moment. "From what we know of the medical procedure used by paramedics, is it not a fact that they will try to revive victims upon reaching the site of an accident?"

"Yes, that's their duty when they respond to a 9-1-1 call."

I nodded pleasantly. "We know that the body of the deceased must have been manipulated by the paramedics to check for a pulse to perform CPR. They would then use a defibrillator to try to induce a heartbeat, correct?"

"Yes."

"Only after those interventions failed would the paramedics have returned the body to its original position?"

"Yes."

"Could we then not hypothesize that the progression of lividity in this case would be a somewhat inconclusive indicator? After all, the body's position had been changed for an extended period of time. *Livor mortis* could have been delayed or hampered by the ministrations of the medical team," I suggested respectfully. "Would you agree?"

"Possibly," said Lippi with a curt nod.

"So Senator Monnehan could have died an hour or two later, right?"

Lippi thought for a minute. "I would have to say that the time of death could extend to a slightly but not significantly broader range than stated originally."

"Aah…Thank you, Doctor."

"Redirect?" asked Ramsey.

Ribisi rose to his feet. "We have no further questions for the doctor. Thank you, Dr. Lippi."

The judge looked at Dr. Lippi and nodded. "You may step down, Doctor."

Ribisi called his next witness. Dr. Moses Stringer took his time getting to the witness box, not just because of his heft and bulk, but also because of his aggrandized sense of importance. Stringer was indeed famous for his forensic expertise, more so even than his colleague, Dr. Lippi. As the Chief Forensic Examiner of the NYPD, he had served its ranks far longer than Lippi and had distinguished himself in some of the most notorious and lurid murder cases in the city's history. With his corpulent trunk, short stubby legs, and black-rimmed glasses, Stringer reminded me of an overgrown panda. He inserted his bulk into the witness stand—a large round peg in a square hole—and focused his myopic glare on Ribisi.

After a mind-numbing recitation of Stringer's credentials, during which I noted with satisfaction the slight glazing over of the jurors' eyes, Ribisi approached Stringer. "Doctor, I would like to reexamine the issue of GSR, which Dr. Lippi touched upon."

Stringer began, "Well, as you know, GSR, which is the nomenclature for gunshot powder found on a body as well as—" Ribisi raised an apologetic hand. "Sorry, Doctor, we have already been apprised by Dr. Lippi of the nature of the particles and the significance of their presence on the defendant." I smiled inwardly, knowing that Ribisi had a tough job ahead of him. Stringer was known for his propensity to run on and pontificate about the intricacies of his profession. Ribisi had to maneuver delicately between showing deference towards his illustrious witness and trying to keep him on a short leash.

Dr. Stringer scowled. "What is it, then, that you wanted me to clarify?"

Ribisi flashed the witness a placating smile and hastened to clarify. "Sorry, Doctor, it is our loss that we have to focus just on the specifics of your analysis of the GSR."

Unmollified, but in full command, Stringer responded: "We found comparable gunshot particles on the chest of the deceased and the sleeves of the defendant's blouse, and to a lesser extent on the defendant's right hand."

"And there is no doubt in your mind that Mrs. Monnehan shot the firearm?"

"None whatsoever!" Succinct, polite, and authoritative.

"How about the stippling of the bullet hole?"

At this, you could almost feel Stringer's lungs inflate with pomposity. "Actually, it was I who pointed out to Dr. Lippi the evidence of stippling around the wound." He directed his glance towards the jury box and amplified, "The irregular shape of the wound and its import."

Ribisi yielded the floor to Stringer. "Can you please tell the court what, in your expert opinion, this evidence tells us about the shooting?"

Dr. Stringer looked at the judge and rose to his feet. "May I?" He pointed towards a large screen, which was being set up.

Ramsey nodded as Stringer alighted slowly from the box, picked up a small laser pointer, and waited for Ribisi to distribute a number of glossy photographs to members of the defense and the foreman of the jury. The screen came to life with an image of the Monnehan bedroom, featuring the bed with its white covers thrown halfway across it and several decorative pillows stacked on a nearby armchair. The bottom edge of the duvet was splattered with crimson spots, and Senator Monnehan's body lay sprawled on the floor. With the red dot from his pointer dancing on the screen, Dr. Stringer started to talk, now obviously in his element.

"All the blood that you see here and here," he explained, swinging the laser beam from the blood under the Senator's head to the edge of the white duvet cover, "was collected and belonged to the deceased, except for one other miniscule blood sample, too small for comparison, which we found at the edge of one round decorative pillow. Luminol testing proved negative for blood elsewhere." Dr. Stringer took a long, deep breath. "We conducted blood pattern analysis with highly accurate and sophisticated software that superimposes an ellipse over a scaled close-up image of a bloodstain, then automatically calculates the angle of impact. In our work, the analysis of the spherical shape of blood in flight is important for the calculation of the angle of impact."

Ribisi waited for the witness to take a breath and interjected before the forensic pathologist could segue into another elaborate lecture. "Dr. Stringer, could you please walk the jury through the next photograph?" asked Ribisi, as a magnified diagram was projected onto the overhead screen.

"After a detailed and thorough examination of the crime scene and the position of the body, my assistants and I have created this graphic exhibit. This illustrates what I believe happened that night." He focused the red little dot on the heavy black outlines, drawn on a white board, showing a kneeling figure and a standing figure holding a gun. There were small notations of measurements and angles covering the margins of the diagram. The discrepancy between the two figures' heights was delineated with a strong diagonal red line, which connected the two figures and apparently marked the angle of the bullet.

Dr. Stringer cleared his throat as he began. "I believe that the victim was kneeling when he was shot. There are two substantiating pieces of evidence to corroborate this hypothesis. One is that the bullet entered the chest at a downward angle of about 30 degrees." The computer screen changed to another diagram with the same outlined figures, but now covered with numerical markings at the margins. Dr. Stringer's pointer followed the red line on the diagram. "The deceased's height was six foot one, or seventy-three inches; for the shooter to hit him at that particular angle, he or she would have had to be either extremely tall, or standing on something. This shot at this angle could not have been made if both figures were standing upright."

Ribisi pointed to the projected image. "Can you tell the court what the notation on the side refers to?"

"It means that the angle of the bullet can be easily explained if the victim was about forty inches away from the floor, which corresponds more or less to the height of the defendant's chest when he was shot."

"And what does it tell you?" asked Ribisi.

Stringer paused for the briefest moment. "The victim could have been pitching forward at an awkward angle to reach the shooter, or more likely—and I believe this is a better scenario—he was kneeling, and the shooter was standing over him." Stringer glanced at the jury, fully aware that he was in command of everybody's total attention. "The second substantiating piece of evidence is that there was no exit wound, further supporting the theory that the bullet penetrated the Senator's chest at a downward angle."

While Stringer clambered back to the witness box, Ribisi nodded gravely and asked the court reporter to turn off the projector. He then approached Stringer and asked, "Doctor, I would like to re-address the issue of the gun powder found on the defendant's hand and clothes."

"Yes, the GSR," concurred Stringer. "As I have already stated, there is clear indication that the defendant handled the shooting gun."

Ribisi picked up the plastic-encased firearm, marked with a large Exhibit B label. "You are referring to this gun?"

All eyes locked on the gun.

"Yes."

"Did you find the defendant's fingerprints on this gun?"

"Yes. Although some of the prints were smudged, there were enough significant matches of ridges and points of minutiae to correspond to Mrs. Monnehan's fingerprints."

"You are aware that false positives and false negatives can occur in the science of fingerprint matching?" Ribisi was deftly preempting my forthcoming challenges.

Dr. Stringer, narrow-eyed and slightly truculent, answered, "Of course."

Ribisi smiled placatingly. "The reason I brought it up, Doctor, is because Mr. Conor is probably going to cast doubt on the findings of your lab and is going to quiz you about the possibilities of false positives in Mrs. Monnehan's case. The state wants to make sure that your investigation has established the correlation between Mrs. Monnehan's prints and the prints on the gun without a shadow of a doubt."

Dr. Stringer shot me a withering glance, and then like a sovereign granting a nod of reprieve to a lowly peon, cast a benevolent smile at Ribisi. "There was no instance of either false positive or false negative in our investigation," he added forcefully. "Mrs. Monnehan's prints were on the gun that shot Senator Monnehan."

"Besides fingerprints, I was told that a small hair shaft was found on one of the decorative pillows."

"Yes, but extracting nuclear DNA from that sample was impossible due to the missing follicle. Contrary to what people assume, hair samples are not ideal unless we also have the root."

"Thank you, Doctor," said Ribisi, smiling and walking back to his seat.

Feeling strangely light, I rose slowly to my feet. I was going to use the evidence that Ribisi took such painstaking time to extract and turn it around to dispute the State's conclusions. *Let the games begin.* When I approached the witness box, Dr. Stringer gave me a slight nod and a condescending smile. I smiled in return. "Good afternoon, Doctor. Your findings seem to be quite conclusive."

Despite the supercilious expression plastered across his face, his tone was mild as he answered with a succinct, "Yes."

"Dr. Stringer, could you please tell us what tests you have conducted in relation to this case?"

Stringer re-crossed his legs and stared at me impassively as he answered, "We lifted and tested fingerprints taken from the gun and essentially from all surfaces in the bedroom. We examined the fibers on both the victim's and the defendant's clothes. We checked the bedding for additional DNA, and we conducted firearm analysis."

"Can you elaborate on your findings, Doctor?"

"The ballistics report is pretty self-explanatory: our investigation confirmed the bullet and the type of the gun fired as a .45mm Beretta. To be exact, the model is a .45mm Beretta PX4 Storm Inox. The firearm was found at the scene. Fingerprints collected were those of Mrs. Monnehan."

"I understand that this type of gun takes a magazine of 17 rounds?"

"That's correct."

"In addition to the bullet lodged in the deceased's chest, there were still sixteen rounds left?" I inquired.

Stringer stared at me long and hard, then said, "No, actually there were only fifteen rounds left."

I shot a quick, sidelong glance at Annika, who was studiously displaying no reaction. "So one other bullet had been fired from the gun?"

"Yes."

"But you found only one?"

"That is correct," Stringer acknowledged grudgingly. "It was not for want of looking."

"You never found the missing cartridge?" I was letting the jury process this revelation, which the prosecution had not deemed necessary to share. "Could you establish whether that missing bullet was fired on the same night?"

"No. The gun had definitely been fired, but as to whether it was fired once or twice on the same night is impossible to determine."

I asked slowly, "And you searched the house…"

"Yes."

"How about hair specimens?" I asked.

"We collected hair specimens that matched those of the deceased and those of the defendant."

I stared at Stringer and asked with a subtle emphasis, "All these specimens belonged to the couple then?"

Stringer cast a fleeting glance at Ribisi but merely said, "As I've indicated, we collected one additional, unidentified hair specimen."

"Did you find any correlating matches in the Combined DNA Index System?"

"No."

"Not in any of the DOJ list of candidates' matches—the primary DNA database, the largest in the world?" My tone of incredulity seemed to irritate Stringer.

"No. There was no root attached to the small strand." Curt and dismissive.

"I presume you collected samples from the staff and anyone who had access to the residence?"

"Of course." Stringer's face grew stony.

"And you found no matches?"

"No."

"Where was this single hair strand found?"

"It was caught in the side zipper of one of the throw pillows," came the reluctant response.

I paused, letting the fact that a specimen had been found but remained unidentified hover in the pregnant silence. I returned to the defense table and leafed through my notes at a deliberate, slow pace.

"Let us return to the blood samples your lab analyzed," I continued.

"We collected blood and oral swabs for all the standard typing inclusions." The curt tone implied that I was wasting the court's and the witness's valuable time with unnecessary questions.

"And what did these blood samples reveal?"

Stringer sighed audibly. "There appeared to be no blood or skin under the fingernails of the deceased; the spattered blood on the carpet and the bed skirt was type A+ and belonged to the deceased."

"How about the defendant's blood type?"

"Mrs. Monnehan's blood is Type O."

"Any A+ blood found on the defendant's clothes, other than the right sleeve of her blouse?" I asked nonchalantly.

"No."

"Yet you and Dr. Lippi have testified that the defendant was close to the deceased when she allegedly shot him. Wouldn't the lack of any blood spatter on Mrs. Monnehan seem unusual in that scenario?"

When Stringer answered, I noticed the quick intake of breath as he struggled to keep his voice unaffected. The almighty criminal forensic expert was slowly losing his cool. "It can happen that the bullet's trajectory is such that blood disperses away from the shooter," he answered acerbically.

I sensed, rather than heard, the buzz behind me. It felt as if my fingers, parrying painstakingly on the lock of a safe, were dialing the secret combination. I was listening to the small clicks of the tumbler as they dropped from within.

"Let us turn to your testimony on the assumed trajectory of the bullet," I resumed. "The bullet, according to Dr. Lippi, was still lodged in the body when she conducted her post-mortem."

"Yes."

"This led you to hypothesize about the trajectory of the bullet's path?"

"That and as I have already testified, the stippling of the wound," Stringer added dismissively.

"But according to your own testimony, the disparity between the deceased's and the shooter's heights could also be explained by Senator Monnehan stumbling toward the shooter, thus shortening the distance between his chest and the floor."

Dr. Stringer gave me a long, hard look. "It is possible, but not probable. I have already stated that Senator Monnehan was probably kneeling at the time he was shot."

"But you don't know that for a fact," I persisted gently. "He could have been pitching forward in the dark."

A long pause. "Perhaps, but not likely."

"But still, it could have happened that way?"

A sphincter-clenching smile. "Yes."

"Wouldn't such a motion also account for the GSR found at the bullet's entry?"

"How do you mean?"

"I mean, if the deceased was stumbling in the dark and was moving rapidly forward while the shooter was simultaneously advancing into the room, couldn't such a scenario account for the close-range gun residue found on the body?"

Dr. Stringer did not answer for such a long time that Ramsey leaned forward and prompted, "Doctor?"

Stringer looked at the judge and then turned to me. "Yes. But both Senator Monnehan and his wife would have had to move at precisely the same time."

"But," my voice softened, "assuming that both the shooter and the intruder were moving in tandem, could that account for the close range?"

Not waiting for Stringer to answer, I hurried on. "Isn't it possible then, that if Mrs. Monnehan shot her husband, it was because when she walked into the bedroom, she found an advancing figure of a man, and she fired in self-defense?"

"Objection!" Ribisi shot out. "Counselor is leading."

Ramsey gave me a hard look. "Mr. Conor, I warned you about limiting your questions to evidentiary facts and not establishing defense theories."

I smiled disarmingly at the judge's stern countenance. "Sorry, Your Honor."

"Stick to the facts, Counselor."

I silently savored an inward smile; I was casting breadcrumbs, hoping at least one juror would follow the path.

"Let me rephrase the question. Dr. Stringer, the victim had to be as close as three feet or less from the shooter in order for him to exhibit the gunshot residue on his skin, is that correct?"

"Yes."

"Could a scenario such as the one I described earlier—of the two figures advancing at the same time—account for the point-blank range and the gunshot powder around the bullet's entry wound?"

"It might," said Dr. Stringer in a clipped voice.

I turned towards the stand and regarded him. "Coming back to the GSR. Are you aware, Doctor, that Mrs. Monnehan tried to revive her husband, and that only after futile efforts realized that he was dead?"

"I was informed of that," Stringer said curtly.

"Is it likely that contact with the victim would result in the gunshot residue being deposited on her hand?"

"Yes, there is a possibility that she could have gotten some gun powder on her hands from contact with the bullet wound." Stringer looked at me truculently. "But there was quite a significant amount of residue on the sleeve of her blouse as well."

I nodded. "I see." I smiled thinly at Stringer's irritable expression and asked, "Tell me, Doctor, in theory, can you transfer GSR from one person to another—and I don't mean from a victim."

"In theory, yes, but we are dealing with factual findings in this case." Stringer was hard pressed to hide the scathing tone of his voice.

Unperturbed, I went back to the defense table and examined my notes. I turned to Stringer. "Let us examine that last bit of your testimony," I said affably.

Stringer gave me a quick nod. He was watching me with equal amounts of wariness and haughtiness. "All right."

"You have testified that Mrs. Monnehan's prints were lifted off that gun." I pointed to the black gun on Ribisi's table.

"Yes."

"Yet you mentioned that the prints were also smudged."

"But there were enough direct matching points to conclude, without a doubt, that Mrs. Monnehan handled the gun."

"Isn't it a fact that in your analysis, you found some other unidentified smudges on the gun?"

"We found one or two extremely small smears," Stringer demurred.

I gave him a quizzical look. "How do you explain that, Doctor?"

Stringer hesitated for a moment, and then chose his words carefully. He and Ribisi were clearly aware of the problematic nature of this finding. "It could be that the defendant smudged her own fingerprints, by wiping them either deliberately or unknowingly."

"So, these smudges were remnants or partly obscured prints of the defendant?"

A longer hesitation this time. I knew Stringer was not about to tarnish his stellar reputation, not even for the District Attorney. We were glaring at each other, each daring the other to look away. Stringer finally turned away to give Ribisi a quick look and then said, "No. The partials did not seem to match those of the defendant."

I let the little bombshell explode quietly into the silence of the room.

"What you are saying is that there was a second set of fingerprints on the gun that shot Senator Monnehan, albeit smudged and unrecoverable, but still different from those of the defendant?"

"Yes."

"Did you compare the fingerprints of the victim with those unidentified smudges?"

Stringer gave me an exasperated glance but answered in an even tone, "Yes."

"And they did not match?"

"No."

"Let me recap, then," I said smoothly. "You testified that the only fingerprints found in the bedroom were those of either the deceased or Maddie Monnehan, is that correct?"

"Yes."

"Yet you found partials of more than one person on the gun in question?"

"You have to understand, Mr. Conor, that we did not have a single viable fingerprint to analyze accurately; there were simply smudges of one partial."

"But still, whatever you found did not match Mrs. Monnehan's fingerprints?"

"That's correct."

"And they did not match Andrew Monnehan's?"

The haughty expression was gone; Stringer sighed and answered in a weary tone, "No."

"No?" I asked with as much incredulity as I could inject into that little word. I could feel everyone's gaze on my face. "You mean to say that there is a possibility that someone else was holding the gun, or even shooting it?"

The fact that Stringer did not suggest an alternate scenario, such as past handling of the gun by a person or persons unknown, confirmed the findings of our own expert Dr. Morgan. It was time to close in for the kill. "Doctor, isn't it also a fact that the second set of prints were adjacent to Mrs. Monnehan's fingerprints, suggesting that someone else handled the gun during, or after, the shooting?"

Ribisi leaned forward on the table as he called out, "Objection!"

The judge looked at him with a scowl. "On what grounds, Counselor?"

Ribisi rose to his feet as he said, "Your Honor, Dr. Stringer has testified to the fact that these prints were unidentifiable and that no scientific inferences could be drawn from such degraded evidence."

Ramsey's face held a disgruntled expression. "I will allow the question, since it addresses neither the validity nor the identification of the fingerprints, but is strictly concerned with what the court is fairly sure that Dr. Stringer could discern without difficulty. Objection overruled."

Dr. Stringer looked at me with an aggrieved expression. "While there is some indication of another fingerprint, it is extremely hard to determine that to be a fact." Another slight pause as he directed his gaze at the jury. "It is pure fantasy and extremely irresponsible to allude to the presence of some phantom shooter based on some indeterminate partial."

I deliberately prolonged the pause before I asked, "But you cannot exclude that hypothesis?"

Dr. Stringer cleared his throat. "No, but it is still a gross conjecture and beyond the realm of what the situation in this case indicates. A small…"

"That is all, Dr. Stringer," I interrupted, unperturbed. "No further questions." As I walked to my seat, I was gratified to see that most of the jurors were taking notes.

Ribisi rose to his feet energetically and asked his witness, "Dr. Stringer, you were about to say something when you were interrupted by Mr. Conor."

Stringer looked at me and said, "I was about to tell Mr. Conor that not only could we not establish the origin of the second set of partial prints, we couldn't determine the time they might have been deposited on the gun."

"In other words," added Ribisi, "there is no way to tell who touched the gun and when. In theory, the partials could have been deposited well before the shooting incident—even days before the night of March 11th. Is that correct?"

"As I have already testified, there is no way to determine either fact." Dr. Stringer sounded testy; he was not about to be led to drink from the trough against his will.

I felt a small jolt of pleasure. Ribisi was ignoring one of the bedrock rules of questioning witnesses: you can never compel your own witness to self-incriminate.

I sensed the jurors were starting to have less than total faith in the State's findings.

Court was adjourned. Since I was quite pleased with the day's proceedings, it was with some surprise that I noticed Maddie's rigid expression. By now, however, I was able to discern the subtle signs of suppressed anger. We walked out of the courthouse, swam against the tide of reporters until we managed to clear the corner. Annika, like a quicksilver tuning fork, slid into the back seat of the waiting car, her head averted and eyes fixed on the windshield. Maddie did not even wait for the door to close before she turned to face me. "What is it that you were getting at in there?" she whispered.

"I'm formulating a defense for your acquittal," I answered in a cold voice.

"The unidentified hair sample, a minute smudge of a strange print—what is it that you're trying to establish?" she asked with a voice as brittle as glass.

I met her icy stare with equal frost. "We need to rebut every one of Ribisi's iron-clad suppositions and disprove his evidence."

"I told you what happened! Work with that," Maddie said witheringly.

As tight-lipped as Maddie had been on occasion, I had only seen her this irate once before and I wondered what it was that had set her off.

"I'm trying to puncture holes in the prosecution's case, Maddie."

"By conjecture and sleight of hand?"

"If necessary," I said harshly.

"The idea that someone else was present is ludicrous."

"Is it?" I asked. Maddie said nothing.

I let the silence grow between us. Finally I said, "If you noticed, I haven't actually pointed the finger at a third party. I have merely cast doubt in the minds of the jury.

"Are you forgetting that I've already confessed to shooting Andrew?"

"I don't forget much, Maddie. You have to trust me on this. A trial is a contest. Not necessarily a contest searching for the absolute truth, but nonetheless, a contest in a court of law. We all profess to be fighting for the truth, but truth is not an objective end. We compile facts in a way that makes it possible to convince ourselves and others of what we need to prove."

I saw that she understood, yet felt the steely resistance underneath.

"Can we not establish a viable defense based on the castle doctrine?" Maddie asked.

"We can and we will, but there's nothing wrong with casting additional aspersions on the prosecution's case. I was trying to establish that the prosecution's physical evidence is ambiguous: forensics, time of death, all of that…there are too many unknown variables."

I regarded Maddie's inscrutable expression as she took it all in, then continued, my voice a notch lighter. "I've merely cast an alternate defense theory. As inconceivable as it might sound in light of your confession, I might have tapped into the one juror emotionally invested in acquitting you. He or she might prefer to entertain the notion that you lied and accept the presence of another shooter. That's all I need—one juror who's going to tip the scales of justice."

"All right," said Maddie in a tired voice. "I will trust you, but I wish that you would fashion your argument on my version of events."

"I intend to," I replied. But I wondered about Maddie's choice of words. Was her "version" a script we were all required to follow?

I left her at the corner of Madison and 75th and saw her turn back to stare at us as we drove away. A still and alert figure girded for battle.

I wanted this woman with a ferocity I had never known. I wanted her safe, acquitted and free, and I needed her to trust me. To know that I would stand with her in the shallows and fight the good fight. All at once, I thought of Padrick – the essence of all that I thought of as good and heroic, and a memory stirred in the back of my mind.

We are sitting at the edge of the pier. Padrick's head is tilted up as he squints at the endless, cloudless sky. He turns his eyes, a brilliant robin's egg blue, to look at me. He is unusually quiet and pensive as he says, "You're really smart, Nicki. Sharp as a whip." He smiles into my startled eyes.

"Not as smart as you!" I reply instantly.

He waves his hand dismissively. "I'm more brawn than brain." A flash of brilliant white teeth. "Also lots of charm and street smarts. But you, Nicki, you're the real thing. If you learn to control your anger, you'll be grand."

"I can't help it if things make me want to fight back." My voice trails off in disappointment. "You want me to run?"

"No, Nicki, I know you. There are those who run and then there are those who stay and fight. I just want you to fight with your brains and not

with your fists." He looks down at my bunched hand. "Anyway, there's little to brag about your fists that I can see." He chuckles.

"It's not the size," I protest indignantly. "It's the will."

A full-blown grin. "Yeah, it is the will. It's the heart, and that you have in spades." He cuffs my neck and then snakes his arm around my shoulder. We stay sitting like that for a long time, gazing at what is waiting out there in that wide blue beyond.

I found myself thinking of the guilt and remorse that had affected every decision I'd made since I was sixteen. Moira, Ma, and Padrick: my Holy Trinity. These were the crosses I'd been bearing all my life. This, more than anything, made my love for Maddie so momentous. The notion that Maddie and I were meant to be had lodged itself inside my head. That my life as it was, its entire purpose, had been to hold unto what Padrick called "the heart". Padrick never quit, never ducked from adversity or a challenge, and without ever saying so, expected the same of me. Everything Padrick tried to pass on to me came back: the dictates to stand strong, be focused with purpose, to fight the good fight yet be courageous enough to lay oneself bare to hope and love. To not lose the sense of who I was. I was finally ready for a reckoning I did not invite nor could I prevent. I was ready to lay claim to a new paradigm: a new troika – Hope, Love and Faith.

CHAPTER 21

Not knowing when dawn will come,
I open every door.

    —Emily Dickinson, *The Complete Poems.*

We watched Leo O'Shaunessy stride down the aisle to take the stand. If possible, the courtroom seemed even more crowded than the day before. It was, after all, a sexy scandal. Judge Ramsey seemed unusually bright-eyed and alert.

As usual, O'Shaunessy looked distinguished in his elegant, three-piece suit, pinstriped shirt, and jaunty maroon bow tie. His eyes flickered towards Maddie as he stepped into the witness box. His ramrod-straight spine added height to his otherwise diminutive form. After being sworn in, O'Shaunessy recounted to the court his detailed *curriculum vitae,* which would have impressed even the most indifferent listener.

Ribisi dove right in. "Mr. O'Shaunessy, can you please tell the court in what capacity you were acquainted with the deceased?"

O'Shaunessy cleared his throat and responded in his famous, mellifluous voice. "My firm has been retained by the Monnehan family for thirty-seven years. For the last twenty-five, I have acted as the sole advisor to the Monnehans, and for the last six years, upon the death of Mr. Monnehan Sr., I have worked with Senator Andrew Monnehan exclusively."

"You were involved in all matters pertaining to the late Senator's concerns. Isn't that so?"

"Yes," said O'Shaunessy dryly.

"Commercial, legal and..." A pause. "Personal. Is that right?"

"Yes."

"When did you first meet Madeline Wallker?"

O'Shaunessy was assiduously avoiding eye contact with Maddie. "I met Mrs. Monnehan upon her engagement to the Senator."

"Can you tell the court the circumstances of that meeting?"

Another throat clearing. "Senator Monnehan had asked me to draw up a prenuptial agreement."

Ribisi paused for several seconds. "Hmmm...a prenuptial agreement? Can you tell us briefly what that contained?"

Leo O'Shaunessy finally turned to look at Maddie. His composed expression could not hide the twinge of regret in his eyes. I felt pity for the man. It was apparent that he resented being here, and out of the corner of my eye, I caught Maddie's slight nod, a gesture of reassurance, and not for the first time I wondered what the true nature of the relationship between my client and her attorney was.

"The contract stipulated, in no uncertain terms, that if the marriage was dissolved for whatever reason other than death, Mrs. Monnehan could not lay claim to the estate."

"In other words, if the couple divorced, Mrs. Monnehan would not be entitled to any other financial divorce settlement; is that correct?"

"Well, she would receive an annual stipend of one hundred thousand dollars, but could not lay claim to anything beyond that amount."

"Could you tell us what his estate is worth?"

"I believe in excess of one hundred-eighty million."

"Thank you, Mr. O'Shaunessy." Ribisi nodded with a small smile and returned to his seat.

There's motive for you. One hundred-eighty million reasons. I rose unhurriedly from behind the table. "Good morning, Mr. O'Shaunessy." I smiled pleasantly into his attentive eyes.

He offered a gracious nod. "Good morning, Mr. Conor."

"About that prenuptial agreement, was there anything unusual about it?" I asked.

"No, nothing at all," he said in that rich voice, smiling for the first time. "It was certainly incumbent on Senator Monnehan to have such an agreement. It is quite common among the very affluent who marry late in life."

I nodded somberly. "And the future Mrs. Monnehan, how did she react to this arrangement?"

"She seemed altogether unconcerned and quite indifferent when they came in to sign the papers. I did admonish her to read the contract, but she just went ahead and signed it without looking at it."

"She was aware of what it contained, then?"

O'Shaunessy nodded. "Oh yes, she knew what she was signing; as I said, she seemed utterly unconcerned."

In my most languid tone I asked, "Mr. O'Shaunessy, you testified that you had on occasion met with Maddie Monnehan when she came to your office with her husband?"

"Yes."

"Was there any time when you met with the defendant privately, other than with Senator Monnehan?"

"Yes, I met separately with Maddie on two occasions."

"Could you please tell us about those meetings?"

That honeyed voice dropped a register when he answered, "Mrs. Monnehan approached me with questions about starting divorce proceedings."

In my peripheral vision, I caught a sudden, involuntary movement at the prosecution table, as Ribisi half rose in his chair before realizing that he himself had opened the door to this line of questioning and therefore was barred from objecting. O'Shaunessy and I watched the prosecutor slide back into his seat. For the first time, Ribisi was genuinely taken by surprise. I kept my own face as impassive as my witness's, while I appreciated the small prick in Ribisi's inflated ego.

"Mrs. Monnehan approached you to start divorce proceedings against her husband?" I injected a note of bewilderment into my voice.

"Yes, she came to me to file for divorce."

"When was that?"

"On February 2nd of this year," said O'Shaunessy readily.

"That's the date she filed for divorce?"

"Actually, she called me two days later and asked me to defer action."

"Do you know why?"

"She told me she had spoken with her husband, and he had asked her to delay filing until after the election so it wouldn't affect his chances for re-election, and she agreed."

"But as far as you know, Mrs. Monnehan wanted to end her marriage at least five weeks before the tragic events of the night of March 12th?"

"Yes."

"Did she offer any explanation or reasons for her decision to end the marriage?"

"She cited irreconcilable differences."

"Thank you, Mr. O'Shaunessy. I have no further questions."

Ramsey looked at Ribisi, "Cross, Counselor?"

Ribisi remained at his desk while he addressed the witness. "Mr. O'Shaunessy, in your sworn statement, you failed to inform the prosecution about any of this."

Leo O'Shaunessy impaled him with a stern look. "You never asked, Counselor."

Ribisi gave a lighthearted shrug. "No matter. The fact remains, however, that Mrs. Monnehan backed out of filing for a divorce, isn't that so?"

"Yes, as I have explained."

Ribisi waved his hand dismissively. "Yes, we know what Mrs. Monnehan told you, but we only have her word for it."

O'Shaunessy remained silent.

"By the way, you mentioned that there were two occasions in which you met Mrs. Monnehan privately; what was the second meeting about?" Ribisi looked coolly at O'Shaunessy. "Counselor?"

The attorney spoke in a slow, pensive manner. It was clear to me that he was carefully choosing his words, but the answer seemed too innocuous to merit this kind of deliberation. I felt the undercurrent of some hidden agenda that neither Ribisi nor I were privy to.

"Mrs. Monnehan asked me to set up her last will and testament," said O'Shaunessy.

"Her last will and testament!?" Genuine surprise.

"Yes."

"Did Mr. Monnehan make a will at the same time?"

"No, he never got around to it." O'Shaunessy grimaced as if to imply that notions of death were anathema to Andrew Monnehan.

"But he was aware that his wife went to your office to set one up?"

O'Shaunessy stared at Ribisi as he answered evenly. "I wouldn't know if he was; he never asked me about it."

"Yet he was your client." Ribisi said musingly.

"So was Mrs. Monnehan," came the quick retort.

"I see… She retained your legal advice and your services separately from her husband?"

"Yes."

"Wasn't there an issue of conflict of interest?"

"No." O'Shaunessy voice was even as he met Ramsey's eyes. "Mrs. Monnehan informed Senator Monnehan of her wish to start divorce proceedings as soon as she had hired me."

"And the will?"

There was a flicker of something in O'Shaunessy's expression. "As I said, I have no idea if Mrs. Monnehan shared that with her husband."

Ribisi paused, then smiled at O'Shaunessy. "Thank you. That will be all."

"You may step down, Counselor," said Ramsey, who announced a twenty-minute break.

I wondered what it was about O'Shaunessy's testimony that made me uneasy. The crafty old geezer would never obfuscate or lie under oath, but I was almost certain that he managed to deflect the prosecutor with less than full disclosure. Once again, I was unable to account for the strange feeling that there was more to the relationship between Maddie and O'Shaunessy than meets the eye.

As soon as the courtroom emptied out, I rose and stared at Maddie coldly. "You told us of your application for divorce, but didn't mention the other meeting with O'Shaunessy?"

"I didn't think it was relevant."

"When did you discuss the details of the will?"

"A few days before I approached Leo to start the divorce papers."

"Did you talk to your husband about it?"

Maddie said with a sigh. "No."

I stared at her, weighed down by what I did not know. My misgivings were a direct reflection of Maddie's inherent mistrust. My need to defend her kept ramming into the wall she had built around herself.

I jotted another note on my legal pad; the damn questions kept piling up. I saw Annika's frown as we exchanged a quick glance. What need was there for someone like Maddie—a woman in her prime, childless and bereft of any kin, whose husband of less than two years was as rich as Croesus and intent on preserving his wealth—what need was there for such a woman to make her will in secret?

For the duration of the break, Annika and Matthew were busy writing notes while Maddie and I sat side by side in silence. I tried to concentrate on my notes and the prosecution's next witness. This woman was turning me inside out.

Marvin Mollis was, by far, the most nondescript man I had ever encountered. Of medium height and medium weight, with brown eyes and brown hair and a face you could easily pass without noticing, he could have blended into any crowd as easily as a teju lizard disappeared against the frond of a palm tree.

Ribisi studied him for a moment. "Mr. Mollis, can you tell us what you do for a living?"

"I'm an attorney at the firm of O'Shaunessy, Warren and Rosen."

"And how long have you been with that firm?"

"Nine years."

"What is your area of expertise?"

"I am a senior associate in charge of Family and Divorce law."

"Did you have occasion to meet Mrs. Monnehan before today?"

Marvin Mollis stared at Maddie with fascination. "No, I never had the pleasure." There was real regret in his voice.

"But you met with Andrew Monnehan?" Ribisi asked as smooth as butter. I felt the familiar tug in my gut and was bracing myself for whatever the unremarkable Mr. Mollis was going to say to distinguish himself.

"Yes."

"Can you tell the court in what capacity you met with the deceased?" Ribisi turned on his heels and focused his laser eyes on Maddie.

"Mr. Monnehan approached me to start divorce proceedings against Mrs. Monnehan."

Here was the smoking gun. I looked down at Maddie's lap where her white-knuckled hands tightened reflexively, the only indication that she was affected in any way. She was utterly still as she met Ribisi's stare with unwavering eyes. It was clear to me that she was not as indifferent to this piece of information as she seemed, either now or at the office when we first read Mollis's sworn affidavit.

Ribisi pivoted back to his witness.

"Can you tell the court when this meeting between you and Mr. Monnehan took place?" Ribisi asked.

"Well, I met Mr. Monnehan on the first of March this year, when he stopped by my office, introduced himself, and asked a few questions about no-fault divorce law in New York. He was particularly interested in finding out what the allowable time period was to file for such a divorce." Mollis cast a quick look at our table. "I told him that since 2010, New York State has effectively permitted no-fault divorce in any marriage that has lasted for at least six months."

"He asked you to start the divorce process?" Ribisi inquired.

Mollis's thin lips seemed to disappear altogether as he frowned at the prosecutor. "Not at the time. He actually asked me to start the proceedings when he called back, a week later."

"And that was when?"

"I believe it was the fifth of March."

"You spoke to him on the phone?" asked Ribisi.

"Yes."

"And there was no doubt as to what Mr. Monnehan wanted you to do?"

"No. None at all."

"And this was on March the 5th? Six days before he was killed?"

"Yes." Mollis's Adam's apple bobbed as he swallowed hard and now looked, not at Maddie, but at the gallery, at Leo O'Shaunessy, whose features betrayed nothing at all.

"Thank you, Mr. Mollis."

By now, the jury had heard a tale of a failed marriage which both parties were intent on ending. Ribisi's calculated opening statement was understandable. In view of both the prenup and Monnehan seeking a divorce, it theoretically provided a clear motive on Maddie's part. Coupled with her incontrovertible admission that she shot him, the State had an open-and-shut case. A case of a wife who, standing to lose everything, had opted for a "quickie divorce."

Judge Ramsey looked at me. A frown hung on his face. "Let's break before your cross, Mr. Conor."

"That's fine with me, Your Honor," I responded.

The judge called for a lunch break, and the courtroom emptied slowly. Observers lingered, trying to catch sight of Maddie, but she stayed seated, while Matthew and I busied ourselves with papers. Annika, as responsive as ever to my moods, knew to hang back, so the four of us were the last in the empty courtroom.

We had a little over an hour before we had to return to court. Maddie declined our offer to join us for lunch and left. Matthew had brought his own sandwich and opted to stay put, so that left only Annika and me to take the elevator upstairs to the lunchroom reserved for court personnel.

Annika gave me a long look and then asked, "Can we talk honestly?"

I nodded. My cheeseburger tasted foul, so I washed it down with Coke, which was cloyingly sweet. I pushed away both the plate and the soda.

"The jury lapped up O'Shaunessy's and Mollis's testimonies. They know now that the marriage was not as solid as the public was led to believe." Annika didn't have to add that our client had failed to update her own attorneys about the state of her marriage.

"I'm aware of that." I said.

Annika chose her words slowly. "Regardless," she paused briefly, "the prosecution still has the burden of proving that Maddie acted with intent."

I nodded in agreement. There was no refuting the fact that the State had established motive.

"I wish I could tell you that I trust our client like you seem to, but you know I cannot tell a lie." She gave me a rueful smile.

I nodded slowly. "I know Maddie's been selective with the facts, Annika. I know she's been keeping some things hidden, but in the end, we'll discover the whole truth, you know that and I know that."

We stared at each other, both reluctant to continue. Finally, Annika looked down at her salad and started pushing at the tiny slivers of red peppers. "I hope it won't be too late when that happens, Nick."

A strange silence settled over the rest of lunch, a first in our long association.

When we returned to court, I spotted Oscar in the last row, and Matthew and Maddie were already seated at the defense table. Maddie had a small notepad open in front of her, the first page of which was covered with strong, slanted handwriting. Her eyes rose to meet mine.

"I'd like the truth, Maddie. You told us you knew nothing about Andrew and Marvin Mollis. Was that the truth?" I asked with a voice so low and clipped it sounded like a stranger's.

She looked at me, her voice flat as she asked, "Do you trust me, Nick?"

"No. I don't trust as a rule. It takes me a long time to trust." I added dryly, "I haven't known you long enough."

Maddie considered my response and nodded. "Trust is in short supply." Then she said, "I knew nothing of Andrew wanting a divorce."

There was very little Maddie could read in my face as I replied, "Is that what you're going to testify to when Ribisi asks you about it?"

"Yes." I recognized the steel lacing the word.

"All right, then," I said, sitting down.

Marvin Mollis was recalled to the stand and reminded that he was still under oath. I approached him with a smile. "Mr. Mollis, you testified that you'd never met Mrs. Monnehan before, is that correct?"

"Yes."

"But you've seen her in the office with Mr. Monnehan?"

"Yes, I saw them when they came to consult with Leo."

"Were you aware of the prenuptial agreement that Mr. O'Shaunessy drafted?"

"Not until Mr. Monnehan called me to handle the divorce."

"Were you surprised when Mr. Monnehan asked you to start divorce proceedings?"

Mollis gave me a perturbed look and hesitated before answering. "To tell you the truth, I was, a little…"

"And why was that?" I asked encouragingly.

His thin shoulders jerked upwards. "I didn't expect it. I mean, they were married for a very brief time and…" He paused and glanced at Maddie. "Mrs. Monnehan is so beautiful." The color rose in his cheeks, and he seemed lost for words.

I decided to rescue the poor man and smiled easily. "Yes. Mrs. Monnehan is an exceptionally beautiful woman. But beautiful people can experience marital difficulties just like plain folks."

"Yes," came the awkward answer.

"Was there any other reason for your reaction?"

"Objection." Ribisi stood up. "Your Honor, I fail to see the relevance of this line of questioning."

I looked at Ramsey. "I'm trying to find out whether Senator Monnehan's call to Mr. Mollis was a sudden and impulsive act, and in what context he made that startling decision."

Ramsey studied me and said, "I will allow it." He directed Mollis, "You may answer."

Mollis shifted in his chair. "No, not really."

"You don't know what caused Mr. Monnehan to call you that day?"

"No."

"He didn't give any reasons?"

"No." And of course Mollis would never question Andrew Monnehan.

"Do you know if the deceased discussed this matter with his wife?" I was aware that I was holding my breath.

"I don't know, he never mentioned it."

"So, upon reading your deposition, Mrs. Monnehan could have been just as surprised as you were then, to find out that her husband was initiating a divorce?"

Ribisi lunged to his feet, "Objection! Speculative and beyond the realm!" he called out indignantly.

"Sustained," said the judge. "Mr. Conor, please don't confuse cross-examination with defense arguments."

I nodded and then asked, "Mr. Mollis, you don't know whether Senator Monnehan was determined to proceed with the divorce?"

He looked at me uncertainly. "Well, he did ask me to draw up the papers."

"But the Senator could have stopped you from filing, just as Mrs. Monnehan did earlier with Mr. O'Shaunessy?"

"Objection," called Ribisi. "We don't know if Mrs. Monnehan intended to go through with the divorce in the first place."

"Sustained," said Ramsey.

"When Senator Monnehan called you, did he tell you when he intended to meet with you to sign the papers?"

Marvin Mollis pondered my question and then in a slightly bewildered tone, replied, "No, we never got to make an appointment."

"So, you don't really know whether Senator Monnehan intended to pursue the matter beyond the phone call?"

Mollis cleared his throat and suggested timidly, "He might have expected me to call him when the papers were ready."

"How long would it have taken you to prepare them?"

"The papers could have been ready in a matter of hours. The existence of the prenuptial made the divorce papers strictly perfunctory, pro forma."

"I'm assuming the deceased was aware of that?"

"Objection!" said Ribisi. "Calls for speculation."

"Sustained."

"Were you aware that Andrew Monnehan had a law degree and that he had had a successful legal career before he turned to politics?"

Mollis nodded. "Yes."

"Would someone who practiced law understand the ramifications of the prenuptial when filing for divorce?" I asked flatly.

"Oh, yes," answered Mollis without hesitation.

I gave him a thin smile. "So, everyone in the court can assume that Andrew Monnehan was well aware that his papers could be ready in a day at the most?"

"Yes."

"But he did not contact you after his initial telephone call, not the next day or the day after?"

"No."

"Wouldn't that indicate reluctance on the Senator's part to pursue the matter?"

I was ready for Ribisi's objection, but I had done what I could. The jury could contemplate the different possibilities. I returned to the counsel table and Ribisi called his next witness.

Helen Morley, the Monnehan's housekeeper in New York, was sworn in and took her seat. She wore all black, with crepe-soled shoes. I could imagine her lurking about the Monnehans' residence, as silent as a ghost and just as unsettling.

As Mrs. Morley answered the standard questions about age, occupation, and personal history, I unobtrusively studied the jury. Mrs. Wilkinson, the kindly housewife from Queens, was eyeing Helen Morley with a furrowed brow. Mr. Shue, the only Asian American juror besides Emily Long, was watching with an expressionless face, but was unusually alert. Even Mr. Grimaldi, the leader of the pack, had a strange frown plastered on his face.

Helen Morley was not an appealing person by any means. She was stiff and her clipped voice off-putting. Yet it was not her manner or appearance, but her testimony that concerned me.

"So," began Ribisi, "you were in the employ of Senator Monnehan for more than seventeen years before Maddie Walker married him?"

"Yes."

"What did you do before you worked for the deceased?"

"I worked for twelve years for Glenda Fowler, the Senator's sister."

"Are you still employed by Mrs. Monnehan?"

"I'm not sure." Mrs. Morley's expression did not change, but her curt tone left no doubt in anyone's mind that the status of her present employment was unclear.

"Were you aware that Senator Monnehan wanted to terminate the marriage?" Ribisi asked cordially.

"No," Mrs. Morley answered brusquely. "But it does not surprise me," she added.

"Why is that?" asked Ribisi.

For the first time, Mrs. Morley's eyes shifted towards Maddie, and the small gleam of malice was replaced by a look of righteous indignation. "Well, the Senator was extremely busy dividing his time between New York and Washington, D.C. It seemed to me that he could have used more support from his wife."

Ribisi appraised her speculatively before he prodded, "You did not think that Mrs. Monnehan was the right helpmate for her husband?"

Helen Morley's thin lips compressed tightly against her teeth. "I certainly didn't think so at the time!"

"What made you think that?"

"Well, for one thing, Mrs. Monnehan never accompanied her husband to the capital. He stayed in D.C. on his own, for days at a time."

"Did Senator Monnehan ever voice displeasure at being left on his own?"

Mrs. Morley shook her head. "Senator Monnehan was too much of a gentleman to air his private grievances, even to me, but I could tell he was unhappy when Mrs. Monnehan stayed behind to do whatever she deemed more important than joining her husband."

From the corner of my eye, I saw, to my astonishment, a suppressed smile on Maddie's lips. But I heard little to smile about. Given Andrew Monnehan's free-for-all lifestyle in Washington, I seriously doubted that he was aggrieved by Maddie's absence. But I also knew that Helen Morley's testimony had the power to taint Maddie's image. Perception was as crucial as facts.

Returning my attention to Ribisi, my stomach dropped. I saw the eyes of a tiger just about to pounce, and I thought I knew where Ribisi was leading his witness.

"Was there anything else that you felt was indicative of Maddie Monnehan's lack of interest in her husband's career?"

Mrs. Morley met Ribisi's eyes, and I saw the tiny nod of approval he bestowed on her. "Oh, yes," she said, looking at the jurors. "I felt that Mrs. Monnehan was cultivating a life totally separate from that of her husband, especially when he was away."

"What do you mean by that?"

"I mean that Mrs. Monnehan led an active social life when Senator Monnehan was away."

"I see…can you tell us a little about it?"

Again, that quick look of derision and animosity. "Mrs. Monnehan entertained different men while her husband was in Washington." I saw Ramsey's lips twitch as he contemplated the witness.

"You mean she was seeing men other than her husband?" asked Ribisi curiously, as if he were entirely ignorant of Helen Morley's forthcoming testimony.

Mrs. Morley emitted a noise that sounded like a cross between a bark and a snort. "There were a few men who came to the house, and Mrs. Monnehan not only received them, but left in their company."

"Did you recognize any of them?"

I stood up. "Objection."

"On what grounds, Counselor?" growled Ramsey.

"Relevance, Your Honor. The fact that Mrs. Monnehan had friends and socialized with them has no bearing on this case."

"On the contrary!" rejoined Ribisi, "We intend to show that there were ample reasons for the deceased, Andrew Monnehan, to end his marriage and that one of the obvious ones was Mrs. Monnehan's extra-marital relationships."

Ramsey contemplated Maddie and then said firmly, "I concur, there is enough reason to find out the nature of the relationship between husband and wife. I will allow."

Ribisi asked, "Mrs. Morley, would you like me to repeat the question?"

Mrs. Morley favored the prosecutor with a smile. "Not necessary. I remember the question, and the answer is that I did recognize Mr. Christopher Logan and Mr. Giles Romney, as they were the most frequent guests."

A collective gasp from the spectators. The two names belonged to two very well-known individuals. Giles Romney had won last year's Wimbledon tournament, and his face had graced the covers of various tabloids for the past two years. His reputation as a "bad boy" helped sell both tickets and magazines, and his handsome pouting visage had recently been appropriated by a successful ad campaign for men's underwear. Chris Logan's boyish good looks and his meteoric rise in politics had catapulted him to national celebrity. He was destined to go far—even to the highest office in the land.

Ribisi let the reactions ripple, milking them for all their worth. The judge pounded the gavel and ordered the courtroom to settle down. We now had the making of a full-blown melodrama. As Annika leaned against the back of her chair, I saw behind her Matthew's pained expression.

Maddie's eyes darkened. That I had warned her of this eventuality was no consolation. We had to deal with this, and damned if I wasn't going to call Chris Logan to the stand and refute any allegations of wrongdoing.

"You are referring to the Attorney General of the State of New York?"

"The same."

"And Giles Romney, the tennis champion."

"Correct."

"And both these men were frequent visitors to the Monnehan residence?"

"Yes."

"How about when Senator Monnehan was there; did these men call on him as well?"

"Sometimes, but it was mostly when he was away."

"Did Mrs. Monnehan go on any trips by herself?"

"She mostly went to their villa at the beach on Long Island. She did leave for Florida at one time, but returned after two days."

"Did the couple stay often in their beach house?"

"Mr.…sorry, I mean, Senator Monnehan, did not care for the beach; he very rarely went out there. It was mostly Mrs. Monnehan."

"When Mrs. Monnehan left for Sag Harbor and Senator Monnehan stayed in D.C., did you and the cook stay in the Manhattan residence?"

"Sometimes, but more often than not, we were given those days off to do as we pleased. We had to make sure, of course, that we returned a day before either one came back, and we were available on our mobiles at all times in case Mr., sorry…" a quick frown, "Senator and Mrs. Monnehan had a change of plans."

"On the night of March 11th of this year, neither you nor Mrs. Piacelli, the cook, were on the premises?"

"That's correct. I was visiting my sister in Yonkers, and Mrs. Piacelli had gone to see her daughter."

"What time did you leave the house?"

"I left about fifteen minutes after Mrs. Piacelli, around three o'clock."

"Was Mrs. Monnehan still in residence?"

"No."

Ribisi turned to the counsel table and leafed through his notes. He raised his eyes and asked, "One more question, Mrs. Morley. The alarm system in the house, were all four of you able to arm and disarm the system?"

"Well," Mrs. Morley paused, as she mulled over the question. "Mrs. Piacelli never touched the alarm. The alarm was always disarmed by the time she started her day."

"Who else besides you and the Monnehans had access to the code?" asked Ribisi.

"No one. Anyway, Senator Monnehan kept changing it, almost every two to three months. So, even if someone knew it at one point, the code kept changing."

"And why is that?" Ribisi asked, genuinely startled.

Mrs. Morley sighed loudly. "Senator Monnehan kept forgetting the code, and the monitoring company kept resetting it."

Ribisi smiled at Helen Morley. "Thank you, Mrs. Morley; you've been more than helpful."

On many levels, despite the surliness of Morley's voice, this testimony was pure gold for the prosecution. It was time to shake the compost and see what crawled out from underneath.

I faced Helen Morley with a courteous smile. "Good afternoon, Mrs. Morley. I promise I'll make it brief; just a few questions."

Mrs. Morley watched me, motionless. "That's all right. I have all the time in the world."

"Mrs. Morley, you testified that Senator Monnehan had been commuting between New York and D.C.?"

"Yes."

"How long had that been going on?"

"Ever since he was elected to the Senate."

"Senator Monnehan had been travelling back and forth for the last six years?"

"Yes. It was only in the last three months that he was staying in D.C. for longer periods of time."

"Did the pattern of his stays in D.C. change when the Senator married Mrs. Monnehan?"

"Yes, Senator Monnehan tried to stay longer in New York City."

"Do you know if that was because it was the Senator's preference, or because of Mrs. Monnehan's wishes?"

Mrs. Morley pursed her lips. "I have no idea. Like I said before, Senator Monnehan never discussed his private affairs."

I nodded; I was establishing a slow and easy rhythm, my questions intentionally routine and inoffensive. I wanted Helen Morley settled into a comfortable lull.

"When Senator Monnehan was called away, would he inform you of his plans ahead of time?"

"Yes, for the most part. He sometimes didn't know ahead of time, so we would be informed of his plans by his secretary."

"But that was before the Senator was married?" I posited gently. "Surely Mrs. Monnehan was the one to let you know if the Senator was going to be away?"

"Yes." I saw her lips tighten with displeasure and affront.

"And Mrs. Monnehan would also inform you and Mrs. Piacelli when the Senator was due back?"

"Yes."

"So, on March 11th, it was Mrs. Monnehan who told you that her husband was called away?"

"Yes."

"Did she also tell you when he was supposed to come back?"

"She told us he was due back on Thursday, the 14th."

"And she gave you Tuesday and Wednesday off?"

"Yes." The relentless sourness of Helen Morley's responses worked well for the defense. I hoped the jury was capable of discerning the discontented nature of the witness.

I went over to the defense table and rifled through some papers. While scanning my notes, I asked with a distracted air, "In the past, did it ever happen that Senator Monnehan would cut his stay in the capital short and come home unexpectedly?" I felt the beat of my heart as I waited for the response; so much depended on Helen Morley's answer.

The pause seemed interminable, but when Mrs. Morley finally said, "No, never," I quietly expelled the breath I was holding. Annika and I exchanged glances.

I raised an eyebrow as I turned to face Mrs. Morley. "Never? You mean Senator Monnehan never surprised the household? He never returned unexpectedly?"

After another slight pause, Mrs. Morley answered with a blatant burst of dislike. "No. Senator Monnehan always made sure that we knew when he was due back in New York. He was considerate to a fault."

I was filled with gratitude as I approached the witness stand again. "You testified that Mrs. Monnehan had friends who visited when she was home alone?"

"Yes."

"Are you aware of the fact that Mr. Logan is an old friend of Mrs. Monnehan?"

Mrs. Morley eyed me suspiciously. "No, I wasn't aware of that."

"Yes," I continued pleasantly, "Mrs. Monnehan and Mr. Logan were friends long before she ever met and married the Senator."

Helen Morley remained silent.

I ignored the frost and smiled benevolently at her hostile expression. "They knew each other long before Mrs. Monnehan moved to Washington." I paused to look Mrs. Morley straight in the eye. "Actually, it was Christopher Logan who introduced Andrew Monnehan to Maddie; did you know that?"

The beginning of a flush appeared on Helen Morley's cheeks, but she answered in the same bland tone. "I wasn't aware of that."

I was gratified by the utter stillness in the room and let my own silence linger a bit longer. "Do you think it's possible that being a friend of Mrs. Monnehan's, Christopher Logan felt duty-bound to visit Mrs. Monnehan, who, being a stranger in New York, would likely feel lonely in her husband's absence?"

If ever there was a grudging acknowledgment of a hypothesis, Mrs. Morley's tone conveyed it to the hilt when she said, "I suppose." The expression on her face was sullen.

"How often did Mr. Logan call on Mrs. Monnehan?"

Helen Morley was slow to answer. She was now aware that she needed to choose her words carefully. Her eyes dropped. "Perhaps once a week," she said at length.

"Every week?" I pressed.

She gave me a hard look. "More or less."

"In the last three months, how many times did Mr. Logan visit?"

"I can't remember exactly."

I did not change my tone of voice. "Before, you testified that Mr. Logan was a frequent visitor. How many times did he visit to merit your description as a 'frequent visitor'?"

"Objection!" Ribisi called out. "Counselor is badgering the witness."

"Sorry, Your Honor," I grinned unabashedly. "I'm just trying to understand the witness's own terminology."

Ramsey grumbled. "I will overrule, but you are walking a thin line, Counselor; the witness is not a linguistics expert."

"Yes, Your Honor."

I turned to Mrs. Morley. "How many times did the New York State Attorney General visit, would you say?"

Helen Morley's voice rose with each answer. "I can't remember exactly."

I said pensively, "Well, let's see…there are approximately four weeks in each month; so, would you say Mrs. Monnehan saw Mr. Logan twelve times during those three months?"

"No, not that many."

"Ten?"

"Maybe less."

"Six?"

"Maybe six or seven," Mrs. Morley finally conceded.

"We spoke to Mrs. Piacelli, and she agrees with you; Mrs. Monnehan saw Mr. Logan at the residence six times since before Christmas, but on two of those occasions, the Senator himself was present."

If looks could kill!

I waved my hand magnanimously, as if I did not just make porridge out of gristle.

"How about Giles Romney? Was he also a frequent visitor?" I asked innocently.

The burst of laughter in the crowd was a welcome sound.

I smiled. "I withdraw the question. I think we have a fair picture of Mrs. Monnehan's teeming social life. Thank you, Mrs. Morley. As Mr. Ribisi has already said, you have been very helpful."

I saw the frown on Ribisi's face linger while he was debating whether to re-direct, but he wisely decided against it. Better hope that some of Morley's testimony still resonated with the jury, rather than dig himself into a deeper hole.

When I sat down, Matthew leaned over and whispered, "You nailed it!"

As I smiled at Matthew's bright face, I noticed on Maddie's face a look somewhere between respect and wariness—and I figured she and I were about to lock horns on the issue of Logan. Annika slid me a folded, handwritten note that read, "Well done." No exclamation mark, just a plain acknowledgment, a small high-five, and I smiled.

CHAPTER 22

You just can't beat the person who won't give up.

—Babe Ruth

Julie McGuire entered the courtroom with the studied air of a woman aware that all eyes were on her. She was wearing a tight-fitting jacket over a flouncy silk skirt, and her high heels made a soft clicking sound as she sauntered towards the stand. She gave the jurors a quick smile, which produced a pair of impish dimples in her otherwise smooth cheeks.

After she was sworn in, Ribisi rose to greet his witness. "Mrs. McGuire, could you please tell the court what you do for a living?"

"I run a non-profit organization called Hand in Hand. We sponsor various women's shelters and soup kitchens for the homeless."

Ribisi nodded respectfully. "Is that how you met Senator and Mrs. Monnehan?"

She nodded. "Alex, my husband, and I met Andrew Monnehan seven years ago. Andrew was extremely keen on any organization whose charter was women's issues. We found ourselves running into him at various charity events, and as he and Alex discovered a shared enthusiasm for golf, we ended up socializing quite a bit. When Andrew married Maddie," Mrs. McGuire smiled brightly, "we naturally welcomed her with open arms. We saw them quite frequently."

"So, you were quite close to the deceased and his wife?"

An elegant shrug and a nod. "Yes, both Alex and I liked them."

"Were you aware of any marital troubles between Senator Monnehan and Mrs. Monnehan?"

Julie McGuire's red lips formed a cupid-bow's pout, which she must have been told had an adorable effect. "Well," she articulated slowly, "Andrew told us in confidence…" She stopped.

Ribisi interjected soberly, "The Senator is dead, but I'm sure he would have liked you to be forthcoming with any relevant information, if it could shed light on the events leading to his death."

Mrs. McGuire cast a furtive glance at our table, but did not make eye contact with her "good friend" Maddie Monnehan. "Andrew came over one night, when Maddie was apparently at their Sag Harbor beach house, and told us that he was thinking of ending his marriage."

"When was that, do you remember?"

"It could have been a week before he was shot."

"Did he confide in you as to the reasons why?"

Julie McGuire uncrossed and re-crossed her legs. "Well," she continued, looking slightly embarrassed, "he didn't actually say so, but he intimated that Maddie's affections had waned and wandered."

"What did you infer from this?"

"Objection." I rose and leveled my eyes on Mrs. McGuire. "Speculative and beyond the scope."

Ramsey, whose attention was focused on Julie McGuire's pretty features, turned to Ribisi. "Counselor, you'd better rephrase."

"Yes, Your Honor," said Ribisi. "Did Senator Monnehan allude to anything else?"

The small dimples made a brief appearance, followed by the magic pout. "Well, Alex and he had a private talk, and Alex later told me…"

"Objection." My voice had equal amounts of courtesy and harshness, as I looked at Ramsey. "Hearsay, Your Honor."

Ramsey picked up his pen, made a notation in his diary, and declared: "Sustained."

Ribisi smiled at his witness, as if they had each been rapped lightly on their knuckles. "Mrs. McGuire, did you have occasion to speak privately with the deceased after that evening?"

"No. Unfortunately, that was the last time we spoke with Andrew privately. We did, however, have dinner with the Monnehans the evening before he died."

Julie McGuire pulled out an embroidered handkerchief from her handbag and dabbed her eyes delicately. It was a peculiarly old-fashioned, but extremely effective gesture. The vulnerable damsel in distress unable to cover a show of genuine grief. I heard a quiet sound from Annika's corner, rather like a muffled snort. Maddie hadn't moved an inch but was eyeing Julie with equal parts indifference and amusement.

Ribisi was too adroit a manipulator not to capitalize on this small windfall and lowered his head in a show of sympathy. "I'm sorry; we're about to wind down. But if you need a moment…?"

Mrs. McGuire gave him a grateful, teary smile and said, "No, I'm fine. Please continue."

"Coming back to that last dinner with the Monnehans and the Watkinses, did anything unusual happen that night?"

"As I went to the restroom to powder up, I saw Andrew and Maddie huddled in the small vestibule behind the main dining area."

"What were they doing?" asked Ribisi.

"They seemed to be engaged in a heated conversation."

Ribisi watched his witness and asked slowly, "Heated conversation? How could you tell?"

"Well, I was not about to eavesdrop, but Andrew's voice was certainly loud enough to carry."

The air in the room hummed like a band about to snap. I was as intrigued as everyone else. We did have the testimony of two eyewitnesses who claimed to have seen the Monnehans arguing, but I had no idea what Julie McGuire was about to say. Ribisi's somber voice cut through the tension. "We know you would not deliberately invade the privacy of your friends, but can you share with the court what you inadvertently overheard?"

Inadvertently, my foot.

Julie McGuire sent an apologetic look in Maddie's direction. "I heard Andrew say, 'I will not let you get away with that.'"

"Did Mrs. Monnehan reply?"

"She must have, but I couldn't hear her words; her voice was barely above a whisper."

"How do you know that she replied?"

"Because in the next moment, in response to something Maddie said, Andrew grabbed her by the arms and started shaking her."

Out of the corner of my eye, I caught the sudden stiffening of Maddie's shoulders.

Julie continued, "That was when I decided to go over; I thought I could diffuse the situation—until I heard Maddie speak."

She turned her dark, woeful eyes toward Maddie and dabbed beneath them.

"And what is it that you heard Maddie say?" asked Ribisi.

Pausing as if to recollect the exact phrase, she said, "'Don't be such a petulant little boy, Andrew!'"

There was a prolonged murmur in the room. My gaze remained frozen on Julie McGuire's handkerchief as she lifted it again to dab at invisible tears.

"What happened then?"

"I saw Maddie wrench her arms free and turn towards the dining room. When I joined our table, Andrew was already seated next to her. She seemed composed as she was conversing with Elena Watkins, but Andrew, I could tell, was angry. The dinner broke up soon after; we all felt the strain in the air."

Knowing when to quit, Ribisi looked in my direction and declared. "Thank you, I have no further questions, Mrs. McGuire."

I sat watching Julie McGuire, trying to decide the best tack to take. She had made headway with the jury, I could tell, and I certainly didn't want to alienate any of them by appearing insensitive to her vulnerability.

"Just a few questions, Mrs. McGuire," I said.

She nodded slowly.

"You have testified that you and your husband were friendly with the Monnehans?"

"Yes."

"In fact, after Andrew married Maddie, you socialized quite a bit?"

She nodded again. "Yes."

"Dinners, opera, and, of course, charity events?"

"Yes."

"During that time, did you notice anything to suggest that the relationship between the Senator and his wife was troubled?"

"No. They seemed to be fine. They seemed comfortable in each other's company."

"Did you witness any arguments prior to that night at the restaurant?"

"No."

I stepped closer with a warm smile. "You've been married for twelve years, I understand."

The dimples and a flash of white, even teeth. "Yes. Happily married."

"I guess no arguments, then?"

She actually fluttered her lashes. "Oh, we've had some doozies."

I returned her grin. "Did you think the argument between Andrew and Maddie was peculiar or odd in any way?"

"No, not really. All couples argue." She turned towards the jurors and actually giggled. "I'm sure everyone here knows that arguments can lead to the sweetest make-ups."

"Thank you, Mrs. McGuire, I have no more questions."

Ramsey glanced at Ribisi.

"No more questions for this witness," said Ribisi.

Julie McGuire left the stand with the same aplomb with which she had made her entrance, the smart heels clicking jauntily against the floor as she sashayed down the aisle.

Before Ribisi could call his next witness, Ramsey called for a twenty-minute break and the courtroom began to empty out.

"Is there anything I need to know about that argument?" I asked Maddie warily.

She glanced at me, then turned to look at Annika, whose intense examination of Maddie was almost as tangible as a touch. "No."

I drummed up a smile. "You know, Maddie, I've had hostile witnesses more willing to talk to me than you. It's incredible to me that not only do you not help your own defense, but actively seem to impede it."

"There was nothing about that argument," said Maddie in a measured voice, "that need concern my defense." The rest of her sentence could well have been, "or that need concern you."

As the noise in the courtroom receded, I bit out, "What was it about?"

Maddie gave me a hard look. "I told Andrew that I reconsidered and was filing for divorce the following week."

"He did not take it well, I gather."

Maddie said levelly, "You could say that."

I looked at her while considering this latest bit of info. I was off balance, unsure of the terrain, but for now I had to let it go. I collected my papers from the table and with the same cold control I had mastered my whole life, said, "All right, Maddie, later today we'll talk. Maybe you'll remember other things you've failed to mention to us." I glanced at Annika and Matthew. "I'm going to step out for ten minutes. I need to make a call."

When I returned, Maddie was the picture of composure.

Elena Watkins was a striking brunette, hawk-eyed and thin-lipped. She resembled archetypal illustrations of Mayan women, famous for their attenuated and conical heads. The long, strong neck and the chiseled cheekbones harkened back to some noble Spanish blood in her lineage. Mrs. Watkins's posture on the witness stand was just as regal, a queen granting an audience. She regarded Ribisi with equanimity and curiosity, but did not return his smile.

"Mrs. Watkins, thank you for coming in."

"I had no choice. You subpoenaed me, Mr. Ribisi."

Ribisi chose not to respond, but I noticed the sudden alertness on the jurors' faces. This was the first witness who clearly had been subpoenaed against her will.

Ribisi chose a friendly, conversational tone as he said with a smile, "We only have a few questions."

Elena Watkins waited.

"You and your husband were friends with the Monnehans?"

"Yes. My husband knew Andrew years before he turned to politics. He and my husband practiced law in the same firm."

"How about Maddie Monnehan?"

"When Andrew wed, his wife was more than welcome."

"Were you friends with Maddie Monnehan?"

Elena Watkins turned away and looked at Maddie pensively. "No, not really. I do not know Maddie that well." She paused. "But I like her."

Ribisi watched Elena with interest, but remained silent, waiting for her to continue. She smiled dryly. "Most women try to exert their presence in the company of men. Especially beautiful women. They seem to think everyone is interested in what they have to say." She glanced at Maddie. "Maddie is an exception in that regard. She listens well and says very little."

Trying to quash my uneasiness, I wondered what it was that had induced Ribisi to call Mrs. Watkins to the stand. There was obviously more to her testimony than documenting a friendship between couples and the last dinner they had shared with the Monnehans. As gracious as Elena Watkins was trying to be, it was clear to all that she was testifying reluctantly.

"Could you please tell the court what you shared with your husband a few months back?"

From the corner of my eye I saw Annika pick up a pen and twirl it nervously around her fingers. We seemed to share the same nameless dread.

Mrs. Watkins looked at Maddie with something akin to regret. "What I told Bill was in a private conversation, not to be bandied around, and certainly not to cast a poor light on whomever you intend to, Mr. Ribisi."

Ribisi's smile remained frozen on his face. "We only intend to get to the truth, Mrs. Watkins."

"I don't see how my conversation with Bill plays any role in determining the truth of Mrs. Monnehan's guilt or innocence." There was a slight derisive tone to her answer.

The smile plastered on Ribisi's face did not soften the brusqueness of his voice. "Let us be the judge of that, Mrs. Watkins. So, will you enlighten the court as to what you told your husband?"

Without preamble and in a tone as hard as Ribisi's, Elena Watkins said, "I saw Maddie and Chris Logan enter Hotel Gansevoort in the meatpacking district one afternoon."

"When was that?"

"I cannot recall exactly, sometime in September or October."

Ribisi wore an air of mild disinterest as he asked, "Was there anything unusual about seeing Mrs. Monnehan in the company of Mr. Logan?"

"No, by itself it wouldn't have registered," she added softly, "but I had seen them once before enter the lobby of another hotel, The Lowell on 64th Street, and that time, it was around 9 p.m."

There it was: the glimpse behind Door Number One.

The ripple in the crowd mushroomed into a loud buzz, which the vigorous cracking sound of the judge's gavel could not staunch for a full minute.

Because Elena Watkins had the grace to look as uncomfortable as she did, her testimony had the disastrous effect of a well-timed detonator. I saw the jurors' eyes turn to look at Maddie, who, sitting straight as a gymnast, met their eyes with an expression as inscrutable as a Chinese magus.

Ribisi was clever enough not to overplay his hand; he knew that besides the money issues embedded in the case, his side had just tossed out a hot potato, insinuating why Maddie would want to get rid of a husband twenty years her senior. And all thanks to this elegant and formidable woman.

I remained seated. "No questions, Your Honor." My voice rang strong in the now-subdued courtroom. Mrs. Holloway, a heavy-set African American woman in the jury box, stared at Maddie with fierce disapproval, a sentiment indubitably shared by others. We were slowly losing our sympathetic jurors.

"The people would like to call Samuel Prentiss to the stand," said Ribisi.

I could not stop the relentless progression of incriminating evidence. I was well aware of who Mr. Prentiss was, as his name appeared on the State's list of witnesses. I hoped I could undermine his forthcoming testimony, but we had little ammunition against cold facts. Oscar, the masterful purveyor of information, had kept us well informed of the facts that would implicate Maddie.

Samuel Prentiss was a trim man of about fifty with a distinguished, long face and a closely clipped moustache so thin and straight it seemed drawn on by a pencil. His lively blue eyes roamed the room, and he smiled engagingly at Judge Ramsey, Paul Ribisi and the jury, in that order. He was the manager of The Lowell and had served as such for the last eleven years.

"Could you tell us, Mr. Prentiss, if you are familiar with Mr. Christopher Logan?" asked Ribisi.

"Oh, yes!" Mr. Prentiss's vigorous nod underlined his response. "Mr. Logan has been a guest of the hotel."

"He is a frequent guest?"

"Not exactly frequent, but I would presume to say a steady customer. I think Mr. Logan spends more time in Albany than in New York City."

"Have you seen him at the hotel with other guests?"

"I have seen him on occasion conducting meetings in the dining room. Sometimes he set up these meetings in the private Pembroke Room if there were a large number of participants."

"Have you seen Mrs. Monnehan in the company of Mr. Logan?"

"Yes, I have."

"More than once?"

Mr. Prentiss looked at Maddie and smiled. "I'm not sure; I might have."

"Do you remember seeing Mrs. Monnehan with Mr. Logan at the hotel on more than one occasion?" asked Ribisi in an insistent voice.

At least five times! According to Oscar's benighted information.

"I can't remember." Mr. Prentiss smiled again. "Sorry, I just know that I have seen Mrs. Monnehan."

Ribisi's frown hung unattractively on his face. He had anticipated a different response. He was struggling to remain calm. "Try to remember, Mr. Prentiss. Also remember that you are under oath."

Mr. Prentiss pursed his lips and smiled apologetically. "Sorry, I don't want to mislead the court. I truly don't remember."

"When I spoke to you earlier, you indicated that the defendant was at The Lowell more than once."

"Yes, I know, but I had time to reflect and I think I might have confused seeing Mrs. Monnehan's picture in the papers with seeing her in person," Prentiss said contritely. "Her face is everywhere. All I remember definitively is that I saw her with Mr. Logan that one time when they had a late supper."

"I see." Ribisi was between a rock and a hard place. If he prodded Prentiss any further, Ribisi was in danger of badgering his own witness.

"Can you tell the court when this event took place?"

"I can't be totally sure, but I think it was sometime in early September."

"You might want to work on your memory skills," said Ribisi acerbically. "I can recommend some mental exercises for the brain."

There was chortling in the courtroom, but Mr. Prentiss only smiled and seemed unruffled. "It comes with age, Mr. Prosecutor," he said genially.

Ribisi turned with annoyance. "I have no more questions for this witness."

I remained seated as I smiled at Mr. Prentiss. "I have no questions for this witness either, Your Honor."

"You may step down, Mr. Prentiss," said Ramsey. "It is now 3:15. Mr. Ribisi, would you like to call your next witness and run the risk of having his testimony interrupted?"

Ribisi leaned over to Bennett and after a quick consultation turned to the judge. "We'll defer our questioning until tomorrow, Your Honor."

"Very well," said Ramsey. "Court is adjourned. Tomorrow morning, we will start at 8:30 sharp instead of 9:00 a.m."

Oscar was waiting in the car in his usual hiding place behind the courthouse, and Matthew, Annika, and I slid into the back seat. Maddie slipped into the passenger seat next to Oscar.

Maddie turned to Oscar. "I saw you in court today. How is it that you managed to get to the car and have it ready?"

"I try to be in the courtroom as much as possible, especially when I think the testimonies will be interesting for our case. So today I stayed for the entire day. As for the car, I pay a guy to sit behind the wheel and bring it around as soon as I call him."

Oscar looked at me in the rearview mirror but said nothing. I smiled. "Interesting testimonies" was Oscar's euphemism for statements loaded with minefields.

I leaned over Maddie's shoulder and said, "Annika and I need to clear up a few things, so instead of dropping you off, I'd like you to come with us to the office."

"All right."

I knew Maddie was not about to ask what issues needed clearing up. She was smart enough to realize that we needed to address the issue of Chris Logan. I tried to ignore the onslaught of pain, anger and jealousy and frustration warring inside. I took a steadying breath as I was girding up for battle.

Maddie, Annika, and I retired to my office. I nodded at Annika, giving her the floor. I knew she would try hard not to sound argumentative or snide.

"Maddie, we need to undermine the implication of a liaison between you and Mr. Logan," Annika said kindly.

Maddie watched Annika silently, waiting. So did I.

"We need to know the nature of your relationship with him," continued Annika

"I've told you before, we're friends," said Maddie flatly.

"Friends who meet in hotels? You must realize how it looks," added Annika in a quiet tone.

"Appearances can be deceiving," offered Maddie impassively.

"We found out that you visited with Chris at The Lowell on at least five different occasions."

"I don't recall," said Maddie. "But it means nothing." She paused to scrutinize Annika's face. "Anyway, Mr. Prentiss had no such recollections."

Annika grew quiet.

"Apparently, Mr. Prentiss changed his testimony," I injected.

"Perhaps."

Did you or the Attorney General have anything to do with it?

I could not ask the question; the answer might reveal witness tampering. I would be duty-bound to inform the court of my findings. In addition to the moral ramifications, failure to do so could get me disbarred.

"You slept with Christopher Logan, didn't you?" I couldn't hide the bite in my voice.

"Who I sleep with is nobody's business but my own."

"Maddie," Annika interjected softly, "you must realize that if you had, or are having a romantic relationship with Mr. Logan, this is a terribly damning piece of evidence and extremely beneficial to the State's case. They can use it to establish motive. It will be an open-and-shut case of homicide in the first. We need to be prepared."

Instead of answering Annika, Maddie looked at me across the table and for a moment her eyes lost their fierceness. "It's not what you think."

I heard my own coolness. "I need to know if information regarding an affair is liable to come out during the trial. You can't be so naïve as to not expect the prosecution to pounce on this."

"It will never come up," Maddie said flatly.

"How would you know?"

"Because it's not true."

I let the information sink in. "You could have said that in the first place," I said dryly.

"I could have." There was a tiny gleam in Maddie's eyes. "I hate it when people push me around. It brings on my mad."

Annika and I exchanged a glance. "So, Christopher Logan and you are truly and strictly just friends?"

"Yes."

"Oscar discovered that the two of you also frequented the James in Soho."

"Yes."

"Any reason why your friendly rendezvous are conducted mainly in hotels, Maddie?" I asked.

"Chris likes the privacy."

I sighed. "All right, Maddie, we'll take your word for it. Are there any other hotels that might come up in the investigation?"

"Maybe just the Plaza," she answered as she stared, unblinking, into my eyes.

"How about Giles Romney?" I asked, the words spewing out like little ice pellets.

"What about him?" asked Maddie.

"What is the nature of your relationship with Giles Romney?" The game was getting excruciating, but I refused to let it hurt beyond a certain point.

"I don't know him well; we've only gone out a few times. He's a charming conversationalist and is quick-witted and fun to be with."

Annika looked at Maddie with a bemused expression. "Didn't your husband object to your 'going out' with unattached men?"

Maddie's smile was a study in irony as she said, "It was Andrew who introduced me to Giles and who asked him to keep me company while Andrew was away."

If Maddie Monnehan was an enigma, Andrew Monnehan certainly deserved the moniker "eccentric." His peculiarities ran the gamut, but this latest surprise was not hard to fathom. The possibility that the Senator was devious enough to set up potential entrapment for his wife entered my mind. Having her followed to establish proof of infidelity was certainly grounds for an uncontested divorce.

The glint in Maddie's eyes confirmed what I had suspected: Andrew's ulterior motives were as transparent to his wife as they were to me. The question was, why had Maddie played along?

"Did you ever meet with Mr. Romney on the sly?" asked Annika, in an attempt to determine the extent of the damage.

"No. I made sure that the few times we were together were in public places."

"I would like to add Mr. Logan to our list of witnesses," I said.

"No," came the sharp retort.

"We need him to deny any suggestion of an affair between the two of you."

"No," she responded decisively.

"The prosecution will do its utmost to unearth all the unsavory details of your marriage and to establish the existence of an affair between you and Mr. Logan. I need his testimony to thwart that speculation."

"No," repeated Maddie with sudden weariness. "I do not want Chris to appear in court." The tone brooked no leeway to object. "If there are no other issues to discuss, I would like to leave."

It was Annika who rose to her feet first. "I think I'll work with Matthew for the rest of the afternoon," she said, adding courteously to Maddie, "See you tomorrow morning at 8:30."

We watched Annika leave. Maddie raised her hand and said in a low voice, "I don't want to argue about it, Nick. I've had my final say."

I was too furious to respond.

CHAPTER 23

He even whispered in my ear: "You will suffer; you
will suffer more.
But this time I am on your side. You will be free.
You will, I promise you.

— Henri Charrière, *Papillon*

I decided to take the subway rather than drive to Brooklyn for my meeting with Moira. If I timed it right, I could get to the Brooklyn Academy of Music just as she was done. I haven't seen Moira for a while, so when she called that afternoon, I knew I needed to make time to see her. For the past two months, Moira had been attending the Brooklyn Conservatory of Music supplementary classes in the field of Music Therapy. Moira was an experienced, licensed, and credentialed music therapist. She worked with children who were not only challenged economically, but who had special developmental and psychological needs. She had told me, often enough, how gratifying she found the work, and she never failed to regale me with success stories of "her children." It was apparent to me that her interaction with them was a welcome salve, and I was intensely thankful for it.

Moira came rushing out the front door. "Hey you," she said smiling softly.

"Hey, *chailín mo chroí.*" I hugged her tightly.

I felt her smile burrow into my shoulder. "How come you remember so much of Ma's old tongue?"

I stepped back and grinned. "I've got this good memory, remember?"

She shrugged. A small, pleased nod. We started walking.

"How are your classes?" I asked.

She turned to look at me and smiled. "We're polishing up our assessment skills."

"What kind of assessments?"

"It's fascinating really, how much we're still learning about the psyche." She paused, her features intent. "Well, we're often faced with children from broken homes with a multitude of dysfunctions. We need to separate the wheat from the chaff in order to better understand their triggers and overcome the hurdles in communication."

"Sounds interesting." I wondered what these tests would reveal about my state of mind.

We took a booth in the back of the diner. The waitress, a thin-lipped, peroxide blonde with black roots and black-rimmed eyes shuffled over to our table. She placed two tall glasses of ice water with straws and stood gawking at Moira's face. I felt my own harden as I turned to look at her. She met my eyes and slunk away.

I watched Moira as she carefully unwrapped the paper tip off the straw and took a long sip of her drink. "How are you doing otherwise?" I asked.

"With Da gone I have more time for my music. I've been practicing like a fiend."

"I worry about you. I'm sorry I missed our last two dates…" I continued lamely, "I'm in the midst of this major trial…takes up all my free time. I'm sorry."

I saw her swallow and then force her lips into a lop-sided smile.

"You don't have to be, you know," she said. "Worrying doesn't accomplish anything. It doesn't change things…."

She reached her hand across the table, her long fingers covering mine. I studied our linked fingers. She said, "You bear too much, Nicki. You always have. It kills me to know you never have peace. It was so long ago…"

She drew in a long breath, but before she could resume, the waitress, pointedly fixing her stare strictly on my face, brought over our Greek salads layered with grilled chicken. We waited until she retreated behind the counter.

I said quietly, "I'm all right. It's you who bears the brunt of it."

Moira made an effort to sound casual as she sliced through her chicken breast. "Can we talk about something else for a minute? Can we talk about you for a change? You tell me so very little about yourself."

"What would you like to know?" I flashed her a grin. "Legal practice is not as glamorous as portrayed on Law & Order, you know."

Moira's downcast eyes refused to meet mine; she said gently, "I wish you could be happy, Nicki. One of us should have the right to claim some joy outside of our work."

It was my turn to reach for her hand. "I'm okay. We can't be constantly worrying about each other. Let's agree that we're both doing well." *Cast in a sea not of our making. But survivors, nonetheless.*

Moira pushed her food around her plate. She seemed sad and distracted.

"I thought you said you were hungry?" I said, trying for a lighter note.

Moira twisted her napkin in her lap. "I've been having some bad dreams lately."

"Want to talk about it?"

Moira searched my eyes, then sighed, "Ever since Da died, I've been remembering things…How it was…"

My heart rapped hard against my ribs. "Sweetheart…" I started. But she shushed me with a hand. "Don't! Let me say this before I lose my nerve…I don't know how, but my mind shut down some of the awful memories of our childhood. In a sense, it was a relief not to recall and relive them." Moira's voice broke and she heaved a deep breath. "I know that you and Padrick and Ma experienced abuse the way I never did. You made sure of that… I was insulated from it and perhaps that's why it was easier for me." Moira's cheeks were wet. She swiped impatiently at her tears.

"Sweetheart, nothing good will come from dredging up memories that are best forgotten."

She swallowed hard. "But I do remember. I remember… snippets really…:" She inhaled and exhaled in a rush. "I remember once at night, I walked in on Ma and Padrick. It was so quiet in the house, you were sleeping and Da was away. I was thirsty, I heard Ma's muffled voice in the kitchen. … she was brushing some liniment over Padrick's raw back. It was horrible…"

I swallowed bile in my throat and forced myself to take a sip of the water. "It's done with, *mo chroi*. Please, let it go. What good would it do to rehash any of this?"

She seemed not to hear me. As if from a far-away distance I heard her continue, "But the one night I remember clearly, the one that keeps playing over and over in my head is the night of my thirteenth birthday." Her voice broke, and she had abandoned all pretense of control and started crying in earnest. I rose and slid beside her, holding in check the string of oaths simmering on my tongue. I skimmed my hand over her hair and gathered her tight against me. I felt the hammering of a muscle below my eye. My mind was reeling, battered by the memories, the countless trips to different emergency rooms, the painful stitches, the broken ribs, the dislocated bones. The night of Moira's thirteenth birthday flashed against my lowered lids.

I was fourteen, and Ma was waiting for her ribs to heal. We were celebrating Moira's thirteenth birthday, and she was leaning against Padrick, his arm slung over her shoulders. As always, I found it strange to see Moira's white-blond long tresses against the sleek black of Padrick's. Yet there was no mistaking their kinship—the shape of their eyes, their intense blueness.

The table was laden with Ma's fancy cooking: a shepherd's pie for me, a cabbage dish that we could never be without, and steamed potatoes with cream. There were pickled tomatoes and Padrick's favorite—a lamb stew. The air was filled with the mouth-watering aroma of mysterious seasonings and spices.

"Greg's dad told me he heard great things about you, Padrick," I said with my mouth full, as I sat beaming at my brother.

Padrick shrugged and grinned at me.

"Soon he'll be asked to join the Detective Bureau." I said to Ma, who was watching Padrick with eyes equally brimming with love.

Padrick smiled at her. "If you believe the lad, I'm about to become Chief of Police." He cut a piece of lamb and chewed it appreciatively. "I just try to do good, Ma," he said quietly.

"Tell us about your citation!" I pressed on, basking in the glory of the moment. It was Ma's eyes that alerted me to the sense of dread in the room. I glanced furtively at Da. The ugly expression on his face froze my puppy-dog enthusiasm.

Da gave a short laugh that sounded like a bark. "Ye coming to gloat, boyo?" His beady, venomous eyes were boring holes in Padrick's flushed face.

I saw Padrick's jaw line tighten, his eyes grow hard. "Why don't we try to have one decent meal under this roof?" His tone was flat.

"You think the uniform makes ye a man? Gives ye the right to talk back at me?" It was clear that Da was itching for a fight.

Padrick didn't answer. The air grew heavy around us. I wished I could have taken back my words.

"Frank," Ma's soft voice spilled into the room, desperate, "it's Moira's birthday. It's your daughter's birthday."

Da's voice turned mean as he looked at Ma. "I remember, Molly. You be always reminding me." Ma looked at Da silently, her stricken gaze growing more desperate by the minute. I sat between them, unsure of anything but the need to deflect the impending storm.

"*Da, nobody means to give you lip!*" I hated my voice; it sounded weak and panicky.

"Don't," Padrick said coldly. "Don't let him get to you."

Those nasty eyes focused on Padrick's face. "Why don't ye remind me, boyo, that it be your sister's birthday?" growled Da. There was so much menace in his tone that I half rose to my feet.

Ma touched Moira's shoulder gently. "Dearie, why don't you get us some more bread from the kitchen?"

Moira, who'd been staring at the table, rose obediently to her feet.

"Sit!" ordered Da, his voice deadly.

Padrick stood away from the table. "Let her be. It's between you and me, old man."

A broad, satisfied smile grew on Da's face. It was strange how it twisted his features, rendering them almost unrecognizable. "Damn right, boyo. It's always ye, ain't it?"

Da rose abruptly to his feet and slapped Ma as hard as he could. Ma's sharp scream pierced the air as her chair toppled backwards. Her arms windmilled as she tried to protect her head before she hit the floor with full force. Padrick lunged forward, a growl escaping his lips. Rob's arms shot out and grabbed Padrick from behind. Rob, who'd always stood silently by when things got uncomfortable, and whose way of dealing with Da was to mollify him at all times, now looked coldly down at his brother.

"Let it go, Frank!" he said forcefully. "Let it go, Frank." Rob repeated. "You've done enough fer tonight." At first I thought Da didn't hear him, but then I saw Da's heavy shoulders slump as he sagged back into his seat.

Padrick wrenched himself free of Rob's iron vise and joined me on the floor and we lifted Ma slowly and propped her carefully between us. I was consumed by both rage and helplessness, and my body started trembling. Padrick was speaking, but all I could hear was the noise in my head. It was only after we had laid Ma on the bed that I noticed the taste of tears in my throat. I looked away, knowing that if Padrick glanced my way I would come unraveled.

But Padrick kept talking to Ma, his voice soothing and gentle. He laid his palm on Ma's arm. "It's okay; everythin's all right, Ma. Just take a deep breath…Lie back…Do you need me to retape your ribs?"

I saw Ma's startled eyes turn towards me.

"I told him; he knows," I choked back.

She shook her head despondently.

Barely breathing, Padrick's body was like a clenched fist. Only the flared nostrils betrayed the turbulence within. "It's okay, Ma," Padrick repeated; his voice was growing stronger. "I'll be going now, don't you fret."

Silently, Ma reached for his hand and I saw Padrick's smile as he looked down at our mother, a sad little tug of lips. "I love you, Ma," he said, "I've asked you to move out with me, so many times… I could take care of you and Moira and Nicki… I can't abide seeing you here." I heard the gravel in his voice.

Ma was shaking her head. "Oh, my Paddie, hush…"

His face grew colder, hard. "I'm like the fuse to ignite his fire, Ma. His demons come out when I'm come to visit you. And it's always you he punishes when he sees my face."

Ma closed her eyes, lying very still.

Padrick kept staring at her face, his own filled with a blade-like viciousness, the eyes unnaturally bright. "I'm never coming back here, so don't you be asking me again."

I saw Ma strain against his words, the instinct to protest, but then she let go of his hand and said with a weary voice, "I love you, my Paddie. I love you with all my heart."

"I love you too, Ma, I will call," he said and turned away.

Padrick and I walked back to the sitting room. I was still fighting against the rush of tears when I heard the deafening sound of shattered dishes. My brother had swept everything off the table with a calm and deadly swing. The quick savagery of Padrick's move was so shocking, that Da, who'd been placidly enjoying the meal, sat blinking stupidly into *my brother's face. Padrick said with a cold smile, "I think you've enjoyed enough, you bastard!" And walked out of the apartment.*

I forced myself to pull away from the past to meet Moira's tear-drenched face. Her expression mirrored my own: grief and shock and love.

"I'm so sorry, sweetheart, I'm sorry you have these memories and that they bring you so much grief." I drew in a harsh breath. "I would take it away, if I could. I know what it feels like… I think of Padrick and Ma so often, they've become a part of me." My throat felt dry, I found it hard to speak, but I needed to let it out. To make Moira hear what I had only lately come to understand. "I've come to think that these remembrances are part of a healing. Bitter medicine we need to swallow in order to mend. I realized that in remembering only the bad I had forgotten the good that Ma, Padrick, you and I shared. I let the nightmare take over my life…" I made an effort to smile into Moira's sad eyes. "But now, somehow, I feel as if I've just been given the go-ahead signal, to let go of all that misery…to remember what we did have, to hold on to the good."

I felt the strain ease out of her shoulders. Her voice gentle, she whispered haltingly, "I remember the good… Ma and you and Padrick. I remember Padrick…His stories and his laughter… I remember his voice… I remember thinking that he smelled of the sea and sunshine and all that was strong and healthy. And I remember that when he was with us he never forgot to let me know how proud he was of me…" She exhaled softly. "He was special, Padrick, wasn't he?"

"Yes."

Surprised to feel wetness, I brushed my cheek and stared down at Moira. The blue in Moira's good eye was so much like Padrick's.

"Yes. "I repeated. "He was something else." I smiled with relief, with gratitude. "It feels good to remember him together."

Then I got to my feet. "Let's get you back to your place."

I accompanied Moira on the train ride back to the Commons and walked her to the door. We were exhausted. But our silence was not uncomfortable; our steps, a familiar rhythm, echoed on the pavements of our childhood.

"Sleep tight," I said as I bent to kiss her cheek. "I'll call. I promise."

"Thank you, Nicki," she exhaled softly. With her marred side turned away, she looked beautiful in the moonlight. Young and innocent and whole.

CHAPTER 24

The sandy marsh below my feet
As I labor to come undone.
One more step I cry,
But the shoals wait nigh.

—Maddie Walker, *Against the Shoals*

Annika and I returned to court the next morning, the quiet between us loaded with unspoken words. Annika was withdrawn and I was edgy. I was about to unleash a hornet's nest and add Christopher Logan to my witness roster. I was thinking of Maddie's poems, and new doubts started to seep into my mind. Maddie and Logan's relationship felt like the shallows to me, the undertow looming like a dark threat.

Little did I expect that the first witness for the people would be Christopher Logan! Behind me, I felt, rather than heard, the stir in the courtroom, the gasp morphing into a wave as it spread throughout the hall. We were all watching Christopher Logan walk down the aisle with swift, confident strides. He cast a long, encouraging look at Maddie.

The Attorney General of the State of New York was sworn in and provided his credentials in a clear and thoughtful manner. Regardless of the air of indifference she was affecting, Maddie was tensely alert. I, too, sat still as I watched the innate grace and composure of the man in the box. Logan's quick smile in Maddie's direction disappeared the instant Ribisi approached the stand. He eyed the prosecutor in a courteous manner.

"Thank you for responding so quickly to our request, Mr. Logan. I know you're a busy man and promise not to keep you long," said Ribisi obsequiously.

Chris Logan inclined his head politely and replied, "I'm here to assist in any way I can."

Ribisi rolled his tongue under his upper lip as he paused thoughtfully. "During our investigation, Mr. Logan, it has come to our attention that you and the defendant have a long-standing relationship."

The courtroom was still, as we all watched the Attorney General choose his words carefully. "Yes, Maddie and I have been friends for quite some time," Logan answered smoothly.

"I believe you met in San Francisco?"

"Yes," The voice was amiable, but the expression guarded.

"And the relationship continued while she lived in Washington, D.C.?"

"Yes."

"And it continued after she married Senator Monnehan?"

"Yes."

"Could you expand on the nature of your friendship, Mr. Logan?"

"As I said earlier, Maddie and I are friends. I find Maddie to be singularly smart and well versed on a large number of topics. She is steadfast in her dedication to some of the causes I'm interested in." He paused briefly as he scanned the faces of the jurors. "It's true we come from dissimilar backgrounds; she – from the world of academia, me– from the discipline of law, but we found we shared a common passion for advocating change in the legal and social systems addressing the issues of domestic and child abuse. I find her commitment to these and other social blights commendable. I think Maddie is exceptional."

The jury sat enthralled by Logan's quiet and authoritative commendation of Maddie. In fact, even the spectators were hushed, as if Logan's testimony were being delivered within the sacred walls of a cathedral.

Ribisi nodded respectfully and approached the prosecution table to pick up a few densely-typed sheets of paper. "Mr. Logan, I have here a few of the dates that you and Mrs. Monnehan saw each other. Perhaps you could assist us with these?" I wondered if Ribisi repeated Logan's initial choice of words in an attempt to sound sardonic.

"I will if I can, but I would suggest you get in touch with my secretary, who has a record of all my scheduled meetings."

"Your secretary keeps a record of your personal meetings?" Ribisi asked with a note of disbelief.

Chris Logan's grin was easy. "Yes, she does. My days are too hectic and fraught with last minute scheduling for me to keep track of all my appointments." *Extremely prescient of a man set on a long political career.*

Ribisi decided to change tack. "We also have some of the locations of your rendezvous with Mrs. Monnehan."

"Objection." I stood up and locked eyes with Logan.

"On what grounds?" asked Ramsey.

"On the grounds that this line of questioning is irrelevant to the crime that Mrs. Monnehan is accused of."

Ribisi countered, "The people intend to show the relevance, Your Honor, if we may continue."

Ramsey contemplated Ribisi, then looked at Logan. "I will allow the question, but get to the point quickly, Counselor."

"Thank you, Your Honor."

Ramsey waved his hand and asked the court reporter to repeat the question.

Logan's smile flashed wide across his handsome face. "Is there a question in there, Counselor?"

Ribisi finally chucked caution to the wind and asked forcefully, "It seems that for the most part, you and Mrs. Monnehan preferred meeting in the dining rooms of certain hotels."

Logan turned serious. "I repeat, Counselor, is there a question somewhere?"

I had a sudden urge to grin; the wolf advancing on a sleepy house-cat had suddenly found himself confronting a leopard.

Ribisi smiled tentatively at his witness. "What I meant to say is that it is odd that you and Mrs. Monnehan met in these private places."

I rose to my feet. "Move to strike, Your Honor. Counselor is not asking but proffering personal biases."

Ramsey nodded his assent. "The jury will disregard Mr. Ribisi's last statement, as it expresses an opinion rather than poses a question."

Chastened but undeterred, Ribisi looked at Logan. "*Why* did you and Mrs. Monnehan meet in hotels?'

"For exactly the reason that you mentioned before, Mr. Ribisi. I find restaurants in hotels much more private, discreet, and less accessible to the press. I try to find some measure of privacy away from my otherwise public persona as Attorney General. My appearances are documented, photographed, and scrutinized daily by all sorts of journalists."

Logan smiled good-naturedly at the jury. "Even an Attorney General deserves to have an undocumented dinner with a friend, once in a while."

"These assignations, away from the intrusive eyes of the public and the media, were strictly to have private dinners with Mrs. Monnehan?"

"Objection!" I rose from my seat. "I move to strike the question, Your Honor. Mr. Ribisi knows better than to use suggestive terminology while questioning his own witness."

Ramsey scowled at Ribisi with irritation. "Counselor, you have been warned before. I caution you. One more infraction and I will move to strike Mr. Logan's testimony in its entirety!" Ramsey directed his eyes towards the jury box. "The jury will disregard Mr. Ribisi's last question and its suggestive language!"

I noticed the coolness with which Chris Logan followed the last exchange and thought I saw the ghost of a smile on his lips. He was a picture of casual curiosity; underneath that charm and air of bonhomie, the man was gifted with nerves of steel.

It was clear to me that if Ribisi was determined to get answers from Christopher Logan, he had to resort to plain language and risk antagonizing the Attorney General of the State of New York. I caught a crack in Ribisi's polished façade as he approached Chris Logan.

"Mr. Logan, far be it from us to disparage your or Mrs. Monnehan's character, but you must agree that given the circumstances of Mr. Monnehan's death, it behooves us to explore any and all of Mrs. Monnehan's relationships outside of her marriage?"

I saw Logan's jaw tighten. "As I have already stated, Maddie and I are old friends." Logan narrowed his eyes, but continued in the same smooth tone, "Unless you care to imply otherwise?"

Ribisi was quick to respond with an ingratiating smile. "We're not implying anything, Mr. Logan; we are just trying to establish a picture of Mrs. Monnehan's actions before the fatal shooting of her husband."

Logan regarded him for several seconds. "I'm sure you will find that Mrs. Monnehan is blameless in the tragic events that led to her husband's death. As for me, I can assure you, I have no doubt that Maddie will be exonerated of any wrongdoing in regard to the shooting."

Ribisi had to concede defeat. It was not for lack of trying that the prosecution had failed to uncover any evidence pointing to an affair between Maddie and Logan. Due in part to the failure of Mr. Prentiss to provide corroborative evidence, Ribisi had only conjectures that he could not prove. By now he must have realized that he had no hope, short of turning his superior into an enemy, of prying any incriminating information out of Chris Logan. And Ribisi was not about to commit political suicide. He had to let his witness go.

I, on the other hand, felt utter pleasure listening to Logan's resolute testimony. The loftiest legal voice in the state had assured the court of his faith in Maddie's innocence; I couldn't have asked for more.

"Again, I want to thank you for coming in, Mr. Logan. I have no further questions," said Ribisi curtly, this time without a smile.

"No questions at this time," I said, my voice a polished agate. "But we reserve the right to cross at a later date, Your Honor."

Logan glanced again at Maddie before he rose unhurriedly from his seat. She met his gaze and kept staring at the witness stand long after he had left the court.

We had just sidestepped another land-mine, but we were plagued by the same questions. I knew that if in his ongoing investigation, Ribisi found any proof of what he was so desperately trying to have Logan confirm, he would not hesitate to produce it in court. He would do so in order to validate his theory and incriminate Maddie, even if it meant bringing the wrath of Khan upon his head. I desperately needed to find my own answers.

Ribisi rose slowly to his feet. "Your Honor, the State calls Dr. Bruce Plinny."

Dr. Plinny was as thin as a broomstick. His bony shoulders jutted out from underneath his limp brown suit, which had seen better days. He marched down the aisle without looking at anyone, and when he settled his scrawny body into the box, he eyed Ribisi with a dour expression, giving the impression that he felt greatly put upon and expected to conclude his business post-haste.

"Dr. Plinny, can you please tell the court what you do?" asked Ribisi, plainly ignoring the supercilious expression of the witness.

"I run a forensic psychology practice. I am a board-certified psychologist and specialize in Post-Traumatic Stress Disorders and Abused Woman Syndrome.

"Dr. Plinny, you conducted an interview with the defendant, Maddie Monnehan, at my request, isn't that so?"

"Yes. I met with Mrs. Monnehan on the morning of March 14th, 2012 and conducted an unstructured interview, which allowed me to observe Mrs. Monnehan and assess her testimony in time for her grand jury hearing."

"What was the reason that you conducted this interview?"

Dr. Plinny looked down his long, thin nose and gazed blankly at Ribisi. "You asked me to evaluate Mrs. Monnehan's state of mind and assess the reliability of her testimony."

"Did Mrs. Monnehan respond willingly to your questions?"

"Yes. I assured her that the interview would naturally not touch upon any evidentiary details pertaining to the fatal shooting of her husband."

"You saw the defendant prior to her pre-trial hearing?"

"Yes." Dr. Plinny bared his teeth in a condescending grimace. "I saw her right after I met with her lawyer." A quick, expressionless glance in my direction.

"And what did you conclude at the end of the interview?"

"Mrs. Monnehan displayed none of the symptoms of trauma. She was alert and calm, and exhibited neither anxiety nor confusion. She exhibited a sense of self-possession and her answers revealed a sharp and keen mind."

"There was no display of grief or remorse?" asked Ribisi in a theatrical tone of incredulity.

"Objection!" I called. "Leading the witness."

"Sustained," snapped Ramsey.

"Let me rephrase: Did the defendant display any emotions during the interview?"

The witness hesitated a moment. "Well, she admitted that, as far as her emotions went, she felt quite numb; so, short of coercing Mrs. Monnehan and over-stepping the guidelines, I could not determine Mrs. Monnehan's emotional state."

"I see. But did Mrs. Monnehan manifest any symptoms that would indicate she had been or was experiencing a shutdown?"

"She was calm and manifested no symptoms of confusion or dis-association and helplessness in the face of what had occurred—all of which are signs of shock and can point to a dissociative fugue state."

I rose to my feet. "May we approach the bench?" Ramsey nod-ded and waved us over. Ribisi raised an eyebrow, but waited for me to speak. "Your Honor," I said, "with all due respect to Dr. Plinny, his testimony in regard to Mrs. Monnehan's emotional state is purely hypothetical. He knows that an unstructured and informal interview overlooks crucial areas of anyone's emotional and mental state. If he had indeed wanted to gauge my client's state of mind, he should have administered specific normed assessment tests, which other profes-sionals in the field of forensic psychology employ and depend on in their evaluations of their patients. Tests like the TSI, Trauma Symptom Inventory are specifically designed to gauge and evaluate the impact of a seminal event upon the psyche of a survivor. Because Dr. Plinny failed to do so, his testimony is within the realm of mere conjecture." I continued on smoothly, without allowing Ribisi to cut in, "To say that Mrs. Monnehan exhibited no symptoms of trauma without the benefit of the standardized tools of his profession renders his evaluation invalid. I respectfully submit that Dr. Plinny's testimony should be stricken from the record."

Ramsey looked at Ribisi. "Counselor?"

Ribisi cleared his throat. "Your Honor, the witness has evaluated thousands of patients over the course of twenty-three years; his 'con-jecture' in this case is based on vast experience and knowledge of the gamut of symptoms that a person suffering from Post-Traumatic Stress Disorder would exhibit."

Ramsey looked at Ribisi thoughtfully. "But did Dr. Plinny conduct any tests specific to the evaluation of trauma effects?"

"No, he did not, I—" Ribisi was interrupted by the judge's dismis-sive wave of a hand. "We will allow Dr. Plinny to answer questions about Mrs. Monnehan's general state of mind during his interview, but he will confine himself to the contents of the interview and not extrapolate into the realm of trauma."

"Thank you, Your Honor," we said in tandem.

Ramsey turned to the jury. "The jury will disregard Dr. Plinny's last answer regarding Mrs. Monnehan's emotional state."

Dr. Plinny looked at Ramsey with a peeved expression; not many, I thought, had dared contradict or question the doctor's opinions. I swallowed a small smile as I watched Ramsey give as good as he got. Two curmudgeons facing each other with mirrored sanctimony, except that here in court, Ramsey was holding the gavel.

Ribisi approached Dr. Plinny, slick as a seal. "Dr. Plinny, can you tell the court what essentially was the reason I asked you to interview Mrs. Monnehan?"

Eyeing him with the now-familiar hauteur, Dr. Plinny said tersely, "You stipulated that I should look at Mrs. Monnehan's report of the shooting, specifically the gap between the time of death and the time of her call for help, and that I should try to clarify what had actually transpired in that time frame."

"And what did you conclude?"

"She indicated there was a long-time lapse between the actual death of her husband and her 9-1-1 call. She was unable to recall or to furnish any details about the gap."

"And what, if anything, did you deduce from that?"

"Normally, patients who sustain memory loss as a result of a traumatic event tend to slowly regain their memory. Certain pieces of information will crop up after a few days, even after a few hours, especially as one recounts the seminal event. Memory loss due to trauma is typically transient. Not so in Mrs. Monnehan's case, who claimed she had not regained the lapsed memory.

"In your opinion, what does that mean, Doctor?"

The witness impaled Maddie with stern, accusatory eyes. "I do not believe that Mrs. Monnehan suffered from memory loss. I don't know why there was a gap of more than an hour between the time of Senator Monnehan's death and the time the police were informed. But I believe that Mrs. Monnehan was fully cognizant of the passage of time."

"Thank you, Dr. Plinny," said Ribisi.

An odd hush descended on the hall. I was watching the expressions on the faces of the jury, and I recognized Dr. Plinny as the one witness who, instead of chipping away at our proposed line of defense, was actually heaving a wrecking ball at it. I avoided looking at Maddie. Dr. Plinny had essentially called her a liar. I knew that I needed to do damage control—quick—and that, unfortunately, time wasn't on our side. It was Friday afternoon and it was unlikely that I could start my cross of Dr. Plinny. His testimony would, disastrously, hover in the minds of the jurors for three days like the stagnant odor of rancid meat. Ribisi had maneuvered us into a sinkhole. The judge, unsurprisingly, turned to me and in a tone I was well familiar with, instructed me to return Monday morning for my cross of Dr. Plinny.

Ramsey adjourned court for the day, admonishing the jury once again to abide by his guidelines over the weekend. They filed out, clearly tired and relieved to return to the normalcy of their lives. The courtroom was starting to clear as I dialed Oscar's number. After leaving a brief message to meet us at the office, I fought against the tide of humanity that swarmed around Maddie as we exited the courtroom. Maddie hailed a cab. I barely had time to suggest she call me in the morning before she yanked the door shut and the car took off. When Annika, Matthew, and I walked into the office, Oscar was already waiting for us. He acknowledged our grim expressions with a philosophical look, himself looking more than usually down in the mouth.

"You look tired," Annika observed.

Oscar smiled and answered, "Covered a few miles since yesterday." He turned a raised eyebrow in my direction.

I was unable to hide the weariness in my voice. "I wish I could say we have nothing to worry about, but the prosecution has been building a pretty solid case." Oscar nodded, and I felt the vise tighten inside my chest.

"Annika, why don't you, Matthew, and Dennis brainstorm awhile for Monday morning's cross while I chat with Oscar for a few moments? He looks dead on his feet."

They left, and Oscar and I sat facing each other at my desk. When he started to speak, his voice was low, but the words came out quickly and precisely, without hesitation or uncertainty. "I've been to Lewistown, Montana, where Maddie's mom had supposedly spent her last years. The people at the address Maddie gave us knew nothing about a doctor or a Hungarian woman with a child—not surprising since the house had changed hands eight times in the last twenty years! I finally hit gold: it seems that all Hungarian residents had been required to register at the town hall. I found documentation of a marriage between a Dr. Hume and Ilonka Erdos." Oscar passed a weary hand over his brow. "From there it was 'Do not pass Go' and straight on to Arco, Idaho. That's where Maddie and her mom spent the better part of three years. The town is small. As per the census of 2010, there were about 905 people living there in 417 households."

I nodded silently. I had the sinking feeling that somehow Oscar had stumbled on Maddie's nightmarish past.

"The mother was apparently very beautiful, and she had a small daughter, equally beautiful, by the name of Magdi."

"Maddie?"

"Yes. As far as I could ascertain, Ilonka Erdos met this widower, a doctor by the name of Herbert Hume, who was vacationing with his son someplace on Lake Michigan. He married her after a whirlwind romance, sold his parents' home in Lewistown, and brought his new wife and her daughter to Arco."

I felt my muscles tense; I sat still, hearing Maddie's words, as she spoke in that dead voice: "The good doctor… rotting my insides, day after day." Aware of Oscar's sharp look, I unclenched my jaw and said, "So, Magdi became Maddie; did the doctor also give her his name?"

"As far as the records show, she was enrolled in school as Magdi Erdos."

"Why Arco?" I asked.

"As you know, one third of the nation's potatoes are produced in Idaho, but are you aware that the state is also noted for its nuclear research and experimentation?"

"You're talking about the Idaho National Laboratory?" I asked, interested in where this was leading.

"The Idaho National Laboratory complex is located between Arco to the west and Idaho Falls. Apparently, the history of nuclear energy for peaceful application has principally been written in Idaho. Throughout its lifetime, there have been more than 50 one-of-a-kind nuclear reactors built by various organizations at the facility. The doctor was a member of the medical staff at the Idaho National Laboratory, tending to the needs of the scientists engaged in experimental and research projects. He also had a private practice on the two days he was away from the facility."

Oscar paused and took a long breath. "Some people are born with a black cloud over them; Ilonka Erdos Hume was one of those luckless souls. I don't know what reasons drove her to leave a husband and a home and immigrate to a country where she barely spoke the language and where she survived by taking the most menial jobs. But when she had apparently found some stability and security, she became sick with leukemia." Oscar stopped and I waited.

I sensed the slight resistance in his voice as he deliberately picked his words. "There was a fire, apparently a blaze so fierce it consumed the house in a matter of minutes. Maddie and the doctor's son were the only survivors."

"The doctor and his wife?"

"The wife, it seems, was already dead when the fire broke out. The doctor, who had accidentally set off some flammable canisters in his basement, perished in the inferno."

"What happened to Magdi/Maddie?"

"Social Services came and scooped her up, and she was never heard from again."

"She disappeared into the system?"

Oscar shook his head. "No. She was never in the system. She just vanished. Literally vanished into thin air." He gave me a thoughtful look, his voice edged with perplexity. "I can't find a single trace until the day she enrolled at Yale under the name of Madeline Walker. I think she started to reinvent herself when she left Arco. New name, new ID, and everything it included."

I conjured up the image of Maddie leaning over my bedside. Her words swirled in my mind. I knew where that desperate fourteen-year-old girl had disappeared to, at least for a while.

"How could a fourteen-year-old create a whole new persona, with a new name and new records? She went on to some great schools, has been teaching in some of the best! Christ, she won a Pulitzer!" I snapped.

Oscar shrugged and cleared his throat, his expression unreadable but his jaw was tight as if crunching down on something hard and unpleasant. "I guess she's got some ball-busting, iron-clad papers. Besides, I don't think anyone has ever thought to question her credentials."

"How much of this do you think the prosecution knows?" I asked.

"I don't think that Ribisi is concerned with the past; he is blinded by the open-and-shut case of the present," said Oscar tersely.

"If what you are suggesting is verifiable, we're sitting on a tinder box. Ribisi will expose Maddie's duplicity and fake identity."

Oscar sighed and stood up. "As I said, I don't think Ribisi is concerned with Maddie's past." He shrugged, picked up his pack, and left. The unuttered question hovered between us: *But are you?*

I experienced a sudden yearning for innocence, for a time when I wasn't aware of life's cruelties. I could well imagine the young girl Maddie had been when her mother died and understood the need to escape the past, to survive. All I could feel inside was compassion for a fourteen-year-old girl, and a sense of clarity that made everything else pale in comparison.

CHAPTER 25

'Come,' he said, 'come, we must see and act.
Devils or no devils, or all the devils at once, it matters not; we fight him all the same.

—Bram Stoker, Dracula

The prosecution's case, the police report, the collected evidence, the witness interviews, the background checks of anyone connected to the Monnehans, none of it had the impact of Dr. Plinny's testimony. As we walked into court on Monday morning, nothing was plainer than my need to lay to rest the anxiety that dogged my every step since that first interview with Maddie.

In my mind, I was going over the same ground ad nauseam. From the first, Maddie's account of the shooting was suspicious in my eyes. I knew that the time lapse in her narrative was critical and that it could sow seeds of doubt in the minds of the jurors. Initially, I did not buy the possibility of trauma-induced memory loss or a convenient fugue state to explain the hour-long delay before calling the police. But now, privy to the abuse in Maddie's past, I could conceive of how traumatized, how paralyzed she might have been. In light of her history of abuse, the delay made sense to me.

I could understand the fight-or-flight reaction that Maddie must have experienced when she confronted Monnehan in the dark.

Believing him to be a threat, a ghastly echo of the past, Maddie likely had acted reflexively because of her years of abuse. It must have been a huge effort to reach the semblance of control I had witnessed in her that night.

I had to demonstrate somehow that Maddie's inertia and memory loss could be viewed as normal defense mechanisms. But short of exposing her long history of abuse and its undeniable impact on her psyche, I had little to bring to the cross-examination of a witness whose entire career was based on exploring trauma-induced symptoms. If I posited that certain aspects of Maddie's childhood were germane to her reaction, I was compelled to reveal the horrors of her past and expose her assumed identity. A veritable catch-22.

Maddie was already at the defense table and turned to look at me as I walked down the aisle. She looked like a cool, tall glass of water. Let us dispense with the past! I thought savagely. *Such as we are made of, such we be!*

I looked at her and smiled gently. "Hello." I tried to infuse my voice with all that I could not express just then—my support, my love, my pledge to defend and protect her. I fought that cruel, cold voice that insisted I use any means at my disposal to exonerate her. It would be so easy to win the jury's sympathy and understanding if I could set Monnehan's death in the context of Maddie's past. But deep inside, I knew that I would cut my heart out before exposing Maddie's past to the voracious eyes of the world.

We watched as the jurors were led into the courtroom. There seemed to be a bounce in their steps and their eyes betrayed an air of eager expectation. Judge Ramsey sprang onto his podium, reinvigorated after the weekend. Dr. Plinny took his seat in the witness box and eyed me with the same condescension he'd shown the prosecutor.

Ramsey put on his rimless reading glasses and riffled through the papers on his desk. "Dr. Plinny, you will remember that you are still under oath."

"Good morning, Dr. Plinny." I rose to my feet. "I trust you had a restful weekend," I inquired agreeably.

"Yes, thank you."

I took comfort in the fact that I had incurred the same disfavor as Ramsey and Ribisi before me. We were all equal, and inferior, in the disdainful eye of the doctor.

"Mrs. Monnehan stated that she killed her husband because she feared for her life," I said.

Dr. Plinny barely moved his lips as he rejoined, "I am well aware of Mrs. Monnehan's statement. I was present at the grand jury hearing."

"Taking a life…Such an act surely would be horrifying and extremely shocking to any person?' I inquired.

"Yes, I am sure it would be," Dr. Plinny allowed.

"Such an event would constitute what you consider a trauma?"

"Yes."

"Your expertise, in fact, lies in the field of diagnosing and treating victims of trauma?"

"Yes. I have already testified to that effect." Dr. Plinny was clearly annoyed.

"Common among survivors of trauma is a heightened sense of anxiety and disconnectedness that can present as different coping mechanisms, isn't that so?"

"Yes."

"In fact, reading about Post-Traumatic Stress Disorder, or PTSD, I understand that although the disorder is normally associated with battle-scarred soldiers, some overwhelming life experiences can also trigger PTSD," I offered.

"Yes," Plinny answered, adding, "especially in cases where the event was unpredictable and beyond one's control."

"You interviewed Mrs. Monnehan before her hearing and sat in on the grand jury hearing in which she testified that she was indeed confronted by such an event, a danger she could not predict, correct?"

Dr. Plinny thought for a long time. "Yes, that was her testimony," he finally said.

"Would you agree, Doctor, that after the traumatic experience of facing what she considered mortal danger and then discovering that she had killed her own husband, Mrs. Monnehan's mind and body could be in shock?"

He answered slowly, "Yes, it is possible, but then I wasn't there to conduct an examination for the purpose of diagnosing PTSD. My interview with Mrs. Monnehan was conducted for the purpose of ascertaining whether Mrs. Monnehan's narrative and state of mind were congruent with the facts." *Ahh.* I felt the slow breath escape my lips.

From the corner of my eye, I noticed the stiffening of Bennett's shoulders. I was somewhat surprised that it was he rather than Ribisi who understood where I was heading.

I nodded easily, never breaking the even rhythm of our Q&A "Following such trauma, one can remain in psychological shock?" I proffered smoothly.

"Yes, it is possible," Dr. Plinny replied. These were, after all, matters of acknowledged medical and scientific research.

"I had the pleasure of reading some of your articles in the *Journal of Consulting and Clinical Psychology,*" I continued respectfully. "In one particular article, you mentioned that the patients' memories of what happened to them, and their feelings about it, were disconnected in the extreme. You cited some cases of women suffering from domestic abuse in which these victims had either forgotten some of the abuse or were unable to talk about it in a coherent manner." I paused to look inquiringly at the doctor.

The muscles in Plinny's face tightened. The man might have been vain as a peacock, but he was no fool. He was aware of the small, gentle proddings that would end in an inevitable conclusion that he, as a man of medicine, could not deny.

"Isn't it true, doctor, that some of your case studies show distinct avoidance techniques by patients when dealing with their traumatic experiences?"

"Yes," Plinny said tersely, his voice rising slightly, "but these were patients diagnosed and treated by me for PTSD."

"Yes," I agreed. "Mrs. Monnehan has not been offered such consideration or treatment, yet she has demonstrated memory loss, avoidance, and disconnectedness similar to the patients under your care."

The courtroom was still. For once, Dr. Plinny's look of certainty wavered. "I only saw Mrs. Monnehan three days after the trauma, and my interview had nothing to do with PTSD," Plinny offered sullenly.

"Precisely," I offered equably. "Had Mrs. Monnehan been seen by a professional right after the incident, isn't it possible that she might have been found to be suffering from acute shock?" I asked, my tone becoming stern as I continued. "Had she been thoroughly examined by a physician, she might have displayed such physical reactions as a pounding heart, rapid breathing, nausea, muscle tension, sweating— all responses associated with fear and helplessness and lumped together in the diagnosis of Acute Stress Disorder, or ASD."

Dr. Plinny remained silent, watching me as one watched an uncoiling cobra.

I decreased the distance between us, making sure Dr. Plinny read the grimness in my eyes. "Isn't it true, Doctor, that when the symptoms of ASD last more than a few days and become an ongoing problem, they are diagnosed as PTSD?"

Except for the slight pinking tips of his ears, Dr. Plinny appeared utterly impassive. "Yes, that is very often the case," he conceded.

I pointed at Maddie. "For all we know, Mrs. Monnehan has been and still is experiencing symptoms of Post-Traumatic Stress Disorder and consequently is unable to account accurately for the time that elapsed between her husband's death and her 911 call. Had you been consulted from the first, you would have been able to ascertain that, isn't that so?"

Dr. Plinny's voice lost its breezy confidence when he replied with a quiet "Yes."

"Thank you, Doctor, no further questions." I walked over to Maddie and sat down. It was only when the tension had left my shoulders and the constant band of pain across my chest had eased up, that I realized they had been there in the first place.

Ribisi was on the horns of dilemma: if he chose to redirect his witness, he would have to concede his own obvious negligence in failing to provide Maddie with immediate psychiatric and medical assistance. If, on the other hand, he let my cross stand, I'd made my point that Maddie's memory lapse was possible.

After a prolonged silence, Ramsey finally snapped at Ribisi, "Counselor? Redirect?"

Ribisi rose heavily to his feet and slowly announced, "We have no further questions at this time, Your Honor."

Judge Ramsey nodded brusquely and broke for lunch.

I was heading towards the door when I felt a tap on my shoulder and looked back to see Ribisi's flushed face. "Nick, can we talk?" he asked.

I regarded him thoughtfully. It seemed doubtful that he was about to propose negotiation; it was too early in the game and he had too much to lose. Yet he was obviously eager to talk.

"Sure," I answered, "why don't we retire to your office?"

I followed Paul Ribisi down the long corridor to his office. It was identical to the many work spaces in the district attorney's fiefdom. It lacked charm, warmth, and light. A long, ungainly desk dominated the room, strewn with files and folders.

"We have a new problem," said Ribisi with a sigh before he sat down. "Some new evidence has come to light."

"What new evidence, Paul? Isn't it a bit late for playing catch-up."

"This witness was unavailable till now; she has just turned up," said Ribisi.

"The time for discovery is long gone. It's a pretty shabby tactic, even for you, Paul," I said frostily.

"When court reconvenes later, I'm going to ask Ramsey to meet in his chambers. We'll let him decide." Ribisi looked at me with an odd expression. "I wanted to give you a heads-up."

"Decent of you," I responded sarcastically. "How about a name?"

"Edith Clayton."

"See you in court, then." I stood up and left without a parting glance.

Everyone was waiting for me in the conference room adjacent to the courtroom. Annika's smile died on her lips when she saw my face. Maddie, too, seemed aware of my unease but as usual remained inscrutable. It was Dennis leaning from behind, who broke the silence with an enthusiastic voice. "I thought you kicked ass!" he said, grinning broadly.

I drummed up a quick smile to meet his grin, but then announced quietly, "The prosecution has a new witness by the name of Edith Clayton. I have no idea who she is, but I have a suspicion that this is what Ribisi's been waiting for all along. He's going to present his arguments to the judge as soon as we reconvene."

Oscar broke the silence that greeted my words. "It's too late to find out what the prosecution has, but I had my suspicions all along. I've been watching the detectives on the case. Ribisi's man and Lachey's team have been loitering near the Monnehans' house for weeks now."

I narrowed my eyes. "An eyewitness, you think?"

Annika shook her head. "Witness to what?" she asked, careful not to look at Maddie directly.

"Any idea who Edith Clayton is and what she could possibly testify about, Maddie?" I heard the sharpness in my voice.

Maddie simply said, "I don't know anybody by that name and I have no idea what she's going to say."

No one stirred. "There's nothing to do, then, but start digging," I said tightly.

I watched as Oscar unfurled his long, bony legs and without a word left the room. I turned to Dennis. "Why don't you and Matthew go over the list of neighbors and anyone else we collected data on? If Oscar's and my suspicions prove right, it's a person from the neighborhood. I want that list vetted." Looking at my watch I added, "You have a little less than an hour to work miracles."

Dennis and Matthew left the room. Maddie, Annika, and I remained at the long empty table. Annika's voice was non-deferential and speculative. "Maddie, we never found any eyewitnesses to corroborate your movements that night." Her intelligent gaze met Maddie's cool, remote stare.

"You did speak with Thaddeus Constantine, the diner's owner," Maddie responded calmly. "Did he not confirm my presence at the diner shortly before closing that night?"

I appreciated her poise under fire. I suddenly wondered how accomplished a liar she had become over the years. Annika and I were trudging through what felt like a syrup of half-truths, but could find little traction in any possible explanation. Maddie confessed to killing Andrew Monnehan. There was no subterfuge in that, but underneath that admission I sensed something off.

Annika said, "Yes, we spoke to Mr. Constantine and he confirmed the time. As for the rest, Maddie, all we've got is your word." She paused. "Over the years, Nick and I…we've represented many clients. Frankly I'm at a loss…."

Annika met my gaze, heaved a sigh, and said, "It's obvious that the prosecution has some kind of stick to beat us with. Ribisi has wanted Murder One since day one. The question is, what do they know that we don't?"

"I cannot help you there," said Maddie lightly. The matter-of-factness of her tone prevented any further inquiries.

When we entered the court, Ribisi was already seated at the prosecution table, his back rigid and his features taut; he was waiting for Ramsey to make his appearance.

"All rise!" the bailiff's voice boomed out, and moments later, Judge Ramsey entered, took his place, waved his hand and with a gruff voice ordered, "Be seated!"

I watched Ribisi get to his feet and address the judge. "Your Honor, may we approach the bench?"

Ramsey grunted, threw a quizzical glance in my direction, and with a quick blur of his hand, motioned us to approach.

Ribisi said, "Your Honor, it has come to our attention that a witness we have been unable to locate until now has finally come forward."

Ramsey studied the prosecutor for a moment, then nodded decisively. "In my chambers, gentlemen. I will hear your arguments in private."

Once there, he hung up his gown and sat down heavily in his wide, worn-out leather chair. Ensconced in his sanctuary and without his gown, he looked younger and more at ease. He regarded Ribisi with an undisguised frown on his face. "Counselor, you better make a good case of it, otherwise I will find this maneuver a waste of my time and yours."

Ribisi nodded his head briskly. "Your Honor, I beg the indulgence of the court to allow this witness to testify. My office has known about this witness for some time now, but unfortunately, we've been unable to locate her. The witness's name is Edith Clayton; she is the housekeeper of Mr. and Mrs. Frankenthaler, residing at 396 East 75th Street. Mrs. Clayton is a witness of utmost importance, as she can furnish the court with new information she herself witnessed on the night of March 11th. On the morning of March 12th, Mrs. Clayton left for Jamaica, supposedly intending to return within a month, but extended her stay due to some complications with her father's care. She has just this past weekend returned to New York and offered to come forward and testify about what she saw the night before her departure."

"Your Honor," I said, "this is outrageous, and the prosecutor is well aware of that. We have had no knowledge of this purported witness; we have absolutely no idea what she is going to say, and have no means to establish the veracity of her testimony, which might well have been the prosecutor's intent."

I saw Ribisi bristle at my tone and my slur on his reputation. "Your Honor!" he rejoined with heat, "I assure you that the facts are exactly as I have presented them. Detective Lachey and his team have been canvassing and interviewing all the Monnehans' neighbors for weeks. Mrs. Frankenthaler of 396 East 75th Street had suggested that her vacationing housekeeper might have seen something on the night of the shooting, but despite our continuous attempts to find her, we failed. We ask that Your Honor allow the witness to come forth."

"I must protest again…" I said. "This is 'trial by ambush'!"

Ramsey raised his hand in a silencing motion. He sat deep in thought and eventually said, "I am well aware of the standard trial order and due process. However, as both counsels are also aware," he pierced the two of us with a glaring look, "the court is afforded broad discretion in deciding whether an undisclosed witness should be allowed to testify."

Ramsey stopped to collect his thoughts and continued. "Over the years, I have come to realize that to preclude the testimony of a witness who might provide essential information in a case is a drastic sanction, and that preclusion could be an abuse of discretion if the facts of the case do not warrant it. Furthermore, a trial judge may properly allow a previously undisclosed witness to testify if the presenting party has diligently attempted to find said witness and was unsuccessful."

Ramsey shifted his gaze to me. "I have known Mr. Ribisi for more than ten years, and none of his cases has shown a history of violating court orders. The late production of a witness, in and of itself, does not amount to bad faith or willful disobedience of court rules. Bad faith could be found if Mr. Ribisi had engaged in a pattern of dilatory behavior, but this argument presented to me by Mr. Ribisi is an isolated occurrence. Consequently, I am granting the State's request."

"For the record, Your Honor, I strongly object to this ruling," I said.

The frown hung on Ramsey's face, but his voice was unusually mild when he replied, "Duly noted, Mr. Conor. If you have any problems with my ruling, you may save your objections for your appeal."

Thus it was that Edith Clayton was led into the courtroom and was sworn in. Mrs. Clayton was a tall black woman of about sixty. She was big, not fat but solid and robust. Her face had a kindly, alert expression, and her brown eyes viewed the court with interest and a complete lack of intimidation.

"Please state your name for the record," requested Ribisi, still sitting at his table.

"Mrs. Edith Clayton," replied the witness, her words flowing with a strong Jamaican lilt.

"Where do you reside?"

"I live at 396 East 75 Street, where I work as a live-in housekeeper for five and a half days." She said to Ribisi with pride. "But I have my own place in East Orange, New Jersey, for the days I'm off." Edith Clayton's voice carried into the hall like a lush melody—drawn-out syllables and a fluid intonation.

Still seated, Ribisi regarded the witness and asked, "And how long have you been employed by the Frankenthalers?"

"For four years."

Ribisi sorted through some thick folders lying on the counselor's table, pulled out what looked like a discovery file, and eventually retrieved a large envelope. He raised his eyes to Ramsey. "May I, Your Honor?" he asked.

Ramsey nodded his assent and Ribisi got to his feet. He proceeded to set a photo in front of Mrs. Clayton, repeating the process with Mr. Grimaldi, the jury foreman; he then walked slowly to our side to deposit a large, glossy photograph of Senator Andrew Monnehan's smiling face.

Ribisi approached the witness stand and pointed at the photograph. "Mrs. Clayton, are you familiar with the man in the photograph?"

"Yea, mon, that is Mr. Monnehan."

"You have seen him before?"

The close-cropped head nodded animatedly as Mrs. Clayton said, "Yea, I see Mr. Monnehan on the street many times when I walk Lulu."

"Lulu?" asked Ribisi.

"She is a wee poodle, real friendly. I walk her in the morning and at night."

"You walk her regularly, then?"

Same vigorous nodding of her head. "She is like a clock. Seven-thirty in the morning and ten at night for a walk, a visit in the back yard at four."

"Every day?" asked Ribisi. "I wish I were that regular myself." He smiled as soft chuckles flitted across the courtroom. "So, March 11th, the night before you went on your vacation, you took Lulu for her usual walk?"

"Ten o'clock just like every evening."

"Where do you usually walk to?"

The big shoulders shrugged. "We usually walk to the corner of 75 Street and Fifth Avenue. Sometimes we go all the way to the Museum and back; sometimes we go to 72 Street and walk a little into the park, it's irie." Mrs. Clayton smiled.

I assumed *irie* to mean nice or pleasant, and although Ribisi himself seemed uncertain about the term, he was not about to break the flow and rhythm of his questioning. This was neither the time nor the place to learn patois.

"How long do you usually stay out?"

"Lulu and I, we stay for twenty minutes." Mrs. Clayton gave Ribisi another big smile. "If it snows or rains we come back sooner."

"March 11th this year was a nice dry night," offered Ribisi thoughtfully.

"Yea mon, it was nice for three days that week. I remember, 'cause I was upset the next morning when it began to rain just when I was leaving for the airport."

"Can you tell us what you saw on the night of March 11th?" asked Ribisi.

Mrs. Clayton's dark brown eyes were grave. "I saw Mr. Monnehan walk up the steps to his house." A deep furrow creased her forehead.

"What was Mr. Monnehan doing?"

The courtroom fell into a hushed silence. We were all staring at Mrs. Clayton. The air hummed with the unknown. I was keenly aware that Mrs. Clayton, in her soft, melodic cadences, was about to unleash something powerful and irrevocable into the room.

Edith Clayton shook her head from side to side. "He was talking over there with a woman beside him."

I was ready for almost anything but that. I felt the piercing shock of disbelief. Maddie, on the other hand, displayed no reaction at all. For a split second, I thought, astonishingly, that she was not the least surprised. The notion that she was not surprised dug the knife in deeper.

"You saw a woman?" repeated Ribisi, careful not to look in our direction.

"It's true, she was right there with him."

"Did you recognize the woman?" Ribisi asked, and that hollow feeling when your heart plummets unexpectedly hit me as I waited with helpless certainty for Edith Clayton to point her finger at Maddie.

Mrs. Clayton swiveled her entire body to stare Maddie in the face. "It was Mrs. Monnehan."

It was as if a sound wave hit the room, letting loose a force that ricocheted against the walls. As hard as Ramsey's gavel smacked his desk, he was unable to restore peace. I saw Maddie pick up a blank sheet of paper and with clear, strong strokes write and underline a single word: _NO._

NO what? I felt a violent urge to take Maddie by the shoulders and shake her.

"Are you sure?" repeated Ribisi forcefully.

Mrs. Clayton smiled sadly at Maddie. "Yea mon, I'm sure."

"Do you wear glasses, Mrs. Clayton?"

A wide flashing grin. "No sir, eyesight is 20/20."

Ribisi returned her grin with one of his own. "Around what time was it that you saw Mr. and Mrs. Monnehan at the front steps of their house?"

"We just came back, Lulu and me; we came around the bend and I saw them, probably fifteen-minute after ten or so," she answered.

"One last question, Mrs. Clayton: how is it that you have just now come to tell the court about this?"

Mrs. Clayton leveled her calm eyes on the judge and said, "I went to Kingston to visit with my family. I knew nothing about the killing before Mrs. Frankenthaler told me about it when I come back, so I called the police and told them what I saw."

"Thank you, Mrs. Clayton." Ribisi smiled, a cat licking the milk, the butter, and the cream off its whiskers. He did not add his familiar parting sequitur of how helpful the witness's testimony had been. It would have been overstating the obvious. Mrs. Clayton had single-handedly blown Maddie's case to smithereens. The room fell silent; there was a lack of sound so elemental it felt like the aftershock of a blast.

It seemed to me I was constantly setting my sights on moving targets. I had to remind myself that I got to where I was by sheer hard work and resourcefulness. I was good because I hated losing. Intellectual probity aside, my true asset was my ability to get back up after being knocked down. Like Gardner's Perry Mason, I often heard myself respond to the question "And what is it that you do, Mr. Conor?" with his famous one-liner, "I fight."

"Your Honor." I rose to my feet. "We request a recess to allow us time to prepare for a cross. We did not have Mrs. Clayton's name on the witness list and have been totally blindsided. We request the court's indulgence to give us a few days."

"One day, Mr. Conor. That should give you time enough. After all, the prosecution has had the same amount of time to meet with the witness."

"Thank you, Your Honor." I wondered if my sarcasm was noticeable.

Armed only with that single underlined *NO* as my directive, I picked up my papers and waited for my perplexed team to gather their thoughts and belongings.

Back at the office, Annika, Matthew, Dennis, Maddie, and I sat huddled around the large conference table. Oscar was already interviewing the Frankenthalers and probably waiting for Edith Clayton to return from court. But short of discovering that Mrs. Clayton was lying about her perfect eyesight or addle-brained enough to mix up times and dates, there was little he would be able to provide to discredit her testimony. I would have loved to use Cousin Vinnie's ploy of holding two fingers far enough away to establish a witness's failing eyesight, but Ribisi had preempted that option quite deftly, thank you very much.

"Have you ever spoken to Mrs. Clayton?" I asked Maddie.

"I never met the woman."

"But she knows you."

Annika offered quietly, "She must have seen Maddie's picture in magazines and such. Maybe even seen her in the neighborhood."

"You sure you've never bumped into her in the street?" I leveled a cool look at Maddie.

"I don't bump into people," answered Maddie calmly. "Besides, I would have remembered seeing her. She's quite distinctive. Wonderful features."

"And did you stand with your husband at the door of your house at 10:00 o'clock on the night of March 11th?"

"No."

"All right." I stood up. "Why don't all of you get into research mode, while I think of our next move. Maddie, if anything comes to mind, let me know. I'll call you tomorrow night."

I asked Kim to get me Dr. Borodian on the phone. Dr. Iliya Borodian was a cognitive psychologist we had occasionally called as an expert witness when we needed to confirm or debunk the testimony of witnesses who had participated in the judicial process known as eyewitness identification—more commonly known as a police lineup.

Dr. Borodian's thick Russian accent came on the line. "Nicholai, *Zdrvstvujte*. How many summers?

"*Zdrvstvujte,* Ilyusha. Yes, been busy."

I heard his hearty laugh. "Me, I only play."

"Listen, Iliya I need to pick your brain. You got a few minutes?"

"Fire."

"I have a witness who has identified my client as being someplace where she could not have been. I need to set the record straight. What can you suggest?"

"Well," his heavy voice filled the air, "who's your client?"

"Maddie Monnehan."

He breathed out loudly, "Oh, *malchik*, a beautiful lady."

"Yes."

There was long pause on the line, then Borodian chortled. "Many pictures in the newspapers."

"Yes."

"Is good. What we call in the business 'transference.'"

"Like in psychoanalysis?" I was intrigued.

"No. We're talking eyevitness identification." He barreled on. "Sometimes witnesses make a mistaken identification because they saw the person they identified on other occasions, like in magazines or newspapers."

"I see. Anything else?"

"The witness, what can you tell me about her?"

"She's a Jamaican woman of about—"

"Stop." Borodian's voice sounded like a whip. "Cross racial identification. Sometimes witnesses are not so accurate when they identify someone of a different race. I'm not saying this is the case, but you can maybe build on that."

I can certainly do that.

"Thanks, *priyatel,* I owe you."

"Wait, wait! You can ask 'quick glance' or 'long look'? Can make a difference."

Yeah. "This is something I can work with. Send me the bill."

"A bottle of Yamaskaya and you can call me anytime."

"You got it. Thanks."

I called Annika in and we sat down to work out a plan.

* * *

Two days later, all the pieces in place, I walked down the aisle and watched appreciatively the play of light on Maddie's yellow silk blouse.

"I hope this meets with your requirements?" said Maddie with a straight face.

"It's perfect." It was.

The court came to order; the jury was in its box, Ramsey was on his throne, and Edith Clayton was comfortably seated on the witness stand. I needed to establish Maddie's account and somehow debunk Mrs. Clayton's testimony. I made my face relax into a smile as I walked towards Edith Clayton. She smiled back at me, patently kind and caring. Her smile suggested that she knew that her testimony had stirred up a maelstrom of emotion in the court, but that she had little understanding of why.

"Mrs. Clayton, at ten o'clock at night, isn't it difficult to see things clearly?"

She raised her big hand toward me, the palm pinkish and callused. "there's always light in the street."

"Always?" I asked dubiously.

"Yea mon; also, Mr. Monnehan's house, it has them lights in the wall." Her brows lifted almost to her hairline in concentration, then, "Sconces, they be called. There are always sconces shining down the steps." *Fuck. A well-deserved slap on the wrist for asking an open-ended question.*

I moved on smoothly. "Do you remember how long the Senator and the woman stood by the door?"

"A few seconds, maybe."

"So you just glanced across the street and saw them?"

"Yea."

"A quick glance?"

"Objection. Leading," said Ribisi.

"Sustained."

"Did you have a long look at the Senator and the woman?"

"No, not long, but I knew them."

"You know Senator Monnehan and Mrs. Monnehan?"

"Yessir."

"You've seen them around?"

"More the Senator, not the missus so much."

"But you know Mrs. Monnehan, you've seen her on TV maybe?"

"I've seen pictures, sure."

Ramsey scowled at me. "Counselor, where are you going with this?"

"Your Honor, I'm just trying to establish the fact that Mrs. Monnehan's face was familiar to the witness."

Ribisi stood up "Your Honor, Counselor is trying to insinuate that Mrs. Clayton identified Madeline Monnehan because she looked familiar."

Ramsey waited. I hurried to respond with an easy smile. "Not at all Your Honor, just trying to verify facts."

"Get on with it then," ordered Ramsey.

"Mrs. Clayton, on the night in question, how far were you from Senator Monnehan's house?" I asked with a smile and as gentle a voice as I could muster.

"Like I told Mr. Ribisi, we were rounding the corner when I saw them."

"You were on the other side of street?"

I smiled at that familiar vigorous shaking of her head. "Yessir, we were across the street."

"You were almost at the end of the street then?"

"Well…" Mrs. Clayton creased her face in concentration. "Yea, a few feet away from the corner."

I turned towards the rear of the courtroom and walked about fifteen feet away from the witness. I turned to face her and asked, "Would you say you were as far as this from the Monnehans' house?"

Mrs. Clayton shook her head. "Nah, we were further."

I resumed my walk and reached the large, heavy entrance door and leaned against its polished surface. I raised my voice, aware of being the focus of every eye in the audience. "Were you this far away, Mrs. Clayton?"

"Nah, a little more, I think."

I opened the door and stepped into the bright corridor; it was at least fifteen feet long. I walked the length of it, and my voice louder still, I called out, "Do you think you were this far away, Mrs. Clayton?"

No shake of the head this time; Mrs. Clayton was frozen in concentration as she looked back at me down the length of the courtroom and into the corridor beyond. "Yea, I think it's about right," she said, her genial face serious and focused on mine.

"Do you see me well enough?" I asked.

The white teeth flashed at me from across the room. "Yea mon, I see you *irie.*" I took a piece of chalk out of my pocket and drew a straight line on the floor. The Judge was watching me, intrigued, and Ribisi, as much as he wanted to jump up with objections, had no leg to stand on. After all, his witness was complying beautifully with the facts he himself laid out.

I walked back toward my table. "Your Honor." I fixed my stare on Ramsey's face. *You cast this surprise witness in my path. You better play ball, or I'm moving for a mistrial, you miserable son of a bitch.* "Since we did not have the benefit of asking the witness to make her identification in the proper judicial process of a line-up, I would beg the court's indulgence in allowing my client to walk back to the chalk mark."

Ramsey's face was a study in equivocation, uncertainty, contemplation, and speculation. Reason finally won out. "I will allow it. Bailiff, please escort the defendant all the way to the back corridor. If I hear any sound in the courtroom," boomed Ramsey's voice, "I will clear the room! Is that understood!?"

Maddie's heels clicked softly against the floor as she walked towards the back of the room, long limbs, long muscles, an elegant, purposeful stride. When she finally reached the mark, she pivoted silently to look at Mrs. Clayton.

My eyes never left Ramsey's face. "Your Honor, at this point, I would like to present the witness with a sequential line-up." I saw the momentary hesitation on his face, but he regained his judicial, dignified expression as he waited for me to proceed.

"Mrs. Clayton," I said clearly, "I want you to look at Mrs. Monnehan and take a few minutes before you answer." We were all watching Maddie. She was standing still in the bright, well-lit hallway just beyond the open doors of the courtroom. Tall and straight—her chin up and her shoulders back.

"In a minute, I will ask another woman to take her place; all you need to do is look at that woman and compare."

Ribisi finally jumped to his feet. "Of all the harebrained, unprofessional, underhanded, scheming hocus-pocus and pyrotechnics…" He finally ran out of breath. I was actually worried for him. His face was red and he was gasping for air.

Ramsey, strangely unmoved by the prosecutor's outburst, regarded him coolly. "I assume you are objecting."

"Yes. Thank you, Your Honor." Ribisi was surreptitiously loosening his tie.

"On what grounds?" asked the judge.

"On the grounds that these shoddy tactics, designed to undermine the witness's credibility, have no legal basis."

"On the contrary, Your Honor," I intervened, "sequential line-ups have been an accepted legal device for the purposes of identification by law enforcement all over the United States. As a matter of fact, many law enforcement agencies have been advocating the supplanting of the traditional simultaneous lineup with—"

Judge Ramsey waved his hand. "I'm acquainted with the pros and cons of the debate. Go ahead, Mr. Conor, I'm curious to see how you proceed."

I approached Edith Clayton. "Mrs. Clayton, please take your time and look at the woman now standing in the hallway. Is *this* the woman you saw beside Senator Monnehan that night?" Time stood still as she regarded another pretty, tall blonde, wearing an identical outfit to Maddie's.

I could almost slice through the rapt attention that settled on the room.

Another pretty woman, same coloring as Maddie's, same clothes. Same question. Easy and slow. An orderly procession. There were five women in total, all pretty, all slim, all dark blond, and all wearing identical outfits. Five models Annika had sourced with promises of exorbitant fees.

I heard the rapid beating of my heart as I made myself face Mrs. Clayton. A moment that felt like a lifetime.

It was the slight shadow that crossed her face, a soft wondering look that made my heart lurch. When she finally spoke, her words trickled out cautious and slow. "My…I'm not so sure now…They all look alike …It could be one or the other…" Edith Clayton's voice trailed off in bewilderment. "I was sure till now, but I'm thinking maybe someone like Mrs. Monnean, maybe not her…I mean…"

My quiet exhale was drowned by the riotous sound exploding around us. I saw Ribisi's face lose its color. Even Ramsey seemed to have lost his perennial aplomb. Pens were scribbling furiously, the room echoed with the sound of rushing feet – journalists scampering towards the door, scurrying to send the newest sound bites into the air. Amid the cacophony of sound, I saw Ribisi jump to his feet and shout above the furious din, "Objection!"

Ramsey, in control once more, pounded the gavel. He directed his narrowed gaze first at me, then at the prosecution's table. "If order is not restored in the next minute, I'm going to make good on my warning!" Ramsey turned to the two uniformed men standing to his right and in a voice loud and firm ordered, "Officers, please be ready to escort the public out of the courtroom in…" He looked at his watch "…Forty-five seconds." When, on cue, the courtroom fell silent, Ramsey impaled me with a long, hard look. "Mr. Conor, please escort your client back to her seat. I'm not going to tolerate further disturbances that disrupt the orderly progress of this case, is that understood?"

"Yes, Your Honor," I said. I went out and walked Maddie back to her seat. Ribisi was still standing, his pallor replaced by splotches of red on his cheeks. "Your Honor," he said, "I am repeating my objection."

"On what grounds?" Ramsey seemed genuinely curious.

"Your Honor, defense counsel has used – for lack of a better word – theatrics to manipulate Mrs. Clayton and undermine her testimony!" Ribisi exclaimed with outrage.

Ramsey's elegant eyebrow lifted. "In what way, Counselor?"

I have rarely seen Ribisi at a loss for words, but the red turned deep crimson as he tried to form a coherent argument "I believe Mrs. Clayton was put on the spot. How could she tell under those circumstances? I believe that, Mr. Conor using that shoddy tactic, was intimidating the witness!"

"Do you believe," countered Ramsey, "that the witness's normal visual acuity in daylight from the distance she specified of fifty feet could be less sharp than her vision from the same distance on the night in question?"

Ribisi remained standing, unsure how to respond.

"Sit down, Mr. Ribisi. Mr. Conor, you may continue with your cross."

Edith Clayton offered me an apologetic, bashful smile. I returned her smile with a reassuring one of my own. "Mrs. Clayton, would you please take another look at Mrs. Monnehan, just to be sure?" Overconfidence was sometimes a killer, my gut instinct told me Mrs. Clayton's wrongful identification had to be reconfirmed. I didn't want to risk leaving a single doubt, now that Maddie's underlined NO! had been validated.

Mrs. Clayton shook her head, "I'm sorry, Mr. Conor. I was so sure before, but maybe…I was looking at Mr. Monnehan so I was thinking it was Mrs. Monnehan, but these women…" she pointed towards the back hallway. "they all look like Mrs. Monnehan. It could be one of them, maybe it was one of them that I saw."

The pragmatic pyrotechnics of a defense attorney! I smiled. "That's all right, Mrs. Clayton. I'm sorry to have put you in this position, but I had to make sure. I have no further questions, thank you."

Edith Clayton mulled over my statement. She had a simple dignity about her. "Thanks. Sorry."

After a long pause, Ribisi gave a short nod as if concluding an internal dialogue. "Thank you, Mrs. Clayton, I have no further questions at this time."

Mrs. Clayton looked at the judge. He said simply, "You may step down, Mrs. Clayton."

"Yessir," she said, and stepped down. Giving Ribisi a shy, timid smile, Mrs. Clayton walked out of the courtroom.

"The State rests, Your Honor." Ribisi's face remained expressionless as he moved to his table and sat down.

Ramsey said, "Mr. Conor, there will be a fifteen-minute break. Please be ready to call your first witness."

"Thank you, Your Honor."

I looked down at Maddie's folded hands. All I said was, "Maddie, you are next."

She lifted her eyes and answered simply, "Yes."

CHAPTER 26

A man so painfully in love is capable of self-torture
beyond belief.

—John Steinbeck, *East of Eden*

I studied my notes while fending off the temptation to feel prematurely confident or self-congratulatory. The case kept shifting. So far, I had calculated my every word and move, but I could not predict the next dip or twist of this rollercoaster ride.

By the time court reconvened, I was ready and so was Maddie. It was now five months since she had been arraigned and indicted in the shooting death of her husband, and she was finally about to tell her story. I called Maddie Monnehan to the stand. The talisman clasped deep inside – for me there was nothing else but this woman.

Maddie took the stand, her yellow blouse crisp against the black jacket, the ubiquitous coral brooch pinned once more at her throat. In my mind, I knew I had to work with the double-edged sword of her looks. Maddie played well into any fantasy. She personified that primal female image in the hearts of all red-blooded men, the unattainable goddess, yet I also needed to circumvent the human instinct toward envy and resentment, the urge to stigmatize and malign anyone who stood so far apart.

"Please state your name for the record." I wondered whether Maddie could detect beneath the cool of my words my ferocious need to take care of her.

"Madeline Monnehan." The voice, magnificent and full-blown, dark velvet with a hint of smoke.

"Mrs. Monnehan, can you please tell us in your own words what transpired on the night of March 11th of this year?" My tone equaled hers in composure.

She described arriving at the house, taking a bath, being startled by a noise, the looming intruder, the grip of shock and dread, the gun, and the final realization that she had just killed her husband. I let her speak, never once interrupting the steady flow, her voice starting softly, then becoming resolute and firm.

I was keenly aware of the jurors' rapt attention; they seemed to hang on her every word. Yet I could not tell if Maddie's testimony was a tad too smooth. Whether it was her words or the voice that seemed to captivate. My usual ability to predict the juror's reactions was blown to smithereens. I was too far gone to read anyone's biases, especially given my own.

"…So, I called the police and I waited." Maddie's voice finally died, and I heard the collective expulsion of held breaths from the jury box.

"Mrs. Monnehan," I asked, "when you placed the emergency call, what went through your mind?"

Maddie went still; I had thrown her a curve ball, a question that we had never discussed. Good, I thought. I watched her hesitate and for the first time, pick her words carefully. Unrehearsed and a little unsteady, she replied, "I don't know that I was thinking very clearly. I was totally numb. The only thought I had was that Andrew's dead body lay at my feet. I wanted to look away." I saw sympathetic looks on two of my favorite jurors, Mr. Murphy and Mrs. Wilkinson.

Maddie went on, her voice shaking slightly. "When I called, I think I wanted to scream, but I made myself speak quietly and coherently."

She paused and looked at the jurors as if to make sure they were following her train of thought. "I was looking at my hand… my fingers… they were shaking so badly."

I walked over to the defense table and picked up our copy of the audio disc. "Your Honor, we would like to submit this disc as Defense Exhibit A and ask the court's indulgence in letting the jury hear it."

Ramsey nodded and turned to the court reporter, "Sandy, please set it up."

We waited for a few minutes while Sandy hooked the CD player to a small speaker, slid the disc in, looked at the judge, and pushed the play button. I marveled at the surprisingly strong and rich sound produced by a black box smaller than my shoe. Maddie's voice, low and infused with emotion, filled the hall. I watched as Maddie inclined her head; she looked deep in thought. The courtroom was silent. Not a rustle of paper, no scratching of pens, no sound other than Maddie and the voice on the other end.

Maddie sounded helpless on the telephone, her words tumbling out breathless and full of pain. "Hello, hello, may I speak to someone about an accident?"

The operator's voice, calm and professional, answered, "Did you say you wanted to report an accident?"

"Yes, please, I need help!"

"This is Officer Miggs, who am I speaking with?"

"This is Maddie Monnehan. I have just shot my husband. I think he's dead."

"Can you tell me where you're calling from?" The officer's tone became slightly more urgent.

Maddie's voice sounded shaky and thin. "I'm calling from our residence. I just shot and killed my own husband. I thought he—"

Miggs interrupted firmly, "Mrs. Monnehan, can you please give me the exact address. I'm going to dispatch an ambulance and help to your home."

"Sorry?" Maddie sounded disoriented, "What?"

"Can you give me the exact address?"

"I'm calling from home."

"Yes. Can you tell me where that is?"

"Oh, yes. It's 11 East 75th Street." Maddie made a sound as if catching her breath. "Please hurry!"

"Just stay put, Mrs. Monnehan. Help is on the way."

The sound of Maddie's ragged breath filled the room, a stifled sob, and then a low-voiced "Thank you." And that was that.

I waited for the audio to end before I rose to my feet and approached Maddie.

"Mrs. Monnehan, we just listened to your call for help. When the officer interrupted you during the call, can you tell the court what you were about to say?"

She took a long breath. "I wanted to tell him that there had been an awful accident, that I mistook my husband for an intruder, and that I had killed him." Total silence. No hyperbole, no tears, nothing else, just the facts and the voice rigidly under control.

"When Detective Lachey asked you what happened, you said, and I quote, 'I shot my husband, I felt his pulse… I knew he was dead.'"

"Yes." Maddie's voice tamped to a whisper.

"Why did you not explain the circumstances in which you shot your husband?"

A long pause. "I was trying to hold unto myself … I was so cold… By then I had no other thought than to hold on to myself… "

"You were in shock?" I suggested gently.

"Objection, your honor." Ribisi said. "Counselor is putting words in his witness's mouth."

"Objection sustained. Move on counselor."

"Yes, Your Honor."

I did not look at the jurors, I knew they all saw Maddie eyes glistening with pain. I thought I felt a slight shift in the air, as if each member of the jury leaned forward and heard something else underneath Maddie's plain words.

"But when Detective Lachey asked you if you were all right, you assured him you were?" I asked with a voice devoid of any inflection, save for the simple need to comprehend.

Chin high, shoulders stiff, Maddie's voice sounded strained. "Asking for help is not something that comes easily to me."

I heard a low murmur ripple through the room—the buzz of, if not acceptance, then acknowledgment that Maddie's statement had a ring of truth.

Maddie felt it, too. Her eyes met mine, a sliver of a look so powerful it barreled into my heart. *I love you*, I wanted to whisper. It seemed I had waited my entire life for this woman. If I could paint, I would do a Klimt—dip this moment into the rapture of enamel and gold.

In the stillness, I heard my voice, clear and deliberate. "Thank you, Mrs. Monnehan."

I turned towards Ribisi. "Your witness."

I sat down and took a truly deep breath for the first time in days.

Ribisi did not smile at Maddie. He wore an edgy expression, his posture erect and tense, as if approaching an unpredictable predator. He seemed to appraise Maddie thoughtfully, as if searching for a vulnerable opening. Maddie, on the other hand, regarded him levelly, her features serene, her expression impassive.

Ribisi asked, "Mrs. Monnehan, you have just testified that you took the 7:25 train from the East Hampton train station, because you missed the 6:02. Is that correct?'

What struck me at that moment was the absolute stillness that came over Maddie. At the same time, I had the impression that Ribisi was proceeding against his better judgment.

Alongside the tension around his eyes, he seemed off-balance. There was something problematic for him in this line of questioning, and I wondered if the D.A. had used his crushing weight to somehow wedge Ribisi into a corner against his wishes.

Maddie's voice was cool, steely. "Yes."

I felt a chill. Again, like in our sit-down at the police station, I heard the undertones of a gifted liar.

"The 6:02 arrives at Penn Station at 8:42, while the 7:25 gets in at 10:05," said Ribisi casually.

"That's correct." Flat and even.

"It has just come to our attention that your driver's car was spotted not too far from the East Hampton train station at 5:56 p.m."

I shot to my feet. "Objection, move to strike."

Scowling, Ramsey asked, "On what grounds?"

"Your Honor, this is the first we've heard of this purported evidence."

"May we approach?" asked Ribisi calmly.

"What do you have to say to that, Mr. Ribisi?" Ramsey snapped over the sidebar. I now understood Ribisi's uneasiness. This attempt to include new evidence on the heels of Edith Clayton's surprise testimony was not going to incur any favors with the judge. Ribisi was well aware that his office had violated the rules of transparency. Choosing not to share discovery was not an unfamiliar tactic, but I'd never known Ribisi to stoop so low.

Ribisi started slowly and carefully. "Your Honor, in our investigation to corroborate the defendant's affidavit, we've been trying to establish the *true* facts of that night." I stared at Ribisi coldly and wondered if Ramsey caught the inflection. "It was imperative to confirm the timelines of both the victim and the defendant. We were successful in so far as Senator Monnehan's movements were concerned. We know when the Senator left D.C. and where he stopped on the way to dine. Mrs. Clayton testified that she saw him at the door of his house sometime around 10:00 to 10:15 that night. By the same token we needed to verify Mrs. Monnehan's account of her time. If she had indeed taken the 7:25 train, she would have arrived at the house after her husband;

however, if she had taken the 6:02 she would have been waiting for him inside." Ribisi looked at me, his lips twitched before he lowered his eyes. *Take your pick!* Either option was pointing to a lie.

"Your Honor," I said, the even spacing of my words accentuating the derision in my voice, "may we remind the prosecutor that no one has, as yet, established as fact that the Senator actually entered the premises at 10 or 10:15!" I saw Ribisi's eyes widen as he tried to speak, but I laid unto him cuttingly. "No. Mr. Ribisi has not proven to the court's satisfaction that the Senator actually entered the house. All we know is that Mrs. Clayton identified him standing at the door. In fact, Andrew Monnehan could have turned to leave for some other destination. For that matter, Andrew Monnehan might have entered his residence only to leave it again for reasons unbeknownst to us." I paused and smiled into Ribisi's perplexed face. "I can offer ten rational reasons to explain simply why Andrew Monnehan returned to his home at a later time. That said," I thinned my lips in displeasure, "it still does not mitigate the fact that Mr. Ribisi keeps popping up with new material that has not been previously shared with the defense."

"Motion to strike is granted!" Ramsey announced summarily. "Mr. Ribisi, the fact that I granted your motion to include the testimony of Mrs. Clayton does not mean that my brain has become addled with age. If you try again to present the court with discovery as yet undisclosed, we will cite you for contempt, if I do not actually choose to impose a harsher measure! The defense would certainly be within their rights to accuse the State of improprieties and present valid motions for dismissal of the case altogether. Is that clear?"

Duly chastised, Ribisi took the rap on his knuckles like a man, and replied stoically, "Yes, Your Honor." It occurred to me that Ribisi was only too aware that he was stepping into quicksand when he tried to introduce this new evidentiary statement. He knew all along that it was a foolish move. I could see his boss Bradley's big paws all over this.

Ramsey turned to Sandy, the court reporter. "Strike Mr. Ribisi's last words from the record!" He then commanded the jury, "You will disregard the last statement made by the prosecution."

Ribisi strode over to the counsel table, took a quick look at his notes and approached Maddie.

"Let us revisit the reasons for your hasty return to the city. You stated that you had to rush back in order to get your medication, is that correct?"

"Yes. As I have said, I am a diabetic and need to inject insulin every evening with my last meal. I had also left my papers in the city. It would have been a total waste of time if I could not work at the cottage." Not a single note of impatience or irritation at having to repeat herself, just a steely reserve.

"Why did you take the train, rather than ask your driver, Louis, to drive you back? Or better still, would he not have been able to retrieve the insulin and your writings from the house by himself?"

"Mr. Kertés was away, and Anthony, the gardener, is normally gone in the evening. It was just sheer luck that Anthony was able to pick me up when I arrived. Besides," Maddie added coolly, "I don't mind the train; in fact, I much prefer it to driving on the Long Island Expressway."

"You did not speak to your husband then, letting him know that you were on your way back?"

Maddie raised an eloquent eyebrow. "I did not speak with him."

"Actually, you did not talk to your husband that afternoon, or that evening?"

"No."

Ribisi continued, "Senator Monnehan never called you to let you know that his meeting had been cancelled and that he was coming home as well?"

"No."

"It seems that your relationship was founded on a very thin 'need to know' basis." There was a clear note of sarcasm in Ribisi's voice.

Maddie answered softly, "Marriage is an institution fraught with irony."

"Coming back to your marriage, were you aware that your husband was filing for divorce?"

"No, not at the time."

"To your knowledge, was there a reason that might have led to this decision on his part?"

Maddie answered with a flat and even tone, "I cannot second-guess Andrew's reasons for deciding to terminate the marriage." I heard the steel beneath that serene exterior. I wished I had told her to be less formidable. I needed her to seem more vulnerable and less self-assured, certainly less willful.

I noted the disapproving glance that Ms. Thackeray, the accountant, cast in Maddie's direction. She was one juror who took copious notes. Her sharp eyes missed little and her dislike of Maddie was clear from the start. She often nodded approvingly when Ribisi delivered salient points for his case. I thought that if I could thaw Ms. Thackeray's prejudices, I would be halfway to winning. It was clear to me that, so far, her clever mind, well-versed in detecting the minutest discrepancies in a balance sheet, was busily tabulating all the deficits in Maddie's narrative. Mrs. Thackeray's reactions were my litmus test, and so far, Maddie was not faring too well.

Ribisi said, "Mrs. McGuire testified that your husband intimated that the relationship between the two of you had cooled off."

Maddie sat in the witness box motionless, waiting.

Ribisi lifted a quizzical brow but there was still no reaction. I saw a hint of annoyance in his otherwise implacable expression. "Mr. O'Shaunessy testified that you expressed a desire to terminate the marriage as well—any particular reason?"

"I think I cited irreconcilable differences."

Ribisi let out a small sound that sounded like a snort, and motioned with an irritated flick of his hand. "Yes, we all heard what

Mr. O'Shaunessy said, but that term can cover a gamut of reasons. I'm asking if there was a specific one. After all, the marriage was only slightly over two years old."

"Perhaps people like us," Maddie replied, "people like Andrew and me, who were inured to a lifelong, solitary existence, find it difficult to live within the bounds of wedlock." Maddie shrugged indifferently. "All I know is that we grew apart, and the contrivances of marriage were no longer desirable for either one of us."

Ribisi looked at Maddie with an indecipherable expression as he asked dryly, "So, it was the institution of marriage that you found abhorrent?"

Maddie studied Ribisi coolly. "Look, Mr. Ribisi, I can certainly expound on my views on matrimony, but I find this line of questioning quite disingenuous. Is this how you are trying to discover if I tried to end my marriage by shooting my husband?"

Maddie's gaze, serene and slightly amused, met Ribisi's shocked expression. I'd never seen a witness slice through the craftiness of a hostile prosecutor to spell out so clearly and nonchalantly what he was so insidiously trying to convey.

For the second time that day, Ribisi was at a loss for words. Finally, with a voice thick with anger, he asked, "Mrs. Monnehan, did you not become tired of Senator Monnehan, rather than the institution of marriage? Did you not realize that there were greener pastures out there?" *To hell with caution, guile, and decorum!*

Maddie took her time before responding. She gave Ribisi a thin smile. "Mr. Ribisi, if you are intimating that I entered into an illicit affair with another man, I can assure you that I did not." The voice grew colder. "I did not have an extramarital affair. When I make a vow, I stand by it."

Ribisi went through the next series of questions with an air of determination. He was leading Maddie through her movements inside the house prior to the shooting. Maddie's responses were civil, but her eyes retained that opaque look that I knew so well. Every question asked was met and answered without equivocation or flourish. Every answer was then parsed and scrutinized, spawning a new question. I had to admire Ribisi's tenacity in the face of something he had never encountered before, beauty as unbending as steel.

"I understand that your husband had received some anonymous threatening calls?" Ribisi segued smoothly, undeterred.

"Yes."

"It prompted him to purchase a firearm, a 9mm Beretta?"

"Yes."

"You went to the shooting range to learn to handle the gun?"

Maddie nodded. "Yes, I did. Andrew insisted on my accompanying him."

"You became quite proficient in handling the Beretta, isn't that so?"

"Proficient? Hardly. I abhor guns. I barely touched the foul thing."

Ribisi looked at his notes. "According to the records of Shore Shot Pistol Range, you signed in on twelve different occasions. I would venture to say that you had acquired more than a basic familiarity with the handgun."

Maddie leaned back against her chair and crossed her legs. A picture of poise, she eyed Ribisi and admitted, "Yes, I did go to the shooting range, always at Andrew's insistence. If you check the records you might find that while I was present for the number of times you mentioned, I didn't actually participate in most of the practices." A slight pause as Maddie seemed deep in thought. "To my recollection, I fired the gun a total number of two times." The smooth and chilly voice warmed up as she smiled amenably into his face. "I'm sure that the facts are verifiable; your office will have no trouble confirming them."

I sat staring at Maddie; we had done our homework, and she was ready for Ribisi. On the table in front of me I had the signed statement from Bruce "Babba" Babchik, the manager of Shore Shot Pistol Range, attesting to the twelve dates on which the couple signed in at the front desk and when Maddie herself had used a firearm.

"But you can handle a gun?" persisted Ribisi.

"I can hold it and shoot; I don't know if I can actually hit a moving target," said Maddie.

Ribisi abandoned the issue of the gun and tackled the shooting itself. When the questioning reached the actual shooting, Maddie's impassivity disappeared, and her tone of voice softened. Her responses were filled with an unrestrained sadness.

"After you shot him, what did you do?"

"I don't know…" Maddie shut her eyes for a moment. "I think I went to the bathroom…" Her eyes flew open, as she stared blankly at Ribisi. "I felt I was going to be sick, so I went to the bathroom. I wanted to splash my face with cold water, but I saw that my hands were red with blood, so I washed them."

"How long was it before you called the police?"

"I don't know. I'm not sure. It could have been ten minutes or an hour."

"Would it surprise you to know that your husband died somewhere between 9:00 and 11:00 p.m. and that your call to the police was logged at 12:08 a.m.?"

"Objection, Your Honor!" I stood up. "With all due respect to Dr. Lippi, the exact hour of Senator Monnehan's death cannot be scientifically pinpointed. We have already elaborated on the variables in this case, and Dr. Lippi herself expanded on that. It would be inaccurate to summarily assume that Senator Monnehan died before 11:00 p.m."

Ramsey regarded me critically. "Mr. Conor, I seem to recall that according to the contents of the victim's stomach and the other variables that you just mentioned, Dr. Lippi stood firm on the question of time of death, it being between 9:00 to 11:00 p.m. Your objection is overruled." Ramsey's acerbic tone mellowed perceptibly, as he turned to Maddie. "Mrs. Monnehan, would you like the court reporter to reread Mr. Ribisi's last question to refresh your memory?"

Maddie, her exquisite features soft and guileless, smiled into Ramsey's face. "Thank you, Your Honor; it's not necessary, I remember the question." I saw the rush of something that looked like sympathy flit across Ramsey's stern features.

Maddie turned back to Ribisi and said quietly, "I was dazed. I did not have any sense of time." She looked at the jury and gave them a faint, helpless smile. "I think I was in shock. I was reeling from the horror of what I had done. There was a total sense of unreality." Another pause and another silent plea directed at the box. She was more than I had anticipated. I watched silently as she so cleverly engaged the jurors in her plight. I hoped she knew not to overdo it.

"It took you a very long time to call for help" Ribisi commented with something close to an accusatory tone. "How did you know he couldn't be helped?"

"I knew he was dead," Maddie said quietly. "I tried to feel his pulse."

"So after approximately an hour and probably more, you made up your mind to call 9-1-1?" Ribisi insisted, careful to keep his voice mild. It would not do to badger a witness who was trying so gallantly to hide her distress.

Maddie shook her head. "Made up my mind!?" She laughed, a small, mirthless sound. "I guess you would have to experience something as traumatic as this to understand that all my faculties had come to a standstill. I was numb, my mind as sluggish as if I were barely conscious. There was no process of rational thought. I don't even know if I was aware of my surroundings. Time stood still. When I finally came to, I called."

Ribisi waived his hand dismissively. "We'll let it go for the time being. Let's talk about where you were when you shot him straight in the heart."

"All right."

"You stated that you were in the doorway when you shot your husband."

"At the doorway or a step or two into the room," Maddie told him.

"Your bedroom is about thirteen feet by fifteen feet."

"I guess. I've never known the exact dimensions of any of the rooms in the house."

Ribisi smiled briskly. "We measured. Your bed is about nine feet away from the door."

"If you say so," answered Maddie calmly.

Ribisi looked at his notes again. "You testified that as soon as you saw the shadow advance upon you from the direction of the bed, you fired."

"Yes."

"How far were you from this 'unidentifiable' intruder?" Ribisi's voice dripped with irony.

Maddie seemed to consider her response and then said evenly, "I don't know how far or near he was at the time. You don't seem to understand how quickly things happened…the darkness, the terror… the threat; all of it happened in a blur, a fast-forward motion. It was over before I could process the horror of it. It's hard to judge distance when you are in the midst of a crisis and when your instincts for survival take over."

A long, deliberate pause. "How would you explain the gunpowder residue discovered around the bullet hole?" asked Ribisi.

There was a small crease between Maddie's brows. "I don't understand the question."

"As has been already expounded on, Mrs. Monnehan, gunpowder residue is found only when the victim is shot at close range. Much closer than you claim to have been standing at the time of the shooting."

Maddie looked thoughtful for a moment; she seemed to contemplate the question with genuine puzzlement. "Are you saying that the man advanced faster than I thought he did?"

I had to suppress a smile. Maddie was doing so well, puncturing little holes in the prosecution's suppositions.

Ribisi was not about to yield. "That is one explanation, I suppose." He made sure his skepticism was apparent to all. "Another would be that you came into the room and stood much closer to the victim. In fact, our contention is that you were so close to him as to easily identify the apparent assailant as your husband."

Maddie listened motionless and poised. When she answered, her voice was level. "I cannot explain the powder marks except to repeat what I have already told you. I did not walk into the room more than a step or two. All I can surmise is that when the intruder…I mean, when, who I took for an intruder at the time, advanced towards me, he must have done so with swift strides. You have to remember that the entire house was pitch black. I cannot say how far we were from one another. Believe me, if I could have discerned anything, it was only the fact that someone was about to kill me in my own house!" *King, Bishop, and Knight! Checkmate!*

Ribisi's grim face relaxed into a sardonic smile. "Mrs. Monnehan, it is our contention that whether you discovered your husband's intention to divorce you and thus deprive you of a lifestyle you had grown accustomed to, or you were prompted by other motives unknown to us, you killed your husband deliberately. I can assure you we will find out the truth before these proceedings come to an end."

"Objection," I called out impassively. "The process of a cross is not a platform for long-winded conjectures."

Ramsey frowned. "Sustained. Mr. Ribisi, please confine your questioning to actual questions!"

"Sorry, Your Honor."

I was convinced that Maddie was fully aware of the depth of Ribisi's animosity. Looking simultaneously haughty and vulnerable, and in a voice tired and resigned, she said slowly, "I understand that you have a job to do, Mr. Ribisi, but all I can do is tell you how the events of that night unfolded. I have told you the truth, the whole truth, and nothing but the truth."

Paul Ribisi glared at Maddie, then turned on his heels and announced, "No more questions for this witness at this time. Reserve the right to recall."

The silence in the courtroom grew noticeable. I rose slowly to my feet, knowing I should leave well enough alone, but needing to dispel the hovering cloud of suspicion. I asked, "Mrs. Monnehan, did you take the 7:25 train from East Hampton?"

"Yes. I did."

"Because you missed the 6:02?"

"Yes."

"The train arrived at Penn Station at 10:05?"

"Yes."

"What did you do then?"

"I took a cab to the Upper East Side."

"To your home?"

"Yes."

"Did you go directly to the house?"

"No, I first went to the diner on 75th Street and Madison."

I let the silence roll. "3 Guys Restaurant?"

"Yes."

I saw Bennett scanning Maddie's affidavit to the State. There was no mention of the sugar-free muffin.

"Did you notice the time?'

"It was about 10:15 or so; there was hardly any traffic heading uptown."

"What did you do then?"

"I spoke to Thaddeus, the owner, for a few minutes. I bought a sugar-free muffin, then walked around the corner to my home."

"Was the alarm on when you entered the house?"

"Yes."

"Was anyone in the house?"

"No. As I have told you and Mr. Ribisi, there was no one. I was alone."

You had to love the easy ebb and flow, the even rhythm of our voices. The jurors followed the exchange: heads swiveling back and fro, eyes tracking the bouncing ball. It was a heady feeling, this harmony between Maddie and me. Neither of us betrayed the slightest emotion—just a strict, vigorous, fact-finding exchange.

"You didn't expect anybody to be there?"

"No, as I explained, I came home, took a bath and went to bed. Shortly after, I heard a noise, realized I had not reset the alarm, and went downstairs. Not seeing anything amiss, I armed the system and went back upstairs."

"That's when you saw the shadow in your bedroom?"

"Yes."

"And you feared for your life?"

"Yes."

"You fired the gun in self-defense?"

A long silence as Maddie lowered her head; she raised her eyes laden with unshed tears and said quietly, "Yes."

"Thank you, Mrs. Monnehan." I let out a long steadying breath.

Court was adjourned.

As the room started to empty out, we remained sitting as was our custom. "Maddie," I said quietly, "Oscar came back from Arco yesterday."

A quick probing glance, a slight shadow of resignation. "You want me to come with you to the office." It was not a question.

"Yes."

Maddie inclined her head. "All right."

I walked her into my office and closed the door, careful not to touch her. By tacit agreement we had stayed away from each other since the trial began, and I knew that the smallest touch would unleash a tidal wave that would be impossible to stop.

"Please sit," I said quietly.

I watched her sit, back straight and hands folded neatly in her lap.

She closed her eyes wearily for an instant, then she said, "Go ahead." Her face revealed nothing but a ferocious courage. No one had ever faced me so openly and valiantly.

I started by recapping Oscar's account of his investigation—Dr. Herbert Hume marrying Ilonka Erdos, the move to Arco, her mother's terminal illness, the fire, and finally her disappearance. "It was determined at the time that the fire was accidental. The police discovered two dead bodies, burned to a crisp. The young daughter of Mrs. Hume was turned over to Social Services and subsequently disappeared into the system without a trace." I grew quiet.

Maddie's eyelids shut against the burning anger. She didn't raise her voice, but the sound of it made my jaws clench. "Mother married Dr. Hume when I was ten." A bitter smile crossed her face. "The good doctor... The good doctor, he was very well-respected in our community." I heard the suppressed emotion in Maddie's voice. "You have to remember that, other than a select few, most residents worked in the potato industry. Very few had more than a high school education. Dr. Hume's background, urbanity, and profession were enough to set him apart and above his patients. I always thought that his eagerness to help his fellow men stemmed from his own sense of superiority."

There was a long silence. "He kidnapped my childhood," she said. My heart pounded against my chest.

"For nearly two endless years, I had been praying for someone to come and save me. Creating a landscape of my own, imagining a world where I was free. I didn't know it then, but that was the fountainhead for any of my future writing." Maddie's voice fell.

"Then your mother died..." I said so softly it was the merest breath of a sound.

"Yes, my mama died, and then there was the fire," she whispered. Suddenly her voice grew stronger and harsher, "Mama died, and I was finally free. I let them take me away, and I slipped out the first instant that the ever-so-kind, well-intentioned social worker left me alone." Maddie finally stopped talking, and we sat in silence.

"You were just a child then…" My voice sounded strange to my ears.

Maddie looked at me with unfeigned indifference. "No, not for a long time, Nick."

"You started running then?"

"Yes."

"Since you were fourteen…?"

"Yes."

"You reinvented yourself." I swallowed against the parchment in my mouth.

"Yes."

I hadn't turned on the lights in the room and in the fading light, Maddie's eyes held something close to a question as she contemplated my face.

I thought of Maddie's book, the poetry of the dislocated, the alienated, and the forgotten. Her words painted an intimate journey through hell. I had always likened it in my mind to Marquez's spiritual odyssey, but unlike his writings, Maddie's poems were bereft of any redemptive tokens of hope and love.

I said softly, "The past is done with. It's dead and buried, Maddie. We're here now, together…you and I. Against the odds…you and me. I want you to remember that."

Save for a widening of her eyes, Maddie hadn't moved. I didn't touch her, I didn't need to. My words were more binding than any embrace, the room a hush of hope.

All at once I was seeing the long journey which had led me to this juncture. I was thinking of all that had preceded this day: my shitty childhood, the blows that marked me at an early age and the decisive moment when my path, as derailed as it had suddenly seemed, righted itself towards a new purpose. I smiled at the memory of myself

– an ardent youth whose application to law school was more of a Hail Mary than any sober recitation of merit. I thought that even after years of practicing law, I would not change a word of it. Unbeknownst to Maddie, it was precisely that application that defined me and the reason for fighting my fight. Her fight.

The words danced in my head:

For as long as I remember I knew I would join the police force. My brother was a cop. To me he was a hero. He exuded conviction and hope, smarts and confidence. I knew that if I followed in his footsteps, I would be doing right. I had the forms all filled out, my application perfected. I was ready for my destiny – then my brother died. He was murdered. My light of conviction dying with him.

I learned then of the inherent vulnerability of police work, the built-in inadequacies of the law in the hands of law enforcement officers. I witnessed first-hand the cruelty and brutality of violent men and the frustrating processes that enabled culprits to go free. The solution? I decided then that I was in dire need of legal education. I had a simple goal: to pursue the law as a means to vanquish all that is wrong or evil in man. I believed then and I believe now in the intimate link between morality and the law. In becoming an advocate and a prosecutor, I hoped to be engaged in a process that reflected my values, as well as invested me with the power to affect change.

My purpose in the world was to champion justice and to ultimately find self-fulfillment and redemption. Justice is and will always be the fulcrum of all that I worked for. By pursuing criminal law, I believe that I will embark on what my brother has always deemed to be a "life worth living".

CHAPTER 27

Do not go gentle into that good night.
Rage, rage against the dying of the light.

—Dylan Thomas," *Do Not Go Gentle into the Night"*

I was ready for my last witness of the day. For two days I had presented the jury with character witnesses who testified to Maddie's integrity, compassion, and unstinting commitment, whether to her professional career or to various domestic violence support groups. Bobby Hershing, her publisher, testified to Maddie's loyalty as a client and friend. Jonathan Amiel, an English professor at UC Berkeley and a former colleague of Maddie's, testified about her depth of knowledge and brilliant mind. "She was a great addition to our English Department. We were sorry to lose her." He said with a respectful nod towards Maddie.

The Vice President of Safe Harbor talked about Maddie's allegiance to the organization and its various shelters throughout the five boroughs of New York City. He spoke about her generous contributions and her unfailing support. "Mrs. Monnehan was been passionate in her efforts to provide a safe haven for children and teens affected by violence and abuse."

I regarded my last witness with curiosity. Thaddeus Constantine was a sixth-generation Greek. Two hundred years of a certifiable lineage was nothing to scoff at and he carried his heritage proudly as he walked into court to take the stand. Tall and muscular, he had the aquiline nose, the swarthy complexion, and the black eyes I associated with his ancestors. Constantine gave me a wide grin as he swore to tell the truth, the whole truth, and nothing but the truth.

"Mr. Constantine, can you tell us what you do for a living?" I asked.

"My brother Costa and I own a restaurant on Madison and 75th Street," he responded in an unabashedly proud voice.

"Are you acquainted with Mrs. Monnehan?"

He grinned again. "Yes. I know Mrs. Monnehan. She is sitting right there beside the lady lawyer."

I smiled. "How do you know Mrs. Monnehan?"

"My sister-in-law is a baker; she bakes for the restaurant these sugar-free muffins." Another flash of teeth. "They are wonderful! No aftertaste! Mrs. Monnehan has been buying our muffins ever since she moved to the city."

"On the night of March 11th, do you remember selling the last muffin to Mrs. Monnehan?"

"Yes."

Ribisi rose hurriedly to his feet. "Objection, Your Honor. Are we seriously asked to believe that the witness can accurately recall the sale of his last muffin on a date more than five months ago? I can't remember what I had for breakfast yesterday!"

Before Ramsey had a chance to address the issue, Thaddeus Constantine waved an expressive hand. "I can explain!" he exclaimed before I could rise. I had to hide my appreciative smile; more witnesses like Mr. Constantine and defense arguments could well be dispensed with.

"Go ahead!" Ramsey said, glaring at him.

Undaunted, Constantine continued: "Six months ago my restaurant was broken into, and the cash register was emptied of a full week's earnings. The police came but we had no suspects."

"I fail to see the relevance, Mr. Constantine!" snapped Ramsey with a glowering look that could intimidate even the most stalwart witness.

"Well, you see, Your Honor, after the robbery, we decided to install a surveillance camera in the place. Once burned is bad luck, my grandma used to say, but twice burned is out-and-out stupidity."

I interrupted smoothly as I picked up a small USB. "The defense would like to submit Exhibit B, Your Honor. This video recording submitted by Mr. Constantine will validate his testimony."

Ramsey glowered at me as he allowed, "Go ahead!"

The court reporter connected the small device to the computer, and the screen came to life. We watched Maddie as she was talking to Thaddeus Constantine standing behind the counter. There was no sound, but Maddie was clearly reaching for the single muffin covered by a glass dome. She was wearing a camel-hair coat and looked tired, but her smile at Mr. Constantine was full of warmth. The camera then followed her movements as she paid, said her goodbyes, and walked out of the empty restaurant. The date stamp said 3.11.13, the time 10:38 p.m.

Thaddeus Constantine smiled benevolently at the judge. "You see, Judge, even if I had forgotten, I still have my digital memory. I check it every weekend, and I don't erase. Maybe that goddamn heartless bastard who robbed us will try again."

"No more questions," I said coolly.

Ribisi did not get up. "None here, Your Honor."

Ramsey studied Thaddeus Constantine with a bemused expression. "You may step down, Mr. Constantine." Was there a gleam of acknowledgment in Ramsey's eyes as he looked at me, Maddie's timeline was no longer hypothetical; this was incontrovertible physical evidence, impossible to deny.

Thaddeus Constantine walked out of the court, trailed by a long hush. It had been a long and productive day, so instead of returning to the office I begged off: Oscar had called and asked to meet at the

Chinese restaurant around the corner from my apartment. It took him twenty minutes to join me in the back.

"Hi." He gave me his lopsided grin, and I smiled in return.

"You look much better than the last time I last saw you," I said.

"A good night's sleep with the help of that amber ambrosia can do wonders after two days of not sleeping," Oscar rejoined tartly. "I've been busy, however," he added.

"Productively?" I asked.

He nodded. "Yeah, I think so. First, the prenuptial agreement."

"What about the prenup?"

He extracted a large manila envelope from his backpack. "I got a copy of the agreement that the Monnehans signed two days before they got hitched."

"We went through this already. Can you give me a quick run-down?"

Oscar took out some additional papers and handed them to me. "Our in-house accountant discovered some titillating new information; it was a pretty impressive estate.

"Yeah, he was doing well, the late Senator, and you have to remember this is just a rough estimate!" He paused briefly and leveled his gaze on mine. "Without the existence of a will, the widow would stand to inherit a pretty hefty amount."

"About three hundred fifty million dollars give or take, before taxes," He said slowly.

"The question is, to what extent was Maddie aware of her husband's net worth."

This time a full-blown grin spread across Oscar's long face. "That's the beauty of it, Nick. Ribisi would have a hell of a time trying to prove that Maddie knew anything about the extent of Monnehan's estate. The Senator was wily enough to keep his holdings spread out. There's no indication that anyone knew how disgustingly rich he was. Monnehan had actually employed two different accounting firms, somehow separating the income he got from his inheritance from his current investments and finances."

I digested the information and concluded that it stood to reason that after years of splendid bachelordom, Monnehan might well have found it difficult to share with Maddie any information about his finances. As far as I knew, Maddie was unaware of her husband's extensive holdings. And the same was probably true of O'Shaunessy.

Oscar braced his hands on his knees and continued, "I looked into Ribisi's evidence that you successfully quashed. His office gave me a hard time, but I managed to make a copy of this." Oscar pulled out another envelope from his bag. This one contained a 5x7 grainy black and white of a black SUV and a woman alighting from the passenger side. I could barely make out Anthony's blurred features, but Maddie's profile was clearly visible. She was leaning towards the open window talking to the driver, one elbow bent at the side of the car, the other holding a large shoulder bag. She was wearing a camel-hair coat, the ubiquitous coral brooch pinned to its lapel. I let my eyes linger on the photo. I could tell nothing from Maddie's expression. At the lower right side of the photograph in clear white print I could read "3.11.12 5:56 p.m."

I gave him an inquiring look.

"There are no surveillance cameras in the parking lot of the station, but there are numerous cameras posted in the vicinity," Oscar said. "This is a still taken from Fresno, a restaurant not too far from the railway station."

"How far?"

Oscar hiked his bony shoulders. "If she hurried, she could have made the 6:02 train."

"Why do you suppose she got off at the restaurant instead of directly at the station?" I asked, my eyes never leaving the picture.

"I dunno, perhaps there was traffic and she thought she could reach the station faster by foot. Perhaps it was intentional." Oscar paused,

"Plausible deniability, you know. No one could actually testify that she did enter the station on time, not even Anthony—not even me, for that matter."

Oscar saw something in my face that prompted him to add in a cautious voice, "I checked the rest of the film. This photo is the only one of the car and Maddie, the next shot pans into an empty lot. It's all guesswork, Nick." I felt an internal wince; Oscar rarely called me by name. It felt like an intimate gesture of support. "She might have gone into the restaurant, who knows? She might have had to use the restroom, or stopped to buy a sandwich. Even if she headed directly to the train, she might not have made it in time. I spoke to the conductor, no recollection of a solitary beautiful blonde. According to him the train was practically empty. No other witnesses that I could locate, but I'm still looking." Oscar's voice died, and we faced each other in silence.

My mind replayed the thousand images of Maddie, the tilt of her chin, the pure oval of her face, her eyes green and bottomless. The hard flash of desire, the jolt of yearning so powerful it turned to anguish. I looked away.

"All right," I said hoarsely, reaching for the glass of water and taking a long slug.

"Third item on my list," Oscar said. "I was unable to find any trace of Maddie between her disappearance from Arco and her enrollment in Yale's liberal arts program."

"All right," I said, eyeing Oscar expectantly.

"So, I followed the only leads I had: the two names on the recommendation forms." Oscar pulled out another sheet of paper. "Dr. Martin Linsky was the chairman of the English Department at Columbia University in 1992, when the requisite form was submitted on behalf of one Madeline Walker. He passed away twelve years ago."

"And the other?"

Oscar frowned. "The other is alive and well. You might have heard of her, Dr. Diana Sylvan."

"The host of 'Masterpieces in Focus'?"

"Yeah, that's the one."

"I watch that show sometimes. She spends the whole half-hour on a particular piece of art."

"She's the chairman of the Art History department at Columbia; hers was the second letter of recommendation."

"Two professors from the same school?" I said speculatively.

"Exactly. So I went to see this art history maven. She agreed to meet me without hesitation. Cordial, and slick as oil on water. A cold fish. She told me she knew very little about Maddie, except for the fact that in 1992 she was lecturing at New York University where Maddie attended a special program. Students entering their junior or senior year of high school could apply to take college-level courses for credit. Maddie was such a student, and since she was brilliant, she caught Dr. Sylvan's eye. She became her advisor. When I asked about Linsky, she admitted that she had asked her good friend to accept Maddie into one of his English poetry classes and the rest is history. Both professors were more than eager to have Maddie as an acolyte. A year later, Maddie applied to Yale, and on the strength of two glowing recommendations from these highly-respected scholars, she was accepted, at a very young age, to Yale's undergraduate program."

I took it all in. It was more than feasible, yet I felt Oscar's unease.

"What is it, Oscar?"

He sighed. "Remember when you asked me to look into Maddie's past acquisitions of artworks?"

"Yes."

"Diana Sylvan invited me up to her apartment on the West Side. I sneaked a peek into the living room. Two lithographs of Picasso hung on the wall."

"All right," I said, "What about them?"

"The two lithos belonged to a series auctioned five years ago at a London gallery. They were part of sixteen rare lithographs made by

Picasso as early as 1947. I don't have the final auction figures, but these prints were going for large sums of money, the prices ranging from 12,000 to 150,000 British pounds."

"So, the woman is solvent," I retorted.

"Those lithos, one titled Tête De Femme and the other Femme Assise et Dormeuse, were among Maddie's listed possessions. I can see that maybe one of the lithographs might be part of a trio depicting the same image, but the other one was a single unique image, and I know for a fact that when I last checked, it belonged to Maddie."

"She sold them to Ms. Sylvan," I proposed.

"Makes sense," Oscar concurred, "except that Ms. Sylvan denied having seen Maddie for the last ten years."

"An intermediary?"

"Perhaps, but I could find no records of any sales. And then why avoid mentioning it if we were specifically discussing Maddie?"

We stared at each.

Oscar said with a sour scowl, "Maybe Maddie's artwork found its way into Diana Sylvan's hands as a form of payment, or even as hush-money."

I stared at Oscar curiously. "Hush-money for what?"

"I bet ya Dr. Sylvan has no problem finding a master restorer. It would be a simple leap to procure some fucking bona-fide documentation for a young runaway. I'm liking Diana Sylvan for making Magdi Erdos Hume disappear and become Maddie Walker with stellar credentials."

"Okay." I said slowly, trying to wrap my head around Oscar's over-developed sixth sense.

Oscar grimaced, "Want me to pursue this?"

I found little merit in investigating Diana Sylvan; I had to concentrate on the issues at hand. "No," I said firmly and opened the menu.

"One last item." Oscar added.

I lifted my eyes wearily.

"I got in touch with Tim."

"Your poker buddy?"

"Yeah, his company, UGT, is focused on security technology, primarily to do with mobile protection," said Oscar.

"I remember."

"It seems that right before a phone dies, it sends a signal like an S.O.S. It's like it's saying 'I'm dead, this is where I rest.' In reality the signal tells the nearest cell tower that it's the last signal it will put out."

I nodded silently.

Oscar continued, "Tim's company uses the world's largest mobile data bank and cloud technology to protect the networks and their services, but they can place the newer devices in a radius of five miles from their last signal."

"Okay."

"I asked him to triangulate the location of Maddie's cell phone before it died. The last call she made was from her home, on March 11th. Her phone had not been charged when she left for Sag Harbor that day."

"So, she was telling the truth. She never got Monnehan's call."

Oscar's long finger tapped the table, before he met my eyes. "I asked Tim to access Maddie's call record. He came up with a few numbers for March 11th."

"Okay."

"She received three calls that day. None from her husband, one from Louis Kertés and two unlisted." A few seconds ticked by before he continued. "I asked Tim to track down the unlisted calls. It will take some time. I also asked him do a reverse phone lookup for Kertés."

Oscar's edginess finally caught up with me. I asked, "Get on with it, Oscar."

"Kertés received a call from Maddie's landline as soon as she arrived at the villa."

"Nothing odd about that. He's her driver after all, and she knew he had some family trouble."

Oscar nodded. "He received another call that night at 10:32 p.m."

"From Maddie?"

"An untraceable, Tim says probably from a payphone."

"And this is bothersome, why?"

Oscar shrugged, but there was nothing nonchalant about the gesture. Oscar was troubled. "I asked Kertés about that late call, nothing doing, no idea, no clue, no problem, wrong number probably, ya da, ya da, ya da. In the meantime, I found out Kertés bought a new phone and changed servers. Claims the old device broke."

"Coincidence?"

"I don't believe in coincidences." Oscar's voice was devoid of any emotion.

The minutes ticked by while we both mulled over the "things known, the things unknown and the door in-between."

I studied Oscar's brown eyes and heavy eyebrows. I liked this man and I trusted him. "I spoke to Maddie about the fire." I said.

The silence stretched for a moment. Oscar nodded, expressionless.

"I think the matter will not come up during the trial," I said carefully. "I was wondering if O'Shaunessy is somehow privy to Maddie's past."

Oscar lifted his gaze and nodded. "I'll look into it. There's that damned question of Maddie's will. O'Shaunessy was pretty reluctant to discuss it."

Oscar seemed lost in thought, and then picked up another envelope and pushed it across the table.

"You can put Chris Logan on the back burners, Nick."

Again, the use of my name.

I pulled out an eight by ten color photo. I was looking at the smiling faces of Christopher Logan and Giles Romney. Dimly lit by candlelight, there was no mistaking the linked hands and the open affection between the two men.

Oscar said, "It's been hard for the Attorney General of the State of New York to meet with someone he's truly interested in…"

I nodded slowly. "Maddie has been acting as a go-between?"

"Yes." Oscar smiled grimly. "She's been making it easy for the two men to meet. What better guise is there than a rendezvous between a beautiful woman and a prominent political figure?"

"It's the twenty-first century, for heaven's sake!" I muttered.

"Not if you're aiming for the sky," responded Oscar in a quiet voice. "He'll probably marry someone just to be on the safe side."

"Why would Maddie be willing to play a game that offers her nothing in return?"

"I was wondering the same thing, but it occurred to me that Maddie might have an understanding of Logan's circumstances. The man is trapped. I've always felt that Mrs. Monnehan's self-control betrays similar past experiences." Oscar smiled openly into my guarded eyes. "I think you should ask her. I'm pretty sure you'll find out that Mrs. Monnehan has a softer side."

I slid the photograph back into the envelope. "Who else knows about this?"

"Only you and I, for the time being. And Maddie, of course."

"He'll have to be pretty damn careful," I said.

"One does what one needs to." Oscar's response echoed my thoughts. One did indeed do what one had to. Whether to survive, or escape, or conform.

Silently I pushed the envelope back into Oscar's hand.

"I'll get rid of it," he said and tucked it out of sight.

CHAPTER 28

There is only one good. And that is to act according
to the dictates of one's conscience.

—Simone de Beauvoir, *All Men Are Mortal*

When I walked into court the next morning, Matthew, Annika
and Maddie were already at the defense table. I turned to Maddie,
my low voice devoid of any emotion and asked, "How much does
O'Shaunessy know?"

Eyes flickering with something akin to panic, she replied,
"O'Shaunessy?"

"What does he know?" There was no mistaking the controlled fury
in my tone.

"What do you mean?" She could barely form the words.

One look at Maddie's stricken expression and it was clear to me that
O'Shaunessy had known about her new identity from the start and
had been protecting her all this time. The reasons were, for the time
being, obscure, but damned if I wasn't about to tear the old geezer limb
from limb to uncover the answers. My voice trembled against the urge
to shout. "What does O'Shaunessy know about your past? Your true
identity. Your assumed name, the fake papers, the falsified credentials."

Maddie's expression softened for a moment. I ignored the quick tinge of pity. "I want to talk to you about O'Shaunessy later." I said coldly as I laid my briefcase on the table.

I was thinking of my conversation with Annika last night. It had been a long day and an even longer night. We were both punch-drunk with fatigue and exasperation. About to leave, Annika stopped, eyes darting inquisitively to my face. She knew I had been wrestling with something unspoken and dark. I was in the midst of sharing with her Oscar's discovery of the photograph of Maddie in front of Fresno's when she said, "Man to man?"

"What's on your mind?"

Annika said quietly, "I know you think I'm being a negative Nancy, but I, for one, don't want to be led down the garden path. I'd like Maddie to explain this."

"Me, too." I said. "We'll talk to Maddie tomorrow in court."

I recognized my own misgivings as Annika had broached hers. After all, I was way ahead of her. The notion that Maddie misled us about her movements the evening of the shooting had dug its talons deep into my head from the start. I saw contradictions in every picture I projected, but I fought hard to believe the truth of Maddie's claim of self-defense. What I imagined was a scenario in which Maddie, beset by ghosts of her past, stood facing her own husband's sexual aggression, and in a terror-filled moment defended herself from a new threat of abuse. But short of revealing Maddie's childhood traumas—which she had adamantly barred me from disclosing—I couldn't offer Annika or anyone else this explanation.

Now, in the light of day, sitting with Maddie and Annika, I had to lay to rest all the niggling doubts. I looked at the large clock on the opposite wall, it was approaching eight forty. Twenty minutes to resume what had become by now my line of defense. I was aware that Ribisi was primed to challenge my next witness, and I was expecting his motion for dismissal.

Ribisi rose to his feet as soon as Ramsey took his seat. "Your Honor," he started with a firm voice, "we realize that defense counsel has obtained a court order to compel the next witness to testify. We have submitted motions to suppress the testimony of the witness."

The judge looked down and scanned the papers on his desk. "I've examined and considered the various motions for dismissal, and I would like both counsels to approach the bench. The matter will not be heard in open court until it is resolved to my satisfaction."

"Your Honor," said Ribisi as soon as we reached the bench, "we ask the court to strike the name of Dr. Wildenstein off the witness list for the defense. His testimony is not only irrelevant, but will be defamatory and extremely offensive to the memory of Senator Monnehan."

River's brow lifted. "Mr. Conor?" he inquired.

"Your Honor, the testimony of Dr. Wildenstein is crucial and goes directly to the credibility of my client."

"I understand that Dr. Wildenstein is a Washington-based psychiatrist. I still do not understand how his testimony is relevant to Mrs. Monnehan's statement," said Ramsey.

"Dr. Wildenstein has been treating Andrew Monnehan for a variety of deep-seated emotional issues, besides his physical problem," I offered.

"That is precisely why the State put in a motion for dismissal!" interjected Ribisi hotly. "We fail to see the relevance of airing Senator Monnehan's so-called psychological difficulties in public. The man is dead, and whatever evidence Dr. Wildenstein will offer the court will only result in maligning the deceased and hurting the surviving family members."

Ramsey looked at me inquiringly.

"Your Honor," I responded coolly, "far be it from the defense to want to slander the victim, but the doctor's evidence will support Mrs. Monnehan's testimony by shedding light on the reasons for Senator Monnehan's startling appearance in their bedroom."

"We vehemently object, Your Honor! The defense is trying to muddy the waters and turn the jury's attention from the defendant to Senator Monnehan."

I stared at Ribisi hard and said bitingly, "Your Honor, Mr. Ribisi is well aware of the Brady Rule, which pursuant to Brady v. Maryland 373 U.S. 83 of 1963, states that irrespective of the good or bad faith of the prosecution, all information in possession of the prosecution has to be included in discovery. In the case of Dr. Wildenstein, the prosecution has, by omitting his name, flagrantly failed to do so."

"But Dr. Wildenstein has never been considered a viable witness!" retorted Ribisi. "His testimony is not germane to the charge of murder!"

"Yes," I answered with an acerbic tone. "But his testimony would prove favorable to our defense. The ruling in Giglio v. U.S. 405 U.S. 150 of 1972 made it clear that the Brady Rule applies to information that relates to the credibility of a witness, in this case, Mrs. Monnehan." I raised my voice. "Furthermore, if Mr. Ribisi is going to claim that the defense has not requested disclosure of discarded information, I will refer him to United States v. Agurs 427 U.S. 97 (1976) which indicates that the prosecution's duty to disclose any and all discovery, under Brady, does not require a specific request by the defense."

Ribisi's face turned red. "Are you accusing my office of trying to suppress evidence?"

"I'm saying that whoever interviewed Dr. Wildenstein on behalf of your office and vetted and discarded the information should have disclosed it to my office." The issue of prosecutorial suppression of exculpatory evidence lingered between us.

I turned to Ramsey. "Due diligence on our part has uncovered the relationship between Senator Monnehan and his therapist, Dr. Wildenstein, no thanks to the prosecution's good or bad faith. Your Honor, the sworn testimony of Dr. Wildenstein will attest to several behavioral fetishes that Senator Monnehan was displaying at the time of his death, one of which was the acting out of certain fantasies.

Dr. Wildenstein's testimony is paramount to the credibility of Mrs. Monnehan's testimony. The defense has also lined up two other witnesses who would corroborate Dr. Wildenstein's findings."

"We have filed objections with the court and submitted written motions to strike these witnesses off the witness list." Ribisi's tone was controlled once more.

"I shall rule about those objections after I hear the testimony of Dr. Wildenstein," announced Ramsey. "I will allow the doctor's testimony with specific caveats: he will not produce a full account of Senator Monnehan's private therapy. He will be allowed to testify strictly to issues that have relevance to Mrs. Monnehan's testimony. Mr. Conor, you are hereby forewarned that should I find that Dr. Wildenstein's testimony is nothing but an effort to slur the good name of the deceased, I will put a stop to the proceedings and strike it off the record. Is that understood?"

"Yes, Your Honor. Thank you." When I reached the defense table, I said, "The defense calls Dr. Craig Wildenstein."

Dr. Craig Wildenstein had a full head of barely-tamable hair—riotous masses of white, gray, and black curls. He wore a pair of tortoise-shell glasses, which seemed to perch precariously on the bridge of his long, thin nose. He was clean-shaven and fairly young, given his illustrious reputation and thriving practice. He walked down the aisle quickly and took the stand, looking at me guardedly.

I knew that Dr. Wildenstein was reluctant to testify and that he disapproved of his appearance in court—both of which he did not fail to communicate to me. He was extremely sensitive to issues of doctor-patient privilege and was disinclined to testify when I had first met with him. He was here by court order and pretty much against his will.

"Doctor, can you tell us how you knew Senator Monnehan?"

"I've been treating Andrew Monnehan for the past five and a half years." The doctor's voice was pleasant and his expression as genial as he could make it, but I knew he was wary of me and my forthcoming questions.

"What were you treating him for?" I asked politely, maintaining steady eye-contact with him so as not to glance at any Monnehan family members.

Dr. Wildenstein looked at the jury, utterly aware of the impact of his next words, and answered in a slow measured tone. "Senator Monnehan suffered from erectile dysfunction. This dysfunction evolved into a neurosis, which unfortunately had far-reaching consequences. I was treating the Senator for both his physical and psychological disorders."

In the hushed courtroom, Dr. Wildenstein's voice was the only sound.

"You were treating his physiological disorder with medication?" I asked.

"Yes."

"What kind of medication?"

"I subscribed sildenafil citrate in conjunction with an anti-depressant."

"Can you tell the court what sildenafil is indicated for?"

"It is sold as Viagra or Revatio and under various other brand names. It's a drug used to treat erectile dysfunction, as I am sure most everyone in this courtroom and in the country knows by now."

"Senator Monnehan came to you for psychotherapy because of his sexual dysfunction?"

"Yes."

"Can you describe to the court the course of the Senator's treatment with you?"

Dr. Wildenstein explained in a courteous manner the kind of neurosis that Andrew Monnehan developed after a bout with syphilis that had rendered him virtually impotent, but still left him with a strong sex drive. The fragile and inadequate erections that the deceased experienced had driven him to explore different sexual stimuli.

"Senator Monnehan equated his sense of self and his self-worth with his sexual vigor," the doctor said. "His sexual pathology was such that he was constantly in search of sexual stimulation. He was obsessed with his virility and went to extremes to recapture it."

"Could you give us some indication of the nature of Senator Monnehan's forays into regaining his lost vigor?" I asked.

"Objection, Your Honor!" Ribisi called out. "As we have already argued, the defense is trying to create a salacious picture of Andrew Monnehan's private life without showing any relevance to this case!"

"Your Honor, if I may? The next questions will make the relevance all too clear."

Ramsey narrowed his gaze. "I will allow it, but beware, Counselor."

"Thank you, Your Honor," I said. "I will try to be brief and to the point." I turned to Dr. Wildenstein. "Doctor, can you tell the court how Senator Monnehan's obsessive attempts to regain his virility manifested themselves?"

The courtroom went silent. I fully sympathized with Dr. Wildenstein's earlier reluctance; he knew that his testimony would probably become the lead headlines. The details of Monnehan's trysts and titillating peeks into the lives of his sexual partners would be disclosed by any pissant blogger. I shared the doctor's distaste, but had no regrets. His testimony was pivotal to Maddie's defense. If the good name of the deceased was going to be damaged, it was something I could neither avoid nor prevent.

The doctor seemed to choose his words carefully before answering. "For a long time, the only sexual stimulation Andrew Monnehan could achieve with women was to stage scenes of dominance in which the elements of surprise and danger figured preponderantly."

"So this type of disorder, which Senator Monnehan suffered from, manifested itself in seeking male dominance and requiring theatrical acting-out of certain scenarios?"

A longer hesitation this time. "Yes. Senator Monnehan had discovered that he could achieve potency and sexual gratification through playacting and staging fantasies of bondage and domination. However, in the last four years, I thought we'd made headway in our sessions. Since Senator Monnehan's election to the Senate and his subsequent nomination to the Committee on Finance, coupled with his recent nuptials, I felt that his view of his own self-worth had improved, diminishing the need to exert his virility artificially." Dr. Wildenstein sighed audibly, and a furrow appeared between his brows. "It was by no means a straight path to recovery; there were definitely relapses, but we had made strides…."

"Could a relapse explain the Senator's actions on the night of March 11th? Is it possible that the Senator tried to enact a scenario of an intruder/rapist to fit in with his fantasies?"

Ribisi rose to his feet. "Objection, Your Honor, argumentative."

Ramsey studied Dr. Wildenstein carefully, then said dryly, "I will allow. Objection overruled."

Dr. Wildenstein's voice had an edge. "Yes. The use of this fantasy scenario of intruder/rapist was part of the victim's sexual pathology."

I willed myself to ignore the quiet gasps of more than a hundred stunned spectators.

"Mrs. Monnehan testified that on March 11th of this year, she was confronted by a menacing intruder in her home, and fearing for her life, she fired in self-defense. Unfortunately, on the night in question, Senator Monnehan's playacting led to his death; he died pursuing a fantasy. Would you concur that such a scenario was a possibility?"

The doctor paused and regarded me somberly. "As I have already stated, Andrew Monnehan's feelings of inadequacy drove him to simulated fantasies. If indeed he mimicked an intruder in his own home, it was but a symptom of his fractured inner life. And it is my deepest regret that I was unable to help him resolve his emotional turmoil."

"Thank you, Doctor; we appreciate your coming in and testifying." I smiled respectfully.

Dr. Wildenstein merely nodded but said nothing.

Ribisi stood. "Just a few brief questions, Doctor."

Dr. Wildenstein nodded again.

"You testified that because of sexual dysfunction, Senator Monnehan developed certain emotional conditions, which had affected him adversely, namely in his relationships with women?"

"That is correct. The male-female relationship that Senator Monnehan was capable of maintaining changed inexorably as his ability to have intercourse deteriorated, but so had his attitude towards women."

"How so?" asked Ribisi.

The doctor answered slowly, "Senator Monnehan came to realize that he disliked women and viewed them as objects of threat to his dwindling self-image. His only recourse was to overcome his animosity and find release by intimidating and subjugating women to his will."

I saw a flash of anger in Maddie's otherwise shuttered face.

Ribisi nodded gravely. "Then how do you explain his courtship of Miss Maddie Walker and his subsequent marriage to her?" Ribisi turned on his heel to look at Maddie as twelve pairs of eyes followed his. "How would you explain, Doctor," asked Ribisi, "a marriage between this beautiful, vibrant woman and Andrew Monnehan, who, for all intents and purposes, could not establish a viable relationship with a woman?"

It suddenly occurred to me that Maddie had married Monnehan with full knowledge of his impotence—in fact, that was essentially the reason she had agreed to marry him in the first place. Secrets upon secrets, layered and tangled as deep as sea kelp, but impossible to traverse.

"Well…" The doctor grew pensive, "I think that at the time, Andrew Monnehan was injected with a new zest for life. As I mentioned earlier, he had made strides in recovering his sex drive and physiological vigor, and perhaps he felt that Miss Walker would be supportive in his recovery."

Ribisi took a moment to carefully form his next question. "Let me understand, Doctor. When Andrew Monnehan was embroiled in sexual scenarios of his making, he must have had consensual partners who participated willingly in these fantasies?"

Dr. Wildenstein was unhappy but responded with a laconic "Yes."

"The Senator had confided in you to that effect?"

"Yes."

Ribisi segued seamlessly to his next question. "Could the Senator's sexual pathology have remained an open secret between husband and wife?"

I was about to object, but the quick look the doctor cast in my direction made me hesitate. It had an odd quality of command.

A long, deliberate pause, then the quiet voice: "I have to admit that Senator Monnehan hardly spoke about his relationship with his wife. Any answer I would give at this point would be in the realm of conjecture only."

Ribisi smiled thinly. "I find it inconceivable that such a psychological disorder, such an obsession, in your words, could be kept hidden from one's spouse!"

Dr. Wildenstein said patiently, "If you're asking me whether it is possible to hide a deep psychological disorder from someone close to you, I would have to direct you to a long list of extremely capable psychopaths who led double lives with great facility."

Marriage is an institution fraught with irony. Maddie's words echoed in my head.

When Ribisi finally conceded defeat, I stood and asked, "Doctor, you are aware that Senator Monnehan commuted between New York and Washington?"

"Yes. In the last two years he traveled quite frequently between the two cities."

"Temporal and geographical factors allowed the Senator to pursue his sexual fetishes away from home, is that not so?"

The doctor nodded. "Yes, probably."

"Once he satisfied these compulsive needs, he could feasibly return home and lead a perfectly normal life?" I asked matter-of-factly.

"Yes. It would have been possible for him to lead a sort of double life."

"Mrs. Monnehan could have been totally in the dark, as far as his sexual forays were concerned?"

Dr. Wildenstein gave me a small smile. "It is entirely plausible that Mrs. Monnehan was unaware of her husband's neuroses."

"Thank you again, Doctor," I said and walked back to my seat.

Annika muttered softly, "The jury doesn't seem particularly fond of the deceased now; they will never go for pre-meditation!"

Judge Ramsey leaned forward and addressed the jury: "As today is Friday, court has a shorter session. We will forgo calling the next witness." He shot an impenetrable glance at Ribisi and turned to me directly. "Court will convene Monday morning at 8:30 a.m."

I turned to Maddie. She sat staring into space; her eyes had an odd look, intent and serious. She seemed entirely oblivious to anything around her.

CHAPTER 29

When the light hits the ripples
The ray, a fragile arrow, dies without a sound.

—Maddie Walker, *Against the Shoals*

Oscar called me at one in the morning. His voice sounded tinny, as if calling from the inside of a tunnel. He uncharacteristically apologized for calling so late, but said he thought I needed to get this information ASAP. He was going to leave it with the concierge. From Oscar's tone, I knew it was important, but before I could prod him for more, we were cut off. While I waited for him to call back, I tried to fall back to sleep, but he never called.

The rest of the night was spent wrestling fitfully with my thoughts. When I finally got out of bed, hollow-eyed and strung tight as a piano wire, I saw the first glimmers of light through the heavy drapery. I showered, shaved, and wondered if I could find a place open for breakfast at this ungodly hour. As I approached Ernesto's desk, I saw the large manila envelope tucked into my mail slot. I leaned over and took it, then retrieved my car from the garage. The streets were empty. I pulled over and opened the envelope. It contained a typed sheet of paper folded tightly around three photographs. The smaller photographs featured the Monnehans' Lexus, its plate readable through what seemed to be the photo lens of a toll-booth. Behind the wheel, Lou

Kertés's features were clearly visible. Oscar's typed memo was brief: "I've been tracking the car and driver since day one. The old geezer has been cagey from the start. Couldn't reconcile some dates and the whereabouts of the car, most importantly on March 11th. Apparently, he knew enough not to use the EZ Pass. I've finally traced his movements—modern technology is a bitch."

I put down the sheet of paper and looked at the large photograph. It was obviously taken with a zoom lens. I was looking at Maddie's face, but on second glance I realized it wasn't Maddie at all. It was as if Maddie had regressed in time, shedding decades. It was a picture of a young girl, her beautiful face adorned with golden hair, cut in a sleek pageboy.

Dr. Stringer's words were bouncing in my head: "There was a smudged unidentified partial...a hair shaft in the pillow." I heard the faint clink of metal as the penny dropped. The doctor's words ran through me. I looked at the strong cursive handwriting on the back. It was an address.

The queasiness never left entirely, but it was now coupled with a sense of fierce purpose as I put the car in gear and pointed it out of the city. Two hours after leaving New York City behind, I was driving through a different country: small clustered towns, clapboard houses, well-tended and fenced-in front lawns with glimpses of rural land beyond. I raced along Interstate 84, cutting through fields and meadows as the landscape around me changed. The housing thinned out and gave way to farmland. The topography was largely flat, the roads mostly straight. There was little traffic on a Saturday morning.

I pulled over to eat a bland breakfast, barely tasting the food, but the coffee was strong and hot and just what I needed. I passed fewer and fewer homes, a couple of gas stations, several large barns, and enclosed pastures where clusters of cows lay indolently in the early dawn. I was like a homing pigeon flying towards the secret that Maddie had been protecting all along.

The town sat right on I-84, and although the surrounding farm-land increased the sprawl geographically to a good 60 square miles, it had a small-town ambiance. I drove slowly, taking it all in, delaying the moment of coming face-to-face with something that would finally open the lock, and at the same time be irrevocable. I passed the traditional town square with its quaint park in the center. Some of the stone benches were already occupied by groups of women rocking baby carriages, enjoying the beauty of the early morning.

The Convent of the Sacred Heart was tucked away from the commercial center of the town. The small church was dwarfed by two long arms extending towards the back. I found parking near a sign that said "Administration" and walked up the steps into the dim hall of what was clearly an old and well-used building. I was greeted at the door by a nun, whose habit set off a face dominated by a pair of quiet, grey eyes and a thin unsmiling mouth.

"Reverend Mother Superior is expecting you," she whispered as she motioned for me to follow. My footsteps on the scrupulously polished marble floor echoed noisily. The place was eerily quiet, more suitable to a place of worship than to an institution for the developmental and educational needs of young adults.

My guide knocked on a heavy wooden door, waited an instant, then stepped aside to let me precede her into the room. She closed the door behind me. I stood facing the Mother Superior who was seated behind an almost bare elegant desk, its gleaming polish shining like wet glass. The single red folder in the center looked like an open wound.

"Please sit down, Mr. Conor," said Mother Superior. Her voice was utterly in command. She was well over seventy, and signs of patience, sorrow, and wisdom were etched in her face, like watermarks. She studied me warily, her large hands motionless atop the folder.

"Mr. Conor, I'm afraid you've made a long trip for nothing." She waved one white hand to stop my protest. "I know. You told me on the phone that you represent Maddie Monnehan, but I fail to see the reason for this visit."

I said nothing but took out the photograph and slid it across the desk.

The Reverend Mother looked without touching it, her face inscrutable.

"I'm here because I think that this"—I pointed to the picture lying between us— "is crucial to the defense of my client."

"Does Mrs. Monnehan know that you are here?" she asked calmly.

"No. I left very early, too early to call."

"Mr. Conor, this is a school, a boarding school to be exact, but it is also something else, and by the power vested in me it would be unprofessional and unconscionable to provide you with any information about any student."

"There is no teacher-student privilege that I'm aware of," I answered, my voice as even as hers.

She gave me a long, considered look. "I'm referring to doctor-patient privileges."

I sat in silence, perplexed and unsure how to proceed.

She took pity on me and smiled gently. "I realize that you or your associate did not have sufficient time to research our facilities. Let me give you some background. This place was founded fairly early in the 20th century and at first was strictly a convent. It was only in the fifties – with the resurgence of public and private interest in issues of mental health and the lack of schools for mentally challenged children – that the mission of the church changed. The abbey became an accredited institution for children whose disadvantaged families were unable to pay for their care. Today, it is a well-established diocesan school, housing more than 150 children with disabilities up to the age of eighteen. Then they are either turned over to the state institutions or returned to their families. It is also a strict, all-girls Catholic school, which is housed in a different wing."

I nodded slowly. "The girl in the picture has been living here…"

"Yes," she said gently.

Her hazel eyes studied me carefully. I saw the gradual, weary lines of resignation; she had made a decision. She did not care much for it, but apparently deemed it necessary.

Without prevaricating, she asked, "Mr. Conor, why is this picture important to you?"

Like great big bats, my thoughts whipped around in black swirls. There were so many answers, but in the end only one mattered. Only one was desperately right.

"I am defending Maddie Monnehan," I said. "I know she is innocent of murder, but circumstantial evidence, combined with her confession, make it almost impossible for me to protect her." I heard the involuntary break in my voice. "I love her, Reverend Mother, I need your help…"

We sat in silence so deep that all I could hear was the beating of my heart.

"Her name is Ivy," she finally said. "She's Maddie's daughter and has been in my care for the past twenty-three years. She suffers from a variety of debilitating deficiencies. As a baby, she experienced delays in physical growth, cerebral atrophy, and abnormal brain development. Later, she was diagnosed with ASD—autism spectrum disorder."

The shocks came quick and cruel, my heart slamming against my rib-cage.

Reverend Mother's voice became flat. "There are no clear indications as to why Maddie's baby was born this way. Research indicates that certain toxins can affect the health of an unborn child. Maddie confided to me that, while pregnant, she went through a grievous period, living in sometimes inhuman conditions. The fact remains that Maddie, at the age of fourteen, gave birth prematurely to an infant girl who required urgent medical and long-term care. I have an old school friend—we've kept in touch—and although she'd lambast me for it, I think she's deeply spiritual in her way." Reverend Mother smiled gently. "She brought Maddie to my doorstep."

As if hearing my unbidden thoughts, Mother Superior continued, "After the delivery we became concerned for the welfare of both mother and child. Maddie was recovering too slowly, almost reluctantly, and there was a feeling among the medical staff that we were losing her. She was but a wee child herself and seemed to wrestle with more than physical damage. It took a long time for Maddie to mend, but when she did," a smile flared around the creases of that worn face, rendering it young and vibrant, "it was a thing to behold."

I spoke into the silence. "She's strong." *So strong, even then.* I understood Maddie's resolve, her inherent need to barricade and deflect, to hold onto that overwhelming secret.

Mother Superior nodded. "Yes, whatever she was, she was that. It was apparent then that she was unable to let us in, but that she cared about the babe. She was, however, incapable of taking care of Ivy." Mother Superior rose from the desk and walked over to the window. I thought it was the closest to pacing she allowed herself. "After Maddie left with my friend, things seemed to settle into an arrangement in which we handled Ivy's care, and as things progressed from bad to worse, the decision to leave Ivy here was inevitable."

Another slight pause. She turned to face me, speaking softly into the room. "I had hoped when Maddie married, that she could finally have Ivy with her. That it was at last time for Maddie to quit moving around, to stop running and after such a long wait, be able to take care of her child."

I felt the silence stretch painfully between us.

Mother Superior turned once more and looked towards the squares of light streaming through the windows. She said, "I don't know how Ivy figures in your defense of Maddie, Mr. Conor, but I think Maddie deserves a break. If you think Ivy could provide some assistance, I will not stand in your way."

"Can I see her?"

"You would need to proceed very slowly and with care. It's not only her limited mental capabilities; Ivy tends to get highly agitated. When she gets emotional, she's not easily controlled. It takes a long time to settle her down."

I thought of the continuing custodial care for Ivy, which Maddie had to support secretly and alone. "All these years…" I said haltingly, "all these years Maddie has been alone with this…"

"Yes," Mother Superior responded, there was grief beneath that quiet tone. "All alone, all these years. Ivy is the only one I kept on beyond the usual enrollment period of the school. Maddie is one of the two outside faces that Ivy has grown accustomed to." She grew silent and studied me for a long moment. "I want you to know that Maddie loves Ivy deeply; there's nothing she wouldn't do for her."

I marveled at how smoothly all the pieces of the puzzle were starting to fit together. Maddie had done everything in her power to conceal her past while also taking care of Ivy, including marrying a man who could support them both comfortably.

"Mother Superior," I said quietly, "you knew Senator Monnehan?"

She nodded somberly. "I met him when Maddie first married him. She brought the Senator to meet Ivy, believing it was important to introduce him in an environment in which Ivy felt secure. At that time, she was thinking of taking Ivy to their home, so she thought gradual exposure to the Senator would help acclimate Ivy."

"But she did not. Maddie never took Ivy to New York." It was not a question.

"No. She never did. She visited much more often, and I think she kept promising to take Ivy out of school, but I always thought Maddie hoped Ivy would forget the promise."

"You met Andrew when he came with Maddie, but did the Senator ever visit on his own?"

"Sometimes."

Bells in my head started to chime ominously. "Did he ever take Ivy off the premises?"

"Sometimes. When weather permitted, he used to take her to the park. Ivy didn't seem to mind, so I saw little reason to object." She looked at me quizzically. "I saw nothing wrong with them spending some time together."

"No," I said with a note of reassurance that I was far from feeling. "On the day that Senator Monnehan died…" *Out of the sunlight and into the shadows.* "…he came to visit?"

I knew the answer before she replied. "Yes. He came that afternoon and took Ivy back to New York. He told me he wanted to surprise Maddie, and Ivy was happy. I made him wait while I called Maddie."

"But Maddie was unavailable," I said softly.

"Yes. Maddie did not pick up the phone, so I called Lou."

"You called Lou Kertés." Another tumbler falling into place.

"Yes. I kept them at school as long as I could, waiting for Maddie to call back. But eventually I had to let them go. He was, after all, Ivy's stepfather, and Ivy was practically skipping on her way to his car. I called Lou when they left. Lou was the other constant in Ivy's life."

"Was the Senator's driver waiting?"

Again, that small vertical crease. "No, the Senator himself was driving. I watched as Ivy took the passenger seat; she had such a wide grin on her face."

"Lou called you from the road?"

Frowning at me, she responded, "If you've spoken to Lou already, why are you asking me?"

I tried to summon my winning smile, but I knew what a pitiful attempt it had been. "Mother, please indulge me."

"Yes," she answered sternly. "Lou called from the road and asked me how much time had elapsed since the Senator and Ivy had left."

"Reverend Mother, have you been following the trial? You do know Senator Monnehan was shot that very night?"

Her voice was soft as she answered, "God rest his soul…A true tragedy. I pray for Maddie every day." There was a lifetime of pain and compassion in her expression.

I pressed on. "Lou never showed up that night, did he?"

"Oh, yes, he did," she replied.

For an instant I was startled, but then the last piece of the puzzle fell neatly into place. I said impassively, "Lou returned much later that night, bringing Ivy back with him."

"Yes, it was close to one a.m. when they showed up."

"What happened then?" I asked.

"Happened? Nothing. I put Ivy to bed. She was catatonic with fatigue, and although I invited Lou to stay the night, he declined and drove back to Long Island."

The unidentified overlay of another fingerprint on the gun, the second hair specimen, the misidentification of Maddie on the front steps. I was conscious of the accelerating beat of my heart and the need to inhale slowly.

"Mr. Conor!" Mother Superior said, "you don't look well! You're white as a sheet!" She rose and laid a large hand on my shoulder. It was oddly comforting.

When the silence became uncomfortable, I cleared my throat. "Thank you, I'm fine. I haven't been sleeping well, I'm afraid."

The hand lifted, and I felt a sudden child-like desire to reach for it again.

"Whatever else, I can see that you care very strongly for Maddie and Ivy," Mother Superior said softly.

There was nothing to say. I pushed my chair back. "I'd like to speak with Ivy, if that's all right with you."

She nodded slowly. "Why don't you walk over to the park? It should be quite lovely this time of year. I'll have Ivy brought to you there."

"Thank you." I smiled wearily. It occurred to me that I might not be up to conversing with Ivy.

I chose an empty bench overhung with leafy branches and waited. I turned around to see a little girl being escorted by an older woman. As they approached, I realized with shock that the slight figure was not a little girl—it was Maddie's twenty-three-year-old daughter, Ivy. It was hard to reconcile the body and face with what I knew to be the facts. She was certainly Maddie's daughter, but she had the blurred edges of someone unformed, amorphous. All lost potential, like a clump of raw, unmolded clay.

"Hello," smiled the woman and extended her hand. "I'm Gertrude and this" –she let go of the girl's hand – "this is Ivy."

I shook Gertrude's hand while my eyes were trained on Ivy. "Hi Ivy," I said softly. "I'm Nick Conor. I'm a friend of your mother's. I wanted to come and talk to you. Would you like to sit down?"

The tilt of her head sent a stab through my heart: the image of Maddie's face cut through me like a blade.

Gertrude smiled tenderly into Ivy's clouded expression. "It's all right, Honey. Why don't you sit next to Mr. Conor on this bench?" She patted the bench, and Ivy's eyes turned dutifully toward it as if noticing it for the first time. But Ivy didn't move.

Gertrude said gently, "I'll be close by, Honey, sitting right there." She pointed to a nearby bench, and Ivy followed the finger. Without a word, she sat down on the bench.

"Thank you, Gertrude," I said and sat next to Ivy, careful to stay as far away as the bench allowed.

Ivy lifted her face to gaze up at the sky. A slip of a girl, a child, really. A breathtakingly lovely child with Maddie's beautiful features. Except for her short, fair hair, she looked startlingly like her mother. She was staring blankly into space. I sat silently looking at her, her sun-dappled golden hair an almost iridescent silver-white. Ivy sat in some strange, unreachable universe, oblivious to me and my searching eyes. Her left leg dangled over the bent knee of her right; it was swinging rhythmically and incessantly as if the limb were independent of the torso. The light skittered across her face, but when she turned to stare at me, her resemblance to Maddie died. Ivy's eyes were as empty and flat as those of a porcelain doll. It was unnerving to look at this replica of Maddie, so achingly lovely, yet lacking the soul of the dazzling original.

"Can I talk with you for a few minutes?" I asked gingerly.

Ivy ducked her head and picked at the grass on the side of the bench. She put a blade between her lips and started to chew. I thought I was grossly ill-equipped to reach into that void. Just then an ice cream truck turned the corner, its gay music piercing the quiet garden.

"Would you like an ice cream cone?" I asked.

Ivy stopped chewing the blade of grass; there was a glint of something.

"What flavor do you like?" I asked with a faint smile.

She looked at me, puzzled, as if trying to recall an elusive memory.

"That's all right," I hastened to say. "I'll get you both vanilla and chocolate."

This was going to be harder than I had anticipated. I wondered how limited Ivy was. I was seized by such sadness that I was thankful for the few moments I had to wait at the ice cream truck.

When I returned, Ivy was still perched dutifully at the edge of the bench. She looked forlorn and lifeless. When I handed her the ice cream cone, her expression barely changed. She took it compliantly and started to lick the melting ice cream. Aside from the vacant look in those disturbingly windowless eyes, she was captivating. A girl on a park bench. I marveled again at Maddie's strength and capacity to bear pain—to be within arm's length of her child, never able to truly reach her.

"Do you like it?" I smiled tentatively into Ivy's blank eyes.

A ghost of a smile touched her pale lips.

"I bought you a bottle of water," I said and added, "Why don't I set it down till you feel like a drink?" Holding the bottle by its neck, I set it down carefully on the bench between us.

"Is it all right if I ask you a few questions?" I asked.

Ivy looked at me distractedly, her tiny pink tongue swirling nimbly around the cone.

"Is that all right, Ivy?" I asked. "Just a few questions about the time when Mr. Monnehan came to take you to New York."

Something took hold, a sudden awareness, as Ivy repeated, "New York…" in a small, dreamlike voice. The first sound Ivy had uttered in my presence. I felt the flush of gratitude and had the overwhelming desire to hug her to my chest. The chocolate was dripping down the corner of her pretty lips. I grabbed a napkin and said gently, "I'm going to wipe that little smear of chocolate, okay?"

She nodded stiffly, and I patted the corner of her mouth. Her eyes flew to mine and for one instant, I thought she truly saw me. Ivy spoke in a low, hesitant voice, "I like the chocolate better."

"Next time, I'll buy you a double chocolate cone." I grinned; we were communicating.

Afraid to lose her, I said hurriedly, "Do you remember when Andrew came to pick you up?"

Ivy nodded, intent on eating the crumbling cone, her tongue darting in and out and around the wafer.

"Do you remember when Andrew took you to your mother's place?"

"Andy," she whispered and looked forlornly at the last of the ice cream as it melted all over her fingers.

"Yes." I felt my heart skip, and I stayed very still. "Can you tell me anything you remember about that night?"

Ivy looked up. "He told me to call him Andy. He said it was all right. We were family."

After a very long pause, wading through shark-infested waters, I asked, "You went with Andy to see your mother?"

"Mama…" Ivy said in a voice like a sigh.

"Yes. To see Mama… Do you remember that night, Ivy?"

A shadow slid down her cheek. I laid my hand gently on hers. "What did Andy do, Ivy?" I prodded softly.

A slow, blank stare. I felt the tightness in my chest as I waited, desperate for Ivy not to lose the thin thread.

Ivy was licking her fingers absently, "Andy… He…came to the school and picked me up." The lower part of Ivy's face was smudged and sticky, but I was afraid to move. She became silent.

"Ivy?" I repeated, "Do you remember when Andy came to pick you up?"

Ivy took a deep breath "…He came…" She blinked fast and then looked down at her lap.

"So, he came to pick you up. Did he tell you why?"

A small frown. "He said Mama wanted me to come and visit… she was lonely."

Again, she grew quiet. I realized that she had to be prompted. Speaking freely seemed alien to her. She reached for the water bottle and waited for me to open it. She gripped the bottle with two hands and took several long gulps.

I shut my eyes, the acrid taste of revulsion hot against my tongue. I could not tell whether it was because of what I needed to ask next or because I didn't want to know the answer.

"And did you see Mama?" I asked.

Ivy swallowed hard before whispering, "Mama was angry." She repeated in a voice so forlorn and lost that for a moment I wanted to stop her. "Mama was angry…"

"Angry with you?"

A puppy-dog look full of hurt. "Mama …she did not like what Andy was doing…I was scared… I forget…" Ivy's voice died.

I reached over and touched her hand tentatively. I felt the quick little tremors as they coursed under my palm. Ivy lowered her eyes, her long eyelashes fanned against her smooth cheeks. She raised her palm as if to ward off something in the air. When she raised her eyes, I thought I saw panic blooming in her stare. I leaned over and whispered, "It's all right Ivy; we don't need to talk anymore. It's all right… Let's just sit here and enjoy the sun."

"Don't be a petulant little boy!" Those were Maddie's words to Monnehan the night before he died. I imagined Monnehan seething with impotent rage and thought I could envision the poison flowing in his veins. Monnehan had married a woman whose obdurate strength was more than he had bargained for. But Ivy was easy prey! Ivy, the weak, available duplicate, an easy victim for subjugation, for revenge.

From the beginning, suspecting that Maddie was guilty of something, I knew she was hiding a world of secrets. The answer stared me in the face, right there, sitting on a wooden park bench. My stomach dropped as I tried to imagine the scene: Maddie walking into a nightmare, so horribly familiar it must have pierced her heart. The shock of it, the enormity of what she was witnessing! The simultaneous instinct to protect her child, and at the same time, annihilate the ghost of her stepfather. I realized that in her desperation to protect Ivy, Maddie had created a fictitious timeline, fabricating a scenario of self-defense. And who was to say that it was not self-defense? Maddie was defending that pure, precious part of herself incapable of defending itself…

And then, despite the warmth of the day, I felt a chill as it occurred to me that there could be an alternate narrative. I recalled Mother Superior's words about Ivy's bouts of unruly agitation. Could Ivy have then, in a moment of sheer panic, lost control for an instant and committed an act of violence for which Maddie constructed a whole web of lies? Was Maddie taking full blame for an act by a woman-child who knew no better?

I opened my eyes to find Gertrude standing over me, her eyes politely quizzical. "I'll be taking Ivy back now, Mr. Conor. I believe Ivy has grown tired. She does tend to tire easily." She added kindly, "Be sure to come and visit Ivy again. She seems to like you."

I smiled at the woman and child, for I would always think of Ivy as such. "I believe I will," I said. Ivy had already averted her gaze, and at Gertrude's touch, clasped Gertrude's hand. Woman and girl turned their backs and left. I pulled out a large plastic bag and, careful not to touch the water bottle, inserted it into the bag.

Hours later, when I reached Sag Harbor, I took a deep breath and walked down the path to the cottage. Maddie was kneeling beside a bed of yellow roses. They were not all in full bloom yet, but the air hung heavy with their heady fragrance. Watching me approach, she straightened up, a slow languid movement, her eyes never leaving mine. We had learned, Maddie and I, to read each other's faces.

"Hi," she said softly. She laid the basket she'd been filling down at her feet. I looked at Maddie and then said quietly, "I went to see Ivy."

I caught a whiff of Maddie's scent. She was silent for a very long time, still holding one long-stemmed yellow rose in her hand. When Maddie finally spoke, her voice was low and halting. "After my mother died, I thought everything in me had died. All feelings shriveled. And then I found out I was carrying the seed of a monster inside me, and I thought I would go insane. I tried to kill the life inside of me. I threw myself down a flight of stairs. I swallowed pills, which made me sick for a week. I starved myself for days but it still lived! I was alone in the basement of an abandoned building when I stole a coat hanger and tried to kill it with metal inserted into my vagina so deep that I thought I would die."

Maddie smiled bitterly. "I almost did die. I wound up in a hospital; the squatters who found me dragged me to the street, scared witless by all that blood. When I was found, I was hemorrhaging so badly, I was told it was a miracle I survived. And when I was discharged, I was warned to come back for pre-natal tests. They had all assumed I was a foolish teenager in trouble, hiding the truth from her family. They cautioned me to return with parental guidance for my next visit." Maddie glanced blindly at the rose still clasped in her hand.

Her gaze turned inward, remote and unseeing, watching a memory. "The baby lived. I was fourteen years old when Ivy was born. Regardless of how she was conceived, when I looked down at that helpless, peach-fuzzed head, at that stubborn, fragile body, I let myself feel a love so intense it hurt."

Maddie hesitated for a moment. "Until I met you, Ivy was my only bridge to being functionally human, if human means having a heart." Maddie's voice fell. "I told you that I was incapable of love. That was untrue. I love Ivy very much." Maddie stopped and turned away, looking out over the sloping lawn and the trim flower beds, away from me and my probing eyes.

Until I met you. I wondered whether under the strain of coming clean for the first time in twenty-four years, Maddie knew what she had inadvertently let slip out.

I narrowed my eyes against a light too bright. "Does Leo know?"

Maddie said nothing, but I persisted, "Does Leo know? He's always been so protective."

The air reverberated with the silence between us. *Tell me, damn you! Trust me!*

"He knows about Ivy." She finally said in a soft voice. "He helped me set up a trust fund for her life-long care."

"How about the night of the 11th of March?"

"He knows what I told him. He believes what I told him about that night." Her shoulders drew back and her expression hardened. "I don't want Ivy to be called. I don't want her to be part of my defense."

"I need her to testify." I paused. "She was there that night."

Maddie's lips tightened. "I acted in self-defense. I was frightened, and I shot Andrew."

"No," I said softly. "You did everything with the intent of protecting Ivy." I saw Maddie's eyes widen with alarm. She knew we were past the fabricated version, but she remained silent and on guard.

"Did Ivy kill him?" I asked softly, knowing how improbable that would have been.

Maddie did not answer. I knew she would not.

"I'm going to call Ivy to testify Tuesday afternoon." My voice as implacable as Maddie's.

"I won't allow it." Maddie's voice was quiet and deadly.

I spoke with exaggerated patience. "Ivy is at the heart of this. She is the key to your acquittal."

"No!" insisted Maddie, and for the first time there was a quality of despair in her voice. "If you saw her, you know she is incapable of coherent thought processes, let alone a valid testimony!"

I fought the need to pull Maddie tight against me. Instead, with a voice as gentle as that used to coax a trapped deer, I tried to make myself heard. "Maddie, listen to me, I know what I'm doing. Trust me!"

She dropped the rose and walked away, leaving me by the side of the house in the clutches of the midday sun. I bent down and picked up the yellow rose.

I thought I understood now what O'Shaunessy was protecting. The "why" was easy to fathom. He must have felt instant kinship with Maddie: two parents struggling with the heartache of loving damaged children, never being able to fully understand the broken psyches of their offsprings. It was immaterial when and how Maddie had confided in O'Shaunessy; I understood her need to secure Ivy's future by turning to O'Shaunessy for help.

O'Shaunessy, I thought, had probably been taking care of all of Maddie's needs, like a father would, secretly and protectively, to safeguard his daughter's happiness.

CHAPTER 30

Like Venus I have to rise
Stripped of faith and bare to hope.

—Maddie Walker, *Against the Shoals*

"The defense calls Dr. Burton Morgan," I said. In the charged recesses of my mind, I was getting ready for the kill. Maddie's calm eyes scanned my face.

I turned around to look at the packed courtroom. I saw Oscar and Jim sitting close to the back door. Jim nodded curtly with a small smile. Oscar sat sphinxlike; he knew I was hurtling towards the end. The Monnehans – mother and three daughters and their spouses in attendance for the full three weeks – filled an entire row. I saw the gawkers and the reporters and the lawyers sitting shoulder-to-shoulder with an air of anticipation. Like a masterful showman, I was about to present a veritable Jacobean drama, featuring Maddie as its fallen star.

I turned to look at Maddie, certain she had noticed the regret on my face. Then I glanced at Dr. Morgan, who didn't look the worse for wear, although I knew he had been at the lab at dawn that morning.

Dr. Burton Morgan, world-renowned forensic expert, took the stand with swift, confident strides. His intelligent face was devoid of all expression except for professional acuity. Before I could elaborate on his illustrious credentials, Ribisi stood up and waived his right to challenge the doctor's qualifications, acknowledging Dr. Morgan's education and experience in the field of forensic medicine.

Dr. Morgan had a comfortable, lived-in face, a weathered and leathery complexion attesting to a life-long love affair with the outdoors. He was close to seventy but still spry, and his lively, sharp eyes gleamed with intelligence and forbearance behind his glasses.

"Dr. Morgan, at my request, you have collected specimens from the home of the deceased?" I asked.

"Yes. As soon as the police re-opened the premises, I and my assistants visited the scene. We were also granted access to evidence collected by the NYC Forensic Department."

Dr. Morgan was careful not to use the common sobriquet of "scene of the crime," for which I was most grateful.

"Can you tell us what tests you and your team performed?"

"We inspected the residence for trace evidence, measuring the width and depth of the blood stains."

"You also subpoenaed some of the physical evidence in the possession of the prosecution?"

"Yes. Obviously, we had to wait for the Forensic Department to conclude their own tests." Dr. Morgan's bushy eyebrows were as expressive as his dark blue eyes. They seemed to have a life of their own, animated and full of quirky twitches.

"It was suggested by the prosecution's expert witnesses that there was a marked discrepancy in height between shooter and victim, is that also your opinion?"

A quick dance of his eyebrows, "Oh, yes. Senator Monnehan appears to have been shot from a gun pointing at a downward angle."

"And there is some dispute about the distance from which the firearm was shot."

"Yes, I am aware of that."

I let out a small, steadying breath; this line of questioning was as fragile as the delicate tracery of wind flow. I had to sow the seeds of doubt in each and every member of the jury. The prosecution's duty was to establish facts to the exclusion of everything else. Mine was to establish the reasonable doubt inherent in every scenario. Against the ostensibly open-and-shut case of the State, plausible deniability was my weapon of choice.

"The State is claiming that Mrs. Monnehan was but a few feet away from her husband –close enough to leave gunshot residue on his chest." I paused. "The defense posits a different hypothesis to explain the deposit of these traces," I said levelly.

Dr. Morgan looked at me in silence, waiting for me to continue.

"Mrs. Monnehan has testified that she walked into the bedroom. It was dark, and she barely saw the outlines of an advancing figure she believed to be an intruder."

"Yes, I am familiar with the circumstances." Dr. Morgan's rich baritone voice was notably devoid of any inflection.

I knew that the next questions were crucial, and aware of the stellar integrity of my witness, I was more than cognizant of the risks in asking them. Dr. Morgan had never confirmed or denied the prosecution's allegation as to how the burn marks could be accounted for. Yet I knew that in his cross, Ribisi would pounce on the issue; I had no choice but to bite the bullet. "Is there anything in the scientific evidence to preclude the possibility that the figure was quickly stepping forward at the same time that Mrs. Monnehan was entering the room?"

Dr. Morgan speared me with sharp eyes. "No, there is no scientific evidence to contradict such a theory."

"Could he then…" I paused, "at the moment of discharge…could Senator Monnehan have been bent forward to allow for the difference in heights and distance?"

Dr. Morgan nodded soberly. "Yes, that is also within the realm of reason."

"In the dark, Andrew Monnehan could have been pretty close to the defendant?" I plowed forth.

The frown lines dug deep in Dr. Morgan's forehead, a pronounced vertical gulley between his brows. He regarded me solemnly. "Yes," he finally allowed, "it is possible."

I let out an inaudible sigh.

"Dr. Morgan, could you please tell us what DNA tests you conducted in relation to this case?" I asked.

"There were two hair specimens that we tested. The hair next to the body was definitely Mrs. Monnehan's; the one on the decorative pillow appeared to have different genetic material enclosed within the shaft."

I nodded. "But you could not analyze the second shaft of the hair?"

"No. In order to understand the complexities of extracting DNA from a single strand of hair without the root or follicle attached, I would need to elaborate on the structure of hair in general and the science of DNA investigation in particular." Dr. Morgan's eyebrows twitched, and his lips lifted with humor.

"Briefly, then," I said, "the hair in evidence, despite the meticulous chain-of-custody, could not yield much information?"

"We still carried out DNA analysis despite the low chances of success."

I felt my pulse quickening. I was walking on thin ice, but I was not ready to skate over it yet.

"Let us go on then to the rest of your findings. We'll come back to the hair specimen later." I was breathing in great handfuls of air. Like Lyconides, the hero of Titus Maccius Plautus's play, I was about to retrieve the pot of gold at the end of the rainbow.

"You examined the prints on the firearm used in the shooting?" I asked intently, lifting the small Berretta wrapped inside the evidence bag. "Can you appraise the court of your finding?"

"I documented two separate prints on the handle of the gun."

"Weren't some of these prints smudged and unidentifiable?" I asked curiously.

"Yes, the identity of the second set of prints has remained unknowable so far." The ping of the last two words resonated in my head, but I continued without a break. "Mrs. Monnehan's prints were on the gun?" I asked.

"Yes."

"But there was another set of prints?"

Trust me! I wanted to look into Maddie's eyes, to tell her it was all going to be alright. In the end, it was Maddie's face, the helpless wonder in her eyes as she lay in my arms, the promise of that bright, unequivocal "Until I met you," that kept my shoulders stiff and my voice steady.

Ribisi rose to his feet. "Your Honor, Dr. Stringer has already testified to the evidence purporting to be another set of prints. These could well have been made at a different time, and as such bear no relevance to this case. In addition, I am sure that the doctor is well-acquainted with an alternate explanation for the appearance of a second set of prints. The defendant herself could have accounted for those." He was referring to the technique of transferring prints by lifting them off a glass with an adhesive tape and planting the oil deposits that transfer the prints onto a desired surface.

"Your Honor! I would like to object to the prosecution's spurious allegations. Mr. Ribisi's derogatory remark, intended to suggest improper conduct by Mrs. Monnehan, doesn't even dignify a counter argument. This is outrageous!" Ribisi had not only indicted Maddie for first degree murder, but also seemed prepared to accuse her of doctoring evidence.

Ramsey looked taken aback, the jurors looked puzzled, and only Dr. Morgan, steady and unblinking, looked at Ribisi.

"I would like both counsels to simmer down!" Ramsey pounded the gavel for emphasis. He pondered for a full minute, then looked at Dr. Morgan. "Doctor, is there any reason to discuss these unidentifiable prints?"

Dr. Morgan gave a fractional shrug and took a moment to formulate his answer. "Judge, my lab fast-tracked the fingerprint results, but it is by no means a rush or faulty job." He smiled broadly and benevolently at the prosecutor and then turned towards the jury with a beatific expression. "I have been in the forensics business long enough to realize how important it is to be accurate and careful in the analysis of any data brought to me." Dr. Morgan took a breath and facing Ramsey he added, "Your Honor, if I may, I would like to elaborate quickly on the process in which I have specialized for more than forty years."

Ramsey returned Dr. Morgan's open and friendly gaze and nodded. "Go ahead, Doctor; we can all benefit from your extensive knowledge."

"Thank you, Your Honor." Dr. Morgan inclined his head graciously. His twinkling eyes moved again to the jury box. "When you take two sets of prints at two different times, there are always small differences, even when they are from the same fingers. It's never an exact match; it depends on the amount of pressure when the fingers press the surface. Then there is the quality or the texture of the surface, the angle of the fingers themselves. There are too many variables…" Dr. Morgan paused, reached for his water glass and took a sip. "Fingerprints are one of many forms of biometrics used to identify individuals. The analysis of fingerprints requires the comparison of several features of the print pattern. There are three basic fingerprint patterns: the arch, the loop, and the whorl. The job of the forensic expert is to determine the points of similarity between these patterns in different sets of prints. When you have enough points of similarity of the swirls and ridges, that's when you have a match."

Dr. Morgan paused to make sure that we all had followed his explanation. "The prints lifted off the firearm used in the shooting of Senator Monnehan were definitely deposited at the same time. There was no dryness from longstanding prints, no residue of dust particles or chemicals to indicate a time lapse, or any other substance to indicate the passage of time. My lab uses the most sophisticated equipment, and we do not necessarily rely strictly on optical fingerprint imaging. Ultrasonic sensors, which were utilized in this case, further confirmed the existence of two distinct sets of prints. This ultrasonic device, without boring you with scientific jargon, creates reflected waves forming images of the fingerprint. The benefit of this procedure is that it eliminates the need for a clean sensing surface. In addition," He turned to regard Ribisi with infinite patience, "there were no traces of adhesive or any evidence of trickery involved. There was no tampering with the prints." This was what Ribisi had implied that Maddie had done, and I was still amazed that he had. "These two different prints were made by two separate individuals almost within minutes of each other." Dr. Morgan asserted.

I finally turned around to look at Maddie; she was the picture of stillness. Her cold stare penetrated my being. No matter, I thought: my path was as inevitable as day following night.

"Doctor, a few minutes ago, when you were discussing the results of your tests, you said that the second set of prints remained unidentifiable so far. What did you mean by that?"

"As of earlier today, the prints and the hair specimens were still unidentified by the State's laboratory." Dr. Morgan gave a small, almost self-deprecating, smile. "However, they have now been identified by my own hands."

In the eruption of sound that followed, I felt the taut muscles of my shoulders relax in preparation, like the instinctual shrug of a boxer stepping into the ring.

"Can you tell us to whom the fingerprints belong?" This was the point of no return.

Dr. Morgan turned his gaze in Maddie's direction, his expression sorrowful and grave. "They belong to Ivy Vandor," he said softly. "Mrs. Monnehan's daughter."

An explosive rush of reaction swept through the courtroom. There was no going back. We were careening into the storm, headlong and furious.

"Mrs. Monnehan's daughter was in the bedroom at the time of the shooting?" My voice sounded far away in my ears. Cold. Deliberate. Pitiless.

"Yes." Dr. Morgan glanced at Maddie again, whether to mitigate the impact of his statement or to be rewarded with some sort of response. He heaved a long, sad sigh.

I glanced up at Ramsey; he was watching Ribisi with an unfathomable expression in his eyes. The jurors seemed transfixed – no longer individual men and women with unique personalities and opinions, but fused into one monolithic unit.

"Can you tell us, Doctor, how you have come by this finding?"

"*You* brought me new evidence that facilitated the analysis and identification of this individual." He replied smoothly.

"Objection!" Ribisi jumped to his feet. "We have had no prior knowledge of any new evidence, Your Honor. We were chastised earlier for lack of transparency! The defense has been more than underhanded regarding discovery! We ask that this new evidence be stricken from the record until we have a chance to examine its legitimacy!"

"Your Honor," I responded coolly, "we have just obtained this evidence. Dr. Morgan graciously consented to conduct tests this weekend, which was the earliest I could deliver an identified set of the prints to be analyzed. In point of fact, he has informed me that he was still at it early this morning, making sure his results were accurate and irrefutable."

"Objection overruled," said Ramsey with a speculative gleam in his eyes. "I, for one, would like to get to the bottom of this."

"Thank you, Your Honor," I said. "I apologize again for this unexpected turn of events. I myself came upon this new evidence only this past Saturday."

I addressed Dr. Morgan, who remained totally calm throughout this heated exchange. "Doctor, you are referring to a half-empty water bottle, which I brought to your lab on Saturday evening, is that correct?"

"Yes."

"This bottle bore the fingerprints of someone you had identified as the owner of the other set of fingerprints?"

"Yes."

"I then informed you that they belonged to a girl by the name of Ivy Vandor?"

"Yes. I was then able to extrapolate and analyze all data to confirm the genetic linkage between Mrs. Monnehan and Ms. Vandor. There was no doubt that they are mother and daughter."

I forged on, disregarding the lump in my throat. "Let me recap, Doctor. With the evidence you now have in your hand, are you able to determine, beyond a shadow of a doubt, whether Ivy Vandor was present at the time of the shooting?"

"Yes. The fingerprints on the firearm confirm that Maddie's daughter, Ivy, was there at the time."

"In your opinion, based on this new evidence, would it be possible to determine conclusively who shot Andrew Monnehan?" I asked.

I glanced at Maddie briefly, whose veiled look seemed to reveal more than anger, but a deep sense of sadness.

"The only rational conclusion that this evidence supports is that we do not know what happened on the night in question," Dr. Morgan answered with asperity.

Maddie's eyes remained still.

I said crisply, "Thank you, Doctor. I have no more questions."

My walk back to the counsel's table was agonizingly slow. I sat down heavily next to Maddie.

Her unnatural pallor was as tangible as an early frost. I kept my eyes on the witness stand. Ribisi was, to be sure, still reeling from the revelation of Ivy's existence, but he had no choice but to navigate through

Dr. Morgan's irrefutable evidence. I sat motionless through the cross, hearing only snippets of phrases. I was encased in a bubble of white noise. I had just used the evidence that Ribisi took such painstaking time to lay out and turned it around to dispute both the State's evidence and the prosecution's conclusions, but I felt little more than devastating sorrow.

When Judge Ramsey dismissed us for the day, Annika and Matthew rose to their feet, ready to leave, but Maddie and I remained seated at the table.

I turned to Maddie. "You told Andrew about Ivy?" I said flatly.

"Of course, as soon as he proposed."

"Did you know that he visited her a few times on his own?"

"Yes." A long pause. "I took it as a sign of kindness."

"Until?" I asked tonelessly.

A silence, this one different from any other. I waited, sensing something in the back of my mind. I thought if I was quick enough I could grab hold of it, but it dissolved into the air between us.

"Why Vandor?" I asked.

Maddie smiled softly. "It means a wanderer, a walker. It was my mother's maiden name."

"I believe tomorrow will be my last direct," I said.

Maddie didn't answer. My eyes stopped short, catching sight of the 8 by 10 black and white image provided by the diner's surveillance camera. Maddie in the diner conversing with Thaddeus Constantine, face tired but still beautiful. I was about to add it to the Exhibits folder when my hand froze. The photo showed Maddie from the waist up, wearing the same camel-hair coat wrapped shapelessly around her slender body. The same coat she was wearing when her image was captured earlier on the Fresno surveillance camera, but now without the accoutrement of that beautiful brooch. There might be a myriad of explanations for its absence, I thought, yet it was one more niggling discrepancy to be tucked away with other unanswered questions. I slid the photograph back into the folder and got up to leave.

Maddie, insubstantial as a shadow, rose without a sound and left.

"Well!" said Annika with a dry voice, "it has certainly been a day loaded with explosives!" She sounded peeved but knew better than to voice her discontent in public. She was going to wait until we reached the office to let me know in no uncertain terms how irked she was at not being informed of the latest piece of evidence. In truth, she was right: we'd always worked hand in glove. Yet I had kept the existence of Ivy close to my heart for two whole days, entrusting her name in confidence to Dr. Morgan alone. I had no rational explanation for this impulse. With Dr. Morgan's testimony, her identity would explode into the world. Why had I held it close? Now, looking at Annika, I knew that hard as I tried, I could not explain it either to myself or to Annika.

My mobile vibrated in the inside pocket of my jacket; the screen lit up with Ribisi's name.

"Hi," I said guardedly.

"Nick, are you still in court?"

"Just about."

Annika raised one eyebrow. She watched me mouth Ribisi's name silently.

"I'm sitting here with Bradley in my office. Do you think you can swing by?"

"Now?"

"Yes, if you don't mind. I'd like to run something by you." There was a cautious note in his voice.

If Bradley deigned to bestow his presence on Ribisi, there was trouble in paradise.

"All right. I'm here with Annika Ormond. We'll be in your office in five."

I hung up.

"We never addressed manslaughter per se," I said absently.

"They'll offer four years, the statuary minimum sentence."

"They're worried about their case. If we don't wait for the jury's verdict, we have a good chance to reduce it to two years with some sort of community service." My thoughts kept skipping around. "If indeed this is what Ribisi wants to discuss…"

"You know and I know the case has come to a grinding halt on Ribisi's end," said Annika decisively. "This is what he's calling you about."

Ribisi, now alone, was sitting behind his desk and motioned for us to sit down. He came right to the point. "Self-defense requires that the response be in direct proportion to the threat."

I answered flatly, "Self-defense requires that the response is in direct proportion to the threat as the defendant perceives it to be."

I waited out Ribisi's silence, and was content to let it drag on.

"I'd like to offer a reduction of the charges," he finally said without a smile. "Manslaughter with a recommended sentence of six years."

I gave Ribisi a thin smile. "Even if you offered a deal of involuntary manslaughter with a minimum sentence, I don't think Mrs. Monnehan would take it," I responded evenly.

Ribisi nodded. He had expected this reaction, but he had a script to follow.

He sighed and stood up, his face grim. "Take the offer back to Mrs. Monnehan; let me know as soon as you speak with her." The interview was over.

It was useless to inform him that right from the start Maddie had forbade me to make any deals.

On the way to the office, in the back of a taxi reeking of a combination of spicy Indian food and an unbearably cloying air freshener, Annika said, "It's a good deal."

I said nothing.

Annika studied me warily. "Are you going to recommend it to Maddie?" Lots of tone and undertone in Annika's voice.

"I will present it to her, but knowing Maddie, she won't take it," I said evenly.

Annika smiled briefly and turned to gaze out the window. She then spoke without looking at me, her voice muffled by the din of the traffic. "Juries are unpredictable, Nick. You're rolling the dice with the verdict."

I observed Annika's profile—the hard jaw line, the tight lips—but didn't respond. She was right, of course; it would take only one dissenting opinion to result in a hung jury. For once I had no winning rebuttal. The rest of the ride passed in silence. How could I share with Annika the raw truth that more than a verdict hung in the balance?

To my surprise, when we reached the office Annika begged off and left me to my own devices. I called Oscar to coordinate tomorrow's events and then spent the rest of the afternoon re-reading Ivy's dossier, which Mother Superior was kind enough to have faxed to the office. I read through the agonizing dissection of a young life, page after page filled with prognoses of mental and physical disorders. I read carefully, studiously, as if each word held some kind of cipher. When I was done, I sat motionless in a room grown dark, reflecting on the angry silence in which Maddie and I had parted – and on the heartache I was about to unleash.

My calendar alert chimed into the silence, a rude reminder of the time. When I last spoke to Moira I promised to attend her concert scheduled for that night. I stared at the open folders, the medical dossiers, the sheaves of paper strewn across my desk. Compounding the need to sit and pore over every word and move for next morning was the knowledge that Moira waited and that I could not disappoint. I shook off any residue of weariness and threw on my jacket.

On the few occasions when I had attended one of Moira's performances, often in front of small audiences in tucked-away, obscure little venues, I would feel undone by the relentless grief her playing evoked within me. I avoided Moira's few performances as assiduously as one tries to avoid the sight of open-heart surgery. The rare times that I relented and went to hear Moira perform, I would walk out, whiplashed by the need to escape. I always found Moira's playing a reminder of all that she had lost, all that she could have been and my own damnable part in taking it away.

Tonight, however, I wanted to attend Moira's recital. For months I had found myself wrestling with an avalanche of emotions. Like a man woken from a coma, all my sensory synapses were staggeringly alive. I was struggling with the strangeness of overwhelming feelings: love, hope, and dread. I longed to experience some of that peace Moira seemed to have found in her music.

The last performer of the evening, my sister entered the stage. A slender figure in a simple black dress with long pale arms, as delicate as swaying reeds. She placed the violin against her chin, stroked the smooth, glossy wood as she started to tune the instrument. She nodded towards the conductor and the first soulful notes spilled into the hall. With her eyes closed, she picked up her bow and brushed it against the strings. Her fingers—long, capable, and suddenly powerful—tightened over the neck, her head turned to shift her marred cheek against the violin. Live, puckered flesh against sleek, polished surface. It was a gesture of tender communion; a child's gesture of trust. My eyes stung watching her.

Moira chose *Winter* from the *Four Seasons* by Vivaldi, a piece of music I had often heard her practice when we were young. The notes trembled in the air, sounding like the quiet sobs of a young girl, the winter of Moira's childhood. Then the music's tenor changed, replacing despair with pure notes of solace. The melody became strong with passion as it chased away the pain. Spring and hope to look forward to.

I was watching Moira now, swaying gently on the stage. A swirl of sensation, eyes closed in rapture as her fingers danced on the fingerboard, the bow flying over the strings. Her hands were unleashing a melody so fierce it cut deep. The power of music, I thought, to rip your heart apart even when it soothed and gathered the pieces into a whole.

When the last note died, Moira remained motionless with her head still on the chinrest. She looked peaceful, seeming to listen to the chords as they faded into the distance. She opened her eyes and found me, as if this entire time she had been playing for me alone. Our eyes locked; two solitary blue herons.

I stood in awe as I watched this person on the stage, someone I had always considered as fragile as a sparrow, who I thought could be felled with a single stone. Here she was, my sister, resilient and magnificent. I felt the slow lift of something heavy. The weighty stone of guilt. All this time, I had been hoisting it as it kept dropping down again and again. The poisonous sludge of 'What did I do?' 'Why not me?' and 'If only…' I drew in a deep breath and let my eyes roam around the hall, watching the faces of the listeners: the clear expressions of joy. My wraith of a sister was suddenly more powerful than I could have ever hoped for.

The audience remained still for a second, then the thunderous applause echoed my own responses: the surprise, the acknowledge-ment, and the all-embracing gratitude. A wave of love crested over the room, rushing forward towards that small, lone woman. A woman who seemed to touch the part of each and every one of us that yearned for something beyond our tethered lives. Moira's eyes were brimming as she stared at me across the room. She barely acknowledged the audi-ence. She had spoken to me with the language of music and she had spoken to me alone. For once she was letting me see her as she truly was, as she had become: free and strong and filled with love.

I was waiting outside the stage door when Moira came out. The impulse to hold and be held was overwhelming, and I opened my arms. I held her tight as I whispered, "Thank you" into her hair.

It was Moira who drew away first, pulling her violin case to her side. She raised her eyes. "Let's take a walk," she said. The night air was balmy. I held her hand as we started walking, neither of us breaking the silence. I caught a faint glimpse of a smile as a band of light filtered across Moira's face, a half-crescent lifting of her lips.

"What?" I asked, examining her closely.

"Nothing…" Moira answered quietly, and after a long pause she added, "It's just that you seemed so stunned at the end."

I stopped short and said simply, "Yeah."

She emitted a muffled sound; the lilt of her laugh struck a long-re-membered chord.

She drew back to look at me. "I wanted to tell you this for such a long time, Nicki: we can't change the past. We can't change who we are. But I always hoped that one day you'd be able to hear the same music that I hear."

My unbelievably smart and beautiful sister.

CHAPTER 31

Her voice leaves glass in the wound.

—Federico Garcia Lorca, *Adam*

"The defense calls Mother Cecilia O'Meara, the Reverend Mother Superior of The Convent of the Sacred Heart," I said, my voice unnaturally tight. There was a small, hard knot lodged in my throat, but I was aware of nothing except the sound of doors opening to let the Reverend Mother into the courtroom. The air in the room seemed instantly electrified as all necks craned to watch her slow progress down the aisle. The white coif and the wimple of starched linen could not obscure the calm authority etched on her face. Her walk was deliberate and dignified, her habit gracefully flowing as she stepped onto the witness stand. The cross hanging around her neck gleamed as she sat facing me. I knew Reverend Mother, like all clergy, would not swear on the Bible, considering herself called to a standard higher than some oath. So I was mildly surprised when she said in a firm voice, "I solemnly, sincerely, and truly declare that I will faithfully give true testimony."

I bowed my head for an instant. Then I asked, "Mother Superior, could you please tell the court about The Convent of the Sacred Heart and its mission?"

"The convent's mission has changed over the past sixty years," she began. "The abbey has become an accredited institution, a well-established diocesan school caring for children suffering from a variety of emotional, cognitive, and physical disabilities. These children are brought to us at a very young age, most from disadvantaged families."

"These children board in dormitories under your supervision and ministry?"

"Yes."

"Ivy Vandor is one of your boarders?"

"Yes. She has been with us for twenty-three years." There was a buzz of murmurs, undercurrents of shock.

"Ivy Vandor is Mrs. Monnehan's daughter?" I asked.

The eyes, clear and benign, regarded me calmly. "Yes." The voice matched the gaze.

"Can you tell us briefly why Ivy is boarding at The Sacred Heart?"

"Ivy suffers from a complex set of conditions. She is fundamentally intellectually challenged. Her brain's ability to receive and process information is limited. In addition to her intellectual deficits, she has numerous medical and behavioral issues, and she has been diagnosed with borderline autism."

"I met with Ivy," I said. "Outwardly she displays no physical signs of handicap."

A wondrously beatific smile covered Reverend Mother's face. "No, Ivy is beautiful to behold. But you must remember, Mr. Conor, that most people with an intellectual disability do not show outward signs of it, especially if the disability is caused by environmental factors, such as malnutrition or some sort of toxin."

"Can you tell us how Ivy's disabilities affects her?"

"Ivy has mastered the ability to communicate fairly well within her limitations. But she needs considerable and continuous support. Her comprehension is limited and is very literal; her understanding of abstract concepts is especially impaired." Mother Superior took a long breath and then continued, "Ivy's disabilities, unfortunately, are also developmental and are coupled with a broader spectrum of behavioral difficulties, known today as Autism Spectrum Disorders, or ASD."

"And how do these manifest in Ivy?"

"She has difficulty with social interaction, her memory skills are poor, and she has difficulty learning social mores."

"She has difficulty understanding verbal instructions and communicating meaningfully with people around her?" I asked.

"Yes. She has attention problems and often responds inappropriately to people and other stimulants. Ivy is incapable of understanding the world around her and is unable to explain anything in detail. She can also easily become emotionally agitated and upset."

"Emotionally agitated and upset?" I repeated.

I watched Mother Superior consider my prompt. "Ivy's emotional stability is precarious. She responds well to routine and regular schedules. But she can fly off the handle when she is confronted by something she considers strange and frightening."

"Ivy can be volatile, then?" I struggled on. My voice was a deep, hard rasp.

"Yes, she can be volatile," Reverend Mother allowed gently.

"Violent?"

Reverend Mother's brow furrowed thoughtfully. "It depends what you consider violent, Mr. Conor, but when Ivy is in a state, she needs physical or medical restraint."

I nodded. The feeling of freefalling subsided, I was over the hump.

"Mother Superior, on the day of March 11th, 2012, was there a change in Ivy's routine?"

"Yes. Senator Andrew Monnehan came to visit Ivy and eventually took her with him to New York to visit with her mother."

"He was a frequent visitor?" An equable tone.

"I wouldn't say frequent, but Ivy had begun to feel comfortable in his presence."

"So, on March 11th, the Senator picked Ivy up?"

"Yes."

"Around what time was that?"

"We were just done with dinner, which takes place between 5:00 and 5:30."

"And did the Senator advise you of when Ivy would be returning?"

"He told me she was going to spend the night in New York City," Mother Superior said, her eyes on my face, watchful and sad.

"Thank you, Mother Superior." I smiled and bowed in gratitude. This was not easy. I had cast a small stone into the still waters of a discreet life dedicated to the care of others, and the ripples were only going to expand. Mother Superior and I knew that her church was about to be thrust into national consciousness and become the target of a media blitz. I could only hope that the public's attention span would be short.

Ribisi stood up and smoothed the lapels of his jacket.

"Reverend Mother, Ivy has been your charge since she was born?" he inquired, slow and smooth.

"Yes."

"You knew the defendant then?"

"If you are asking whether I knew Maddie before she gave birth to Ivy, the answer is no."

Ribisi seemed to consider Mother Superior's answer for a moment. I was unsure of his intent and was ready to object, but then he seemed to abandon that line of questioning in favor of another. "You have testified that Ivy is emotionally fragile?" he asked.

"Yes."

"But you also stated that however agitated she can become, she is not considered to be violent?" Ribisi raised a quizzical brow.

"That is correct," Reverend Mother replied evenly. "I have never seen Ivy violent, if you mean trying to bring harm to anyone other than herself."

"Thank you."

"However," Reverend Mother's voice cut through as Ribisi was about to turn away, "I have never seen Ivy truly frightened or shocked, so I cannot in all honestly tell you what her reaction would be if she were thrust into a situation that she was unable to handle."

Never ask a question you don't know the answer to, and never ask an open-ended question! Early on I made that mistake with Detective Lachey, and now I felt Ribisi's internal wince as he made the same mistake.

Mother Superior watched him as he rearranged his features into a gracious smile. "Thank you again, Mother Superior."

She rose to her feet, and seemingly weightless, floated by me and out of the room.

Ramsey gave me an inquiring look. "Mr. Conor, are you ready with your next witness?"

"May we approach, Your Honor?" I asked. I felt the steady beat of my heart as I walked to the bar. "Your Honor, I would ask the court's indulgence in clearing the courtroom of all non-courtroom personnel. I am about to call Ivy Vandor to the stand. As we have already heard, her emotional state is more than precarious. I would like to avoid any extraneous factors that could add to her distress at being called to testify. In addition, although Ivy is biologically twenty-three years old, she should be regarded as a juvenile with limited capacity. Like any juvenile, she is thus in need of the court's protection. Unfortunately, I did not have the luxury of redacting her name, nor of hiding her identity, but I hope the court will see fit to order a completely closed trial for the duration of her testimony."

Ramsey listened intently and nodded. "Mr. Ribisi, any objections?" he asked. "You have the dual responsibility of defending the public interest and protecting the record to avoid error. What do you say?"

When Ribisi spoke, his voice was gentle. "The people would not add undue stress to someone whose mind is as fragile as a child's. We have no objections, Your Honor."

"Very well!" declared Ramsey. "Bailiff, please clear the courtroom!"

I sat down and looked at Maddie. "Trust me," I said again. Maddie's hands on the smooth surface of the table were white as they pressed tightly against each other. Annika looked at me with eyes filled with compassion, but said nothing.

The jury sat waiting in fascination as the room was cleared of all non-essential personnel.

"Your Honor." I finally rose to my feet. I felt the air in the room as an actual weight. "The defense calls Ivy Vandor to the stand."

Maddie shut her eyes, and I heard a moan escape her mouth. The bailiff led Gertrude Robards in through the back door. Hanging onto her hand was Ivy, whose pale face looked ashen with fright.

I stood still. "I'm going to ask Gertrude Robards to sit with us at the defense table. She is Ivy's primary therapist, and her presence is required if we are to keep the witness's distress to a minimum."

"Very well, Mr. Conor, you may proceed." Ramsey stared at Ivy as she was being propelled towards the witness box by Gertrude. She was ushering her charge with gentle reassuring movements, all the while emitting soft cooing sounds. When Gertrude detached herself from Ivy, I saw the momentary flare of panic in Ivy's face, and I walked over—steady and quiet—and smiled into her stricken eyes.

"Hello, Ivy, remember me? Nick?" Her eyes, ricocheting wildly around the room, had a life of their own.

"Ivy," I kept on talking, my voice smooth and sweet, "I know you like chocolate ice cream. I remember."

A momentary stillness as the eyes focused.

I went on, "I promised you a double chocolate cone the next time I saw you. In a few minutes, I'm going to ask" – I pointed towards Matthew, whose expression was almost ludicrously aghast – "that young man to go and bring back an ice cream cone. Would you like that?"

I saw Ivy follow the direction of my finger. There was a soft flicker of a smile on her face when she suddenly met Maddie's eyes, "Mama…"

Ivy breathed into the room, her voice swaying into the air like a rippling strand of soft silk.

My heart was beating fast and hard. I forced myself to slow down. "Ivy," I said softly. I drew nearer and was gratified to see her eyes follow me. I stood as close as I dared.

"Ivy," I heard the crooning of my voice and she visibly relaxed, "Ivy, remember me? I'm a friend of your mama."

Ivy tilted her head to stare at Maddie, and the small pearl-like teeth flashed quickly. "Mama." She pointed at Maddie.

"Yes. Mama and I are friends," I said with that soft lilt. *Were we friends, Maddie and I? More than friends, less than friends? Scavengers and adversaries, lovers and survivors, but no! Not merely friends!*

"Can I talk with you for a few minutes?" I asked.

Ivy sat unmoving, silent and unknowable as a cipher. I was desperate to climb up into those snowy clouds of Ivy's mind.

"Do you remember when I spoke to you about Andy?"

Ivy shrugged, but then the shrug turned into a shudder. I tried to envision how I might proceed. "Andy took you to the house, to see Mama," I said gently. "Remember, when Andy took you to New York?"

"Andy…He said to call him Andy…" Ivy's voice was like the hazy edges of watercolors bleeding onto the page. "He said…he liked me…."

Something cold surged over my skin. "Yes, Andy said he liked you. What else did he say, Ivy?" My voice sounded vague and distant, coming from somewhere deep inside.

"He said Mama wanted me." Suddenly Ivy's eyes darkened, veiled and wary. She looked like Maddie so much at that moment that the resemblance took my breath away. "But Mama was angry…"

I turned to look at Maddie. She was sitting as still as a marble Madonna, as beautiful and as remote.

I felt the catch in my throat as I turned back to Ivy. I was about to betray one of the cardinal rules of law: you never put a witness on the stand before you knew exactly what he or she was going to say.

"Mama was angry, but not angry with you?" I asked softly.

Ivy's distress was palpable as she looked at me and then at Maddie.

"Mama?" Ivy wrenched her eyes from mine, the half sob caught in a voice as soft as the flutter of butterfly wings.

I turned to look at Maddie whose eyes were shimmering with a light so intense I could feel the heat from where I stood. Maddie said with a voice I had never heard her use – rich and warm and swathing the air with velvet and love – "That's all right, Ivika, it will be all right. Don't cry, baby."

Ivy hung her head. I wished I could reach over and touch her hand. But what I said was, "Ivy, can you remember that night, when you and Andy went to see Mama?"

I saw Ribisi's throat work as he tried to swallow. Ramsey did not take his eyes off Ivy, his usually stern features mellow with bewilderment. The room was as silent as a chapel as we all gazed at this pale, elfin face, at this child who was struggling in a web no one could see or understand.

"There was a big door…" said Ivy.

I nodded and smiled. "Yes, there's a big door at Mama's house. Did Andy open it?"

Ivy's head bobbed absently. I thought I was losing her, and I softened my voice to that soft croon that seemed to draw her to me. "Ivy, did you go in with Andy? Did you go inside the big house?"

My gut was in a vise so tight I tasted the bile rising. If I'd known how to pray or to whom, at that moment I would have done so, only to ask that Ivy stay sufficiently lucid and in the moment so that this agony was not in vain.

Her eyes turned vague as she looked blankly into space. "There was a circle inside," she murmured dreamily.

"A circle?" I repeated. "A big circle?"

Ivy tilted her head and for a moment I was sure I had lost her. She then looped her thumb with her index finger and looked through the small circle.

"A small circle?" I fashioned a circle with my fingers and looked at Ivy through the makeshift monocular.

"Pretty…" Ivy said and looked down at her hands. "Pretty red…"

"A red circle?" I asked, but Ivy was already drifting away. *Red? … Red circle…?* I tried to conjure up the stately entrance to the house on 75th Street.

"It … shined in the eye." Ivy grew still and started to pull absently at the fingernail on her thumb. I was going to lose her completely. I couldn't figure out the nature of the red. I stood still, feeling a drop of sweat slide down my back. Then it hit me.

"A red little circle blinking on the wall?" I asked. Bless her heart! Ivy was setting tiny stone markers; I just had to follow the trail.

Again, slower this time, I asked, "Andy turned off the red circle when you walked in?"

She nodded, sucking on her thumb; I saw the raw red of her fingertip.

"So, Andy turned off the red dot and then what happened?"

Ivy turned away; she continued to suck at her thumb. I scrambled desperately for a foothold, for a key, and then I remembered the ice cream.

"Did Andy buy you ice cream, Ivy?"

A huge swell of relief; I saw that small glimmer reappear in the empty mirrors of Ivy's eyes. "He bought you chocolate ice cream?" I asked cautiously.

"I like chocolate ice cream," Ivy said tentatively, as if unsure it was true.

"Andy bought you chocolate ice cream?"

"Lots and lots…" Ivy's voice trailed off into the air, a soft mist, insubstantial and light.

"Lots of ice cream? What else did Andy give you?" I asked uncertainly.

A long, painful silence.

Then as if through a small crack, Ivy started to speak. She spoke in fits and starts, her voice dull and monotonous, her eyes staring through an invisible window. We were shocked into silence as we listened. Painfully faltering sentences painted a picture of a man old enough to be her father who picked her up from school and brought her to a strange place she could neither remember nor identify. My questions were soft, a gentle coaxing, and some of Ivy's answers barely rose above a whisper. Every question stretched out into the air, followed by long, painful silences as I waited, praying for Ivy to stop and at the same time to go on. It was the longest, most heartbreaking testimony I have ever witnessed. I was afraid to look at Maddie.

Ivy's halting answers were excruciating to absorb. I looked at the jury; they were hanging on every painful syllable. The lack of emotion, that dull intoning voice, the power of words uttered by a clueless storyteller, all shimmering in the room like tiny dust motes. Ivy stopped talking and gazed vacantly into the air. Yes, Andy bought her ice-cream, lots of it and Yes, Andy bought her candy, lots of it. And Yes, Andy liked it when she asked for it, and Yes Andy liked it when she knelt down and Yes, Yes, Yes…

I heard the gravel in my voice as I asked, "Ivy, can you remember the last time you saw Andy?"

The look of incomprehension flitted across her luminous features.

"Did Andy pick you up to bring you home to Mama?"

We heard Ivy's quavering voice as if from a very far distance. "Mama was waiting…Andy said Mama wanted to see me…"

"Yes," I said, and felt my constricted lungs scream for air, for relief, for this torture to be over. But I needed to reach the end. I held fast to my certainty.

"Yes, Mama was waiting to see you," I prompted gently.

Ivy lifted her eyes and saw me with a sudden clarity that cut through me like a blade. I felt my eyes fill with tenderness and something so powerful I lost the thread of my thoughts. For an instant I saw it all: Maddie and Ivy and Andrew Monnehan. I felt the change in me as if my blood was slowly turning to ice. I thought at that moment that if Andrew Monnehan was still alive I would have pilloried him before this congregation. No. No, I would have had him drawn and quartered and bleeding to death.

Finally, I turned to look at Maddie. She never once looked in my direction. Her eyes, as if wired and connected by an electric current, were holding on to Ivy.

"Ivy, do you remember when you went to the house?"

A silence alive with unspeakable secrets. I waited as Ivy scrunched up her small face and shut her eyes.

"...I don't remember..." she said at last and opened her eyes.

I swallowed the lump in my throat. "Did you see Mama?"

"Mama was upset...she was angry..." The small catch in Ivy's voice warned me to withdraw soon, *but not yet*!

"She was upset at Andy?"

Ivy looked at me, and her beautiful features started to twist in alarm. "I was scared...I ... I was crying...I don't remember...."

I saw the small tremors of a growing hysteria, but I could not stop. I walked over to Ribisi and picked up that ugly exhibit that had lain on the table for days and that had mocked us with its silence.

The gun felt light against my palm as I lifted it in plain view. I exhaled harshly and forged ahead. "There was a loud noise..." I let the words float into the room; it seemed as if we had all stopped breathing.

Ivy's eyes, the eyes of a terrified, cornered animal, fastened on the glint of metal. She said, "A big noise...My ears hurt..." Ivy began to tremble from head to foot. Her body shook as if caught in a frightful frenzy. A wind-up top that had spun out of control. Her fingers digging into her thin arms, she curled into a small ball and started to moan and gasp in long, drawn-out sobs. A keening wail, the sound of helpless animal terror.

Disregarding courtroom guidelines, I walked quickly to the stand and extended my free hand across the wall. I opened my palm and whispered close, "Ivy, you're safe now, hold my hand…shhh…shhh…you're safe…" *Let me reach into her darkness. Please let me…* I had no idea how long I stood there, powerless, when I felt Gertrude's hand on my shoulder. "Mr. Conor, I got her now," she whispered gently, and she swiftly rose to engulf Ivy in an embrace, to press the soft, white-silver curls to her chest.

Ivy was bawling into Gertrude's ample bosom. The courtroom deputy appeared as if by magic and led the two hunched figures out of sight. We heard the heartbreaking echoes of a child's uncontrollable wailing. Then, absolute silence, as we all tried to breathe.

Every muscle, every bone, and every inch of my skin screamed with fatigue. For the past hour I had been operating in a state of consciousness where I had focused on one thing to the exclusion of all else. I looked over at Ribisi. Was this enough, I wondered? Had I succeeded in making the obvious, obvious? Did I finally succeed in tumbling Ribisi's house of cards to the ground? Did I make it plain for all to see that the night of March 11th was too mired in ambiguities to support an indictment of murder in the first? Was it not clear that the evidence could never point conclusively to Maddie's guilt?

I was unsure now, consumed by doubt and self-reproach. Every thought of failure, every *couldn't, wouldn't, shouldn't* slammed into me. Like a marathon runner, I had hit the wall. All the doubts and fears, regret and pain, roared in my ears. I needed desperately to believe that I had done right. I made myself move slowly as I walked over to the prosecution's table and dropped the gun.

Ribisi was mechanically folding and unfolding a sheet of paper. He felt the weight of my stare and raised his eyes to meet mine. His face looked stricken. Time stood still as we stared at each other.

Ramsey's gavel hit his desk with a force that knocked me back into the room. He coughed and cleared his throat. "We will reconvene tomorrow morning." The controlled sound of his voice rang incongruously loud in the utter stillness of the courtroom.

I turned and walked towards Maddie. She was facing me, standing now. The sharp planes of her cheeks were drawn, and the flint of steel visible in her cold green eyes. She barely moved her lips, a frigid hiss. "Is that what you needed? Did you get what you wanted?" she asked, her voice as violent as a head-snapping slap.

I felt the white tension in my knuckles as I stared into that icy rage, recognizing it as my own; I shut my eyes and inclined my head. The words floated seamlessly in my mind: *I love you…trust me… until I met you…* Over and over like a mantra. My head was still bowed when Maddie left the courtroom.

CHAPTER 32

Millions and millions of years would still not give
me half enough time to describe that tiny instant of
all eternity when you put your arms around me and
I put my arms around you.

—Jacques Prévert, *Le Jardin*

Sleep, which had eluded me for the past two days, came in one crushing wave; I did not merely drift off but collapsed into unconsciousness. The downside of it was that I was awake at five a.m., mind alert and cognizant of what lay ahead. I was staring at yesterday's stubborn images. I had done my best. I had orchestrated all elements in my narrative to be necessary and irreplaceable. Like Chekhov's gun, I had used my trump card, my *deus ex machina* in the person of a damaged child. The ball was now in Ribisi's court.

There was no one else on the runner's lane, the air was still cool in the dawning light. I picked up my pace, but there was little comfort in the echoing sound of my footsteps. I thought sardonically that for the first time I could remember, I resented my stifling solitude. Years of effective, rigorous isolation, the comfort of numbness and the absence of expectations, had sloughed away the moment I met Maddie. Now, immersed in a rush of overwhelming feelings, fully and painfully alive, I was also the loneliest man in the world. I missed Jim and Greg and our steady dialogue; Oscar had intentionally withdrawn to an observer's corner, and I could no longer count on Annika to anticipate my every thought. The woman I loved was as remote as the furthest firmament in the sky, and the child I felt such compassion towards would now cringe in terror at the sight of me. All I was left with was my sister Moira, who, as a result of my efforts to shield her from my pain, was as far removed from my life as everyone else.

The sense of weariness cut deep as I thought that, had I considered the cost, had I anticipated the consequences, I still would have done it all over again. I had never indulged in the metaphysical, never agonized over whether I was righteous or good. All I knew was that I'd been fighting for what I believed to be just. Perched precariously between hope and dejection, I turned back for my apartment, to get ready for what lay in wait.

The jury filed in, wary and overwhelmed, and I wondered if I had overplayed my hand. Ramsey stalked in from his chambers. Apparently sleep deprivation had attacked indiscriminately: both Ramsey and Ribisi seemed hollow-eyed and weary. The courtroom, filled to capacity, had instantly fallen silent. The reporters, alert as bird-dogs, sensed the undercurrent in the air, but being absent from court the day before, they were reduced to mere speculation. There had been as yet no whiff of a leak, and the media was virtually in the dark.

I could feel Maddie's eyes and turned to her. I wondered what she saw in my face. She spoke in a drained voice, undertones of bitterness. "It's almost over, isn't it." It was not a question but a toneless statement.

"Yes," I allowed, simply, my voice calmly detached.

Ribisi rose slowly to his feet. "Your Honor, if we may, we would like to make a statement." Judge Ramsey was about to interject, but then thought better of it, and nodded his consent. In a visible effort to calm himself, Ribisi inhaled deeply and began: "As Your Honor knows, the prosecution's job is, by law, very restrictive. It is this office's onerous duty to follow the letter of the law as stringently as possible. The State is bound to drop the charges if it believes that the accused is innocent, or if there is sufficient reasonable doubt to prevent establishing the defendant's guilt."

Ribisi's voice was grave, as he turned to look at the jury. "We have tried to present our case against Madeline Monnehan without a shadow of a doubt. We felt that the evidence which came before us justified our going forth. The District Attorney's office scrutinized the supporting data, and at the time, concluded that it merited an indictment. In the weeks pursuant to that decision, our search to unearth further evidence to support our charges has been futile. Furthermore, there are disquieting facts that promote doubts as to the absolute culpability of Mrs. Monnehan. It has become apparent that it would be impossible to convict Madeline Monnehan of first-degree homicide on the basis of the evidence at hand."

Ribisi took another deep breath. "As a matter of law, we have no choice but to drop the charges. We therefore move to dismiss the case against the defendant, Madeline Monnehan, and ask the court to discharge her."

Judge Ramsey seemed too stunned to move; he apparently had caught no wind of what the prosecution was about to do. I watched the play of expressions on his face as he was pounding the gavel: shock, weariness, doubt, and finally, the realization that he needed to speak.

Judge Ramsey finally said, "I consider this decision to be brave and just on your part, Mr. Ribisi. You have done your best here, Mr. Prosecutor, but it seems that even your best cannot outweigh the possibility of an error in judgment on the part of the District Attorney's office. We appreciate that rather than extend these proceedings, and waste the Court's valuable time, you have decided to bring this trial to an end."

Ramsey paused as he looked at Ribisi's upturned face. "Your decision does you credit, Mr. Ribisi." Ramsey turned towards Maddie and said simply, "Mrs. Monnehan, you are hereby dismissed; you are free to go. Let the record show that all charges against the defendant have been dropped."

Ramsey then looked at me. "Thank you, Mr. Conor. You have presented your case valiantly and forthrightly. The Court could ask for no more."

The Judge finally turned to the jury. "Ladies and gentlemen of the jury, I would like to thank you for your service. You have certainly set an example of civic duty and for that, the Court and the State are grateful. You are now free to leave. This case is dismissed."

The courtroom erupted into a shattering uproar. Pandemonium ensued, Ramsey's gavel hammering uselessly while he tried to restore order. The clamor refused to die. Finally, the judge rose to his feet decorously, picked up his papers, and left the bench. Ribisi, his face expressionless, turned to leave as well, his assistants in tow. Reporters ran towards the exit to file the breaking news. Shoving and pushing, people were trying to snag their last view of Maddie.

I had gambled on reasonable doubt and on Ribisi's integrity, and he had validated my trust in him. He was faced with two possible shooters and a scenario of self-defense, which he could now not reconcile. He could not prove Maddie's singular culpability, just as he could not fathom Ivy's complicity. The jumbled scenarios must have played havoc in his head: Maddie or Ivy? Maddie in defense of Ivy, or Maddie assuming guilt to shield her daughter? Maddie was innocent until proven guilty beyond a reasonable doubt, and whether innocent or guilty, Ivy was already trapped in her own prison. Confronted by a legal conundrum, a dilemma Ribisi could not resolve, he did the honorable thing and dropped the case. Or perhaps honor had little to do with it. He and I knew that had the prosecution left the verdict in the jury's hands, it would have come to the same conclusion. With an election looming, political expediency and ambition had likely played a large part. A loss of this magnitude would have meant instant death to all his dreams. In the long run, bowing out with grace and integrity would do infinitely more for his political future.

I felt slightly lightheaded as I gathered my notes and stuffed them into my briefcase. I saw Annika and Matthew get up, their faces wearing almost comical variations of shock and disbelief. I felt a momentary stab of pity for Ribisi; it was a staggering defeat for the office of the District Attorney. His open-and-shut case had just slammed shut in his face. It was only a split second of sympathy, however, for I knew he was more than capable of spinning the prosecution's concession into a battle-cry for justice and a moral victory.

I remained seated next to Maddie. She was very still. For the first time, she looked worn-out. She was finally allowing herself to show the strain she had been under. I looked down at her outstretched hand and very tenderly laid mine over hers. I had forgotten how long I had wanted to do that.

Annika and Matthew embraced me. There was a note of wonder in Annika's voice as she said simply, "You did it."

Matthew, his face pink with emotion, was grinning wildly at Maddie. "This is wonderful…so wonderful…I'm so happy for you!" His words tumbled out in a joyful rush, his Adam's apple bobbing in a way that reminded me how young he truly was. He then turned to me. "I didn't understand it yesterday…I didn't understand what you were doing and why, but damned if you didn't present Ribisi with a case he could not resolve!"

I rose to my feet and put my hand on Matthew's sleeve, either to calm him down or in thanks, I couldn't tell. "Go home and take a couple of days off. Both of you. You've earned it."

Annika, grinning at Matthew's outburst, looked at Maddie, her expression and tone turning serious. "Congratulations! Your decision to entrust your case to Nick was by far the best decision of your life."

Maddie stared at her intently. "Thank you. I know this case was not easy for you."

I watched the two women face each other. Annika's voice was gracious and kind as she said, "I always trusted Nick. I just followed his lead." And with that she turned and left. Matthew, still red to the roots of his hair—either from embarrassment or excitement—also beat a hasty retreat.

"Annika never trusted me," Maddie said pensively.

"Does it matter now?" I smiled. We had won. The rest was irrelevant.

Maddie's smile lit up her face. "I'm free!" she said in an incredulous voice.

"Yes. Today is the beginning of the rest of your life." *The beginning of mine, as well.* The spark between us still took my breath away. I loved this woman, and I was going to spend the rest of my life loving her.

Moving slowly as if to conceal how dazed she was, Maddie picked up her handbag and touched my elbow softly. "There will be a circus outside," she said quietly.

I laughed lightly. "Yes. Be prepared."

"I don't think I can address the crowd. I've lost the capacity to formulate clear thoughts. I'll leave it to you."

I felt the slight pressure of Maddie's fingers as they lingered in mine. My chest expanded with a new, wonderful feeling of joy. Outside, shoulder to shoulder, we faced a phalanx of television crews and photographers. Maddie bowed her head slightly and smiled graciously but remained quiet.

Later, I could not remember a single word I uttered. I must have sounded reasonably composed and coherent as I answered the myriad of questions asked. But all I could remember was the familiar catchphrase all winning defense attorneys spouted: "My client is gratified that justice prevailed.... My client is gratified that justice prevailed." There was a sense of weightless euphoria, and I had to caution myself to stay grounded. Maddie and I stood next to each other, our bodies straight and untouching; there was nothing but this moment. There was nothing and no-one else in this moment. A moment of such heady, surreal happiness that it had finally taken my breath away.

I felt slight tremors under my hand as I cupped Maddie's elbow and walked her over to Oscar, who was waiting for us behind the wheel. We slid silently into the back seat of the car. I took hold of Maddie's hand and gripped it, trying to transfer some heat into her chilled-to-the-bone skin. Oscar was grinning at the two of us. "Congratulations! Well done, Boss!" He then gave Maddie an especially benevolent smile. "Don't be afraid to get drunk on freedom! There's nothing like it!"

Maddie, pale and weary, said gently, "Thank you, Oscar. I wonder if you can take me to Penn Station. I would like to go out to the cottage. I'm very tired."

"Sure!" Oscar answered. He whipped around to grab the wheel and plunged into traffic. I raised Maddie's hand to my lips and kissed the underside of her wrist. Her eyes shone bright and luminescent. She bent her head over our linked hands and whispered, "Thank you."

I leaned over and said, "I need to get back to the office; I have some things to take care of. But I'll be coming out as soon as I'm done."

"All right," she agreed simply. We said nothing else the rest of the way.

* * *

It was all behind us now. We were free to love and to be. The day was achingly beautiful. Agi's friendly face beamed at me as she answered the cottage's door and stepped forward to give me a hug filled with the scent of cinnamon and sugar. Her eyes seemed unnaturally bright as she pulled back. "She is down at the beach, Mr. Conor."

I walked down to the water. The sun, the sky, the water, the woman. The glory of everything I was looking at and the happiness I felt in our victory gave rise to a feeling of overwhelming joy. The clear sweep of the beach stretched in front of me. I felt at peace as I walked towards Maddie. She looked carefree and happy as she watched the water lap at her bare toes. She saw me then and froze for a moment, then slowly, almost tentatively, started towards me. Her simple dress, a light, flowing pale green, gave her a look of utter simplicity, but the green blazing in her eyes revealed the dangerous look of a woman fully aware of her power.

Maddie's scarf was flying in the breeze. I lifted the windblown hair off her face and pushed it back, then slid the scarf away, leaving her neck exposed. I pressed my mouth to the long column of her throat, tracing the smooth sweep between neck and shoulder. I stayed there, inhaling her scent, and letting the moment seep in. Maddie laughed and then I took her mouth. When we came up for air, she laughed again, but this time it was just a small, breathless sound.

I waited for a heartbeat, then lifted her chin and stared steadily into her eyes. "I've never felt so sure about anything in my life," I said with a touch of vehemence. "We've earned this. We've earned this by the grace of who we've become and by our capacity to survive our pasts."

"Yes," she whispered. Her eyes half-closed in surrender.

We walked to the house, hand in hand. We climbed the stairs to a room awash with light, a room which I had repeatedly imagined on the endless nights I lay achingly alone in my bed. Maddie stood facing me at the foot of the bed. I stepped closer, but the look in her eyes stopped me as if her hand was suddenly thrust against my chest. I waited obediently; we had all the time in the world. She started to undress—long, languid movements, her eyes never leaving mine. The sheer drapes fluttered against the open windows. The breeze caressed Maddie's hair, soft curling spirals that looked as weightless as air kisses.

The trim flatness of Maddie's hips thrust forward slightly in mocking defiance, as she saw my eyes wander over her body. She raised her arms, spreading them wide with the fluid abandon of a swimmer buoyant on water. Then Maddie smiled and fell naked on the bed, her arms spread, stretched out like wings. The sprawled beauty of Maddie's long, lean body was enough to make my heart stop. I was fully clothed when the length of my body covered hers with my quick responding need. As I kissed her, I heard a tiny sound, not really a word, more a gasp of ecstasy.

"It feels so right," I said quietly, "that it's your body that can give me unbearable pleasure, and that it's my body that can make you lose your unbearable pain. It's the closest thing to a paean I would ever believe in."

Maddie looked up at me, terrifyingly beautiful, and wrapped her arms around me. "Don't leave!" she said, her gaze heavy-lidded. "Don't leave, stay with me tonight." Maddie caught my head and brought my mouth to hers, and then we lost time and place as space disintegrated around us.

We lay spent, the air heavy with our sweat and the sounds of our labored breathing. Maddie held me tight, as if her very being depended on it; I kissed her lips, tasting the salty wetness of her cheeks. She shut her eyes; after a few moments, I heard her breathing deepen.

When we awoke, it was almost dark, the breeze from the ocean cool against our skin. Maddie sat up, and I inhaled the scent of her body, spice and oranges and salt. I pulled her close to me. My voice sounded thick and husky. "I love you, Maddie. I shall always love you." She tensed under my hand but then she raised her head and kissed me. She rolled over, laying her forehead on mine and whispered, "I carry the sun in a golden cup, the moon in a silver cup." I drew Maddie's face down and kissed it. We stayed locked in a moment of sweetness.

"Come!" Maddie sprang gaily to her feet. "I'm famished! I feel like I haven't eaten for days!"

I grinned, watching her, naked, nimble and as lighthearted as I had ever seen her.

"Come." She threw my shirt at my feet. "Come! I'm sure Agi has been waiting impatiently to feed us."

Later, when we walked down to the beach, the sun had disappeared. It was night, the air magically pure, and the sky a beautiful dark blue canvas. The water lapped quietly in the dark—a soothing, rhythmic sound, deep and comforting like a long-forgotten lullaby.

Her eyes swept over me. "What now?" she asked softly.

I replied lightly as I reached for her. "Whatever we wish, whatever we can, whatever we will!" Maddie turned away, her arms wrapped around her as if she were chilled. I pulled her back into my arms, guiding her head to rest against my chest.

Maddie then leaned against the circle of my arms. "I'd like to bring Ivy here, to be with us," she said slowly. I heard the quiver in her voice. She gave me a searching look.

I smiled, awash in a huge wave of love and gratitude. "I would like that," I murmured.

Maddie's eyes went soft. A fierce wonder lit up her face. A single shaft of moonlight pierced the dark to sparkle into Maddie's widened eyes, and for the first time, I sensed the pure gift, the sheer abandonment, with which Maddie had finally relinquished herself to me. My mouth covered hers, her lips supple, warm and welcoming.

The next morning, barefoot and lighthearted and still sleepy, I walked downstairs and out onto the veranda. Maddie was dozing, curled up in the corner of a large chaise. Her eyes opened.

"It's a wonderful morning," she said. The husky voice didn't disguise the storm of emotion. I bent low and touched her lips.

"Good morning, Beautiful," I said softly, feeling a rush of pleasure. Her fingers brushed the back of my head. I could have taken her then and there on that sun-drenched terrace and would have asked for nothing more.

Maddie let out a laugh and stood up. "Go have breakfast first. I'm going to pick up some shells on the beach. I want to make a necklace with Ivy when she gets here."

I grinned. "All right. I'll be coming for you."

I had coffee and a piece of toast. The small television in the kitchen was on, and Agi and I watched the news. Overnight the news that the author Maddie Walker Monnehan had been exonerated of first-degree murder spread like wild fire. The trial was the big story. As we flipped channels we heard the same comments and analysis. "Yesterday was the twentieth day in the trial of Madeline Monnehan, who was accused of shooting her husband, Senator Monnehan, to death in their mansion on 75th Street. The case against Mrs. Monnehan, the recipient of the Pulitzer Prize for Poetry, was dismissed." A shot of Ribisi, pale-faced and blank-eyed, exiting the court and being ambushed by a horde of reporters with mics and cameras. "The people have to sometimes concede that indictments do not always lead to guilty verdicts. The Office of the District Attorney has opted for taking the just path in this case." A shot of Maddie, looking soft and strangely vulnerable, standing in front of a dense row of microphones, thanking me for unwavering faith in her innocence, and thanking the multitude of fans that had showered her with support throughout her ordeal. And then my face, relaxed and smiling into the cameras, looking ridiculously young.

"It has come to this station's attention that Mrs. Monnehan's daughter, Ivy Vandor, appeared as a witness in closed court on the last day of the trial. Although the particulars of her testimony are as yet unknown, it apparently galvanized the prosecution to reach its stunning decision to drop the case." The reporter went on to speculate briefly on the strange denouement of the case and promised a follow-up interview with two legal experts in the following hour. Agi walked over and turned the television off.

Agi's back was turned to me as she started to rinse a cup in the sink, but her voice sounded clear as she said, "It's only a matter of time before one of the jurors will be approached by the tabloids. Ivy's testimony is going to be public knowledge by tomorrow." She turned and sighed. "I know Maddie wants Ivy out here, but I don't think it's a good idea. I think Ivy is better off where Reverend Mother can protect her." Agi lifted her eyes to gauge my expression and then nodded, satisfied. "You will talk to Maddie, yes?"

"Yes," I said quietly and put down my empty cup. "Thanks for breakfast."

"*Isten legyen veletek.*"

I saw Maddie below and started walking towards her, postponing the moment when our eyes would meet. She was shaking off the sand from a shell and was bending down to wash it in the waves. The tide was starting to come in, and she hopped back gracefully as the water rushed in. She laughed, a clear gay sound, and watching her I fell in love all over again.

Maddie saw me then, dropped the shell and walked over to step into my arms.

I raised my face to the sky. Then I asked, grinning, "What does '*Isten legyen veletek*' mean?"

Maddie's delicately arched eyebrows rose as she smiled. "Agi?" she asked with affection.

"Yes. She asked me to tell you that Ivy is featured heavily in the news and to wait awhile before bringing her out here. That was my send-off just before I came to join you."

Maddie said gently, "It means God be with you."

I tightened my arms around her. "I need to return to the city, I'll be gone for a few days. I have to transfer my case load to Jim." In the distance, the line between ocean and sky seemed to waver and blend into a hazy blue. Suddenly I caught a glimpse of a long-forgotten memory – a boy in the water gazing up at the sky, filled with a profound sense of peace. I felt a small tug of love for that boy and closed my eyes. I heard the clarity in my voice as I said softly, "I can't remember when I last took a day off. I don't know how long I'll be able to take off. All I know is that I want to be with you."

"I'll be here."

"You might get tired of me." I searched her face.

"Can a blind person get tired of sight?" Maddie said quietly. A whimsical smile danced at the corners of her mouth. "I'm going to ask

Agi and Lou to stay with Lou's sister for a couple of weeks. I want us to be alone. Just the two of us. Agi is right about Ivy. I'll wait… It'll be just the two of us."

The smile disappeared as Maddie's voice dipped. "I want to ravish and be ravished. When you come back," Maddie's lips twitched merrily, "we'll raid the refrigerator and make like the glutton Romans you love so much."

"Before or after ravishment?"

"Let's leave it to the spur-of-the-moment, shall we?"

"I'm better with planning," I said. "I'm not so good at spur of the moment."

Maddie touched my lips with hers and said, "I have a plan."

CHAPTER 33

Before him he saw two roads, both equally straight;
but he did see two; and that terrified him--he
who had never in his life known anything but one
straight line. And, bitter anguish, these two roads
were contradictory.

—Victor Hugo, *Les Miserables*

It took the better half of four days to put my affairs in order. It was well past three o'clock on my last day in the office when the General summoned me up to his aerie with his familiar abrupt command. I listened absently to his warm congratulatory speech, at the end of which I informed him I was taking my overdue vacation for a duration to be determined. The General didn't even blink in disapproval: I was currently the golden boy.

When I reentered my office, Jim stepped in and hugged me fiercely without saying a word. We were still smiling at each other when Oscar poked his glum face in my door. "Got a minute?" he asked.

Jim reached over and cuffed my shoulder lightly. "Don't hurry back." He smiled at Oscar. "You, on the other hand, stop disappearing! When you're done here, come and talk to me, I'm tired of dealing with the Keystone Kops at Cluny's."

"I'll be in soon."

I looked at Oscar's face and was instantly filled with a sense of dread. "What is it, Oscar?" I asked, fighting against the sudden plummeting in my gut.

"You know, Nick, I think that more than anyone, I was proud of you at the trial." Oscar's voice seemed taut and his smile was just a tight line.

"Thanks," I answered, watching him warily.

He touched his brow absently. "You know me… it's hard for me not to scratch an itch." He took a short breath and continued in a voice sapped of all emotion. "That fire in Arco…now, there was an itch I could not ignore."

I waited silently, watching him.

"Like I told you in my original report, the fire was listed as accidental. But I had this niggling feeling…" Oscar shoved his fingers in his hair. "I fucking wish I hadn't, but it took hold. I went back to Arco right after the trial."

"Okay," I said evenly. "Tell me."

"Like I said, the fire was recorded as an accident at first. The son, Broderick, seventeen at the time, was away at boarding school, and Magdi was at a neighbor's house, working on a school project with a classmate by the name of Sheila Buford."

It was the slow reluctance in Oscar's voice that made me want to ball my hands into fists. "I read your report. We talked about it, you and I."

Oscar looked away. "Both police and fire investigators signed off on it as an accident. The official statement implied that the doctor probably set off the gas canisters on the premises. The accelerant could have been any damn thing; the house had enough materials to blast the premises to kingdom come."

I asked slowly, "But?"

Oscar nodded. "After the medical examiner inspected the bodies, he determined that the doctor's right arm had been fractured– most likely prior to the fire. His investigation shed a suspicious light on the accidental findings. They returned with arson and homicide investigators. In the end, for lack of evidence to the contrary, and having established no motive or viable suspects, the police determined that the trauma to the arm could have occurred when the Doc tried to pry open the metal door in the basement. So, both squads produced the joint, full-on accident report, and the case was closed."

"But you have a different theory?" My heart sank.

"I went back to speak to the Fire Chief, who has since retired. The fire department had originally labeled it arson, and eventually, against his better judgment, Lumas, the Chief, conceded that it could have been an accident. But he told me he was never satisfied with the report's conclusions. You see, according to Lumas, the steel door in the basement was one of the few things that survived the fire. The lock on the door was a double cylinder deadbolt, which has a key cylinder on both the inside and the outside of the door. A key was always required to open the door. The key was always left in the keyhole to ensure safe exit in an emergency. Lumas couldn't find anything resembling a key, melted or otherwise." A long pause. "It's a small town, and they were severely restricted in terms of manpower and investigative tools. But after reading the report and speaking to Lumas …" Silence again, then, "I think the fire was set. I think the basement door had been locked and the key removed, and the doctor was trapped in the inferno."

I nodded silently, waiting for my heart to find its rhythm.

"I spoke to some of the neighbors," he said. "Most of the families had stayed put and remembered the doctor well. According to numerous interviews, the doctor was a respected member of the community. It seems that he was not only highly regarded, but also lauded for his good works and commitment to the town. I couldn't find a single person to badmouth him; so short of blaming the fire on a stranger passing through town, there were no suspects." Oscar emitted a short, harsh laugh. "And believe me, the chances of a stranger passing through that godforsaken town are nil. The last person seen leaving the house was Magdi…"

Oscar met my gaze directly; his eyes never wavered from mine. "She was questioned, as a matter of form, and had little to contribute to the investigation." Oscar drew a long breath and said, "I met with Sheila, Maddie's classmate. It took a while, but I finally convinced her that enough time had passed and if there was anything she could tell me, nothing would come of it."

I watched Oscar carefully. "And?"

"She told me she was afraid of the doctor. She hated going to Magdi's house. She said she didn't know what it was that frightened her about him, but that she was sure that Magdi was just as scared." The air hummed with the silence between us. Oscar said in a low voice, "I think Maddie set the fire, Nick. I don't know why, but I think Maddie did it."

I grew cold as ice. Oscar and I looked at each other. "How is that even possible?" I asked.

Oscar sighed. "She somehow trapped the doctor in the basement and removed the key. As for setting the fire, it's the oldest trick in the book. She set the fire by lighting a cigarette inside a folded matchbook, which would have burned slowly down to the matches, igniting the accelerant and giving her a head start." Oscar spoke slowly and deliberately, granting me enough time to marshal my thoughts. "She had ample time to get to her friend's house. I think that the mother had just died and for whatever reason, Maddie took matters into her own hands and burned the house down."

"How could she have managed it? How much are we talking about?"

"Foreign cigarettes don't have the legal requirement that American brands are bound by of a three-minute burn rate for unattended cigarettes. They can take up to ten minutes for the burn-down. The doctor was known to smoke Gauloises, French black tobacco." Oscar pushed his hair back. "The doctor's basement contained flammable materials. There were oxygen tanks for Maddie's mom in the upstairs bedroom. The explosion would have been horrific, and the fire was probably extremely swift and ferocious."

I could not restrain the savage timbre in my voice, "Christ! She was only fourteen at the time!"

Oscar shrugged, but didn't respond. I never knew Oscar to err in his judgment. I swallowed hard. I knew it was more than feasible to imagine Maddie, desperate to survive, deciding to execute her torturer. I remembered her sitting at my bedside in the hospital, telling me "I waited for rescue but no one came. I wanted to be free." Even at fourteen, Maddie was smart enough, and armed with rage and despair, could have planned it all. She could have set the fire and then watched the house burn down with the doctor and her, by then, dead mother in it.

I felt the jolt of recoil, a quick strike to the heart. It seemed that Maddie had grown into adulthood like Vali, the son of Odin, who in one day morphed from an infant into a god of vengeance. I wondered how one survived that kind of bloodcurdling transformation.

Oscar's body slumped heavily into the chair. We sat facing each other. I forced myself to speak. "There's more?" I asked in the voice of a stranger.

Oscar took out a folder, and I looked at it with sick fascination.

"You know, Boss, how I am when I have a loose end in an investigation?" *No "Nick"?* The sense of dismay intensified.

I nodded mutely; there was nothing to do but wait.

"Ever since we inspected the gun and discovered two cartridges missing, I've been wracking my brains over the missing cartridge. The question lodged itself like a bullet in my brain, no pun intended." Oscar gave me a thin smile and continued almost reluctantly. He pulled a set of at least thirty color photographs out of the folder and laid them on my desk.

I looked at them, uncomprehending and off-balance. They were glitzy magazine shots of the residence on 75th Street, clearly intended to display the over-the-top luxury of the interior. There were seven pictures of that god-awful sterile kitchen, which must have appealed to a certain segment of readers. Monnehan's study fared better, with its lustrous silk drapes set against wood surfaces polished to the hilt. Twelve photos of the library captured dramatically its immense two-story ceiling and plush seating areas. Next came photos of the atrium-like entrance, the domed sky-roof, and the magnificent staircase. Oscar waited quietly for me to look at each photo, to spread them out carefully.

"These were taken as part of a layout illustrating an in-depth article about the newlyweds. You can see the attention to detail with which the photographer shot the master bedroom." Oscar's bony finger tapped the last photos.

I focused on the beautifully-made bed with its pure white satin coverlet and plump, blue-and-white patterned pillows resting against a heavy brocade bolster. There were enough pillows to dress six beds. I lifted my eyes toward Oscar.

He continued. "I found the April 2010 issue of *Architectural Digest* on my desk this morning. I'd forgotten that I had backordered it." He waved his hand, a quick gesture that looked strangely like an apology.

It was like watching the slow spread of blood, unable to stem the flow.

"I still have the key to the Monnehans' house," said Oscar. "Maddie has been at the cottage all of this time and never asked for it back." He spoke slowly and precisely. "I've gone to the residence on several different occasions because it was driving me crazy that I couldn't figure out that missing cartridge."

"Andrew Monnehan might have fired the gun at one time or another," I ventured hoarsely.

Oscar shook his head. "The Senator never took the gun off the premises. I checked at the range, he used one of their firearms."

Oscar pulled out another stack of 8x10 photos from a separate envelope. "Ribisi's office left word with Annika this morning that items removed from the Monnehans' house no longer had any evidentiary value, so I went down to the police station and signed them out. Most of the items belonged in the master bedroom, so I set the room to rights. I had a weird sense that I was missing something, so I decided to take fresh shots of the bedroom. I thought I'd take another look when I got back to the office, but it hit me before I even walked in." He picked out a picture and slid it gently towards me. I pulled it closer and looked. The room looked the same, pillows in various shapes and sizes, same beautiful coverlet. It all looked like it did in the professional photo spread, save for one small exception: the bolster was gone.

"No bolster." I heard the small catch in my voice.

Oscar refused to meet my eyes. "I called Helen Morley and asked her to meet me at the house at four o'clock. I think there might be a simple explanation. She'll clear it up."

"I'm coming with you," I said matter-of-factly.

"Yes." Oscar nodded; he was expecting my response.

On the way to meet Helen Morley, we sat silent as strangers. I was trying to think of all the possible reasons for that idiotic discrepancy in the bedroom's décor. There were so many plausible explanations for the missing bolster: It could have been sent to the cleaners before the night of March 11th. It could have been replaced by cushions. I played with the probabilities like a crap shooter, but my heart wasn't in it. I was still reeling from Oscar's right jab about the fire when his left hook about the bolster knocked the breath out of me. I found myself holding on to the hope that Helen Morley would provide an explanation for the missing bolster. This was the closest I had ever come to praying.

Helen Morley was waiting for us on the stoop. "I hope this will not take long," Mrs. Morley said grudgingly. "I cannot afford to leave my new job for any length of time."

"This won't take long," I managed to say and ushered her in.

The house had an unlived-in feel to it: heavy white tarps covered the furniture in the library, and the balustrades were covered with a thin layer of dust. Our footsteps echoed loud and hollow as we climbed up to the master bedroom; dust-motes swirled indifferently around us.

I entered the room first, in my wake Oscar and then Mrs. Morley. I studied the bed. I asked, "Mrs. Morley, we only wanted to confirm that this was the bedding taken as evidence on the night of the shooting. Would you please take a good look and tell us if anything is missing?"

I tried to breathe against the pressure in my chest.

"Well," Mrs. Morley harrumphed, "you would have to go back to the precinct and ask for the bolster."

"The bolster?" asked Oscar without expression.

"Yes," she scoffed. "It was extremely big and heavy; they couldn't have misplaced it! It weighed a ton!"

I felt Oscar's eyes, but I couldn't speak. It was Oscar who asked, "Are you sure it was on the bed that night?"

"That night and every night! Of course, I am sure! I was here long after everyone left that afternoon. I always made sure that everything was always in perfect order."

There was a long silence. Somewhere outside, a radio was playing a gay little tune.

"Thank you, Mrs. Morley, for taking the time. You've been most helpful." I forced a smile. "I'd like to pay your carfare back to work."

Mrs. Morley glowered. "I can pay for my own cab fare, thank you very much." She looked at Oscar. "If that is all, I will be leaving now."

I heard the sound of those sensible shoes on the stairs and was grateful to Oscar for accompanying her out. I sat on the bed. I remembered Paul Ribisi's opening words: "Murder masquerading as self-defense."

The flickering shadows of doubt—minute flurries of suspicion, which I had willfully tamped down—spun wildly in my mind. But I couldn't arrange them into coherent ideas. I felt rather than heard Oscar in the doorway. He stood still, his voice was excruciatingly gentle. "She must have pulled the trigger and, either intentionally or not, hit the bolster. But then," Oscar hesitated and swallowed, "she knowingly cocked the gun a second time and shot him straight in the heart."

"Yes," I said dully. I thought of the fire in Arco. Deliberate and planned. A decisive act of elimination, and the shooting of Monnehan, just as coldly executed. I knew from my own years of abuse and from years of therapy that damage to the young could be irreversable. My own psychological trauma took shape in the form of emotional alienation and the fervor of a zealot to pursue justice. What toll did Maddie's trauma take on her psyche?

I acknowledged to myself that I had methodically subverted the need to find out. From the first, I had smothered my doubts about Maddie. Now, sitting on this offensively pristine bed, I thought back to what I had always known—one's morality grew out of one's experiences.

"The adult is the grown-up version of the child," I said tightly.

"What?" asked Oscar, still watching me intently.

I pinched the bridge of my nose with infinite fatigue. "Nothing," I answered. "Just talking to myself."

Another long silence.

"I'm sorry, Nick," Oscar finally said.

"Yes," I said. "Why don't you grab a taxi back to the office? I'm going to head straight out to Long Island."

Oscar studied me intently. "Why don't you stay in the city? Sleep on it."

"No," I smiled gently. "Thanks."

Irresolute, Oscar remained at the door. He looked strangely despondent.

"Go," I said firmly. "It'll be all right."

"I'll be home if you want to talk later."

"Yes." There was such dullness in my voice that Oscar gave me another hard look.

"You sure?" he asked.

I mustered a thin smile. "Yes, go ahead, I'll lock up."

After Oscar left, I examined with ruthless honesty the glaring inconsistencies that I had refused to acknowledge: the surveillance camera showing Maddie in plenty of time to catch the 6:02 train, the missing brooch when she was captured on the CCTV camera at the diner, the disarming of the alarm by Monnehan while Maddie was probably waiting for him upstairs.

"The house was dark when I entered; I turned off the alarm and..."

"Do you set the alarm regularly?"

"Every night, when we go to sleep. When we are home, we turn the interior security off; we arm the external one only. But on Tuesday, both alarms were set, so I turned both off."

"Okay. So you walked in, the alarms were neutralized and you did what?"

"I turned on the lights in the downstairs and the upstairs hallways. I went upstairs to our bedroom; I was eager to get my medication from the bathroom."

"So no one was home at that time?"

"That is correct; I was alone in the house. It was too late to call Andrew, so I decided to take a bath and turn in early."

"Mr. Monnehan was not home at that time?"

"No."

"...I realized I forgot to set the alarm..."

...And Ivy with the little red dot winking in the wall... *"There was this red circle..."*

And finally, the missing bolster.

Maddie's betrayal and my mistakes sliced through me, hairline cracks spreading out into chasms, splitting me wide open.

CHAPTER 34

I knelt in reverence, my lord,
I took my vows as you lashed my back
and promised.

—Maddie Walker, *Against the Shoals*

I finally started the car, floored the accelerator, and peeled off into the street. I heard the roar of the engine as I took it through the gears. My Jaguar sat low and hard, its nose like the beak of a bird of prey. Responsive as ever, the car zoomed forward, hurling us towards the endgame. As I got closer to the ocean, I could taste the salt in the air.

I had practiced law for seventeen years, and more often than not I believed my clients to be untruthful to some extent. They tended to exaggerate their attributes and camouflage their shortcomings when they asked for my help. Their lies were sometimes insignificant, occasionally critically important. Yet like any practiced lawyer, I worked around them and eventually could ferret out the truth from any client, no matter how wily.

Except for Maddie.

From the side of the road where I parked, I saw Maddie standing on the bluff above the ocean, outlined against the crisp blue of the sky. Her long white skirt swayed gently in the breeze. She sensed my presence even before turning around. She started towards me, but then stopped and watched me as I approached. I knew that my eyes held hers in a pitiless gaze.

She smiled calmly. "I was waiting for you, ever since Helen Morley called," she said. "I knew you were coming straight from the house." I could detect no traces of pain or regret in that exquisite voice.

"Do you want me to tell you what I found out?" My voice was as level as hers.

"If you wish."

"I do. I think you killed your husband with forethought, malice, and intent. I think that once Lou reached you on the phone, the niggling suspicions reared their ugly heads and you made a quick decision to return to the city. By now you knew who and what Andrew Monnehan was, and you raced back to the house. You activated the alarm and waited for him in the dark. I think you waited patiently for Andrew to be totally engrossed in what he was doing. He probably had Ivy kneel on the floor on one of the throw pillows—that's how the blond strand of hair got caught in its zipper—while he sat spread-eagle, pants around his ankles, at the foot of the bed. You waited in the bathroom, stepped out, and pulled the trigger. You missed him and hit the bolster instead. After all, you're probably less proficient with a gun than Ribisi had suspected. Your husband must have been paralyzed with fear: a pathetic, shriveled man, unable to straighten up. I don't know if you shot him then, but I don't think so. I think you wanted Ivy out of the room. Still pointing your gun at his chest, you must have told him to stay put while you pulled Ivy towards the door. Incoherent with fear, she must have inadvertently grabbed your other hand, which was how her smudged print got on the gun. Once you got Ivy out of the room, you shot Andrew Monnehan in cold blood." My voice sounded eerily calm.

"You planned it perfectly, plotting for all the different eventualities. You must have shot him while you were either naked or wearing a nightgown, which you later disposed of; after Monnehan was shot, you pulled on your clothes. You knew enough to wash your hand, but it must have brushed against some part of your body transferring the gunshot residue back on to your fingers. Then you called Lou, who, following your earlier instructions, was on his way to the city, and you waited about an hour for him to come and get Ivy. That call to Lou from the South Hampton station…" my voice faltered. "Hours before…You already knew exactly what you were about to do."

For one blinding moment, I saw what I could have had with Maddie. The thought was immeasurably cruel. I continued evenly, "It was not easy to pull Andrew's pants back on, but you did it carefully and without leaving a trace. I think you opened the windows to flood the room with cold air, trying to force an erroneous estimate of the time of death. You must have sedated Ivy in order to be able to leave her to dash to the diner. That's why Mother Superior said Ivy was catatonic when she returned. You had the presence of mind to dress once more in your coat, making sure you were clearly visible to the camera overhead. You even made time to chat with Thaddeus, while buying that last blasted sugar-free muffin." I smiled grimly. I thought I could feel my heart breaking. "You needed to make sure he would remember you, and you needed that date and time stamp to corroborate your timeline. You made a slight mistake, Maddie. You left your brooch behind, unaware that there was an earlier image of you wearing it on your trip back to the city."

I took a long breath and watched the rise and fall of Maddie's chest. "Unfortunately, you had to wait quite a while for Lou to arrive; you couldn't call the police before Ivy was whisked away. So you sat in that frigid room, waiting. That was the reason for the long delay between the time of death and the call. When Lou arrived, he took with him your nightgown, the bolster, and Ivy, and then you were free to call. This was well-planned, Maddie. You efficiently eliminated the life of another human being. Save for the two cameras that recorded the slight discrepancies, it was perfect."

I was finally done. My throat was parched; I was exhausted. "The whole drive down here, I struggled with what I knew to be true and whether I could live with it. In my heart, I could have accepted it as justifiable homicide. But then there was the fire."

For the first time, Maddie looked away. "You came because you wanted to confront me first, before you made any decision."

"What is there for me to decide?" I heard my voice, the undertone of bitterness. "I believed in you…I believed in us…" I could not disguise the grief and the utter despair that laced my words.

Maddie stood motionless, the taut lines of her body as unyielding as a drawn bow. I finally understood the nature of that stance: she was a soldier prepared to fall on her sword, the condemned facing her executioner. It had all come to pass, from the first moment I'd entered the Monnehans' library, when, to the exclusion of everything else—the voices, the din, the policemen around us—I first laid eyes on Maddie and wanted her.

Maddie's gaze was level as she spoke. "Would it be more palatable to your sense of moral rectitude, easier for you to digest, if I told you that the fire was an accident, that the doctor and I struggled and he fell and somehow knocked over some combustible substance in that laboratory of horrors that caused the explosion and burned the house down?"

I smiled bitterly, acknowledging the quickness of Maddie's mind. She knew that it was the fire that hacked to the core. She knew me so well.

"Is that how it happened?" I asked softly.

Maddie seemed to reflect for some time, her gaze turned inward. "No," she answered me sharply. "I planned it all. For two years I prayed for something or someone to rescue me. I knew even as a child that my fate was strictly in my own hands. When my mother died that morning and that beast of a man grabbed me and told me that things would stay the same as long as he wanted them to, I knew he had to die."

I could hear the gentle lapping of the waves below as they rushed to the shore. The sun started its majestic descent on the horizon; great sweeps of crimson and orange blanketed the sky. I swept my arm to include the sea, the shore, and the sky. I said, "I want you to know that I've never wanted anything as much as I wanted to be here with you. You were to be my reward for all those damn lost years."

My voice floated between us. "I love you. I love you with every single cell of my being. I loved you when you fought me, and when you surrendered. I loved your mind, your face, the way light changed when it entered your eyes. I loved your body and your hands and that stubborn tilt of your shoulders. I could have loved you for the rest of our lives…but for this—you killed…You killed two men…You not only killed your stepfather, you killed your husband. You planned it, the whole thing, down to the tiniest detail. It was first degree murder."

My muscles shook slightly with the effort to stand still and look at her. I stepped away and gazed at the sea; in the distance it looked calm and undisturbed. "You killed another human being for reasons deemed justifiable to you. You appointed yourself accuser, judge, and executioner."

Maddie's face was frightening, as implacable as stone. "He tried to molest Ivy. I executed him. Do you not think the punishment fit the crime?"

I answered tiredly, "We have courts of law, Maddie."

Maddie and I were both survivors of childhood horrors. The scars we bore were seared deep into our souls, and we had learned to live with them. She was the half that could have made me whole. I closed my eyes for an instant, and when I opened them, I saw Maddie's eyes fill with such tenderness that it cut to the quick.

"On the way here," I said tonelessly. "I tried to let it go. God knows I'm not and have never been perfect. Perhaps I should have better heeded the moral implications of crossing the line with you as my client. Of loving you and yielding to this compulsion to have you despite the boundaries of my profession. But to accept the terrible lines crossed by you will always remain beyond my capacity to condone. I have fought, and always will fight for that which is right and just. Perhaps that is my own cross to bear: being an imperfect man striving to do the right thing in an imperfect world. I can only be true to myself. I have but one true north. If I let go of it, there's nothing left… I cannot, my love!" I knew that I was pushing the only woman I had ever truly loved out of my life and I saw the impact of my words reflected in Maddie's eyes.

"Yes," she said. "I killed them. I killed them with forethought, malice, and intent. I put them down like the rabid dogs they were. In cold blood and with no second thoughts. I'm not sorry for what I did. I want you to know this: I would do it again. If I were faced with the same circumstances, I would do it again." Maddie stopped, and then her voice dropped. "I'm sorry that it hurts you so much."

The exaggerated steadiness of her voice was my first clue that she wasn't as impervious to this pain as she pretended to be. "I'm sorry that you came all the way," she continued, "with the hope that I would make it acceptable for you."

Maddie stopped and her face grew serene. "I love you," she said. "My one regret is that I didn't know it was love I felt. I did not acknowledge to myself that I have loved you from the first. I want you to know that I would have told you the truth, whether you came to uncover it or not."

"It wouldn't have changed how I feel."

Maddie said, almost lightly, "I know. I've known it all along, but I would have tried to make you understand, understand who I am, who I've become." She grew quiet, ready to accept anything I wished to add, anything I wanted to throw at her.

I felt the shock of a single instant when I realized that I still had a choice: I could still protect Maddie and love her with full knowledge of the price I would pay. I could shield her at the cost of losing who I was – relinquishing my compass and my faith in right and wrong – or I could rip Maddie out of my life and uphold the letter of the law.

"The law, Maddie." My voice was barely a whisper. "The law has sustained me my entire adult life and is the reason for my being."

I looked out at the sea. I had invested so much hope in this case and given my heart over to the totally unfounded belief that I could finally love someone with impunity. I thought of that first morning, the morning after meeting Maddie when I sensed, no, *knew*, against all reason, that she would be my undoing. I thought of all that might have been and now could never be. I knew I had reached the end of the line.

I fought against the sting in my throat. "I am who I am, Maddie. Throughout my whole life I've only loved three people: two have died, the third was ruined by my own hand," I said with an effort. "You were the miracle I never thought I deserved. I would give anything for things to be different, but you and I have never succeeded in avoiding reality."

I reached for Maddie, and she came into my arms. I held her body tight against mine like a bandage that could stop the bleeding. When we pulled apart, Maddie's face was expressionless; the only sign of pain was the intense gaze that never left my face.

"Nick," Maddie finally said in an oddly gentle voice. "We can make a go of it, you and I. We were meant for each other. Two damaged human beings who found each other. What are the odds?" She took a bracing breath; her eyes seemed to grow larger. "We each found the single key that could unlock our prison of misery and loneliness. You know that, as well as I do." She waited quietly for me to speak.

"Yes, I do. But at what price?

Maddie's eyes sparkled with what could have been a trick of the light or unshed tears. "I think there's nothing left to say then, is there?" She looked away at the sky, then turned to look at the ocean. "I'm going back to the house. You must do what you must."

I watched Maddie's slender figure, her shoulders held straight and her hair swinging gently as she started walking towards the house. Just as Maddie rounded the corner and before she disappeared from sight, I called out, *"We are our choices, Maddie."*

She stopped; I knew she recognized Sartre's famous quote, his singular tribute to man's inviolate freedom to define himself. She bowed her head as if bracing against a gusting wind, but did not turn around.

The one thing remaining was for me to acknowledge that I had fallen in love with a woman who had lost what I always believed elevated us above the beast—a moral compass. The thought was beyond bearing. *Welcome to the rest of my life.* Yet I knew that I could and would bear it, for the pain would always remind me that I had known love.

My ghosts were stirring, closing in, but now as tender memories — Moira laughing with the abandonment of a child, Padrick singing with that deep beautiful voice, and Ma's gentle hands patting down a lock of my hair.

I slipped off my socks and shoes. The sand under my feet felt warm. I walked over to the edge of the water and looked out at the sea. I started to walk into the foam, the waves lapping at my ankles, as gentle as a child's touch.

It had always been the sea, I thought: Ma, Moira, Padrick, and I, we were children of the sea. I thought I could feel its patience. For a moment I thought how comforting it would be to walk into its welcoming embrace. To sink weightless into the deep, into the calm. And then I turned, picked up my stuff and walked back to the road.

ACKNOWLEDGEMENTS

My thanks go first to my husband, Harry, who has never failed to support and believe in me. For following the progress of this book from its first draft until its last revision with steadfast guidance and conviction.

My beautiful daughter, Sarah, for ideas and inspiration, for the countless talks that encouraged and expressed such unshakable faith in the worthiness of my words. For knowing to impart the right word at the right time. Words cannot express my love and gratitude.

My two great boys, Ron and Etai whose love and encouragement have no bounds. Thank you!

The book would not have found its clear voice without the wit, intelligence and dedication of my editor, Franzeca Drouin, who took my wordy manuscript and used her crafting magic to transform it into cohesive and readable fiction.

The kick-off of *Against the Shoals* would not have been possible without the support, friendship and commitment of Carrie F. Kelly. Without her consummate professionalism and expertise, this book would not have seen the light of day.

Many thanks to the previous readers of drafts: Nancy Ciabattari and Caryl Avery who walked by my side while I took small baby steps tackling this manuscript.

During the research and writing of this book I relied on several professionals who were more than generous with their time and insights.

Though the book is entirely a product of my imagination, the novel is grounded in real-life experiences and real-live individuals. While taking artistic liberties, I tried to stay faithful to the truths of their stories.

ABOUT THE AUTHOR

T. K. Szepesi is a mother, wife, art historian, music lover, and compulsive writer. She grew up in Israel, where her Hungarian parents nourished her love of the arts and insisted on a multi-lingual education, hence her passion for language. Since 1968, Szepesi has been living in the United States, where she received a B.A. from the City University of New York and completed the M.A. program at New York University's prestigious Institute of Fine Arts.

Since then, Szepesi has gone down various interesting and unusual career paths. She was an intelligence officer in the Israeli army, taught at a London kindergarten, owned a New Jersey tannery, dabbled furiously in interior design, and wound up as a curatorial assistant at the Whitney Museum of American Art – and many things in between. However, putting pen to paper has been the one constant in her life: poems, short stories, and half-completed manuscripts. It was only when her young daughter spurred her to focus fully on her writing that this novel became a reality.